Anonymous

Memoir of the Life, Travels, and Gospel Labours of George Fox

Anonymous

Memoir of the Life, Travels, and Gospel Labours of George Fox

ISBN/EAN: 9783337208899

Printed in Europe, USA, Canada, Australia, Japan

Cover: Foto ©Raphael Reischuk / pixelio.de

More available books at **www.hansebooks.com**

MEMOIR

OF

THE LIFE OF GEORGE FOX.

A MEMOIR

OF THE

LIFE, TRAVELS, AND GOSPEL LABOURS,

OF

GEORGE FOX,

AN

Eminent Minister

OF THE

SOCIETY OF FRIENDS.

REPRINTED FROM THE AMERICAN EDITION.

LONDON:

FRIENDS' BOOK & TRACT DEPOSITORY,

12, BISHOPSGATE WITHOUT.

1867.

LONDON:

R. BARRETT AND SONS, PRINTERS,

MARK LANE.

CONTENTS.

CHAPTER IV.—Page 123.
1656—1658.

CHAPTER V.—Page 152.
1659—1660.

CHAPTER VI.—Page 171.
1660—1662.

CHAPTER VII.—Page 189.
1662—1664.

CHAPTER VIII.—Page 209.
1664—1667.

CONTENTS.

CHAPTER XII.—Page 298.

1680—1686.

CHAPTER XIII.—Page 321.

1686—1690.

INTRODUCTORY REMARKS.

In tracing the history of the Christian Church from its earliest establishment, through the periods of its decline, until it reached that long and dark night of apostacy, which for ages preceded the reformation, we find, that in proportion as the life and substance of religion decayed, a multitude of ceremonies were introduced in its place, little, if at all, less onerous than the typical institutions of the Mosaic law. This has ever been the result, when the ingenuity of man has attempted to improve or adorn the simplicity of spiritual religion. There is a natural activity in the human mind, which prompts it to be busy, and can with difficulty submit to that self-renunciation which the Gospel enjoins. It is much easier for a professor of religion to be engaged in the performance of rites and ceremonies, than to yield his heart an entire sacrifice to God. Objects presented to the mind through the medium of the natural senses produce a powerful impression, and

B

are more easily apprehended than those truths which are addressed to the intellectual faculties only, and are designed to subdue and control the wayward passions of the human heart. It is not surprising therefore, that instead of that worship of the Almighty Father, which is in Spirit and in truth, and which requires the subjection of the will and activity of man, and the prostration of the whole soul in reverent humility before God, a routine of ceremonies and forms should have been substituted, calculated to strike the eye and the ear with admiration.

As the period of degeneracy was marked by the great amount and increase of these ceremonies, so, when it pleased the Most High to raise up individuals, and enlighten them to see the existing corruptions, and how far the professed Christian Church had departed from original purity, and to prepare them for instruments in working a reformation, one of their first duties was, to draw men off from those rites by which their minds had been unduly occupied, and on which they had too much depended, instead of pressing after experimental religion in the heart.

This, of necessity, was a progressive work. The brightness of meridian day bursts not at once upon the world. There is a gradual increase of light, from its earliest dawn until it reaches its fullest splendour; yet the feeblest ray which first darts through the thick darkness, is the same in its nature with the most luminous blaze. It makes manifest those things which the Divine controversy is against, and leads back to the state of Gospel simplicity and purity, from which the visible Church has lapsed. And although the light may not be sufficiently clear to discover all the corruptions, nor the state of the world such as to bear their removal, yet those holy men, who act up faithfully to the degree of knowledge with which they are favoured, are worthy of double honour, as instruments for correcting the growing evils of their day, and preparing the way for further advancement in the reformation.

It is interesting to observe, that the different religious societies which have risen since the Reformation, all aimed at the attainment of greater degrees of spirituality and a more fervent piety, than was generally to be found among the sect from which they sprung. The idea, that forms were too much substituted for power, and a decent compliance with the externals of religion for its heart-changing work, seems to have given rise to them all. Each successive advance lopped off some of the ceremonial excrescences, with a view of making the system more conformable to the apostolic pattern. In the early part of the seventeenth century considerable progress was made in this work, tending to prepare the way for that more full and complete exemplification of the original simplicity of the Gospel, which was exhibited to the world by George Fox and his coadjutors. It is no arrogant assumption to assert, that to whatever point in the Reformation we turn our attention, we find the germ of those principles which were subsequently developed and carried out by the founders of our Society, actuating the Reformers, and leading them to results, approaching nearer to those attained by FRIENDS, in proportion to the faithfulness and measure of light bestowed on the individual.

Opinions very similar to those held by our Society, on the subjects of the indwelling and guidance of the Holy Spirit, baptism and other ceremonies, super-stitious rites, war, oaths, and a ministry of human appointment and education, were promulgated by individuals at different periods, antecedent to the rise of Friends, though not advanced as distinguishing tenets by any considerable body of professors.

The Reformation from Popery under Edward VI. was but partial. Many of the errors and supersti-tions of that pompous and ceremonial religion were retained; partly because the dawning light was not sufficient to reveal their true character, and partly in compliance with the popular prejudice in favour of ancient institutions, and of a showy and imposing form of worship. There were, however, men of eminent piety and religious discernment, who per-ceived the degeneracy from primitive Christianity which gave birth to those corruptions, and had since fostered their growth and promoted their increase, until they threatened to supplant vital religion.

On the death of Edward, the hopes which these

had cherished, of further advances towards the original simplicity and purity of Christianity, were extinguished by the accession of Mary, and the barbarous persecution which followed. Many sealed with their blood the testimony of a good conscience, and by faithfulness unto death, not only proved the sincerity of their profession, but prepared the way for those nearer approaches to Divine Truth, which have since been made. If the clearer spiritual light of the present day unfolds to us some points in which the belief of those holy men was defective, it also places in stronger relief, as a noble example worthy of all imitation, the undaunted firmness and integrity of their characters, their love of Christ, and their devotion to his cause. It cannot be viewed in any other light, than as a Divine interposition in behalf of his suffering people, that this bigoted and relentless queen so soon closed her career, after a brief and inglorious reign.

When Elizabeth came to the throne, she found herself surrounded by Papists strongly attached to their religion, and zealous for its support. Her prudence dictated a cautious course in changing the existing order of things. Too great or sudden alterations might have hazarded the peace of the realm, and even brought her crown into jeopardy. Elizabeth, moreover, was fond of magnificence in her devotions; and, in this respect, the pomp of Popery suited well with her inclinations. It is questionable, indeed, whether her preference for the Protestant religion was not as much owing to her affection for her brother, King Edward, and respect for the memory of her father, as to any decided conviction of its nearer approximation to the standard of Scripture truth.

She restored the liturgy and order of worship as established by her brother, and strictly enjoined its observance, though many of her Protestant subjects conscientiously objected to some parts of it. The idol of uniformity, and the long-cherished idea of a Catholic Church, to which the Papists had made such lavish sacrifices of human life, had strong attractions even for Protestants; and Elizabeth, as well as her successors, persecuted, even to death, not a few of her pious subjects, in the vain attempt to coerce the consciences of men, and reduce them to one common standard.

The doctrines and form of worship revived by Elizabeth after the death of Mary, left the minds of many much dissatisfied. They desired a more thorough separation from the errors of Popery; a simpler method of church-government, and a purer and more spiritual religion and worship. These were called Puritans; a name which, though bestowed on them with no good design, yet agreed well with those things for which they contended.

The Protestants who fled to Frankfort, during the persecution under Queen Mary, unanimously concluded to dispense with the litany, surplice, and responses of the Church of England; that public service should begin with a general confession of sins, that then the people should sing a psalm in metre in a plain tune, after which the minister should pray for the assistance of the Holy Spirit, and proceed to sermon. These innovations on the established order of the Service-book, led to warm disputes, which soon spread into England; and though at times the breach would seem nearly closed, yet the controversy was again and again renewed, and efforts made to procure further reformations from the errors of the Romish Church.

Soon after Elizabeth came to the throne, she appointed a commission to review the liturgy as established by Edward. The alterations made in it were rather in favour of the Papists than the Puritans, by many of whom it was viewed as more objectionable than the old Service-book. It was, however, presented to parliament, and adopted as a national form of religion, by "The Act for the Uniformity of Common Prayer and Service in the Church," &c. The same parliament passed an act vesting the entire ecclesiastical jurisdiction in the crown, and empowering the queen, "with the advice of her commissioners or metropolitan, to ordain and publish such further ceremonies and rites as may be for the advancement of God's glory and edifying his Church, and the reverence of Christ's holy mysteries and sacrament."

The act of uniformity was the source of great mischief to the Church. Many conscientious ministers and others could not conform to its requirements, believing them to be opposed to the doctrines and precepts of the Bible. The rigorous enforcement of the act, while it punished the bodies of men, and wasted their estates, did not convince their minds; but rather strengthened their opposition, and alienated their affections from the church.

In the doctrinal views of the two parties, the Conformists and the Puritans, there was little avowed difference. The uneasiness arose chiefly from a conscientious objection to the assumptions of the bishops, the introduction of numerous unscriptural offices and titles in the church—the laxity of her discipline—the prohibition of extemporaneous prayer—the numerous festivals—the use of organs and other instruments of music in time of worship, and of the sign of the cross in the ceremony of baptism—kneeling at the ceremony of the supper—bowing at the name of Jesus, and on entering or leaving their places of worship— the ring in marriage, as well as parts of the words spoken during the rite ;—and the use of the surplice and other vestments by the priest during Divine service. Such were the principal grounds of difference in the commencement of the dispute ; and though the Conformists affected to consider them non-essential, yet they insisted on them with a pertinacity which increased the opposition and widened the breach, until at length it produced an entire separation, from which have sprung the various classes of dissenters.

That the Puritans were conscientious in their objections to the established religion, will not be questioned by such as are acquainted with the piety of their lives, and the patience and fortitude with which they endured persecution for their religious opinions. Connected with these, was a steadfast resistance to the assumed power of the crown, as visible head of the church, to prescribe to, and control, the conscience of the subject, in things not essential. Against this they manfully contended, while the reins of government were in the hands of their opponents. But when the revolution of civil affairs placed *them* inpossession of the power, they too soon forgot the principles of rational and Christian liberty, for which they had formerly struggled, and exercised on others the oppression and cruelty which they had so much condemned in their own case.

Contending for their religious liberty, naturally had the effect to make them more jealous of their civil rights ; and hence, during the subsequent reign, we find them standing forth as staunch opposers of the encroachments of the crown.

That they were instruments in the hand of Providence, for carrying forward the Reformation from the errors and superstitions by which Christianity had been overlaid, cannot be doubted ; yet, as this was a gradual work, accomplished by slow degrees, the corruptions not being all discovered at once, but progressively, according to the faithfulness of those engaged in the work, so others rose up and separated from them, who carried the Reformation still farther.

The first of these was the Society of Brownists,

who contended that the Church of England was not a true church, because of the Popish corruptions which she retained and enforced, and her persecution for the sake of religion—that the power of church-government was in the members—that the ministry was not subject to human selection and ordination, but that any brother who felt engaged so to do, might preach or exhort, and that prayer was not to be limited. to prescribed forms. Their mode of discipline was congregational, every society being distinct and independent of the others; holding intercourse and communion, however, as brethren and professors of a common faith. The severe persecutions which they experienced from the government, induced many of this persuasion to fly to the continent, where they met with little better treatment. They appear to have been a zealous and sincere people, living with strictness and regularity, and preaching with much fervour and energy.

The spirit of inquiry was now abroad, and increasing in vigour and activity. Instead of receiving opinions on the authority of church-canons or dignitaries, there was a growing disposition to bring them to the test of revealed truth. Many which had long been implicitly adopted, and transmitted from one generation to another, were now called in question and warmly debated. As early as 1617, John Selden published his History of Tithes, in which he contends that they are of human, not Divine appointment. It was not to be supposed that those whose worldly interests were affected by such an opinion, would suffer his book to pass without severe animadversion; and as a readier mode of counteracting its effects than the resort to argument, the author was summoned before the High Court of Commissions; and, after various threats, compelled to recant his sentiments.

Another class of dissenters, which took its rise about this time, was the Society of Independents, which grew out of the Brownists. Its name is derived from the system of church-government, in which each congregation formed a distinct body, regulating, independent of all others, its own affairs, judging of the fitness of persons applying for membership, and of the propriety of expelling such as walked disorderly. Their doctrines agreed in the main with those of the other dissenters. During the times of the Commonwealth and Protectorate, they were distinguished by their attachment to toleration, which the Presbyterians denounced as " an hideous monster, the great Diana of the Independents." They were not, however, constant to their own principles; for, when they subsequently acquired the power, they exercised considerable severity toward both Friends and Baptists. They received the patronage and support of Oliver Cromwell, and are often mentioned in connection with the history of Friends.

At a very early period of the Reformation, the subject of water-baptism appears to have attracted the serious attention of pious men, and their researches into it led some of them to differ from the generally received opinions respecting it.

From Fuller's Church History, it appears, Wickliffe held "that wise men leave that as impertinent, which is not plainly expressed in Scripture—that those are foolish and presumptuous, who affirm that infants are not saved if they die without baptism; and that baptism doth not confer [grace], but only signify grace which was given before. He also denied that all sins are abolished in baptism; asserted, that children may be saved without baptism, and that the baptism of water profiteth not, without the baptism of the Spirit."

During the fifteenth century there were a number of persons in England who denied the necessity of water-baptism, and held "that Christian people were sufficiently baptized in the blood of Christ, and needed no water; and that the sacrament of baptism with water, used in the church, is but a light matter, and of small effect." Some of these suffered death by fire, for adherence to their principles; and for a long period afterwards, those who entertained similar views were the objects of severe persecution. In the sixteenth century, the Society of Baptists or Anabaptists took its rise. They objected to infant baptism as unauthorized by Scripture, and re-baptized those adults whom they considered as believers and admitted to the privileges of their communion. Besides their peculiar views on this subject, some of them held war to be inconsistent with Christianity, and doubted the lawfulness of oaths under the Gospel dispensation. They also insisted that the Gospel ought to be free, and denied the right of tithes or other compulsory maintenance for its ministers. They were generally persons of great seriousness of mind and strictness of deportment, searching the Scriptures diligently : and being wearied with the ceremonies and impositions of men, were desirous to practise that form of religion only which they believed to be sanctioned by our Lord and his apostles.

Their views of the Christian ministry did not make it essential that those who took part therein should prepare for it by the acquisition of learning ; but gave liberty for any to speak a word, either in doctrine or exhortation, who believed themselves called thereto and qualified by the gift of the Holy Spirit. Some were zealously opposed to a hireling ministry, declaiming against it in their preaching, by which they subjected themselves to severe sufferings. Many of this persuasion were imprisoned during the fifteenth and sixteenth centuries, and patiently endured their confinement, showing by their steadfastness under suffering, that they were actuated by motives sincerely conscientious. Of this class was the pious John Bunyan, whose imprisonment lasted nearly twelve years.

The first Presbyterian church established in England was in 1572. It consisted of Puritans (then so called), who, among other things, dissented from the government of the church by bishops, &c., conceiving that by pastors and presbyters, or elders, to be more consistent with Holy Scripture. They agreed with the Independents in denying the *divine right* of the bishops to order and direct the congregation: but instead of leaving each distinct, with absolute control over its own members and officers, they associated several churches in one synod, and a number of these again united in forming a general assembly, which is the supreme ecclesiastical body.

This Society comprised a much larger number of members than either of the others we have mentioned; and the part they acted in the revolution which drove Charles I. from the throne, and finally brought him to the scaffold, as well as in the affairs of government during the interregnum, rendered them sufficiently conspicuous.

The persecutions they endured, while the reins of government were in the hands of the church party, we should suppose would have taught them moderation and charity towards the conscientious dissent of others ; but no sooner were they placed in the seat of power, than they began to contend for *uniformity* in faith and practice,—the Moloch of Christendom, to which many of her choicest sons have been wantonly sacrificed.

So fierce was their opposition to toleration, that after a long conference of a committee of parliament, for the purpose of making some agreement by which the Independents might be accommodated in their views of church-government, the scheme was necessarily abandoned; because the Presbyterians refused to concede anything. They who but lately had contended against the divine right of the bishops, were now urgent to make all yield to the divine right of presbytery. The ministers of Sion College pronounced toleration " a root of gall and bitterness ; " others of the sect declaimed against it, as contrary to godliness—opening a door to libertinism and profanity, and that it ought to be rejected as " *soul-poison*." Liberty of conscience was declared to be the nourisher of all heresies and schisms, and most of the sermons preached before the House of Commons, while the question was under debate, breathed the spirit of persecution, and incited the ruling powers to draw the sword against such as would not conform. The Presbyterians little thought that their own arguments would quickly be used against themselves, and the severity they had exercised upon others returned with full measure into their own bosoms. This was lamentably the case after the restoration, when the Church of England having regained her power, exercised it with so little mercy, in the vain attempt to force men's consciences into a conformity with her prescriptions.

We have now noticed the principal sects which existed at the time our Society arose, and to whom the reader will find allusion made in the writings of Friends. They were all strenuously opposed to the Roman Catholic Church; and whilst King James I.

and his son Charles I. were both suspected of favouring that religion, as well as some of the dignitaries of the Episcopal Church, the Dissenters availed themselves of every opportunity to show their dislike to it. This contributed not a little to alienate their affections from the throne, and to widen the breach to which their persecution had given rise.

The violation of their natural and civil rights; the disregard of their often-repeated and respectful petitions, and the frequent breach of promises, solemnly made, tended to make the Puritans suspicious of James, and induced them to watch, with the most jealous eye, every encroachment of the crown. The house of Stuart were remarkable for arrogant and arbitrary assumption, in virtue of their prerogative. However the exigency of the occasions may extenuate some of their acts, there are others which deserve no milder appellations than tyranny and oppression. Against these the dissenters inveighed with boldness and vehemence, and, as is usually the case, the cry of oppression rallied to their side a host of partizans, until at length the king had lost the affections of a large portion of his subjects. Instead of pacifying them by some concessions, and soothing their incensed feelings by gentleness and clemency, measures still more harsh and offensive were pursued towards them.

They were punished as factious schismatics—as enemies to the king and government, and inciters of the people to rebellion—were fined, whipped, maimed, imprisoned, and banished—enduring almost every species of hardship and suffering which cruelty could suggest. It were no wonder, if men who had felt so severely the abuses of regal power, should be in favour of a form of government by which it could be restrained within more just and reasonable limits, and the rights of the subject be more effectually secured.

The disputes between the Puritans and the Church party, which had been carried on with no little acrimony during the reigns of Elizabeth and James I., increased in violence under Charles, and began to assume the most serious aspect, threatening to destroy the peace of the nation. The Puritans had augmented in numbers and importance, and the flagrant outrages committed upon them produced commiseration in the minds of many, who yet were sincere in their attachment to the religion of the church. So little regard was had to law or equity in the treatment of them, that their cause gradually became identified with the preservation of the constitution and laws of the country. To be a Puritan was synonymous with being an opponent of ecclesiastical domination, of the tyranny and encroachments of royalty, under the convenient plea of prerogative, and with being the advocate of the rights and liberties of the subject. In this way politics and religion became blended, and afterwards it was the policy of each party to maintain the connexion.

Besides the matters originally contested, new sources of dissatisfaction and other subjects of dispute became involved in the controversy.

Many of the clergy of the establishment had become corrupt and licentious—they seldom preached —neglected their congregations and places of worship, and were engaged in practices not only unbecoming the sacred character, but in some cases even scandalously immoral. They encouraged, rather than repressed, the licentiousness of the times ; and seemed much more addicted to mirth and amusements than to the duties of the ministerial office. Their example, and that of the court, had a demoralizing effect on others, especially on the lower orders of society.

In order to counteract the opinion that the reformed religion was severe and strict in its requisitions, James published, in 1618, a royal declaration, drawn up by one of the Episcopal bishops, stating, that " for his good people's recreation, his Majesty's pleasure was, that after the end of Divine service, they should not be disturbed, letted, or discouraged from any lawful recreations, such as dancing, either of men or women, archery for men, leaping, vaulting, or any such harmless recreations ; nor having May-games, whitsonales, or morrice-dances, or setting up of May-poles, or other sports therewith used, so as the same may be had in due and convenient time, without impediment or let of Divine service."

This was a source of great offence to the Puritans ;

and when the declaration was republished by Charles, and directed to be read in all the churches, many of the ministers refused to comply.

The license given by the indulgence produced the results which might reasonably have been anticipated. The sports degenerated into noisy and tumultuous revels, with tippling, quarrels, and sometimes even murder. These disorders grew to such a height, that the justices, in some counties, petitioned the judges of the courts to suppress them, which they did. But Archbishop Laud, then primate of England, summoned the judges before the king and council, for invading the episcopal jurisdiction. A sharp reprimand and an order to revoke the prohibition was the result. The archbishop taking the matter into his own hands, was informed by the Bishop of Bath and Wells, within whose diocese the prohibition had been enforced, that the restoration of the wakes and revels, &c., would be very acceptable to the gentry, *clergy*, and common people; in proof of which, he had procured the signatures of seventy-two clergymen; and believed, if he had sent for an hundred more, he could have had the consent of them all. It was determined to continue them, and the King forbade the justices interfering with the people. It may readily be supposed, that such proceedings would have a powerful influence in promoting licentiousness; when, in addition to the command of their King, the ministers of religion joined in encouraging practices, to which the depraved inclinations of the human heart alone furnish strong excitement. We may safely rank this among the causes which contributed to promote the immorality and corruption which so lamentably overspread the nation, and gave rise to the close and sharp reproof, which our early Friends so often found it their duty to administer.

The few parliaments which James and Charles assembled evinced a disposition to apply some remedy to the religious dissensions and grievances which distracted the nation. This was an interference so little agreeable to the crown, that they were speedily prorogued, and a long period was suffered to elapse before another was called, giving rise to the suspicion, that the monarch intended to govern by prerogative only, and without the intervention of a parliament.

The condition of the nation when Charles came to the throne was melancholy indeed. It was torn by internal dissensions; and the affections of a large portion of the people were alienated from the King, by oppression and injustice. The encroachments of the crown—the continued encouragement given to Papists, the unmitigated persecution of the Puritans, and of such as had the magnanimity and courage to resist the arbitrary measures of the court and its minions, together with the failure of some of his military enterprises, tended to increase the murmurs, and to rouse the spirit, of those who regarded the liberties and the religion of the country. Influenced by mistaken notions of royal prerogative, and misguided by his counsellors, Charles, instead of softening the spirits of the Puritans by some concessions, proceeded to still greater lengths, until the minds of many of his subjects were prepared for any change which promised to restore to them their civil and religious rights. From this state of things, it was but a short step to open warfare, and accordingly the nation was soon involved in a civil war, which resulted in bringing Charles to the scaffold, and setting up a new form of government. Numerous negotiations for a settlement of the religious differences took place, but neither the King nor the parliament being willing to accede to the terms proposed by the other, in 1642, they appealed to the sword to settle a controversy which had hitherto been managed only by words. During the course of the war, which continued with various success for several years, the King was often reduced to great extremities, and at last falling into the hands of the parliament, he was brought to trial before his avowed enemies, and condemned to be beheaded as a traitor. This cruel sentence was carried into execution early in 1648.

It was in 1646, during the prevalence of the civil and religious commotions, that George Fox commenced his labours as a minister of the Gospel, being then in the twenty-third year of his age.

After the death of the King, the nation was without any legal form of government; but the parliament, which had assumed the power, and exercised

it at the commencement of the war, still continued to
govern.   The Presbyterians had the control of affairs
chiefly in their hands, and proceeded to model the
religion of the nation to suit their peculiar views.
Instead of the liturgy of the Church of England, they
set up the Directory for Public Worship; and, for-
getting the severity of their own sufferings for non-
conformity when others were in power, they now set
about compelling all to comply with their established
forms.   The arguments they had used against persecution for religion, when smarting under the lash
of the Episcopal Church, were urged upon them in
vain.   Having the power in their hands, they
appeared to consider it as a sufficient authority for
coercing others to adopt that form of worship and
system of doctrines, which they had determined to
be the best.   Never did religious toleration seem
to be less understood, or the great right of liberty of
conscience more wantonly disregarded.

But while the parliament was acting in conformity
with these narrow and bigoted opinions, principles of
a contrary character were at work in the army, where
the Independents predominated, and carried with
them their wonted liberality toward the conscientious dissent of others.   Against this latitude of
indulgence the Presbyterians declared with great
earnestness, as a source of innumerable evils, and
tending to the destruction of all religion.   A long
conference took place between the two parties, for
the purpose of making some arrangement, by which

the Independent form of worship and discipline could be included; but such was the pertinacity of the Presbyterian faction, that they refused to yield anything, and the scheme was abandoned as hopeless.

This arbitrary and oppressive course rendered the sect unpopular; and the Independents, finding they were not likely to obtain much from the parliament, and having the army on their side, with Oliver Cromwell at its head, in the year 1653, put an end to the Commonwealth and the parliament together —the former having continued a little more than four years, and the latter having sat as a legislative body, with some short intermissions, for thirteen years.

It was not long ere Cromwell and his officers struck out a new form of government; and in the latter end of 1653, he was declared Lord Protector of England, Scotland and Ireland, &c. The principles of the new government, relative to religion, were more liberal and Christian than any which preceded it. The articles of the constitution embracing that subject, contain the following, viz.:—

" That the Christian religion contained in the Scriptures, be held forth and recommended as the public profession of these nations.

" That none be compelled to conform to the public religion, by penalties or otherwise; but that endeavours be used to win them by sound doctrine and the example of a good conversation.

" That such as profess faith in God, by Jesus Christ, though differing in judgment from the doctrine, worship, and discipline publicly held forth, shall not be restrained from, but shall be protected in, the profession of their faith, and the exercise of their religion; so as they abuse not this liberty to the civil injury of others, and to the actual disturbance of the public peace on their parts; provided this liberty be not extended to Popery or Prelacy, or to such as, under a profession of Christ, hold forth and practise licentiousness."

Creditable as these provisions are to the enlightened views of religious toleration, entertained by those who framed them, they are still defective, in making exceptions in regard to two classes of professors.   Had they been faithfully carried out in practice, they would have saved much suffering for conscience' sake both to Friends and the Baptists.   For however favourable the Protector was to granting liberty of conscience to all, it was not the case with the magistrates, justices and others, in whose hands the execution of the laws was placed.   From the cupidity or intolerance of these, Friends were often interrupted in the exercise of their religion, and punished, because they could not swear or pay tithes; though to a much less degree than was afterward the case.

Toward the close of Cromwell's government he was again declared Protector, under new articles of government, in which an attempt was made to narrow the grounds of toleration, by a more close definition of the doctrines to be professed.

In the opening of the second session of the parliament, in 1657, the Lord Commissioner Fiennes "warns the house of the rock on which many had split, which was a spirit of imposing upon men's consciences, in things wherein God leaves them a latitude, and would have them free."—"As God is no respecter of persons, so He is no respecter of forms; but in what form soever the spirit of imposition appears, he will testify against it. If men, though otherwise good, will turn ceremony into substance, and make the kingdom of Christ consist in circumstances, in discipline, and in forms, ... in vain do they protest against the persecution of God's people, when they make the definition of God's people so narrow, that their persecution is as broad as any other, and usually more fierce, because edged with a sharp temper of spirit." "It is good to hold forth a public profession of the truth, but not so as to exclude those that cannot come up to it in all points, from the privilege that belongs to them as Christians, much less to the privilege that belongs to them as men."

These just sentiments, which appeared to be gaining ground in the minds of men, were soon to receive a check by the change of rulers. In 1658, Oliver Cromwell died, and was succeeded by his son Richard; who, finding the difficulties and perplexities

of balancing the power of rival parties, and con-
ducting the affairs of state, little suited either to his
capacity or his inclinations, resigned his high and
responsible station, after having occupied it only
eight months.

A short interregnum ensued, and in 1660 the
kingdom was restored to the house of Stuart, by
Charles II. being proclaimed king.

These frequent changes in the government had a
tendency to keep up the unsettlement which had
long agitated the nation, as well as those violent
party feelings and prejudices, which the political and
religious struggles had engendered. Friends took no
part in the revolutions of government—their principles forbade them from putting down or setting up,
and taught them to live peaceably as good citizens,
under whatever power the Ruler of the universe permitted to be established over them. But though
peaceable and non-resisting in their conduct, they
were neither idle nor unconcerned spectators of the
course of events. Believing that righteousness was
the only security for a nation's stability and prosperity, they earnestly enforced on the parliament and
Protector, as well as on the monarchs who succeeded,
the suppression of vice and immorality, the equal
administration of justice, and the removal of all
oppression. The addresses made to those in authority by George Fox, Edward Burrough and others,
are marked with innocent boldness and good sense,
delivered in a style of great frankness and honesty.

Nor did they omit to warn them of the consequences which would ensue, if they failed to perform the Divine will, predicting with clearness the overthrow of Oliver's government, and some other changes which occurred.

In his declaration issued from Breda, on the eve of his sailing for England to assume the crown, Charles held this conciliatory language, calculated to allay the fears of those who dreaded the restoration of the hierarchy : " We do also declare a liberty to tender consciences, and that no man shall be disquieted or called in question for differences of opinion in matters of religion, which do not disturb the peace of the kingdom."

But plausible as were these promises, and sincere as the king might have been in making them, the event proved how little reliance was to be placed upon the royal word. Devoted to his own pleasures, and with too little application or industry to examine the opinions of his advisers, or enquire into the sufferings sustained by his subjects, he permitted the clergy to pursue their own measures for the promotion of the church ; and they took care to return the measure of persecution meted to them under the commonwealth and protectorate, heaped up and running over, into the bosoms of the dissenters. Conformity was rigidly enforced, and as if the existing statutes for punishing those who dared to differ in their consciences from the prescribed standard were insufficient, new and more oppressive laws were procured.

The persecution fell with peculiar severity on Friends, who were suspected of being unfriendly to the restoration of the king, from their refusal to take *any* oath, and consequently the oath of allegiance to the crown ; though they repeatedly offered, instead, their most solemn declarations to the same effect.

The peaceable and unresisting spirit which governed the conduct of Friends, seemed to embolden their persecutors to oppress them without colour of law or justice, knowing they had nothing to fear from the law of retaliation, and that but few could be found to plead their cause or undertake the defence of their rights.

To give some colour to the severities practised against them, pretexts were drawn from supposed violations of the regulations of civil policy :—" A Christian exhortation to an assembly after the priest had done and the worship was over, was denominated interrupting public worship, and disturbing the priest in his office ; an honest testimony against wickedness in the streets or market-place, was styled a breach of the peace ; and their appearing before the magistrates covered, a contempt of authority ; hence proceeded fines, imprisonments and spoiling of goods.   Nay, so hot were some of the magistrates for persecution, even in Cromwell's time, that by an unparalleled and most unjust misconstruction of the law against vagrants, they tortured with cruel whippings, and exposed in the stocks, the bodies of both men and women of good estate and reputation, merely because they went under the denomination of Quakers."

Several obsolete statutes were brought to bear most heavily upon Friends, though originally enacted with a view of reaching the Papists, who refused to conform to the established religion. Among these was an act passed in the 32nd year of Henry VIII.'s reign, against subtracting or withholding tithes, obliging justices to commit obstinate defendants to prison, until they should find sufficient security for their compliance; also the laws made in Elizabeth's reign for enforcing a uniformity of worship, authorizing the levy of a fine of one shilling per week for the use of the poor, from such as did not resort to some church of the established religion, every sabbath or holy day;—and also another, establishing a forfeiture of twenty pounds per month for the like default. A third law empowered the officers to seize all the goods, or a third-part of the lands, of every such offender for the fine of twenty pounds. And as if these were not sufficiently severe, another was enacted in the 35th year of Queen Elizabeth, obliging offenders in the like cases to abjure the realm, on pain of death.

All these laws were revived, and attempts made to enforce them in the cases of Friends, though it was well known they were designed to bear upon the Papists. As Friends could not conscientiously pay tithes, believing that the ministry of the gospel should be free, according to the express injunction of Christ to his apostles, "Freely ye have received, freely give," great havoc was made of their property by the rapacious priests.

The Society of Friends viewed the positive command of our Lord, "Swear not at all," corroborated by the exhortation of the apostle James, "but above all things, my brethren, swear not; neither by heaven, neither by the earth, neither by any other oath," as being of indispensable obligation, and entirely precluding the Christian from taking an oath on any occasion whatever.

Soon after Charles II. came to the throne, the acts made in the reigns of Elizabeth and James, requiring the subject to take the oaths of allegiance and supremacy, were revived, and visited upon Friends with great oppression.

In 1661, the parliament passed another act, aimed directly at the Society, providing that if any Quaker refused to take an oath, when lawfully tendered, or should maintain, in writing or otherwise, the unlawfulness of taking an oath; or met with four or more other Quakers, above the age of sixteen years, for religious worship, he should forfeit five pounds for the first offence, or suffer three months' imprisonment; doubling the penalty for the second offence; and for the third, he was to abjure the realm, or be transported.

The insurrection of the "fifth monarchy men," as they were called, was the occasion of fresh persecution to Friends. They were a company of infatuated men, who, supposing that the one thousand years of Christ's reign on earth mentioned in Rev. xx. was just commencing, rose in arms and ran about the streets of London, crying out that they were going to overthrow the government of King Charles, and set up King Jesus. Although there was not the shadow of reason for connecting the Society in any way with this wild insurrection, yet the king made it the pretext for issuing his proclamation for the suppression of all unlawful conventicles, or meetings for religious purposes, designating particularly those of the Anabaptists and Quakers. This encouraged the profane and irreligious populace to assail the meetings of Friends, and inflict upon them the grossest outrages and cruelties.

Severe as were the sufferings of Friends under the operation of these oppressive laws, their constancy was not shaken. They fearlessly and openly met for the solemn duty of Divine worship, nothing daunted by the terrors which threatened them. This Christian boldness exasperated their enemies, especially the persecuting priests and magistrates; and another law was procured more prompt and terrible in its operation. It declared the statute of 35th of Elizabeth to be in full force; and that every person taken at a meeting, consisting of more than five beside the household, should suffer three months' imprisonment, or pay a fine of five pounds, on conviction before two justices—double the penalty for the second offence, and, being convicted of a third before the justices at the quarter-sessions, should be transported for seven years, or pay one hundred pounds fine—and in case he returned or escaped, he should be adjudged a felon, and sentenced to death. It also empowered sheriffs, justices of the peace, and persons commissioned by them, to hunt out and break up all religious meetings other than those of the established religion, and take into custody such of the company as they saw fit. Persons allowing such meetings in their houses, barns, &c., to be subject to the same penalties and forfeitures as other offenders. Such as were sentenced to transportation, were to be sent over sea at their own expense; and in default of ability to pay, to be sold for five years to defray the charges. Married women taken at meetings, to be imprisoned for a term not exceeding twelve months, or their husbands to pay for their redemption not exceeding forty pounds.

The next enactment by which Friends suffered, was commonly known by the name of the Oxford Five-mile Act. It was aimed at the Presbyterian and other non-conforming ministers, requiring them to take an oath, that it was not lawful under any pretence to take up arms against the king; and that they would not at any time endeavour to procure any alteration in the government of church or state. Such as refused to take the oath were declared incapable of teaching any school, public or private, under penalty of forty pounds. All non-conforming ministers were likewise prohibited from coming

within five miles of any city, town, or borough
sending members to parliament, or within five miles
of any place where they had officiated as ministers,
unless it might be in passing along a public highway,
under a forfeiture of forty pounds ; one-third of which
went to the informer.

The refusal of Friends to take an oath, brought
their ministers within the scope of this law, and
fines, distraints, and imprisonments were the consequences.

In 1670, there appeared to be a disposition among
some of the officers of government to put a stop to
persecution. The king, on several occasions, had
shown his dislike to it; but being opposed by the
bishops and parliament, he had not the firmness or
resolution to withstand their influence. The former
Act for suppressing religious meetings having expired,
a new one was prepared and passed, making the
penalty five shillings for the first offence, and ten for
the second; the preachers or teachers in such meetings to forfeit twenty pounds for the first, and forty
pounds for the second offence; and twenty pounds
penalty for suffering a meeting to be held in a house
or barn. A single justice was authorized to convict on
the oath of two witnesses, and the fines to be forthwith levied on the offenders' goods, and in case of his
poverty, on the goods of any other offender present
at the same meeting; provided the amount so levied
shall not exceed ten pounds for one meeting. One
third of all the fines to go to the informer, as a

reward for his services. Justices, constables, and other officers, were authorized to break open and enter any house, or place, where they might be informed there was a conventicle, and search for, and take into custody, all persons found assembled there. If any justice of the peace refused to perform the duties prescribed in the Act, he was to forfeit one hundred pounds, and every constable five pounds. And it was further enacted, that " all clauses in the law should be construed most largely and beneficially for the suppressing of conventicles, and for the justification and encouragement of all persons to be employed in the execution thereof."

A more unjust and oppressive law could scarcely be conceived. In the hope of rioting on the spoils of the Quakers' goods, unprincipled men lurked about their dwellings, lodged information against them on the most frivolous pretences, and swore falsely to procure their conviction; the facility for so doing being promoted greatly by the privacy of the trial, and by the decision resting with a single justice, himself often the accomplice of the informer and the sharer of the prey. It would be difficult to conceive a scene of more extensive rapine and plunder, in time of peace and under colour of law, than the execution of this Act produced throughout the nation. Many Friends were reduced from competency to destitution of the very necessaries of life.

In 1672, Charles issued his declaration of indulgence, by which, in virtue of his royal prerogatives, as being supreme in ecclesiastical as well as civil affairs, he assumed to suspend the operation of the penal laws against the non-conformists. The right of the sovereign to exercise this power was warmly contested. Some of the dissenters, and especially the Presbyterians who were extremely jealous of the Papists, and unfavourable to general liberty of conscience, were not forward to accept the boon thus offered, and even wrote against it, on the ground that it would sanction the exercise of the dispensing power in the king.

Friends had suffered more severely during the preceding persecutions than any other class of dissenters. They had stood their ground with unflinching intrepidity, when others fled before the storm. They contended that liberty of conscience was the natural right of all men, and that every interference of the civil power with the peaceable exercise of conscientious duty, was contrary to Christianity and to sound principles of government. They meddled not with the politics of the day, nor professed to be skilled in questions of royal prerogative. The knowledge, that hundreds of their brethren were unjustly lying in prisons, while their helpless families were exposed to the rapacity of merciless informers, was an argument sufficiently powerful to induce them to accept the relief which the king's declaration afforded. An application was accordingly made to the crown for the discharge of those who had been imprisoned for conscience' sake ; and such was the favourable opinion produced by the constancy, and uniformly peaceable and consistent conduct of the Society, that a warrant was readily obtained for their liberation. The success of this application afforded Friends an opportunity of proving the sincerity of their opinions in favour of universal toleration and charity. There were other dissenters confined in the same prisons, and their solicitors requesting the aid of Friends in their behalf, they cheerfully accorded it, and included the names of their prisoners in the same instrument by which their own members were relieved from bonds.

The respite which the declaration afforded was of short duration; for in the following year the parliament compelled the king to revoke it; in consequence of which the sufferings of Friends were renewed, though not to the same extent as before.

If the calamities in which Friends bore so large a share had no other good effect, they evidently tended to convince the nation of the folly of persecuting men for differences of opinion. More than thirty years of suffering had passed over, and not a single Quaker had been induced by it to abandon his profession; they were as prompt and diligent as ever in the open performance of their religious duties, and as ready patiently to submit to the penalties of unrighteous laws. They never resorted to violence or retaliation, relying on the justice of their cause, the truth and soundness of their arguments, and their peaceable and blameless conduct, to effect a change in the minds of those in power.   This change now began to be apparent.

In 1680 a bill was introduced into parliament for exempting dissenters from penal laws.   Friends lost no time in presenting themselves before the committee as the advocates of such a measure, and urging the insertion of such clauses as would afford relief to the members of the Society, on the subject of oaths. So successful were they in these endeavours, that they obtained an amendment to the bill, admitting a declaration of fidelity, instead of the oath of allegiance. But the state of affairs was not ripe for such an important change, and the bill was lost.   Another, however, passed both houses, exempting dissenters from the operation of the statute of the 35th of Elizabeth.   But when it should have been presented to the king for his assent, it was not to be found, having been secreted purposely, as was believed, to defeat the measure.   In the next year the parliament passed the following resolutions, viz. : —

" 1. Resolved, that it is the opinion of this house, that the acts of parliament made in the reigns of Queen Elizabeth and King James, against Popish recusants, ought not to be extended against Protestant dissenters.

" 2.   Resolved, that it is the opinion of this house, that the prosecution of Protestant dissenters upon the penal laws, is at this time grievous to the subject, a weakening of the Protestant interest, an encouragement to Popery, and dangerous to the peace of the kingdom.

These votes showed the growing feeling in favour of dissenters, and mark the gradual progress of those principles of religious liberty, which were more fully recognised in 1688, by the passing of the *Toleration Act*, under William and Mary; a measure which afforded great relief to Friends, though they were still subject to prosecutions for tithes, and for refusing to swear. After repeated applications to the king and parliament, a bill was brought into the house, in 1695, and finally passed early in the following year, allowing the solemn affirmation of a Friend instead of an oath.

Having taken a cursory view of the laws under which the persecution of the Society was carried on, it is proper we should briefly allude to the state of religion in the nation, at the time of, and subsequently to, the rise of Friends.

In treating this subject, the statements of historians are of the most opposite and contradictory character. Clarendon and others, who espoused the royal cause, are unwilling to accord to the Puritans either sincerity or truth. They allege that canting and hypocrisy were the order of the day—that a high profession of religion and great pretensions to sanctity and strictness, were the road to preferment and power, and were therefore assumed from ambitious motives.

The advocates of the Puritan party, on the other hand, represent the established church as extremely corrupt—her ministers destitute of even the profession of religion, and in many cases, guilty of scandalous and immoral behaviour. That she enforced, by severe penalties, a compliance with superstitious ceremonies, while she tolerated practices of evil tendency, and discountenanced everything like zeal or fervour in religion. Allowance, however, is to be made for the bias of party attachments, and the distorted views which prejudice gives of the character of an opponent. That great laxity of morals, as well as neglect of their prescribed duties, had crept in amongst the clergy of the Church of England, cannot be denied. Many of them never preached, and addicted themselves to hunting and other sports; frequenting ale-houses and taverns, and indulging in drunkenness and other licentious practices.

In 1640, the parliament appointed a committee to inquire into the conduct of the ministers of religion, for removing scandalous ministers, and putting others in their places, as well as to procure ministers for places where there were none. A part of the proceedings of this committee was published, containing cases of one hundred who had been tried and ejected; from which it appears that eighty of them were convicted of immoralities. The reputation of some of them had been defended by writers on the side of the Church, though they admit that others were very vicious, and the offences of several so foul that it is a shame even to report them. Baxter says, that " in all the counties where he was acquainted, six to one at least, if not many more, that were sequestered by the committee, were by the oaths of witnesses proved insufficient or scandalous, or especially guilty of drunkenness and swearing. This I know," says he, " will displease the party, but I am sure that this is true."

The writings of Friends frequently mention ministers whose characters were similar to those alluded to in the above statements ; and if the language sometimes used by members of the Society, in addressing them, appears severe, an ample reason for it is furnished by the disgraceful conduct to which too many were addicted. It is not designed, however, to involve the whole body in indiscriminate censure. There were, doubtless, among them persons of sincere piety and exemplary lives, and who, according to the degree of light afforded them, endeavoured to discharge their duties with fidelity.

When the reins of government came into the hands of the Puritans, efforts were made to procure a reformation in the morals of the nation. The licentious practices which had grown out of the encouragement given to games, sports, and revels, on the first day of the week, were checked. Those vain amusements, together with stage-plays, were prohibited ; the observance of the First-day was strictly enforced, and regular attendance at places of worship enjoined.

It was certainly a period when the profession of

religion, and a compliance with its exterior requisitions were held in high esteem ; though it cannot be denied, that there were some who put on the garb in order more effectually to accomplish their ambitious and sinister designs. However just the severe censures of some historians may be, with reference to these individuals, they cannot with fairness be applied to others—nor should the whole mass of Puritans be stigmatized in consequence of the duplicity of some particular professors.

The following observation from Orme's Life of Owen, will serve to illustrate the religious condition of the nation during the protectorship of Oliver, viz.: " Of the true state of religion during the period of Cromwell's government, it is difficult to form an accurate estimate. Judging from certain external appearances, and comparing them with the times which followed, the opinion must be highly favourable. Religion was the language and garb of the court ; prayer and fasting were fashionable exercises ; a profession was the road to preferment ; not a play was acted in all England for many years ; and from the prince to the peasant and common soldier, the features of Puritanism were universally exhibited. Judging again from the wildness and extravagance of various opinions and practices which then obtained, and from the fanatical slang, and hypocritical grimace which were adopted by many, merely to answer a purpose, our opinion will necessarily be unfavourable. The truth perhaps lies between the extremes of unqualified censure, and undistinguished approbation. Making all due allowance for the infirmity and sin which were combined with the profession of religion—making every abatement for the inducements which then encouraged the use of a religious vocabulary—admitting that there was even a large portion of pure fanaticism, still, we apprehend an immense mass of genuine religion will have remained. There must have been a large quantity of sterling coin, when there was such a circulation of counterfeit. In the best of the men of that period there was, doubtless, a tincture of unscriptural enthusiasm, and the use of a phraseology, revolting to the taste of modern time ; in many perhaps there was nothing more ; but to infer that therefore all was base, unnatural deceit, would be unjust and unwise. ‘ A reformation,’ says Jortin, ‘ is seldom carried on without heat and vehemence, which borders on enthusiasm. As Cicero has observed, that there never was a great man *sine afflatu divino* [without a divine in-breathing ;] so, in times of religious contests, there seldom was a man very zealous for liberty, civil and ecclesiastical, and a declared active enemy to insolent tyranny, blind superstition, political godliness, bigotry and pious frauds, who had not a fervency of zeal which led him, on some occasions, beyond the bounds of sober, temperate reason.’ ''

From the dawn of the Reformation, the spirit of religious enquiry had been kept alive and strengthened by the very efforts used to suppress it. The shackles with which priestcraft had attempted to bind the human mind had been in some measure broken, and an earnest desire awakened after the saving knowledge of the truth, as it is in Jesus. This was increased by the troubles of the times. The nation was torn by intestine strife. Civil war, with all its attendant evils, raged throughout the country, and the property, as well as the lives of the subjects, was at the mercy of a lawless soldiery. Many were stripped of their outward possessions; reduced to poverty and want, and often obliged to abandon their homes, and flee for the preservation of their lives.

This melancholy state of affairs had a tendency to loosen their attachments to the world, by showing the precarious tenure of all earthly enjoyments, and by inducing them to press after those substantial and permanent consolations which are only to be found in a religious life.

Where the ecclesiastical and civil power was so frequently shifting hands, the national form of religion changing with every change of rulers, new sects and opinions arising, and different teachers of religion inviting their attention, and saying, " Lo here is Christ! or lo he is there !" it is not surprising that the honest and sincere inquirers after the right way of the Lord should be greatly perplexed. The effect of these commotions was to wean men from a dependence on each other in the work of religion, and to prepare their minds for the reception of the important truth, that however useful instrumental means of divine appointment may be, it is the glory of the Gospel dispensation, that the Lord, by his Holy Spirit, is Himself the teacher of his people. Previous to the commencement of George Fox's ministry, many had withdrawn from all the acknowledged forms of public worship, and were engaged in diligently searching the Holy Scriptures, with prayer for right direction in the path of duty, and frequently meeting in select companies for the worship of Almighty God and their mutual edification. Among these the preaching of George Fox found a ready entrance, and many of them joined in religious profession with him.

The period of which we have been speaking may justly be denominated the age of polemic strife. The war itself had been commenced ostensibly for the redress of religious grievances. In the camp and the field, as well as by the fire-side, religion was the absorbing theme. The Baptists and Independents encouraged persons to preach who had not studied for the ministry, nor been formally ordained; and numbers of this description engaged in the vocation, with unwearied assiduity, often holding meetings in the fields, or preaching in the market-places. The parliament army abounded with them, and preaching, praying, and disputing on points of doctrine were daily to be heard among both officers and soldiers. Public disputations were also common, and were often conducted with a warmth of temper, and harshness of language, which seem hardly consistent with the meek

and gentle spirit of the Gospel. Modern ideas of
courtesy and propriety can scarcely tolerate the latitude of expression which the antagonists sometimes
indulged toward each other, not only on these occasions, but in their controversial essays.

Amid so much strife and contention, and the intemperate feelings naturally arising out of them, it
is not surprising that even good men should have
formed erroneous opinions of the character and sentiments of each other. They judged rather by the
impulses of prejudice and sectarian feeling, than by
the law of truth and Christian kindness. In the heat
of discussion the mind is not in a condition to form
a sound and correct judgment. The weakness or
mistakes of an opponent are seen through a medium
which greatly magnifies them; while his virtues are
either depreciated, or distorted into errors. The controversial writings of the times furnish evidence of the
existence of these uncharitable feelings, among nearly
all denominations of professors; and he who reads
them with the enlightened and liberal views of religious toleration, which now happily obtain, will
observe, with regret, men of unquestionable piety,
unchristianizing each other for opinion's sake; and
lament that such monuments of human frality should
have been handed down to posterity.

Those who judge of the writings of the first Friends
by modern standards of literary excellence and
courtesy, are apt to censure them for their severity.
Much, however, may be said in extenuation of them.

Friends were particularly obnoxious to the hatred of the clergy, in consequence of their unyielding opposition to a ministry of human appointment, to the system of tithes and of forced maintenance. Their views on these subjects, which they fearlessly published, struck directly at priestcraft. Deeply affected by the corruption which they saw among many who assumed the sacred office, they boldly declaimed against their cupidity, licentiousness, and persecution. This course drew upon them a host of enemies, who were not very nice in the choice of means to lessen their influence and prejudice their characters. Friends were assailed with calumny and misrepresentation; opinions and practices were charged upon them, of which they solemnly declared themselves innocent; yet they were again and again renewed with the boldest effrontery. The conduct of some of the visionary sects which arose about the same time was unjustly imputed to them, and every advantage that could be taken was eagerly embraced to prejudice their religious profession. Harassed by this unchristian conduct, and at the same time smarting under a cruel persecution, they must have been more than human, if the weakness of nature had never betrayed them into an unguarded or intemperate expression. A comparison, however, with other controversialists of the times, will show that they were not peculiar in this respect. It should be recollected, too, that language, as well as the regulations of decorum toward opponents, has undergone a great change since that time. Expressions which sound harsh and offensive to modern ears were then considered strictly within the limits of propriety, and appear to have given no offence to those who were the objects of them. This license of the tongue and pen is found also in the parliamentary debates, and appears to have characterized those times of excitement and recrimination. Another practice which prevailed to some extent, was that of going into places of worship, and addressing the congregation during the time of service. Custom had sanctioned the practice of asking the minister, at the close of the service, respecting difficult or abstruse points, which required explanation. This liberty was exercised to a much greater extent, during the period of which we have been speaking, and not unfrequently a dispute followed. The overthrow of the national form of worship, and the consequent termination of ecclesiastical restrictions, had a tendency to induce greater latitude in this respect than comports with our ideas of good order. The manner in which Friends speak of those occasions on which they went to places of worship other than their own, induces the belief that it was not extraordinary ; and in most, if not all instances, in which violence to their persons was the consequence, it appears to have been the doctrine delivered, rather than the time and manner of communicating it, which called forth the angry passions of the assailants. Friends were not alone in this course, and sometimes their ministrations were so acceptable to the audience, as to induce them to remain after the stated preacher had withdrawn.

The religious men of that day are commonly charged with evincing a fanatical and enthusiastic spirit, and Friends of course come in for a large share of the censure. To deny that there were cases in which such a spirit was evinced, would be folly ; but to brand whole communities of professing Christians with those epithets, on account of the excesses of a few members, would be extremely unjust. It is, moreover, difficult for us to judge correctly of the exigencies of the church during that period, and what degree of energy and fervour was requisite, to carry those holy men through the work of their day. We know that a much stronger feeling must have been necessary to stem the torrent of abuse and persecution, and carry forward the reformation, than the present day of outward ease and liberty would probably elicit. It is, moreover, highly unreasonable to allow men of the world, in the pursuit of the comparatively trivial objects of their choice, to display fervour and self-devotion, and yet censure it in those who are pressing after the momentous concerns of salvation, with an earnestness becoming their vast importance.

In the succeeding reign of Charles II. the face of things was greatly changed. The court was devoted to licentious pleasures, while religion and religious things were made a mere laughing-stock. The restoration opened the very floodgates of vice and wickedness. " A spirit of extravagant joy," says

Bishop Burnet, " spread over the nation, that brought in with it the throwing off the very professions of virtue and piety; all ended in entertainments and drunkenness; which overrun the three kingdoms to such a degree, that it very much corrupted all their morals. Under the cover of drinking the king's health, there were great disorders and great riots everywhere." This lamentable state of things was the source of great concern to Friends, several of whom addressed the king on the subject, reminding him of the fate of Sodom and Gomorrah; and that in his own dominions, wickedness had reached a height which must certainly call down the divine displeasure. Many Friends were engaged to go to the courts of justice, and exhort the officers to the discharge of their duties in endeavouring to suppress it; they also preached against it in the markets and places of public entertainment. So contrary were their example and precepts to the prevailing corruptions, and so plain and fearless the rebukes they administered, that they were subjected to much abuse; yet, in many cases, they were the happy instruments of turning sinners from the evil of their ways. The licentiousness which had infected nearly all ranks of society, and was tolerated, if not countenanced, by too many whose duty it was to repress it, furnished ample reason for the close and even sharp expostulations, which are found about this time in the writings of Friends.

In taking a view of the religious principles of the

Society, it is proper to remark, that they have always scrupulously adhered to the position, of proving their doctrines by the testimony of the Holy Scriptures, rejecting whatever was contrary to the tenor of those divine writings. In their ministerial labours, their constant appeal to the people, against the existing errors, was to Holy Scripture. It is a well-known fact that George Fox carried a Bible with him, which he frequently used in his preaching; and in the meeting-house which he gave to Friends of Swarthmore, he placed a Bible, for the convenience of reference and perusal by those who attended the meeting. Samuel Bownas also carried a copy of the Holy Scriptures with him; and sometimes preached with it in his hand; and there is reason to believe that the practice was not uncommon. These facts contradict the groundless accusation which is sometimes made, that those worthy men did not acknowledge the paramount authority of Holy Scripture over all other writings. The Society has always accepted them fully and literally, as a rule of faith and practice, under the enlightening influences of the Spirit of Truth, by which they were given forth. Such is the high character they have ever attached to the sacred text, that they uniformly refused to accept, instead of it, the glosses and interpretations of school-men. It was thus they were led to the observance of the positive commands of our Saviour not to swear, or to fight even in self-defence, as well as to the strict and literal acceptance of those precepts which forbid worldly compliance and indulgence; from the force of which too many professors have sought to escape. It is true that they recommended their hearers to Christ Jesus the heavenly Teacher, who, by his Holy Spirit, has come to teach his people Himself; yet they were careful to support this recommendation by showing its entire consonance with the whole scope of the Christian dispensation.

But while Friends fully admitted the divine origin and authority of the Sacred Volume, and acknowledged the richness of the blessing we enjoy in having it preserved and transmitted to us through the goodness of Divine Providence, they dared not put it in the place of Christ, either as regarded honour or office; an error which they believed they saw in many of the high professors of their day.

They wished the Scriptures of Truth and the Holy Spirit to occupy the places in the work of salvation respectively assigned to them in the Bible itself. It was for these causes that they pressed on professors the necessity of coming unto Christ, that they might have life; even though versed in the literal knowledge of the Bible. That as its precious truths are not savingly known or appreciated by the unassisted reason of fallen man, so it is necessary to seek the aid of the Holy Spirit, which searcheth all things, yea, the deep things of God, to open our understandings, and illuminate the darkness of our hearts, and to prepare us for their reception. In asserting the superiority of the knowledge thus derived through the operations of the Holy Spirit, over that which is acquired by the mere exercise of the unassisted intellectual faculties in the reading of the Sacred Volume, Friends were sometimes misunderstood, and charged with denying the Scriptures of Truth, placing their own writings on a level with them, and professing that equally good Scriptures could be written at the present day, as those which were penned by prophets, evangelists, and apostles. But no sooner were these accusations made than they were met by an unqualified denial, asserting, in the fullest and most solemn manner, the sincere belief of Friends in all that the Scriptures say respecting their divine origin, authority, and use.

The prominent manner in which they believed themselves called to hold up the important offices of the Holy Spirit in the work of salvation, was another source of misapprehension among their opponents. Baxter, in his account of Friends, says of them, " They spake much for the dwelling and working of the Spirit in us, but little of justification and the pardon of sin, and our reconciliation with God, through Jesus Christ."

It is not correct to say that Friends " spake *little*" on the great doctrines of justification and remission of sins, through Christ Jesus, our propitiation ; for they frequently and earnestly insisted on them. But finding that these were generally admitted by all Christian professors, while many either entirely denied or undervalued the work of the Holy Spirit in the heart, they were engaged to call the attention of the people to this, as the life of true religion; without which the Scriptures could not make them wise unto salvation, and Christ would have died for them in vain. But while thus enforcing this important doctrine of Holy Scripture, they were careful to recognize and acknowledge the whole scope of the Gospel, in all its fulness. They declared against that construction of the doctrine of Christ's satisfaction which taught men to believe they could be justified from their sins, while they continued in them impenitent; asserting that the very design of Christ's coming in the flesh was to save people from their sins, and to destroy the works of the devil. Yet they fully. and gratefully acknowledged the mercy of God, in giving his dear Son, a ransom and atonement for mankind; that the penitent sinner might be justified freely by his grace, through the redemption that is in Christ Jesus.

Many of them were persons who had been highly esteemed for their piety, in the Societies with which they had formerly been connected, and several of them had been preachers. In the progress of their religious experience they were convinced that they had been resting too much on a bare belief of what

hrist had done and suffered for them when personally on earth, and also in the ceremonies of religion, without sufficiently pressing after the knowledge of " Christ in them, the hope of glory "—or feeling his righteous government set up in their hearts, and the power of the Holy Spirit giving them the victory over sin in all its motions, and qualifying them to serve God in newness of life. They saw that the Holy Scriptures held up to the view of Christians a state of religious advancement and stability, far beyond that which most of the professors of their day appeared to aim at or admit; a state in which sin was to have no more dominion over them, because the law of the Spirit of life in Christ Jesus had set them free from the law of sin and death. That this was an inward work, not effected by a bare assent of the understanding to the blessed truths contained in the Bible, by hearing sermons, dipping or sprinkling in water, or partaking of bread and wine, but by a real change of the heart and affections, by the power of the Holy Ghost inwardly revealed, regenerating the soul, creating it anew in Christ Jesus, and making all things pertaining to it of God.

Convinced that this great work was necessary to salvation, and yet in great danger of being overlooked amid a round of ceremonial performances, and a high profession of belief in Christ as the propitiation for sins, they zealously preached the doctrine of the new birth; calling their hearers to come to Christ Jesus, the true Light which lighteth every man that cometh into the world, that they might experience Him to shine in their hearts, to give them the light of the knowledge of the glory of God in the face of Jesus Christ.

The offices of the Holy Ghost, or Comforter, as the guide into all truth, as the unction from the Holy One, which teacheth of all things, and is truth, and no lie, was the great theme of their contemplation and ministry, and it stands forth no less conspicuously in their writings.

When we turn to the Sacred Volume, and read there the numerous testimonies borne to the great importance of this doctrine in the Gospel plan, we cannot wonder to find it prominently set forth by a people professing eminently the spirituality of religion. But to infer from the fact of their preaching Christ within, that they designed in any degree to deny Christ without, or to derogate from any part of the work which, in adorable condescension, He was graciously pleased to accomplish for us in the prepared body, or from that complete justification from our sins which is obtained through living faith in Him, as our Sacrifice and Mediator, would be illiberal and unjust.

When such accusations were brought against them by their enemies, they indignantly repelled and denied them; and the official declarations and acts of the Society evince that such opinions were never received or tolerated by it.

In carrying out these views of the spiritual nature

of the Gospel, and of that great work in the soul described as "the washing of regeneration and the renewing of the Holy Ghost," the primitive Friends were led to the adoption of their peculiar sentiments respecting water-baptism and the use of the bread and wine. They found it declared in the Sacred Volume, that as "there is one Lord and one faith," so there is "one baptism;" and that the baptism which now saves, "is not the putting away of the filth of the flesh, but the answer of a good conscience toward God, by the resurrection of Jesus Christ." Corresponding with this is the saying of the apostle to the Romans, "Know ye not that so many of us as were baptized into Jesus Christ, were baptized into his death—therefore, we are buried with him by baptism into death; that like as Christ was raised up from the dead, by the glory of the Father, even so we also should walk in newness of life." Also, that to the Galatians, "As many of you as have been baptized into Christ, have put on Christ;" and to the Colossians, where he declares that those who are in Christ, are "buried with him, in baptism, wherein also ye are risen with him, through the faith of the operation of God, who hath raised him from the dead." Sensible that these blessed effects were not the result of dipping or sprinkling the body with water, and apprehensive that many professors of religion were trusting to the outward ceremony as a means of initiating them into the Church of Christ, while neglecting the necessary work of " repentance towards God and faith in our Lord Jesus Christ," they pressed upon their hearers the necessity of experiencing that one saving baptism, which John describes when drawing the distinction between his dispensation and that of Christ—" I indeed baptize you with water: but One mightier than I cometh, the latchet of whose shoes I am not worthy to unloose: he shall baptize you with the Holy Ghost and with fire."

Convinced that the Gospel is not a dispensation of shadows, but the very substance of the heavenly things themselves, they believed that the true communion of saints consisted in that divine intercourse which is maintained between our merciful Saviour and the souls of his faithful disciples ; agreeably to his own gracious words : " Behold I stand at the door and knock : if any man hear my voice, and open the door, I will come in to him and sup with him, and he with me."

There is a strong tendency in the human mind to substitute the form of religion for the power, and to satisfy the conscience by a cold compliance with exterior performances, while the heart remains unchanged. And inasmuch as the baptism of the Holy Ghost and the communion of the body and blood of Christ, of which water-baptism and the bread and wine are admitted to be only signs, are not dependent on those outward ceremonies, or necessarily connected with them, and are declared in Holy Scripture to be effectual to the salvation of the soul, which the signs are not, Friends have always believed it their place and duty to hold forth to the world a clear and decided testimony to the living substance — the spiritual work of Christ in the soul, and a blessed communion with Him there.

A distinguished trait in the character of the first Friends was, that amid the great political commotions which prevailed, they attached themselves to none of the parties, and entered into none of their ambitious views. It was a principle of their religion to avoid all strife and contention, and to live peaceably under whatever form of government Divine Providence was pleased to permit. When the laws of the land came into collision with their duty to God, and they could not for conscience' sake actively comply with their demands, they patiently endured the penalties. When the nation was in a great ferment, after the death of Cromwell, George Fox, ever watchful for the welfare of his brethren, addressed a letter, exhorting them " to live in love and peace with all men—to keep clear of all the commotions of the world, and not to intermeddle with the powers of the earth, but to let their conversation be in heaven."—" All who pretend to fight for Christ," says he, " are deceived; for his kingdom is not of this world, and therefore his servan do not fight."

Unaided by any alliance with the great or powerful, ridiculed and hated by the world, and everywhere pursued with contempt and cruelty, the principles of Friends silently spread through the kingdom, winning the assent of men who were inferior to none in education, talents, and respectability. Amid the severest persecution, when deprived of every temporal comfort, torn from home and all its endearments, with every probability that they should seal the truth of their principles with the sacrifice of their lives, they faltered not. Though all around them looked dark and threatening, yet there was light and peace within;—they not only met their sufferings with patience and fortitude, in the unresisting spirit of their Divine Master, but, through the goodness of God, were so filled with heavenly consolation, that they sang for joy even in the extremity of their sufferings.

Exposed to almost universal hatred and abuse, their names despised and cast out from among men, the disinterested love they showed for each other excited the admiration even of their enemies. While each one seemed regardless of his own liberty and estate, all were zealous in pleading the cause of their suffering brethren, when occasion presented; freely sacrificing their time and property to promote their comfort, and even offering themselves to lie in prison, instead of those whom they thought could be less easily spared from their families or the Society.

Such fruits of Christian love and forbearance, under protracted and poignant suffering, unjustly inflicted, have rarely been exhibited to the world; and nothing less than the marvellous extension of Almighty Power, could have sustained and carried them through it all, to the peaceful enjoyment of that liberty of conscience for which they nobly contended. Their conduct furnishes the strongest evidence of sincere and devoted attachment to the cause of Christ. It proves that they were true men, earnestly engaged in seeking after truth; while the Divine support they experienced, and the brightness with which they were enabled to hold forth, in their example, the Christian virtues, are no inconsiderable testimonies of the favour of that God whom they delighted to serve.

The character of the founders of the Society has not been duly appreciated, even by many of their successors in religious profession. We look back o the age in which they lived as one of comparative ignorance; and tracing the improvements which have since been made in the arts, and in literature and the sciences, as well as the more liberal views of civil and religious liberty which now generally obtain, we are apt to undervalue the wisdom and attainments of our ancestors. But our opinion respecting them will change when we discover how far they were in advance of the times in which they flourished,—that though many of them possessed but few of the advantages of literary instruction, yet their minds, enlightened by the influences of the Spirit of Truth, and expanded by Christian benevolence, were prepared to perceive and to promulgate these great moral and religious truths which are considered the peculiar ornament and glory of the present age.

One of the earliest subjects of concern to George Fox was the want of moderation and temperance in eating and drinking. " The Lord showed me," says he, " that I might not eat and drink to make myself wanton, but for health, using the creatures as servants in their places to the glory of Him that created them." He also observes, that he was engaged " in warning such as kept public-houses for entertainment, that they should not let people have more drink than would do them good," and in crying against the sin of drunkenness; setting an example of remarkable abstinence in his manner of life. The testimony thus early and zealously enforced has ever since been maintained, and from that period to the present, Friends, as a body, have been a Temperance Society.

No less clear were his views in regard to speaking the *truth* on all occasions, without the use of an oath. " The Lord showed me," says he, " that though the people of the world have mouths full of deceit and changeable words, yet I was to keep to yea and nay in all things, and that my words should be few and savoury, seasoned with grace ;"—and he warned all to deal justly, to speak the truth, to let their yea be yea and their nay nay, and to do unto others as they would have others do unto them;—for " that Christ commanded, Swear not at all; and God, when He bringeth the first-begotten into the world, saith, ' Let all the angels of God worship Him,' even Christ Jesus, who saith, ' Swear not at all.' As for the plea that men make for swearing, viz., to end their strife, Christ, who forbids swearing, destroys the devil and his works, who is the author of strife."

The uniform and consistent example of the first Friends, in respect to a scrupulous adherence to their word, as men of truth, and to strict uprightness in all their dealings, soon gained them a high reputation for those virtues. Their objection to the use of oaths cost them much suffering; but their faithfulness at length triumphed over opposition, and their conscientious scruple was recognized and tolerated by an Act of Parliament. Since that period a striking change has been wrought in public opinion. By late Acts of Parliament numerous oaths have been dispensed with in England.

The benevolent and enlightened mind of George Fox was deeply affected with the sanguinary character of the penal code of Great Britain, and, believing that the benign spirit of the Gospel would lead to save men's lives rather than to destroy them, he was engaged to write to the judges and others in authority, " concerning their putting to death for small matters, and to show them how contrary it was to the law of God in old time; for," says he,

"I was under great suffering in my spirit because of it." In an address "to the Parliament of the Commonwealth of England," setting forth a number of particulars "for taking away oppressive laws," &c., he says, "Let no one be put to death for [stealing] cattle, or money, or any outward thing—but let them restore; and mind the law of God, which is equity and measurable, agreeably to the offence."

This is perhaps the earliest account extant of any proposal for meliorating the severity of penal enactments.

The amiable and pacific principles which produced these views in the founder of the Society, gave rise to corresponding feelings in the minds of other members. William Penn, in framing laws for Pennsylvania, mitigated considerably the harshness of the English code, and it is a well-known fact that Friends have always been the advocates of a mild system of punishment, coupled with penitentiary regulations.

In the improvement of prisons and prison-discipline they also took the lead.

Being frequently confined for his conscientious adherence to the precepts of Christ and his apostles, he had an opportunity of seeing the wretched condition of the gaols in England, and of witnessing the demoralizing effects of associating the novice in crime with the hardened offender. His tender feelings were quickly awakened on this interesting subject, and when about twenty-six years of age, he published a paper, showing " what a hurtful thing it was for prisoners to lie so long in gaol, and how they learned wickedness one of another, in talking of their bad deeds;" and inciting the judges of courts to the prompt administration of law, that the prisoners might as quickly as practicable be removed from the influence of such corrupting examples. In the address to the Parliament, before quoted, he says, " Let none be gaolers that are drunkards, swearers, or oppressors of the people; but such as may be good examples to the prisoners. And let none lie long in gaol, for that is the way to spoil people, and to make more thieves; for there they learn wickedness together." Again he says, " Let all gaols be in wholesome places, that the prisoners may not lie in the filth and straw like chaff," &c.; and, after mentioning some of the nuisances then existing in prisons, he adds, " Let these things be mended."

There are several other recommendations which bespeak the liberality and correctness of his views; such as the following, viz. :—

" Let all the laws in England be brought into a known tongue." Many of them, as well as the proceedings of courts, were then in the Latin language.

" Let no swearer, nor curser, nor drunkard bear any office whatever, nor be put in any place."

" Let none keep alehouses or taverns, but those who fear God ; that will not let the creatures of God be destroyed by drunkenness."

" Let no man keep an alehouse or tavern, that keeps bowls, shuffle-boards, or fiddlers, or dice, or cards."

" Let neither beggar, nor blind people, nor father-less, nor widows, nor cripples, go begging up and down the streets; but that a house may be provided for them all, and also meat, that there may be never a beggar among you."

" And let all this wearing of gold lace and costly attire be ended, and clothe the naked and feed the hungry with the superfluity. And turn not your ear away from the cry of the poor."

About the time that George Fox attained his twenty-sixth year, considerable efforts were made to induce him to join the parliament army, and a cap-taincy over a band of newly-raised troops was offered to him. But his religious opinions would not permit him to take up arms in any cause. The ruling principle of his life was " peace on earth and good will towards men." He, whose commands he esteemed of paramount authority, directed his fol-lowers to " love their enemies;" to do good to those who hated them, and to pray for those who despite-fully and evilly treated them. He had none of that sophistry which could reconcile the horrors of the battle-field, the anger, the revenge, and the cruelty which reign there, with these benevolent precepts. This simple acceptance of revealed truth was strongly marked in the character of the primitive Quakers. They sought not to evade or fritter away

F

the strict and positive injunctions of Holy Writ, because they came in collision with popular opinion, or thwarted the wayward inclinations of the human heart. "I told them," says George Fox, when speaking of the above-mentioned circumstance, "that I knew from whence all wars arose, even from the lusts, according to James's doctrine, and that I lived in the virtue of that life and power that took away the occasion of all wars. But they courted me to accept of their offer, and thought I did but compliment them. But I told them I was come into the covenant of peace, which was before wars and strifes were." Persuasion not effecting their object, they threw him into the common gaol, where he lay for six months, but without shaking his constancy.

When Sir George Booth afterwards rose in favour of the king, the Committee of Safety solicited Friends to enrol and join the army, offering important posts and commands to some of them. But neither the sharpness of their sufferings, nor prospects of honours or preferment, could induce them to violate their Christian testimony in favour of universal peace; and to the present day it has been steadily maintained, at no inconsiderable sacrifice both of liberty and estate.

The situation of the African race, and of the Indian nations in America, claimed much of G. F.'s attention and sympathy. One of his first engagements among his friends, after reaching Barbadoes, was to hold a meeting of conference, in which, among other directions, he enjoined them " to train their negroes up in the fear of God, that all might come to the knowledge of the Lord, and that, with Joshua, every master of a family might say, " As for me and my house, we will serve the Lord." I desired also that they would cause their overseers to deal mildly and gently with their negroes, and not use cruelty toward them, as the manner of some hath been and is, *and that after certain years of servitude they should make them free.*" In one of his epistles he expresses the sentiment that " liberty is the right of all men," and on many occasions he evinced a strong solicitude that the benefits of a religious education should be extended to them, as being equally interested with others in that salvation purchased for us by the Saviour's death.

His mind, expanded by Christian benevolence, reached forth in desire for the salvation of all mankind. So exceedingly precious did he esteem the glad tidings of the Gospel, and so adapted to the wants of man in every situation, that, while in America, he not only preached Christ crucified to the slaves and the Indians, but urged upon his brethren the same duty. " All Friends, everywhere," says he, in one of his epistles, " who have Indians or blacks, are to preach the Gospel to them and other servants, if you be true Christians." " And also you must instruct and teach your Indians and Negroes, and all others, that Christ, by the grace of God, tasted death for every man, and gave himself a ransom for all men, to be testified in due time, and is the propitiation, not for the sins of Christians only, but for the sins of the whole world." Again, he observes, " Do not neglect your family meetings among your whites and negroes; but do your diligence and duty to God and them." In another epistle to his friends, he directs them to go among the Indians, and get the chiefs to assemble their people, in order that they may declare to them God's free salvation through Jesus Christ the Lord.

The same enlarged views are evinced by the letters he wrote to some Friends, who, in pursuing a seafaring life, had been carried captive to the coast of Africa. He advises them to acquire a knowledge of the language spoken in the places where they were situated, in order that they might be able to preach to the inhabitants the glad tidings of redemption, through a crucified Saviour, and to translate works which would tend to promote Christian knowledge.

Nor was this Christian concern for the promulgation of the Gospel confined to George Fox. William Penn, in his frequent intercourse with the Indians, took especial care not only to teach them Christianity by precept, but by a just, liberal, and blameless conduct and example, to prepare their minds for the reception of its sublime truths. Ministers of the Society, at different periods, travelled into remote countries, without the least prospect of temporal reward, in order to declare unto others that free salvation, of which, through the mercy of God, they were made partakers.

In advocating the cause of religious and civil liberty the Society of Friends has always stood conspicuous. During a protracted period of persecution and suffering they nobly refused to sacrifice their conscientious scruples, maintaining a patient but firm and unyielding opposition to the arbitrary intolerance and cruelty of those in power. Their steadfastness and boldness in suffering, not only relieved other dissenters from the sharpness of persecution, but tended to prepare the way for those more correct views of toleration which subsequently obtained.

Baxter, though not favourably disposed towards Friends, bears testimony to their constancy under the cruel operation of the Conventicle Act, observing, " Here the Quakers did greatly relieve the sober people for a time ; for they are so resolute, and so gloried in their constancy and sufferings, that they assembled openly at the Bull and Mouth, near Aldersgate, and were dragged away daily to the common gaol, and yet desisted not, but the rest came next day. Abundance of them died in prison, and yet they continued their assemblies still."

On this passage, Orme, the biographer of Baxter, makes this remark : " Had there been more of the same determined spirit among others which the Friends displayed, the sufferings of all parties would sooner have come to an end. The government must have given way, as the spirit of the country would have been effectually roused. The conduct of the Quakers was infinitely to their honour." In another note relative to Friends, the same writer remarks, " The heroic and persevering conduct of the Quakers, in withstanding the interferences of government with the rights of conscience, by which they finally secured those peculiar privileges they so richly deserve to enjoy, entitles them to the veneration of all the friends of civil and religious freedom."

There is no doubt that the persecutions which disgraced England, during the seventeenth century, of which Friends, in common with other dissenters, bore so large a share, contributed very much toward the introduction and establishment of those more liberal and correct views of toleration and civil liberty which succeeded, and so happily distinguish the present times. The constancy of Friends under suffering, their uniform testimony in favour of liberty of conscience to all, the boldness with which they exposed the rapacity and illegal proceedings of the persecuting priests, justices and judges, and their repeated and earnest applications to the king and parliament were eminently instrumental in preparing the way for the passing of the Toleration Act, under William and Mary, in 1688.

It was not as a boon for themselves that they urged the adoption of this great measure : they took the simple ground that liberty of conscience was the right of all men; and that all interference of the government in matters of religion, by which the subject was debarred from the exercise of this right, provided he did not molest others, was contrary to Christianity, to reason, and to sound policy.

In framing the government of Pennsylvania, William Penn adopted these principles, and carried them out to the fullest extent; not only tolerating every religion which owned the existence of a God, but making the professors of all eligible to offices.

Sir James Mackintosh, in his History of the Revolution in England, in explaining the part which William Penn took in defending the declaration of indulgence issued by James, a measure which, however just the rights it granted, was nevertheless denounced as an unconstitutional and arbitrary assumption of power, has these observations: " The most distinguished of their converts was William Penn, whose father, Admiral Sir William Penn, had been a personal friend of the king, and one of his instructors in naval affairs. This admirable person had employed his great abilities in support of civil as well as religious liberty, and had both acted and suffered for them, under Charles II. Even if he had not founded the Commonwealth of Pennsylvania, as an everlasting memorial of his love of freedom, his actions and writings in England would have been enough to absolve him from the charge of intending to betray the rights of his countrymen. But though the friend of Algernon Sidney, he had never ceased to intercede through his friends at court, for the persecuted. An absence of two years in America, and the occupation of his mind, had probably loosened his connexion with English politicians, and rendered him less acquainted with the principles of the government. On the accession of James he was received by that prince with favour, and hopes of indulgence to his suffering brethren were early held out to him. He was soon admitted to terms of apparent intimacy, and was believed to possess such influence, that two hundred supplicants were often seen at his gates, imploring his intercession with the king. That it really was great appears from his obtaining a promise of pardon for his friend, Mr. Locke, which that illustrious man declined, because he thought that the acceptance would have been a confession of criminality. He appears in 1679, by his influence on James, when in Scotland, to have obtained the release of all the Scotch Quakers who were imprisoned, and he obtained the release of many hundred Quaker prisoners in England, as well as letters from Lord Sunderland to the lord-lieutenants in England, for favour to his persuasion, several months before the declaration of indulgence. It was no wonder that he should be gained over by this power of doing good. The very occupations in which he was engaged, brought daily before his mind the general evils of intolerance and the sufferings of his own unfortunate brethren." "It cannot be doubted that he believed the king's object to be universal liberty in religion, and nothing further. His own sincere piety taught him to consider religious liberty as unspeakably the highest of human privileges, and he was too just not to be desirous of bestowing on all other men that which he most earnestly sought for himself. He who refused to employ force in the most just defence, felt a singular abhorrence of its exertion to prevent good men from following the dictates of their conscience."—p. 289.

Previous to this period William Penn had written and suffered much in defence of liberty of conscience, and it was to be expected that, when thousands of his friends were suffering imprisonment and spoliation by merciless informers and magistrates, he would eagerly embrace the relief afforded by the king's indulgence without a very profound investigation of the disputed point of royal prerogative, or the secret motives which influenced the crown.

Another subject which claimed the early attention of George Fox was the promotion of useful learning. He recommended the establishment of two boarding-schools, which were accordingly opened, one for boys and the other for girls. Although the Society has always contended that human learning was not an essential requisite for the ministry of the Gospel, yet it has, from a very early period, been careful to provide for its members the benefits of education. The following recommendation was issued by the Yearly Meeting as early as the year 1695, viz. :—

" Advised, that school-masters and mistresses, who

are faithful Friends and *well qualified*, be encouraged in all counties, cities, great towns, or other places where they may be needed ; and that care be taken that poor Friends' children may freely partake of such education as may tend to their benefit and advantage, in order to apprenticeship." From that period to the present time the subject has frequently been earnestly enjoined on the attention of Friends, and large sums expended in founding seminaries for their youth. Soon after the settlement of Philadelphia, William Penn founded a grammar-school for Greek and Latin, and incorporated a board of education, which is still in operation, under the title of " The Overseers of the Public School founded by charter, in the town and county of Philadelphia, in Pennsylvania ;" with a corporate seal, bearing this inscription : " Good instruction is better than riches."

It would not be practicable, in this brief sketch, to do justice to other members of the Society, who aided in carrying out the liberal views which we have endeavoured to portray. It is sufficient to remark, that those views were the general characteristics of the Society, and some of them peculiar to it. For a long period they maintained many of them single-handed and in opposition to the general voice of the community. That their faithful labours in these great works of Christian benevolence have contributed to bring them to their present condition, cannot be denied ; nor yet that the principles of the Society of Friends, and the practices consequent upon them, are eminently calculated to promote the religious and moral improvement of mankind, and to augment the sum of human happiness.

It is no less the privilege and interest than it is the duty of Christians to be diligent in the use of those means which a merciful Providence has placed within their reach, for attaining a correct knowledge of the principles and practices of our holy religion.

If we have a proper sense of the shortness and uncertainty of life, of our responsibility as accountable and immortal beings, and of the vast importance of the concerns which relate to the salvation of the soul, we shall not rest satisfied without a careful inquiry into the truth of those doctrines and precepts by which we profess to regulate our conduct, and to build our hopes of future happiness, in a world that will never have an end. We shall frequently ponder the inspired pages of Holy Writ, as the divinely authorized record of the Christian religion, and raise our hearts in aspirations to our Heavenly Father for the light of his Holy Spirit, to illumine our darkness, and give us a saving knowledge of the Truth as it is in Jesus. Nor will it be less interesting to us to trace out the result of these principles, as exhibited in the examples of those who have gone before us. To enquire what fruits of holiness they produced in their conduct and conversation,—what support they derived from them, amid the trials inseparable from mortal existence, and what consolation and hope they yielded in the hours of disease and of death. If, in the course of our researches, we discover that they were remarkable for their justice, their integrity, their meekness and humility—were patient under suffering, even when wrongfully inflicted; zealously devoted to the cause of Christ, and cheerfully given up to spend their time and substance for its advancement; "blameless and harmless," "in the midst of a crooked and perverse generation, amongst whom they shone as lights in the world," we may be assured that the tree whence these fruits of the Gospel sprung could not be evil. The faith which showed itself by such works of righteousness must be that by which the saints of old "obtained a good report," and which was their victory. If we follow them to the chamber of sickness and to the bed of death, witness the tranquillity and composure of their spirits, their humble, yet steadfast reliance on the mercy of God, through Jesus Christ, their peace and joy in believing, and their hope full of immortality and eternal life, we shall not only derive the strongest evidence of the soundness of their Christian belief, but, in admiration of its blessed and happy effects, be incited to follow them as they followed Christ.

Differing, as Friends do, in some points, from their fellow-professors of the Christian name, construing the requisitions of the Gospel with especial reference to the spiritual nature of true religion, and its non-conformity to the fashion of " the world which lieth in wickedness," their peculiarities in doctrine, manners, and phraseology, have, ever since their first rise, subjected them to greater or less degrees of misrepresentation and obloquy. For, although they have uniformly appealed to the Holy Scriptures as the standard and test of all their doctrines and practices, freely rejecting whatever should be proved to be inconsistent with their Divine Testimony, yet, either through ignorance or prejudice, or the force of sectarian attachments, their repeated declarations have been disregarded or perverted, in order to represent them as slighting those Sacred Writings, and their principles as scarcely deserving the name of Christian.

It is often more easy to disparage the character of an opponent, by loading him with opprobrious epithets, than to refute his positions by sound and solid arguments ; and mankind are generally so prone to adopt this course, rather than take the trouble of impartial investigation, that it is not surprising the terms enthusiasts, fanatics, Jesuits, and others of similar or more odious import, should have been freely bestowed on Friends and credited by too many. Those who have not had the opportunity, or who have disliked the task of ascertaining their real belief, and whose impressions have been chiefly derived from caricatures, drawn by persons whose object and interest it is to place them in the wrong, could scarcely fail to form opinions unfavourable to them as a body, however they might respect the piety and sincerity of individual members. Nor would it be surprising if the frequent and confident reiteration of grave, though unjust charges, should have the effect to awaken doubts, even in the minds of the uninformed members themselves; to lessen their esteem for those devoted Christians who were the instruments, divinely fitted and made use of, in founding the Society; and to induce the apprehension that the way and the people, thus "everywhere spoken against," must indeed have little claims to Christianity.

It may not be inappropriate to remind the reader that the Son of God himself was "set for a sign that should be spoken against;" and such has been the lot of his Church from the earliest periods of its existence. Had the propagation of the Gospel, in the days of the apostles, depended on the estimation in which they were held by the wise, the learned, and powerful of this world, or on the report which they gave of its character and design, it must have made little progress; but there were many others beside the Bereans who were more noble than to be influenced by such means, and who searched for themselves "whether these things were so."

Happily for the Society it has nothing to fear from investigation, conducted in the spirit of candour and fairness. The various accusations against it have been fearlessly met and refuted; and of those who may entertain doubts respecting the soundness of its faith, it asks a calm and dispassionate attention to its authorized vindications, and to its official declarations of faith. Whatsoever ambiguity may hang over the essays of some of its writers, arising either from the heat of controversy, the redundant and loose phraseology of the times, or from unduly pressing an argument in order to discredit the premises of an antagonist, by exposing the consequences deducible from them, the declarations of faith and the official acts of the Society prove conclusively, that on the points where they have been most questioned, their views are clear and scriptural. The records of the Society also show a long list of worthies whose dying hours and sayings bear ample testimony that the principles in which they had lived, and by which they endeavoured to regulate their actions, did not fail them in the near prospect of death and eternity; but administered all that support, consolation, and animating hope which give to the death-bed of the Christian its peculiar interest.

It is especially obligatory on Friends to be themselves conversant in these matters. Ignorance of them, where the means of information are accessible, is discreditable, if not culpable. We should be prepared to give to every one that asketh us a reason for our faith and hope. If the things which belong to our peace have a due place in our affections, we shall meditate with pleasure on the experience of those who have trodden the path of virtue before us. The fervour of our piety, the strength of our attachment to religious truth, will be promoted by frequently perusing their excellent writings, and dwelling in serious contemplation on the bright example they left us, adorned with the Christian graces, and inviting us to follow in their footsteps.

To whatever department of human pursuit we direct our attention, we perceive that men delight in the productions of congenial minds. He who finds that he has little relish for serious things, and that it is difficult to fix his attention upon them, may safely infer that his heart is not right in the sight of God, nor its aspirations directed towards the kingdom of heaven. The religious man delights to dwell on those things which concern the salvation of his soul. He feels a lively interest in the saints and holy men who have entered the celestial city before him ; and as he contemplates their blameless walk, their faith and patience under trials, their simple obedience and dedication, and above all, the blessed animating hope of an eternal inheritance which shed a bright radiance around their dying-beds, his whole soul kindles with desire to arise and gird himself anew for the journey, and with increased diligence and ardour to press toward the mark for the prize of his high calling of God in Christ Jesus.

Beside the authorities mentioned in the course of the Introductory Remarks, the Editors are indebted to Hume's History of England, Neale's History of the Puritans, ¡Gough's History of Friends, Clarendon's History of the Rebellion.

MEMOIR

OF

GEORGE FOX.

MEMOIR

OF THE

LIFE OF GEORGE FOX.

CHAPTER I.   1624-1647.

Early Life—Religious Exercises—Views of Christian Truth.

GEORGE FOX was born in the month called July, old style, now the Fifth Month, in the year 1624, at Drayton in the Clay, Leicestershire, which appears to be the same place as is now called Fenny Drayton.* His parents were Christopher and Mary Fox, who, though in humble circumstances, were highly esteemed by their neighbours for piety and uprightness.   His father was a weaver, known by the name of Righteous Christer, in consequence of the strictness and sobriety of his life.   Both he and his wife

---

* This sketch of the life of George Fox is chiefly compiled from his Journal, of which Sir James Macintosh says, it is "one of the most extraordinary and instructive narratives in the world—which no reader of competent judgment can peruse without revering the virtue of the writer."

‚ The extracts from G. Fox's writings contained in this volume are, with very little exception, taken verbatim from the folio edition of his life, published in the year 1694.

endeavoured to bring up their children in an exemplary manner, according to the religion of the Episcopal Church, to which they belonged. But it suited neither their circumstances nor situation in life to give their children much learning, and George enjoyed no other literary advantages than those of a plain English education. From a child he was of a religious and observing turn of mind; and such were the gravity and innocency of his spirit, that his relations were desirous he should be educated for the ministry. His mother taking notice of his serious temper, and of his piety and stability, was very watchful and tender over him; endeavouring to cherish his religious impressions, and to strengthen him in good resolutions. When very young he refused to join in vain and childish sports, or to mingle in the company of rude or irreligious persons; and when he saw any behaving themselves lightly, it excited his sorrow, and occasioned him to say within himself, " If ever I come to be a man, surely I shall not do so; nor be so wanton."

" While I was a child," says he, " I was taught how to walk so as to be kept pure. The Lord taught me to be faithful in all things; to act faithfully two ways, viz., inwardly to God, and outwardly to man, and to keep to yea and nay in all things. For the Lord showed me, though the people of the world have mouths full of deceit and changeable words, that I was to keep to yea and nay in all things; that my words should be few and savoury, seasoned with grace, and that I might not eat and drink to make myself wanton, but for health, using the creatures in their service, as servants in their places, to the glory of Him that created them."

Some of his relations objecting to his being made a priest, he was apprenticed to a shoemaker who also dealt in wool. George's business was principally in the fields, tending the flocks of sheep, an employment well suited to his retiring and contemplative disposition, and strikingly emblematical of his future service in the church.

While in his master's employ, much property and money passed through his hands; and being governed by the preserving power of Divine Grace, he was scrupulously careful to wrong none, but to exercise justice and honesty toward all. In his dealings he frequently used the word "verily;" and such was his known firmness in adhering to his word, that it became a common observation among those who knew him, "If George says, 'verily,' there is no altering him."

The simplicity and plainness of his appearance and demeanour sometimes excited the ridicule of rude persons, of which he took little notice; but sober people generally loved him for his innocency and integrity. His tender mind was often grieved with the inconsistent conduct of the professors of religion. On one occasion, when about nineteen years of age, having observed the light and unprofitable conversation and conduct of some, and the eagerness with which others were pursuing the riches of this world, though both made a high profession of religion, his mind was deeply affected; and, withdrawing from the company, he spent the great part of the night alone, in prayer, mourning because of the wickedness which abounded in the world. In this situation, the language was intelligibly addressed to his mind, "Thou seest how young people go together into vanity, and old people into the earth:—thou must forsake all, old and young, and be as a stranger unto all."

About the twentieth year of his age, his exercises increased; he broke off all familiarity with his former acquaintance, and travelled into Northamptonshire and Buckinghamshire, and by Newport-Pagnel and Barnet, to London, seeking for the most religious professors; hoping to find in their society some relief for his tribulated spirit. For a time, however, his distress increased; and Satan, taking advantage of his sorrows, tempted him to despair of the mercy of God in Christ Jesus. Not succeeding in this snare, he tried to draw him into the commission of some sin. But it pleased the Lord, who saw the integrity of his heart and knew his close trials, to support his mind and eventually to deliver him out of them all.

Hearing that his relations were uneasy with his absence from home, he returned, and remained some time with them. They seem to have been in great measure strangers to the nature of his religious exercises; and in order to remove his deep thoughtfulness respecting the everlasting welfare of his soul, and the things which belong to the kingdom of heaven, some proposed that he should marry, and others that he should enter the army. Such proposals, however, were little suited to the state of his feelings, and rather added to his sorrows. He sought lonely places and there poured out his cries to the Lord, from whom alone he expected true comfort.

During this season of conflict, he applied to several ministers for counsel and aid; but none of them could help him, nor indeed did they appear to understand his disconsolate condition. But though afflicted, he was not forsaken; and by the teaching of the Holy Spirit, which our blessed Saviour promised should lead his followers into all truth, his mind was instructed in many of the mysteries of Christian redemption. He gave a striking evidence of this on one occasion, when Nathaniel Stevens, the priest of his native town, asked him "Why Christ cried out upon the cross, My God, my God! why hast thou forsaken me? and why He said, If it be possible let this cup pass from me, yet not my will but thine be done." "I told him," says George, "that at that time, the sins of all mankind were upon Him, and their iniquities and transgressions with which he was wounded, and which He was to bear and be an offering for them, as He was man; but died not, as He was God. So in that He died for all men, tasting death for every man, He was an offering for the sins of the whole world." Thus early in his Christian experience did this faithful servant of the Lord bear his testimony to the truth of that consoling and fundamental doctrine of the Gospel, that our dear Redeemer came into the world to save sinners, and laid down his precious life as a sacrifice and propitiation for the sins of mankind.

In the year 1645 he went to Mansetter, in Warwickshire, then to Tamworth and Coventry; at each of which places he had conversation with those called ministers, respecting the state of his mind; but their attempts to assuage his grief, and the advice they offered, showed them to be very deficient in solid religious experience, and left him without relief. One advised him to take tobacco and sing psalms —and another began to question him as to Christ's parentage. " I told him," says he, " that Mary was his mother, and that He was supposed to be the son of Joseph, but he was the Son of God."

Speaking of his situation at this time, he remarks, " My troubles were so great upon me, that I could have wished I had been born blind, that I might never have seen wickedness or vanity ; and deaf, that I might never have heard vain and wicked words, or the Lord's name blasphemed."

Instead of spending the time called Christmas in feasting and merriment, as was too generally the case, his benevolent disposition induced him to go from house to house, seeking out destitute and needy widows and other objects of charity, to whom he extended relief ; having the means not only of keeping himself from being chargeable, but of administering to the necessities of others. In 1846, he appears to have fixed his residence at Coventry, where he remained for a considerable time.

It is interesting to trace the gradual unfolding of the Christian testimonies now held by the Society of Friends, as they were opened, one by one, to the mind of this eminent servant of the Lord. His attention had been early directed to the Spirit of Christ in his own heart, as the great Teacher under the Gospel dispensation. By obedience to its discoveries he not only grew in grace and obtained the victory over sin, but the Holy Scriptures were so clearly opened to his understanding, that he became deeply instructed in the knowledge of divine things. The perceptible influences of the Holy Spirit in the mind of man, was a fundamental doctrine with him; and it is only by a belief in the same doctrine, and a humble submission to its operations in the soul, that we of the present day can sincerely embrace and practically maintain those religious principles which, through the faithfulness and sufferings of our worthy forefathers, have been transmitted to us.

Of the opinions then generally prevalent among professors, one of the first which was clearly shown him to be an error, was calling persons believers and Christians merely because they made a profession of religion. He was taught that none were true Christians or believers, but such as were really born of God, and passed from death unto life; and that all others, however high their pretensions to religion, were deceiving themselves. The effect of this sentiment was to strike at the root of a formal ceremonious religion; to lead to close self-examination, and an earnest endeavour to experience the great work of regeneration begun and carried on in the heart, that thus they might become true believers in Christ.

At another time, while walking in the fields on a First-day morning, the Lord gave him to see, that being bred at college, or acquiring human learning, was not a sufficient qualification for Gospel ministry; at which he greatly wondered, because the prevailing idea then was, that men could be fitted by education for that sacred office. But he was now convinced

that nothing short of an immediate call and qualification from Christ, the Head of the church, was
a sufficient authority to preach in his name; and
that before persons could properly declare to others
the mysteries of life and salvation, they must become
in measure practically acquainted with them, in
their own experience. That as Christ called, commissioned, and sent forth his apostles, in the beginning
of the Christian dispensation, so all those now who
had a part in the ministry must be called and qualified by Him.   These views were so clearly impressed
on his mind, that he was fully satisfied of their truth,
and greatly admired the Lord's goodness in thus
instructing him.   He perceived that they struck at
the priests' ministry, and he could not go any longer
to hear their preaching, but took his Bible and
retired alone into private places, there waiting on
the Lord in silence.   His relations were troubled at
his conduct, and endeavoured to persuade him to
attend their place of worship; but he could not feel
at liberty to do so, nor yet to join with any class of
dissenters, but became as a stranger to all, relying
wholly on the Lord Jesus Christ.

In the further progress of those openings, he was
shown that '' God who created the world, did not
dwell in temples made with hands,'' and that it was
therefore improper to call the houses erected for the
public worship of the Almighty, '' the temples of
God'' and '' dreadful places;'' or the land on which
they were built '' holy ground;'' which terms were at
that time commonly applied to them both by priests
and people.   He apprehended that the use of such
epithets had a tendency to keep the minds of the

people too much outward, and to prevent them from realizing the truth of the Gospel dispensation, that the hearts of sincere Christians are the temples of the Holy One. Both Stephen and the apostle Paul declared that the Most High did not dwell in temples made with hands, not even in that which He commanded to be built at Jerusalem, after He put an end to the legal dispensation; but that, according to the new covenant of the Gospel, He dwelt and walked in his obedient people. Thus divinely instructed, he could say with David, "Day unto day uttereth speech, and night unto night showeth knowledge." "When I had openings," he observes, "they answered one another, and answered the Scriptures; for I had great openings of the Scriptures."

Yet at times he was still under great conflict of mind, and many temptations beset him, insomuch that when it was day he wished for night, and when it was night he longed for the coming of the day. Early in 1647, he felt his mind drawn to go into Derbyshire, in the vicinity of the Peak, where he met with some friendly people. From thence he went through parts of Leicestershire and Nottinghamshire, where he found a number of tender, seeking persons, with whom he had meetings. Elizabeth Hooton, one of these, appears to have been the first person who openly joined in religious profession with him, and also the first minister in the Society of Friends, himself excepted.

His exercise of mind was not so constant but that he had intervals of consolation; and at times was brought into a state of heavenly enjoyment, which he compares to being in Abraham's bosom. "As I

cannot," says he, " declare the misery I was in, it
was so great and heavy upon me, so neither can I
set forth the mercies of God to me, in my misery.
Oh ! the everlasting love of God to my soul when I
was in great distress ! When my torments and
troubles were great, then was his love exceeding
great. Thou, Lord, makest the fruitful field a barren
wilderness, and a barren wilderness a fruitful field.
Thou bringest down and settest up. Thou killest
and makest alive. All honour and glory be to Thee,
O Lord of glory. The knowledge of Thee in the
Spirit is life."

Not finding in his intercourse with different professors of religion, that comfort and settlement which
he longed for, he continued to live in retirement;
and when all hope of help from man was gone, and
he had nothing outward to look to, he heard a voice,
as in the secret of his soul, saying, " There is one,
even Christ Jesus, that can speak to thy condition."
" When I heard it," he says, " my heart did leap for
joy. Then the Lord did let me see why there was
none upon the earth that could speak to my condition,
namely, that I might give him all the glory. For
all are concluded under sin, and shut up in unbelief,
as I had been, that Jesus Christ might have the pre-
eminence ; who enlightens, and gives grace, faith, and
power. Thus when God doth work, who shall let
it ? And this I know experimentally. My desires
after the Lord grew stronger, and zeal in the pure
knowledge of God and of Christ alone ; without the
help of any man, book, or writing. For though I
read the Scriptures that spake of Christ and of God,
yet I knew Him not but by revelation, as He who

hath the key did open, and as the Father of Life drew me to his Son by his Spirit. And then the Lord did gently lead me along, and did let me see his love, which was endless and eternal, and surpasseth all the knowledge that men have in the natural state, or can get by history or books."

After being thus highly favoured, he was again assailed with temptation to despair, as though he had sinned against the Holy Ghost, and was in great perplexity and trouble, yet still gave himself up to the Lord. "One day, when I had been walking solitary abroad," he says, "and was come home, I was taken up in the love of God, so that I could not but admire the greatness of his love; and while I was in that condition, it was opened unto me by the Eternal Light and Power, and I therein clearly saw that *all was done* and *to be done, in and by Christ;* and how He conquers and destroys this tempter, the devil, and all his works, and is atop of him; and that all these troubles were good for me, and temptations for the trial of my faith, which Christ had given me. And the Lord opened me that I saw through all these troubles and temptations. My living faith was raised, that I saw all was done by Christ the Life, and my belief was in him."

CHAPTER II. 1647-1651.

*First travels as a Preacher of the Gospel—Christian Practices
which he enjoined—Imprisonment at Derby.*

IN the year 1647, when about twenty-three years of
age, George Fox commenced his public appearance
as a minister of the Gospel, at Dukinfield, Man-
chester, and places in the neighbourhood. Some
were convinced by his ministry; and also at a great
meecting held at Broughton, in Leicestershire, where
he attended. The success accompanying his ministry
was great, and the report of his piety and zeal having
spread far, many came from different parts of the
country, to see and converse with him on religious
subjects. · This brought a fear upon his mind, lest he
should be improperly drawn out into words, or elated
by the attention shown to him, and this fear proved
a preservation to him. Others were exasperated at
the reception which his doctrines met with. They
could not endure to hear of perfection, and living a
holy and sinless life; and began to plead for sin and
imperfection, by which the tender convictions and
attractions of the Spirit of Grace are quenched.

" Of all the sects in Christendom (so called) that
I discoursed withal," says he, " I found none that
could bear to be told, that any should come to Adam's
perfection; into that image of God, and righteousness and holiness that Adam was in before he fell;

to be so clear and pure without sin as he was.
Therefore how should they be able to bear being
told that any should grow up to the measure of the
stature of the fulness of Christ, when they cannot
bear to hear that any shall come, whilst upon earth,
into the same power and spirit that the prophets
and apostles were in?   Though it be a certain truth,
that none can understand their writings aright,
without the same Spirit by which they were written."

The universal appearance of the Light of Christ
in the heart, by which he enlightens every man that
cometh into the world, was a doctrine of which
George Fox was early convinced, and which, like
the primitive ministers of Christ, he and his fellow-
labourers in the Gospel frequently declared to their
hearers.   His convictions of this truth are thus
described: "The Lord God hath opened to me by
his invisible power, how that every man was enlightened by the divine light of Christ, and I saw it
shine through all; and that they that believed in it
came out of condemnation, and came to the light of
life, and became the children of it; but they that
hated it, and did not believe in it, were condemned
by it, though they made a profession of Christ."

In describing his commission as a minister, he
says, "Now I was sent to turn people from darkness
to the light"—"to the grace of God and to the
truth in the heart, which came by Jesus,"—"that
all might come to know their salvation nigh.   For
I saw that Christ had died for all men; and was a
propitiation for all,"—"and that the manifestation
of the Spirit of God was given to every man to profit
withal.   These things I did not see by the help of

man, nor by the letter, (though they are written in the letter); but I saw them in the light of the Lord Jesus Christ, and by his immediate Spirit and power, as did the holy men of God, by whom the Holy Scriptures were written. Yet I had no slight esteem of the Holy Scriptures; but they were very precious to me, for I was in that Spirit by which they were given forth; and what the Lord opened in me, I afterwards found was agreeable to them. I could speak much of these things, and many volumes might be written; but all would prove too short to set forth the infinite love, wisdom and power of God, in preparing, fitting, and furnishing me for the service He had appointed me to; letting me see the depths of Satan on the one hand, and opening to me, on the other hand, the divine mysteries of his own everlasting kingdom."

He now travelled more extensively, and laboured abundantly in preaching the word. Many were convinced of the doctrines which he promulgated, and during the years 1647 and 1648 several meetings of Friends were settled. But as the nature of his principles was opposed to the outward and lifeless profession of religion which too much prevailed in that day, tending to draw the people from a dependence on human teaching and external ceremonies, to the work of regeneration by the Holy Spirit in their own hearts, he met with much opposition and cruel usage. His first imprisonment took place in 1648, at Nottingham; where he entered the place of public worship on a First-day morning, and spoke to the people on the subject of the Holy Scriptures, showing that the Spirit of Christ, by which the holy men of old wrote the Scriptures, was that by which only they could be rightly understood. As he was speaking, the officers arrested him and took him to a filthy prison, where he was detained until the sheriff, taking compassion on his uncomfortable situation, removed him to his house. How long he remained there does not appear, but he says it was "a pretty long time;" and after being discharged, he travelled as before, in the work of the ministry.

At Mansfield Woodhouse, in 1649, he entered the place of public worship, and attempted to speak to the people, but they fell upon him and cruelly beat him with their hands, Bibles, and sticks; then put him into the stocks, where he remained some time; and, finally, stoned him out of the town.*

* After the dissolution of the monarchy by the death of Charles, and the consequent suspension of the national form of worship, much greater latitude was allowed to the ministers of religion. During Cromwell's victorious campaign in Scotland, the ministers of that nation objected against him, for "opening the pulpit-doors to all intruders;" to which he replied, "We look on ministers as helpers of, not lords over, the faith of God's people. I appeal to their consciences, whether any denying their doctrines or dissenting from them, will not incur the censure of a sectary. And what is this but to deny Christians their liberty, and assume the infallible chair? Where do you find in Scripture that preaching is included [limited] within your functions? Though an approbation from men has order in it, and may be well, yet he that hath not a better than that, hath none at all. I hope He that ascended up on high may give his gifts to whom He pleases; and if those gifts be the seal of missions, are not you envious, though Eldad and Medad prophesy? You know who has bid us covet earnestly the best gifts, but chiefly that we may prophesy; which the apostle explains to be a speaking

By this unchristian usage he was so injured as scarcely to be able to stand or walk ; but meeting with some persons who pitied his situation, they administered to his relief, and through the mercy of the Lord he was soon healed. From there he went through Leicestershire, by Bagworth, Coventry, Atherstone, Market Bosworth, and Twy Cross, and into Derbyshire, preaching the Gospel of life and salvation, and warning the people to repent and turn from their wickedness.

to instruction, edification and comfort, which the instructed, edified, and comforted, can best tell the energy and effect of.

" Now, if this be evidence, take heed you envy not for your own sakes, lest you be guilty of a greater fault than Moses reproved in Joshua, when he envied for his sake. Indeed you err through mistake of the Scriptures. Approbation is an act of convenience, in respect of order, not of necessity, to give faculty to preach the Gospel. Your pretended fear, lest error should step in, is like the man that would keep all the wine out of the country, lest men should be drunk. It will be found an unjust and unwise jealousy, to deny a man the liberty he hath by nature, upon a supposition he may abuse it. When he doth abuse it, then judge."

This letter shows to what length Cromwell was disposed to go, as respects the license for preaching ;. and taking his sentiments as indicative of the opinions on the subject generally prevalent among the Independents, a great change from the previous restriction is obvious. Whether the practice of going into the places of worship and addressing the assembly, was at all times warrantable, it would be difficult at this day to decide. That it was not uncommon is evident, and the peculiar circumstances of the times furnish reasons in defence of it which do not now exist. It was by no means peculiar to our Society, and in most cases where Friends did it, there is reason to believe they waited until the stated preacher had done, before they attempted to speak.

" About this time," says he, " I was sorely exercised in going to their courts to cry for justices, and in speaking and writing to judges and justices, to do justly, and in warning such as kept public-houses for entertainment, that they should not let people have more drink than would do them good, and in testifying against their wakes, or feasts, their May-games,* sports, plays and shows; which trained up people to vanity and looseness, and led them from the fear of God; and the days they had set forth for holy days were usually the times wherein they most dishonoured God by these things. In fairs also, and markets, I was made to declare against their deceitful merchandize, and cheating and cozening; warning all to deal justly, and to speak the truth, and to let their yea be yea, and their nay be nay, and to to do unto others as they would have others do unto them, and forewarning them of the great and terrible day of the Lord which would come upon all. I was moved also to cry against all sorts of music, and against the mountebanks playing tricks on their stages; for they burdened the pure life, and stirred up people's minds to vanity. I was much exercised, too, with schoolmasters and schoolmistresses, warning them to teach their children sobriety in the fear of the Lord, that they might not be nursed and

* The reader will recollect that James I. had issued a proclamation encouraging these sports and revels, and that it was revived by Charles I. The licentiousness which grew out of the indulgence thus given, furnishes an explanation of the distress of mind which George Fox experienced on account of the prevailing wickedness, and the earnest manner in which he warned the people to repent and amend their lives.

trained up in lightness, vanity, and wantonness.
Likewise I was made to warn masters and mistresses,
fathers, and mothers, in private families, to take
care that their children and servants might be trained
up in the fear of the Lord, and that they themselves
should be therein examples and patterns of sobriety
and virtue to them."

Among other subjects which engaged the attention
of George Fox, was the gaiety and extravagance
which prevailed among the people. He believed
that the Christian religion led all those who faithfully obeyed its requirings, into simplicity and self-
denial in their manner of life. That instead of
being conformed to the world, they were to renounce
its vain fashions and customs, and avoid everything
which promoted pride or luxury. Hence he incul-
cated, by example as well as precept, a plain and
simple mode of living, free from needless show and
expense. Convinced that the use of compliments
and flattering titles, bowing and putting off the hat,
and of the plural number when speaking to one
person, had their origin in the pride of the human
heart which ·seeks honour from man, he was conscientiously bound to refrain from the use of everything of the sort, and to keep to the Scripture language of *thou* and *thee*, to one person, according to
the correct grammar rules. "The Lord showed me,"
says he, "that it was an honour below, which He
would lay in the dust and stain it; an honour which
proud flesh looked for, and sought not the honour
that came from God only. That it was an honour invented by men, in the fall and in the alienation from
God; who were offended if it was not given to them,

and yet would be looked upon themselves as saints, church-members, and great Christians. But Christ saith, ' How can ye believe, who receive honour one of another, and seek not the honour that cometh from God only?' ' And I,' saith Christ, ' receive not honour of men.' . . . . . Oh the blows, punchings, beatings, and imprisonments that we underwent, for not putting off our hats to men. . . The bad language and evil usage we received on this account, is hard to be expressed; besides the danger, we were sometimes in of losing our lives for this matter, and by the great professors of Christianity.'' Scarcely any testimony held by our worthy predecessors caused them more deep and bitter sufferings at their first appearance, but their faithfulness was not shaken; through it all they held fast their profession without wavering.

Believing that none could preach the Gospel but those whom Christ Jesus called, qualified, and commissioned for the work, and that these necessary qualifications were without regard to human learning or ordination, riches, station, or sex, and that all those thus anointed and engaged in the work were commanded by their Divine Master to give as freely as they had received, he bore a decided and faithful testimony against making merchandize of the Gospel, and receiving a pecuniary compensation for preaching. He deplored the covetous spirit which was apparent among many who took upon them the responsible office of the ministry, which induced them to seek for the highest salaries, leaving their flocks and places for greater wages, and pleading a call from the Lord so to do. Against this practice he testified, as an abomination and crying sin. " O," says he, " the vast sums of money that are gotten by the trade they make of selling the Scriptures, and by their preaching, from the highest bishop to the lowest priest! What one trade else in the world is comparable to it; notwithstanding that the Scriptures were given forth freely, and Christ commanded his ministers to preach freely, and the prophets and apostles denounced judgment against all covetous hirelings and diviners for money. But in this free Spirit of the Lord Jesus was I sent forth to declare the word of life and reconciliation freely, that all might come up to Christ, who gives freely, and who renews up into the image of God, which man and woman were in before they fell; that they might sit down in the heavenly places in Christ Jesus."

In the year 1650, he visited Derby and preached to the people, for which the officers arrested him and took him before the magistrates, who, after an examination of eight hours' length, committed him and John Fretwell, who was with him, to the house of correction, where they were confined six months.

During the examination, justices Bennet and Barton endeavoured to draw from him some expression by which they might prove him guilty of holding blasphemous opinions. They asked him, If he had no sin?—to which he replied, " Christ, my Saviour, has taken away my sin, and in Him there is no sin." Then they asked, " How the Quakers knew that Christ did abide in them ?"—and were answered, " By his Spirit that He had given them." Finding nothing in this upon which to ground a charge, they ensnaringly asked, " Whether any of them were Christ ? " To which G. F. promptly replied, " Nay —*We are nothing—Christ is all.*" This full acknowledgment of their own nothingness and the all-sufficiency of the Saviour, defeated their design— but still anxious to convict him, and, if possible, prove a coincidence between the Quakers and the Ranters, they asked, " If a man steal is it no sin ? " —alluding to the monstrous notions of that sect, by which moral good and evil were confounded. G. F. answered them in the words of Holy Scripture, " All unrighteousness is sin." But although he thus cleared himself and his fellow-professors from their imputations, yet they made out a mittimus and sent him and his companion to prison, as persons charged with uttering and broaching divers blasphemous opinions, contrary to the late act of parliament.

His relations were much concerned about his imprisonment, and offered to be bound that he should come to the town no more, if the justices would discharge him. But G. F. told them, that having done no wrong he could not consent to have anyone bound for him, a practice which he and his friends adhered to through all their long imprisonments. One of the justices was much enraged at his refusal, and as G. F. was kneeling down to pray for him, he ran upon him and struck him with both his hands, crying to the gaoler, " Away with him—take him away, gaoler." It was this justice, Gervas Bennet, who first called Friends Quakers, because George Fox bid him tremble at the word of the Lord.

The time of his commitment was now nearly out, and the parliament being engaged in raising troops, a commission as captain of one of the new regiments was offered to him by some of the officers of government. But George Fox objected to receiving it on conscientious grounds. He believed that, instead of war and bloodshed, the Gospel of Christ breathed " peace on earth and good will to men"—that the Son of God came not to destroy men's lives, but to save them, and to teach mankind to love their enemies instead of fighting them—to do good rather than evil to those who hate them, and to pray for those who despitefully use them. " I told them," he remarks, " I knew from whence all wars did arise, even from the lusts, according to James his doctrine, and that I lived in the virtue of that life and power that took away the occasion of all wars." Still they endeavoured to persuade him to accept their offer, and finding they could not prevail, they became angry and ordered him to be thrust into the common gaol, among the felons. This was a most noisome, offensive place, infested with vermin ; and there, among thirty abandoned rogues, he was kept almost half a year.

Many came to see him during this imprisonment, and among others, a soldier who had been a Baptist. This man said to him, " ' Your faith stands in a man that died at Jerusalem, and there was never any such thing.' I was exceedingly grieved to hear him say so," observes G. F., " and I said to him, ' How ! did not Christ suffer without the gates of Jerusalem, through the professing Jews, and chief priests, and Pilate ?' And he denied that ever

Christ suffered there outwardly. Then I asked him whether there were not chief priests, and Jews, and Pilate there outwardly. When he could not deny that, then I told him, as certainly as there was a chief priest, and Jews, and Pilate there outwardly, so certainly was Christ persecuted by them, and did suffer there outwardly under them. Yet from this man's words was a slander raised upon us, that the Quakers should deny Christ that suffered and died at Jerusalem; which was all utterly false, and the least thought of it never entered our hearts."

George Fox early bore a testimony against taking away human life under judicial proceedings. While he was in prison, a young woman was brought there for robbing her master. When she was about to be tried, he wrote to the judges and jury, showing them how contrary it was to the law of God to put persons to death for such offences. She was, however, condemned to die, and he then wrote a warning, to be read at the place of execution, against covetousness and greediness after the things of this world, which lead people away from God, and into many hurtful things. The woman was pardoned, and afterward became a Friend.

CHAPTER III.   1651-1656.

AFTER being a prisoner almost a year, six months
of which he passed in the house of correction, and the
remainder in the common gaol, he was set at liberty
about the beginning of winter, in 1651 ; and immediately resumed his travels, going into Leicestershire, Nottinghamshire, and Yorkshire, preaching
repentance and amendment of life wherever he came.
In several places he met with very cruel usage, being
beaten and stoned so as to endanger his life ; but,
through the goodness of his gracious Lord, he was
soon healed, and, nothing daunted at the hardships
he endured, persevered as a good soldier of Jesus
Christ in proclaiming the glad tidings of salvation
and peace.

He now became known to many of the justices,
some of whom formed a favourable opinion of his
doctrine, and treated him with marked kindness ;
Justice Hotham, of Crantsick, was of this character.
He acknowledged that " If God had not raised up
this principle of light and life, the nation had been
overrun with Ranterism ; and all the justices in the
nation could not have stopped it with all their laws ;

because," said he, "they would have said as we said, and done as we commanded, and yet have kept their own principle still. But this principle of truth," said he, "overthrows their principle and the root and ground thereof; and therefore," he said, " he was glad the Lord had raised up this principle of life and truth."

In 1652, coming to Tickhill, he sat some time with Friends at their meeting, and then went to the public-worship house, and began to address the people. But they immediately fell upon him and beat him—the clerk striking him on the face with a Bible, so that the blood gushed out on the floor of the house: then they cried, "Let us have him out of the church," and accordingly dragged him out and beat him, knocked him down and threw him over a hedge: then they dragged him through a house into the street, stoning and beating him as they went, so that he was covered with blood and dirt. As soon as he could recover himself and get upon his feet, he preached repentance to them, showing them the fruits of their false profession, and how they disgraced the Christian name. After some time he got into the meeting of Friends, and the priest and his hearers coming by the house, he went with Friends into the yard and again addressed them. They scoffed and called them Quakers; but such was the power accompanying his preaching, that the priest trembled, and one of the people called out, " Look, how the priest trembles.and shakes ; he is turned a Quaker also." In consequence of the abuse committed that day, two or three justices convened at the town to examine into the matter, and though the person who shed his blood was liable to a severe penalty, George

Fox forgave him, and would not appear against
him.

In reading these accounts of the sufferings of our
worthy predecessors, it is well for us to contrast the
hardness of their lot with the ease and liberty we
now enjoy; and to remember that our exemption
from suffering was purchased for us by their faithfulness and constancy in bearing testimony to the
truth. The principles we profess are those in support of which they underwent these grievous hardships and imprisoments, and it becomes us to watch
with diligence our steps through life, that we may
not in any of our conduct violate those principles,
or bring a shade over the high profession we are
making.

The next First-day he came to Firbank chapel, in
Westmoreland, where Francis Howgill and John
Audland had been preaching in the morning. While
others were gone to dinner he went to a brook, got
a little water, and then came and sat down on the top
of a rock hard by the chapel. In the afternoon the
people gathered about him with several of their
preachers. It was judged there were above a thousand
persons present, to whom he declared God's everlasting truth and word of life, freely and largely, for
about the space of three hours, directing all to the
Spirit of God in themselves; that they might be
turned from darkness to light and believe in it, that
they might become the children of it, and might be
turned from the power of Satan unto God, and by the
Spirit of truth might be led into all truth, and sen-
sibly understand the words of the prophets, of Christ,
and of the apostles, and might all come to know
Christ to be their teacher to instruct them, their

counsellor to direct them, their shepherd to feed them, their bishop to oversee them, and their prophet to open divine mysteries to them, and might know their bodies to be prepared, sanctified, and made fit temples for God and Christ to dwell in. In the openings of heavenly life he explained unto them the prophets and the figures and shadows, and directed them to Christ the substance. Very largely was he opened at this meeting. The Lord's convincing power accompanied his ministry, and reached home to the hearts of the people; whereby many were convinced, and all the teachers of that congregation (who were many) were convinced of God's everlasting truth.

It does not appear that George Fox was imprisoned during the year 1652, although he was constantly engaged in preaching the Gospel, and exposing the errors and wickedness of the high professors of religion, which produced great excitement against him, particularly among the priests. They procured a warrant for apprehending him, and presented an indictment for blasphemy to the court of sessions held at Lancaster, where about forty of them appeared as witnesses against him. Hearing of this, he thought it best to appear openly in the court, and face his persecutors, without waiting to be taken up by the officers. He accordingly went to the sessions, and when the witnesses came to be examined, they contradicted each other so as to destroy the force of their evidence. The indictment was quashed, and G. F. discharged.

He bore testimony in open court that " the Holy Scriptures were given forth by the Spirit of God," which all people must come to in themselves, in order to experience fellowship with the Father and the Son, and with one another, and without which Spirit they could not savingly understand the Scriptures. This exasperated the priests, and one of them said that the Spirit and the letter were inseparable. To which George replied, "Then every one that hath the letter, hath the Spirit, and they might buy the Spirit with the letter of the Scriptures." This discovery of the error of his opponents, induced Judge Fell and Colonel West to reprove them, observing "that according to their position, they might carry the Spirit in their pockets, as they did the Scriptures." The priest then endeavoured to equivocate and give a different meaning to his words, but the court refused to admit any other than the plain sense of his own expressions. They were thus confounded, and it was proved by witnesses present in the meeting, that no such language had been used by George Fox as they alleged against him in the charge of blasphemy exhibited before the court, and many pious persons praised God that day for the victory which Truth obtained.

At Grayrigg a priest came to a meeting and asserted that "the Scriptures were the word of God." George Fox told him, "they were the words of God, but not Christ, who is the Word," and bade him prove his assertion by Scripture. In this he failed, but sent G. F. a challenge to meet him at Kendal. He sent him word he need not go so far as Kendal, he would meet him in his own parish. At the second interview the priest made the same assertion. To which it was answered, "They were the words of God, but not God the Word." He then attempted to bring proof from the Scriptures, but G. F. keeping him close to his offer, and requiring chapter and verse, he again failed, and ran himself into many errors. G. F. closed the dispute by repeating—that he owned what the Scriptures said of themselves—namely, "that they were the words of God, but Christ was the Word."

The number of those convinced of the doctrines of Friends, and who joined in religious fellowship with George Fox, was now greatly increased. Meetings were settled in many places, and several eminent ministers had come forth, among whom were Richard Farnsworth, William Dewsbury, Thomas Aldam, and Edward Burrough. These were industriously engaged in promoting the cause of religion, and travelled almost constantly, holding large meetings with the people.

At Carlisle, in 1653, George Fox preached at the Market-cross and in the place of worship ; and the doctrines he delivered not being agreeable to some of the people, they stirred up the populace against him, threatening him with beating and stoning. The tumult, however, was appeased by the soldiery, who perceived the injury intended to be done, and rescued him. On the following day the magistrates sent a warrant to arrest him ; G. F., hearing they had granted it, did not wait for the constable to serve it, but went himself before the magistrates. He was committed to prison, "as a blasphemer, an heretic, and a seducer," and cruelly used, being thrust into a common hole, amongst the vilest felons and disorderly persons, without bed, fire, or other accommodation.

While lying in this comfortless situation, he was visited by James Parnell, then a lad of only sixteen years of age, whose mind the Lord had touched by his Holy Spirit, and raised in him strong desires after the knowledge of his blessed truth. He was convinced, and soon became an able minister of the Gospel; and after labouring assiduously in the work, during the short period allotted him, died of cruel usage in Colchester Castle, in 1655, being about nineteen years of age.

He remained in prison until the assizes; and the judges finding that the high charges on which he was committed could not be sustained, resolved not to bring him to trial. It was reported abroad that he was to suffer death, and the parliament ordered a letter of inquiry to be sent to the sheriffs and magistrates concerning him. Through the exertions of Justice Pearson, who visited the prisoner in company with the governor, G. F.'s situation was made more comfortable. The governor was so shocked with the filthiness of the place when he first entered it, that he exclaimed against the barbarity of the magistrates for committing him, and required security of the gaoler for his good behaviour; and the under-gaoler, who had been exceedingly cruel, was imprisoned in the same dungeon. The magistrates, fearing the interference of parliament, soon after released George Fox, as the easiest method of concealing their illegal conduct.*

* These prosecutions on the charges of blasphemy, heresy, &c., were commenced under an act passed by parliament in 1650, designed to reach the Ranters, a visionary sect which arose during the civil and religious commotions of the times,

George Fox, being discharged, resumed his travels, going through Westmoreland, Cumberland, Northumberland, &c. "The everlasting Gospel and word of life," says he, "flourished, and thousands were turned to the Lord Jesus Christ and to his teaching." The success of his labours provoked the envious opposers, who were vexed to see the principles of Friends spreading; and they not only invented and circulated many slanders against them, but prophesied the downfall of the Society. Their predictions, however, failed; and, notwithstanding the sufferings Friends underwent, they flourished in their outward affairs. Their conscientious adherence to strict integrity gained them a reputation among the people, which was surpassed by none. On this subject, G. F. remarks, "The priests and professors had said long before, that we should be destroyed within a month; and after that, they prolonged the time to half a year; but that time being

and published the most wild and blasphemous opinions. They ascribed the attributes of Deity to men—contended that no act, however wicked, was sinful in the saints—that the grossest violations of the moral law were not, in themselves sinful; and that there was no real difference between moral good and evil. Acting on these principles, they committed many excesses, and gave occasion to the irreligious to speak ill of the profession of Christianity. The enemies of Friends, failing in their other accusations, endeavoured to produce the impression that their principles were similar to those of the Ranters, and the parliament having repealed the other penal statutes for religion, they prosecuted them on the charge of blasphemy. But in every instance the charges fell to the ground. So far from agreeing with the monstrous doctrines of that sect, Friends openly protested against them, and Edward Burrough and others exposed their errors in writing.

long expired, and we mightily increased in number, they now gave forth that ' we would eat out one another.' For, many times after meetings, many tender people, having a great way to go, tarried at Friends' houses by the way, and sometimes more than there were beds to lodge in, so that some have lain on the haymows. Hereupon Cain's fear possessed the professors and world's people; for they were afraid that when we had eaten one another out, we would all come to be maintained by the parishes, and so we would be chargeable to them. But after a while, when they saw that the Lord blessed and increased Friends, as He did Abraham, both in the field and in the basket, at their goings forth and comings in, and that all things prospered with them, then they saw the falseness of all their prophecies against us, and that it was in vain to curse where God had blessed.

" At the first convincement, when Friends could not put off their hats to people, nor say you to a single person, but thou and thee, nor could not bow, nor use flattering words in salutations, nor go into the fashions and customs of the world, many Friends that were tradesmen of several sorts lost their customers at the first; for the people were shy of them, and would not trade with them, so that for a time some Friends that were tradesmen could hardly get money enough to buy bread. But afterward, when people came to have experience of Friends' honesty and faithfulness and found that their yea was yea, and their nay was nay; that they kept to a word in their dealings, and that they would not cozen and cheat them, but that if they sent any child to their shops for any thing they were as well used as if they had come themselves, the lives and conversations of Friends did preach, and reached to the Witness in people. And then things altered so that the inquiry was, ' Where was a draper, or tailor, or any other tradesman that was a Quaker ? ' Then that was all the cry, insomuch that Friends had more trade than many of their neighbours. And then the envious professors altered their note, and began to cry out, ' If we let these Quakers alone, they will take the trade of the nation out of our hands.' This hath been the Lord's doings to and for his people, which my desire is all that who profess his holy truth may be kept truly sensible of, and that all may be preserved in and by his power and Spirit, faithful to God and man ; first to God, in obeying Him in all things, and then in doing unto all men that which is just and righteous, true and holy, and honest to all men and women, in all things that they have to do or deal with them in, that the Lord God may be glorified in their practising truth, holiness, godliness, and righteousness amongst people in all their lives and conversations.''

A change had taken place in the government of England, King Charles being deposed and Oliver Cromwell declared Protector. The disturbances and difficulties attendant on a state of civil warfare, reached the peaceable Society of Friends, though they meddled not with political affairs. In 1654, George Fox was arrested at Whetstone, and carried before Colonel Hacker, who, after a partial examination, sent him to Cromwell. The colonel was very desirous to extort from him a promise that he would hold no more meetings, pretending that they were dangerous to the safety of the government. But he was not free to come under such an engagement, and when he found the colonel determined on sending him to the protector, he knelt down by him and besought the Lord to forgive him. He was brought before Cromwell at Whitehall, and they had much conversation on the subject of religion. As he was turning to leave him, Cromwell caught him by the hand, saying, "Come again to my house—for if thou and I were but an hour of a day together, we should be nearer one to the other;" adding that he wished him no more ill than he did to his own soul. He was discharged from his confinement, and, by order of the protector, taken to the dinner-hall and invited to dine with the company; but he declined accepting the offer, sending word to him, that he would "not eat a bit of his bread, nor drink a sup of his drink." When the protector heard this, he said, "Now I see there is a people risen and come up that I cannot win either with gifts, honours, offices, or places; but all other sects and people I can." It was told him again, "That we had forsook our own, and were not likely to look for such things from him."

In the year 1654 and 1655, George Fox continued travelling diligently in England, holding meetings both among his friends and the people generally; and though occasionally arrested or otherwise misused, yet the violence of persecution was in some degree mitigated. In describing the character of his Gospel labours, he says, "I directed them to the light of Christ, by which they might see their sins, and see their Saviour Christ Jesus, who was the way to God, and their Mediator to make peace betwixt God and them, and was their Shepherd to feed them, and their Prophet to teach them. And I directed them to the Spirit of God in themselves, by which they might know the Scriptures, and be led into all truth; and by the Spirit might know God, and in it have unity one with another."

Ignorance and superstition gave credence to many foolish stories respecting him, invented by those who wished to bring into disrepute the doctrines which he promulgated, because of their acceptance by so large a number of pious, respectable persons, in various parts of the nation. For the same reason, others were disposed to criminate him, could they have found any semblance of proof that he was guilty of the offences alleged against him. About eleven o'clock one night, Richard Hubberthorne and he were roused from their beds by a constable, with a hue and cry after two men, a house having been broken into, near a town where George Fox had preached to the inhabitants as he rode through it. They averred that they were honest men and abhorred such acts. The constable, however, carried them in the morning before a justice; but being able to prove by competent witnesses that they lodged that night and the succeeding at the house of a Captain Lawrence, who became acquainted with George Fox when he was carried up to Cromwell, the justice, on examination, said, he believed they were not the men that had broken the house, but he was sorry that he had no more against them. The constable urged him to detain them, saying, they had good horses, and if it pleased him he would carry them to Norwich gaol. A singular circumstance, indeed, that an officer of justice should be sorry to find men innocent, when the object of his station was to lessen crime and promote peace and order within his jurisdiction! They were discharged, and George Fox says a great people were gathered to the Lord, in the town where he preached, and where the hue and cry was raised.

By this time some Friends were settled in the north of Ireland, and William Edmundson, who was a minister and influential member there, being drawn to make George Fox a visit, he wrote the following brief but comprehensive epistle to the newly convinced flock, and sent it by him; the reading of which much tendered those assembled on the occasion.

" Friends,

" In that which convinced you, wait; that you may have that removed you are convinced of. And, all my dear friends, dwell in the life, and love, and power, and wisdom of God, in unity one with another, and with God; and the peace and wisdom of God fill all your hearts, that nothing may rule in you but the life, which stands in the Lord God.

" G. F."

Near the close of the year 1655, George Fox and Edward Pyott were arrested at a place called St. Ives, in Cornwall, by order of Peter Ceely, and sent prisoners under a guard of soldiers to Launceston gaol. An evidence of the resolution and zeal with which Friends pursued their religious duty, occurred on their journey. On First-day, at Redruth, the soldiers would have them proceed on their way, but George Fox told them it was their Sabbath, and it was not usual to travel on that day. Some of the town's-people collecting about them, he held the soldiers in discourse, while Edward Pyott preached to the people; and in turn, Edward Pyott entertained them whilst George Fox preached. At the same time, a Friend who was in company with them got out and went to the steeple-house to address those assembled there. He was abused by the enraged company, and the soldiers missing him, also became much incensed. In the afternoon, the soldiers resolved to go on; but after taking horse and riding to the skirts of the town, George Fox believed it his duty to go back and speak to the man of the house where they had stopped. The soldiers drew out pistols and swore he should not go, but disregarding them, he rode back, and they followed him; and when he had cleared himself he returned, reproving them for their rudeness and violence.

In about nine weeks after their commitment, they were brought to the assizes, before Judge Glynn, and, standing in the court with their hats on, he commanded them to take them off. George Fox desired to be shown, either from the law or by the Scriptures, the propriety of doing so; but the judge becoming angry, cried out to have him taken away, and they were accordingly conveyed back to prison.

During the time they were in the court, their attention was attracted by the constant repetition of oaths, by jurymen, witnesses, and others, directly contrary to the command of Christ and his apostles. George Fox was grieved to observe it, and thought it his duty to give forth a short declaration of his views on the subject; in which he warns them to "Take heed of giving people oaths to swear, for Christ our Lord and Master saith, Swear not at all, 'but let your communication be yea, yea; and nay, nay; for whatsoever is more than these cometh of evil.' .... And the Apostle James saith, 'My brethren, above all things, swear not; neither by heaven, nor by earth, nor by any other oath, lest ye fall into condemnation.' Now you may see, those that swear fall into condemnation, and are out of Christ's and the apostle's doctrine," &c. This paper, which treated the subject of oaths pretty fully, passed about among the jury and justices, until it reached the hands of the judge, who again called George Fox, and asked if that seditious paper was his. The court was crowded with people; and George, being ever ready to embrace an opportunity for spreading the truth, desired the clerk to read the paper aloud, that he and all present might hear whether it contained any sedition, and if it was his paper he would own it. They urged him to take the paper and examine it himself, but he still insisting on its being read, it was at length done. He acknowledged it to be his; and showed them how consistent it was with the Holy Scriptures. Then they dropped that subject, and the judge began again about their hats, ordering them to be taken off. The gaoler took them off and handed them to the two Friends, who put them on again.

Peter Ceely manifested much hostility toward

George Fox, and made several accusations against him, which were shown to be entirely false. Failing to find any cause for further imprisonment, on these groundless charges, the judge fined them twenty marks apiece for keeping on their hats, they to be detained in prison until it was paid. To prison they were accordingly sent, and finding that there was little probability of obtaining a release soon, they determined to demand a free prison and to cease paying the gaoler for their board. This so incensed him that he put them into a hole called Doomsdale, which was so filthy, damp, and unwholesome, that it was remarked that few who went into it came out alive. It was covered with mire and water as deep as the tops of their shoes, and they could not lie down, but were obliged to stand up constantly. For a long time he would not suffer them to cleanse it, or to have any victuals but what was handed to them through the grate : and on one occasion, when a little girl had brought them some meat, he arrested and prosecuted her, for breaking his house.

The sessions being at hand, they drew up a statement of their sufferings, and presented it to the court, at Bodmin. On reading it, the justices ordered the door of the prison to be opened, and that the prisoners should have liberty to cleanse it and to purchase their provisions in the town. Many persons visited George Fox while he was in confinement at Launceston, to whom he preached the Gospel and explained the nature of his religious principles, and so large a number were convinced by his faithful labours, that one of the protector's chaplains remarked, " They could not do George Fox a greater service for spreading his principles in Cornwall, than to imprison him there."

During his confinement a Friend went to Oliver Cromwell, and offered himself to lie in prison instead of George Fox, if the protector would accept him and release G. F. ; which struck the protector so forcibly as an act of disinterested kindness, that he turned to his council and other attendants, and asked, " Which of you would do so much for me, if I were in the same condition?"   After being about half a year in gaol, they were discharged in the Seventh Month, 1656. The gaoler who had used them so cruelly was not only turned out of his office, but came to poverty, and afterwards was himself a prisoner in the same place ; and being concerned in some disorderly conduct while in gaol, was cast into Doomsdale, where he had formerly thrust Friends. The history of this trial and imprisonment furnishes a singular comment upon the administration of law and justice at that period. They were committed as persons " altogether unknown," charged in the course of their trial by the justice who committed them, with a design " to involve the nation in blood," but eventually remanded to gaol by the court, under a penalty of twenty marks apiece, for not taking off their hats.

CHAPTER IV.   1656-1658.

Visits Oliver Cromwell—Answers various objections—Travels into Wales and Scotland—Attends a General Yearly Meeting in Bedfordshire—Remonstrates with Cromwell against the cruelty practised towards Friends.

GEORGE Fox was by no means unemployed during his confinement.   Many Friends coming to visit him, promulgated the truth in Cornwall, Devonshire, Dorset, and Somersetshire.   This induced their enemies to set watches in the highways, on pretence of apprehending suspicious persons ; and accordingly they arrested Friends, to hinder the diffusion of their principles.   Besides two remonstrances against their iniquitous proceedings, he sent forth a warning to the professors of religion in those parts, to awaken them to a sense of their blindness and hostility to the spirit and principles of Christianity.   He also testified against the pride and idleness of many who spent their time in sporting and wantonness, drinking, hunting, and hawking, instead of fearing and glorifying Him who made them, and who will bring all men to judgment.   Of his own religious Society he was not unmindful.   " An Exhortation to Friends in the Ministry," which he wrote, is fraught with weighty counsel, and shows the expanded views of his enlightened mind.—" In the power of life and wisdom, and dread of the Lord God of life and heaven and earth dwell," says he, " spreading the truth abroad, awakening the witness—confounding the deceit—gathering up out of transgression into the life, the covenant of light and peace with God.— Let all nations hear the sound by word or writing. —Spare no place, spare no tongue, no pen. Go through the work, and be valiant for the truth upon earth."

Being released from prison, George Fox and his fellow-sufferers took horses, and rode to a Friend's house, where they had a " precious meeting." After resting two or three days, they went to Thomas Mounce's, where a general meeting for the whole county was held, and the company being too large for any house to contain, they assembled in an orchard. " The Lord's power," says George, " was over all, and a great convincement there was in many places of the county." Passing through Launceston, they visited the Friends who had been convinced by their labours while in confinement, and found them increasing in religious stability, " being established on Christ, their rock and foundation." From thence they went through Oakhampton, Exeter, Collumpton, and Taunton, to Bristol. " Many meetings we had," observes G. F., " and many were turned by the power and Spirit of God to the Lord Jesus Christ, who died for them ; and they came to sit under his free teaching."

From Bristol, accompanied by Edward Pyott, he proceeded to London, holding meetings by the way ; at one of which, at the house of a justice of the peace, in Wiltshire, there were supposed to be between two and three thousand persons present :

the meeting was quiet, and the people went away much satisfied. At London they visited Cromwell, and laid before him the sufferings of Friends in different parts of the nation, and also had some conversation with him on religious subjects. After attending the meetings of Friends in that city and its vicinity, they went into the counties of Buckingham, Northampton, Nottingham and Lincoln, and were joined by Robert Craven, formerly sheriff of Lincoln, Amos Stoddart, and Alexander Parker. The desire to hear the Gospel preached, and to know more fully the doctrines held by Friends, appeared to increase ; and the people flocked to the meetings, many of whom being convinced afterward joined the Society. In those days, there was a large number of serious, seeking persons in the different religious Societies, who were earnestly engaged for their soul's salvation, and could not find in the stated ceremonies and performances to which they were accustomed, that peace and satisfaction which they desired. They found that men could afford them but little assistance in the work of religion, and were therefore anxiously looking for that Divine aid which alone is availing. Few, however, understood the operations of the Holy Spirit in their own hearts ; or had faith to believe in its sufficiency to lead them in the path of peace. They felt something striving with them for sin, and inclining them to holiness, but as yet knew not what it was. In this state of mind, seeking the truth and not finding it, tossed with doubts and fears respecting their spiritual condition, the preaching of George Fox came to them like a message from heaven. It was indeed

glad tidings of great joy, directing them to the light
of Christ Jesus in the conscience, the Comforter,
or Holy Spirit, which He promised to send his
disciples, to bring all things to their remembrance,
and to guide them into all truth. They came to see
that they had depended too much on men, and on
outward performances; overlooking the teachings of
this blessed Spirit in their souls; and they now
turned to it with joy, and in faith received and
obeyed its commands. The hearts of such persons
were like ground prepared to receive the seed of the
kingdom, and to this, under the divine blessing, we
may ascribe the great success which attended the
Gospel labours of the early Friends.

Although large numbers received the testimony
of George Fox and his co-labourers, there were
others who despised their religious profession. Some
believed them to be heretical in principle, and, being
jealous of the growth of a Society whose doctrines
struck at making religion a trade, spread abroad
numerous misrepresentations, which he believed it
his duty to endeavour to correct and remove. What
Christ said of false prophets and antichrists, coming
in the last days, their enemies applied to Friends.
The following statement gives a view of the temper
of the times, and George Fox's mode of replying to
the errors and accusations of the day.

" This message of the glorious, everlasting Gospel,
was I sent forth to declare and publish, and thousands by it are turned to God, having received it;
and are come into subjection to it, and into the holy
order of it. And since I have declared this message
in this part of the world, and have written books of

the same, to spread it universally abroad, the blind prophets, and preachers, and deceivers have given over telling us the false prophets should ' come in the last times ; ' for a great light is sprung up and shines over their heads ; so that every child in the truth sees the folly of their sayings.

" Then they got other objections against us, and invented shifts to save themselves from truth's stroke. For when we blamed them for taking tithes, which came from the tribe of Levi, and were set up here by the Romish Church, they would plead, ' That Christ told the scribes and pharisees, they ought to pay tithes of mint, anise, and cumin, though they had neglected the weightier matters :' and that Christ said, ' the scribes and pharisees sat in Moses's seat, therefore all that they bid you do, that do and observe.' And when we told them they were envious persecuting priests, they would reply, ' That some preached Christ of envy, and some of contention, and some of good-will.' Now these Scriptures, and others such like, they would bring to darken the minds of their hearers, and to persuade them and us, that we ought to do as they say, though they themselves were like the pharisees ; and that we should rejoice when envious men and men of strife preached Christ, and that we should give them the tithes as the Jews did to the tribe of Levi. These were fair glosses; and here was a great heap of husks, but no kernel. Now this was their blindness ; for the Levitical priesthood Christ hath ended, and disannulled the commandment that gave them tithes, and the law by which those priests were made. And Christ did not come after that order, neither did He send forth his ministers after that order ; for those of that order were to take tithes for their maintenance, but his ministers He sent forth freely.

" And as for the Jews paying tithes of mint, anise, and cumin, that was before Christ was sacrificed and offered up ; and the Jews were then to do the law, and perform their offerings and sacrifices which the Jewish priests did teach them. But after that Christ was offered up, He bid them then ' Go into all nations and preach the Gospel ; and lo,' said He, ' I will be with you to the end of the world :' and in another place He saith, ' I will be in you.' So He did not bid them go to hear the pharisees then, and pay tithe of mint, anise, and cumin then ; but, Go, preach the Gospel, and believe in the Lord Jesus and be saved, and receive the Gospel, which would bring people off from the Jews, and the tithes, and the Levitical law, and the offerings thereof, to Christ, the one Offering, made once for them all. O what work had the apostle with both the Galatians and the Romans, to bring them off the law to the faith in Christ !

" And as for the apostle's saying, ' Some preached Christ of envy and strife,' &c., that was at the first spreading of Christ's name abroad, when they were in danger, not only to be cast out of the synagogues, but to be stoned to death, that confessed to the name of Jesus ; as may be seen by the uproars that were among the Jews and Diana's worshippers at the preaching of Christ. So the apostle might well rejoice, if the envious, and men of strife and contention did preach Christ at that time ; though they thought thereby to add affliction to his bonds. But afterward, when Christ's name was spread abroad, and many had got a form of godliness, but denied the power thereof, envious, proud, contentious men, men of strife, covetous men, teachers for filthy lucre, the apostle commanded the saints to turn from, and not to have any fellowship with them. And the deacons and ministers were first to be proved, to see if they were in the power of godliness; and the Holy Ghost made them overseers and preachers. So it may be seen how the priests have abused these Scriptures for their own ends, and have wrested them to their own destruction, to justify envious, contentious men, and men of strife. Whereas the apostle says, ' The man of God must be patient, and apt to teach ;' and they were to follow Christ, as they had them for their examples.

" The apostle indeed was very tender to people, while he saw them walk in simplicity; as in the case of them that were scrupulous about meats and days ; but when the apostle saw that some drew them into the observation of days, and to settle in such things, he then reproves them sharply, and asks them, ' Who hath bewitched you ?' So in the case of of marrying, he was tender, lest their minds should be drawn from the Lord's joining ; but when they came to forbid marriage, and to set up rules for meats and drinks, he called it ' a doctrine of devils,' and an ' erring from the true faith.' So also he was tender concerning circumcision ; and in tenderness suffered some to be circumcised ; but when he saw they went to make a sect of it, and to set up circumcision as a standing practice, he told them plainly, that if they were circumcised, Christ would profit them nothing. In like manner he was tender concerning the baptizing with water; but when he saw they began make sects about it, some crying up Paul, others Apollos, he judged them, and called them carnal, and thanks God he had baptized no more but such and such; declaring plainly, that he was sent to preach the Gospel, and not to baptize; and brought them to the one baptism by the one Spirit, into the one body, which Christ, the spiritual Man, is the head of; and exhorted the church all to drink into that one Spirit. For he set up, in the Church, one faith, which Christ was the author of; and one baptism, which was that of the Spirit into the one body; and one Lord Jesus Christ, who was the spiritual Baptizer, who, John said, should come after him. And further, the apostle declared that they, who worshipped and served God in the Spirit, were of the circumcision of the Spirit, which was not made with hands; by which the ' body of the sins of the flesh' was put off : of which circumcision Christ is the minister.

" Another great objection they had; that the Quakers denied the sacrament (as they called it) of bread and wine, which, they said, they were to take, and do in remembrance of Christ to the end of the world. A great deal of work we had with the priests and professors about this, and about the several sorts of ways that it is taken in Christendom, so called; for some take it kneeling, and some sitting; but none of them all, that ever I could find, take it according as the disciples took it. For they took it in a chamber after supper; but these generally take it before a dinner ; and some say, after the priest hath blessed it, it is Christ's body.

" But as to the matter, Christ said, ' Do this in remembrance of me.' He did not tell them how oft they should do it, or how long ; neither did He enjoin them to do it always as long as they lived, or that all believers in Him should do it to the world's end. The Apostle Paul, who was not converted till after Christ's death, tells the Corinthians, that he had received of the Lord that which he delivered unto them concerning this matter : and he relates Christ's words concerning the cup thus : ' This do ye, as oft as ye drink it, in remembrance of me ;' and himself adds, ' For as often as ye do eat this bread and drink this cup, ye do show the Lord's death till he come.' So according to what the apostle here delivers, neither Christ nor he did enjoin people to do this always, but leaves it to their liberty, (' as oft as ye drink it,' &c.) Now the Jews did use to take a cup, and to break bread and divide it among them in their feasts, as may be seen in the Jewish Antiquities ; so that the breaking of bread and drinking of wine were Jewish rites, which were not to last always. They did also baptize with water ; which made it not seem a strange thing to them, when John the Baptist came with his decreasing ministration of water-baptism.

" But as to the bread and wine, after the disciples had taken it, some of them questioned whether Jesus was the Christ ? For some of them said, after He was crucified, ' We trusted that it had been he which should have redeemed Israel,' &c. And though the Corinthians had the bread and wine, and were baptized in water, the apostle told them, they were reprobates, if Christ was not in them; and bid them examine themselves. And as the apostle said, ' As oft as ye do eat this bread, and drink this cup, ye do show the Lord's death till he come ;' so Christ had said before that He was the bread of life, which came down from heaven ; and that He would come, and dwell in them ; which the apostles did witness fulfilled ; and exhorted others to seek for that which comes down from above; but the outward bread and wine, and water, are not from above, but from below.

" Now, ye that eat and drink this outward bread and wine in remembrance of Christ's death, and have your fellowships in that, will ye come no nearer to Christ's death than to take bread and wine in remembrance of his death? After ye have eaten in remembrance of his death, ye must come into his death, and die with Him, as the apostles did, if ye will live with Him. And this is a nearer and further state, to be with Him in the fellowship of his death, than only to take bread and wine in remembrance of his death. You must have a fellowship with Christ in his sufferings : if ye will reign with Him, ye must suffer with Him ; if ye will live with Him, ye must die with Him ; and if ye die with Him, ye must be buried with Him ; and being buried with Him in the true baptism, ye also rise with Him. Then having suffered with Him, died with Him, and been buried with Him, if ye are risen with Christ, ' seek those things which are above, where Christ sitteth on the right hand of

God.' Eat the bread which comes down from above, which is not outward bread; and drink the cup of salvation which He gives in his kingdom, which is not outward wine. And then there will not be a looking at the things that are seen (as outward bread and wine and water are): for, as says the apostle, 'The things which are seen are temporal, but the things which are not seen are eternal.'

"So here are many states and conditions to be gone through before people come to see that, and partake of that which cometh down from above.

"For first, There was a taking of the outward bread and wine in remembrance of Christ's death. This was temporary, and not of necessity; but at their liberty, 'As oft as ye do it,' &c.

"Secondly, There must be a coming into his death, a suffering with Christ; and this is of necessity to salvation; and not temporary, but continual; there must be a dying daily.

"Thirdly, a being buried with Christ.

"Fourthly, a rising with Christ.

"Fifthly, after they are risen with Christ, then a seeking those things which are above, a seeking the bread that comes down from heaven, and a feeding on that and having fellowship in that.

"For outward bread, wine and water are from below, and are visible and temporal, but saith the apostle, 'We look not at things which are seen,' 'for the things which are seen are temporal but the things which are not seen are eternal.' 'So the fellowship that stands in the use of bread, wine, water, circumcision, outward temple, and things seen, will have an end: but the fellowship which stands in the

Gospel, the power of God which was before the devil was, and which brings life and immortality to light, by which people may see over the devil that has darkened them, this fellowship is eternal, and will stand. And all that are in it do seek that which is heavenly and eternal, which comes down from above, and are settled in the eternal mystery of the fellowship of the Gospel, which is hid from all eyes that look only at visible things. And the apostle told the Corinthians, who were in disorder about water, bread, and wine, that 'he desired to know nothing amongst them, but Jesus Christ, and him crucified.'"

Having performed a visit to Friends in most parts of England, to the comfort and strength of his brethren, George Fox returned to London, in 1656, where he remained some time. Diligently engaged in his Master's cause, he allowed himself but little rest; and when not travelling, much of his time was occupied in writing essays for publication, with a view of spreading a knowledge of the doctrines of the Society, of correcting the false charges which were made against them, or checking the violence of persecution. He was indeed an indefatigable labourer, scarcely allowing himself to take sufficient food or sleep, and wholly giving up temporal business, that he might be more at liberty to serve the Lord.

The Society had now greatly increased in numbers, and meetings were settled in most parts of the kingdom, which Friends were concerned to attend with diligence, notwithstanding the cruel usage by beating, stoning, and imprisonment, which they often met with while there, or on the way.

Persecution served but to strengthen the faith and constancy of the sufferers ; who counted the testimony of truth, and the faithful support of their religious principles, dearer than any earthly consideration, freely surrendering their property, their bodies, and their lives, rather than violate their duty to God. For many years " there were seldom fewer than one thousand in prison in this nation for truth's testimony ; some for tithes, some for going to the steeple-houses, some for contempts (as they called them), some for not swearing, and others for not putting off their hats, &c."

About this period many being constrained to declare the goodness of the Lord in their assemblies, some of whom were in their infancy as to religious growth, this prudent elder wrote an epistle of advice respecting the proper conduct of Friends towards such, containing the following :—

" All my dear friends, in the noble Seed of God, and who have known his power, life, and presence among you, let it be your joy to hear or see the springs of life break forth in any; through which ye have all unity in the same, feeling life and power. And above all things take heed of judging any one openly in your meetings, except they be openly profane or rebellious, such as be out of the truth ; that by the power, life, and wisdom, ye may stand over them, and by it answer the witness of God in the world, that such, whom ye bear your testimony against, are none of you ; so that therein the truth may stand clear and single. But such as are tender, if they should be moved to bubble forth a few words, and speak in the Seed and Lamb's power, suffer and bear that; that is, the tender. And if they should go beyond their measure, bear it in the meeting for peace and order's sake, and that the spirits of the world be not moved against you. But when the meeting is done, if any be moved to speak to them, between you and them, then one or two of you that feel it in the life, do it in the love or wisdom that is pure and gentle, from above; for the love is that which doth edify and bear all things, and suffers long, and doth fulfil the law. So in this ye have order and edification, ye have wisdom to preserve you all wise and in patience; which takes away the occasion of stumbling the weak, and the occasion of the spirits of the world to get up: but in the royal Seed, the heavy stone, ye keep down all that is wrong, and by it answer that of God in all. For ye will hear, see, and feel the power of God preaching, as your faith is all in it (when ye do not hear words), to bind, to chain, to limit, to frustrate, that nothing shall rise nor come forth but what is in the power; for with that ye will hold back, and with that ye will let up and open every spring, plant, and spark; in which will be your joy and refreshment in the power of God. For now ye that know the power of God and are come to it, which is the cross of Christ, that crucifies you to the state that Adam and Eve were in in the fall, and so to the world, by this power of God ye come to see the state that Adam and Eve were in before they fell. Which power of God is the cross, in which stands the everlasting glory, which brings up into the righteousness, holiness, and image of God, and crucifies to the unrighteousness, unholiness, and image of Satan, that

Adam and Eve and their sons and their daughters be in in the fall. Through this power of God ye come to see the state they were in before they fell; yea, I say, and to a higher state, to the Seed,*

---

* In reading the writings of George Fox, we find him frequently using the word SEED with reference to our blessed Lord. The term is derived from that remarkable prediction delivered on the expulsion of our first parents from paradise foretelling the coming of Christ Jesus, as the Saviour and Deliverer of mankind from the consequences of the fall; Genesis iii. 15. "I will put enmity between thee (the tempter) and the woman, and between thy seed and her seed: it shall bruise thy head, and thou shall bruise his heel." George Whitehead, in his preface to the Epistles of George Fox, has the following observations on this subject:—

"In many of the ensuing Epistles, he often mentions the Seed, the Life, the Power of God, and the like; whereby he intends no other than what the Holy Scriptures testify of Christ: which we know, he truly loved and esteemed, and was often conversant in reading of them, and had an excellent memory and spiritual sense thereof given him of the Lord. By the pure holy Seed he meant and declared Christ, the promised Seed; wherein all the promises of God are yea and amen. And as Christ is the Word of life, the Word of faith, He is that immortal and incorruptible Seed, of which all true and spiritual believers and children of the light are begotten to God, and born again; and which Seed or Word of eternal life ·abideth in him that is born of God, and he sinneth not because thereof. 1 John iii. And the generation of God, and children of his kingdom, and of the promise, are called the good seed, and counted for the seed, being born of that incorruptible Seed, or Word of Life, which endureth for ever.—1 Peter i. 23, 25.

"This our deceased friend and servant of Jesus Christ truly testified of Him in all respects, both as come in the flesh and in the spirit, both as Christ was and is our only Mediator and Advocate, and as He was and is God over all, blessed for ever;

Christ, the second Adam, by whom all things were made. For man hath been driven from God. All Adam and Eve's sons and daughters, being in the state of the fall in the earth, are driven from God. But it is said, ' The church is in God, the Father of our Lord Jesus Christ :' so who come to the church, which is in God the Father of Christ, they must come to God again, and so out of the state that Adam and his children be in in the fall, out of the image of God, out of the righteousness and holiness, and they must come into the righteousness, into the true holiness, and into the image of God, and so out of the earth whither man hath been driven, when they come to the church which is in God. And the way to this is Christ, the Light, the Life, the Truth, the Saviour, the Redeemer, the Sanctifier, and the

whom he so dearly loved and honoured, that he often offered up his life, and deeply suffered for Him ; and that in dear and constant love to his seed, that a holy generation might be raised, strengthened and increased in the earth among the children of men. And his knowledge and ministry of our Lord Jesus Christ, being after the Spirit in life and power, did no ways imply any lessening of the dignity or glory of Christ, nor any defect of faith or love to Christ, as He came and suffered in the flesh for mankind; as some adversaries have injuriously misrepresented and aspersed him ; for he highly esteemed Christ's sufferings, death, resurrection, and glory ; and powerfully testified of the virtue, power, blessed and spiritual design, fruit, and effects thereof, as revealed and witnessed by his Holy Spirit.

" Christ Jesus being our spiritual Rock, Foundation, and Head, He is truly precious to us and all true believers, in all states and conditions ; both of his humiliation, and glory, and dominion ; his great grace and goodness appearing in those precious ministerial gifts given by Him (when He ascended up on high) for his ministry and church.

Justifier, in and through whose power, light, and life, who is the way to God, conversion, regeneration, and translation is known from death to life, from darkness to light, and from the power of Satan to God again. These are members of the true church, who know the work of regeneration in the operation and feeling of it; and being come to be members of the church in God, they are indeed members one of another in the power of God, which was before the power of darkness was. So they that come to the church that is in God and Christ, they must come out of the state that Adam was in in the

"And it is very observable, that though, to express Christ's lowly condition and appearance in the world, He is sometimes in Holy Scripture termed the seed, his name is also 'called Wonderful, Counsellor, the Mighty God, the Everlasting Father, the Prince of Peace;' upon whose shoulders the government is laid; and 'of the increase of his government and peace there shall be no end.' Isaiah ix. And it is most suitable to Christ's low, humble, and suffering condition, to make use of such instruments as are most like Himself in humility and lowliness of mind, although they be but low and mean in the world's eye and esteem. God is pleased to make choice of low, mean, and weak things, and of instruments contemptible in the eyes of the high and lofty ones of this world, to confound the wisdom of the world, according to 1 Cor. i. He chose poor shepherds to divulge that great evangelical truth of Christ's birth; and certain women to preach that Gospel truth of his resurrection (Luke ii. and xxiv.), and both from angelical testimony, as well as from their sight of Christ himself. Truth must not be rejected because of such instruments which God in his wisdom is pleased to employ in his work; nor the day of small things despised: from small beginnings of good matters, great things, glorious attainments and perfections, do spring. Glory, honour, and dominion to our most gracious God, and to the Lamb on his throne, for ever and ever."

fall, driven from God, to know the state that he was in before the fall. But they that live in the state that Adam was in in the fall, and cannot believe a possibility of coming into the state he was in before he fell, come not to the church which is in God; but are far from that, and are not passed from death to life, but are enemies to the cross of Christ, which is the power of God. For they mind earthly things, and serve not Christ; nor love the power which should bring them up to the state that Adam was in before he fell, and crucify them to the state that man is in in the fall; that through this power they might see to the beginning, the power that man was in before the heavenly image, and holiness, and righteousness were lost: by which power they might come to know the Seed, Christ, which brings up out of the old things, and makes all things new; in which life eternal is felt. For all the poorness, emptiness, and barrenness is in the state that man is in in the fall, out of God's power; by which power he is made rich again, and in which power he hath strength again; which power is the cross, in which the mystery of the fellowship stands; and in which is the true glorying, which crucifies to all other gloryings. And, friends, though ye may have been convinced, and have tasted of the power, and felt the light, yet afterwards ye may feel a winter storm, tempest, and hail, frost and cold, and temptation in the wilderness. Be patient and still in the power, and in the light that doth convince you, to keep your minds to God; in that be quiet, that ye may come to the summer; that your flight be not in the winter. For if ye sit still in the patience which overcomes in the power of God, there will be no flying. The husbandman, after he hath sown his seed, is patient. And ye, by the power being kept in the patience, will come by the light to see through and over winter-storms and tempests, and all the coldness, barrenness, and emptiness; and the same light and power will go over the tempter's head; which power and light was before he was. So in the light standing still, ye will see your salvation, ye will see the Lord's strength, ye will feel the small rain, ye will feel the fresh springs, your minds being kept low in the power and light: for that which is out of the power lifts up. But in the power and light ye will feel God, revealing his secrets, inspiring your minds, and his gifts coming in unto you; through which your hearts will be filled with God's love, and praises to Him that lives for evermore; for in his light and power his blessing is received. So in that, the eternal power of the Lord Jesus Christ preserve and keep you? And live every one in the power of God, that ye may all come to be heirs of that, and know that to be your portion; even the kingdom that hath no end, and the endless life which the Seed is heir of. So feel that set over all, which hath the promise, and blessing of God for ever.

"G. F."

In the latter part of the year 1656, George Fox went into Wales, and in 1657, visited Scotland, in both of which engagements many persons were convinced and joined the religious Society, and meetings were settled in most places where he came. He met with but little interruption in those journeys.

In Wales he was overtaken by a person of note, who purposed, as he afterwards said, to arrest him and John Ap-John for highwaymen. But before they reached the town they were travelling to, George spake to the man in such an affecting manner, that the divine witness in his conscience was reached, and he invited them to his house and entertained them hospitably. The man and his wife requested them to give Scripture proofs of their principles, which they did gladly. These the man took down and became convinced of the truth of their doctrine, "both by the Spirit of God in his own heart, and by the Scriptures, which were a confirmation to him."

On coming into a town, his companion would pass up and down the streets, preaching to the inhabitants, and frequently was arrested while George was yet at the inn. He soon learned the fate of his friend, and by a bold remonstrance against their uncourteous treatment of strangers, obtained his release.—Such occurrences gave opportunity for discourse with the principal men of the place, drew the people about them, and thus furnished opportunities to impress the doctrines of truth with good effect.

In Cumberland, the people had so forsaken the priests that several steeple-houses stood empty. John Wilkinson, who preached at three of them, had so few hearers left that he held a meeting in his own house, and preached there. Then he held a silent meeting like Friends, to which a few came, and thus continued till but half a dozen were left. At last he would come to Purdshaw Crag, where Friends held a very large meeting, and walk around the house like a person looking for lost sheep. Eventually, George Fox coming there, he, with three or four remaining adherents, were all convinced : he became an able Quaker Minister, and died in fellowship with the Society, in 1675.

On getting into Scotland, he found the people under the influence of the dark doctrine of unconditional election and reprobation. George preached the universal love of God to all mankind, and proved that reprobation was the consequence of sin committed, and not of a personal decree to irremediable perdition. He taught that He who was a propitiation for the sins of the whole world, for reprobates as well as saints, commanded his ministers to preach the Gospel to *all nations*. He died for all, and enlightens all by the manifestations of his Spirit ; but they who vex, quench, and grieve the Holy Spirit, are the reprobates ; and the fault lies at their door, because they have rejected the grace of God, which brought salvation to them. But they who receive and obey Christ, become elected in Him, and partakers of the blessings of his propitiatory sufferings and death. These doctrines alarmed the Scotch priests, and to deter their hearers from entertaining them, they drew up a number of curses, to be read in their public assemblies, for the people to answer, amen. The first was, Cursed is he that saith, Every man hath a light within him sufficient to lead him to salvation ; and let all the people say, Amen. Second, Cursed is he that saith, Faith is without sin ; and let all the people say, Amen. Third, Cursed is he that denieth the sabbath-day ; and let all the people say, Amen.

At Edinburgh, the magistrates issued an order for him to appear before them, which he readily obeyed. When about entering the council chamber, where they were assembled, his hat was taken off, against which he remonstrated; and gave satisfactory reasons for refusing to gratify the pride of man with this mark of homage. On being introduced before the magistrates, he paused a little, and then addressed them—" Peace be amongst you—and wait in the fear of God, that ye may receive his wisdom from above, by which all things were made and created ; that by it ye may all be ordered, and may order all things under your hands, to God's glory." After inquiring into the cause of his coming into Scotland, and the nature of his business there, they issued an order commanding him to leave the country in one week from that time. But in the performance of religious duty, he believed it right to obey God rather than man; and apprehending himself called to further service there, he continued holding meetings and preaching the Gospel, in Edinburgh and its vicinity for a considerable time; and although he returned again to that city, after visiting meetings in the country, yet he was suffered to pass unmolested.

Leaving Scotland, he came to Durham, where he met with a learned man, recently from London, who had come for the purpose of setting up a college to prepare young men for the ministry. George reasoned with him on the subject, showing that human learning, though prosecuted to the greatest extent, could never qualify for preaching the Gospel. That this could only be done through the power and assistance of Christ's Spirit, he being the great Minister of ministers, whose exclusive right it is to call and qualify his servants to preach life and salvation in his name. He reminded him that Peter and John, though *unlearned* men, preached Christ Jesus to Jews and Gentiles with great success; and that Paul·declared he was made an apostle, *not of man*, nor *by man*, neither received he his Gospel *from man*, but by the revelation of Jesus Christ. The man assented to the truth of many of these arguments, manifested much tenderness of spirit, and after further consideration, declined setting up the college.

Oliver Cromwell having issued a proclamation for a fast, on account of the great drought, George Fox wrote a paper to show that the true fast could not be kept in strife and debate, and smiting with the fist of wickedness; or in bowing down the head like a bulrush, or in afflicting themselves for a day. He declared that, according to the Holy Scriptures, the fast which the Lord required was to abstain from every species of evil, to loose the bands of wickedness, to undo the heavy burdens, and to let the oppressed go free, and to break every yoke; to deal their bread to the hungry, to bring the poor that are cast out to their houses, and to clothe the naked. To call for a fast, as a means of drawing down Divine favour, while they were tolerating wickedness, persecuting the followers of Christ, and depriving them of every outward comfort, presented a glaring inconsistency, in which he and his brethren could not unite. The Society has always maintained a testimony against all human requisitions and commandments of man,

L

which intermeddled with duty to God, who only, they
believe, has the right to prescribe the service due to
Himself.

At Leominster, while George Fox was preaching
upon the universality of the Light of Christ, a priest
cried out, " That is a natural light, and a made
light."   George desired the people to take out their
Bibles ; and then asked the priest, " Whether he did
affirm that that was a created, natural, made light,
which John, a man that was sent from God, did bear
witness to, and did speak of, when he said, ' In
Him, to wit, in the Word, was life ; and that life
was the light of man.' "   " Dost thou affirm and
mean," said he to the priest, " that this light
here spoken of was a created, natural, made light ? "
He said, " Yes."   George then showed them by
the Scriptures that " the natural, created, made
light was the outward light in the outward firmament, proceeding from the sun, moon, and stars.
And dost thou affirm," said he to the priest, " that
God sent John to bear witness to the light of the sun,
moon, and stars ? "   He answered, " Did I say so ?"
George requested the audience to turn to the first
chapter of John. From this he proved that Christ, the
eternal Word, created all things ; consequently all
these luminaries in the firmament ; but that He was
himself the true Light, that lighteth every man ; and
that this Light shineth in the heart to give the
knowledge of the glory of God in the face of Jesus
Christ, who declared, " I am the Light of the
world," and commands us to " believe in the Light."
God likewise said of him by the prophet, " I will
also give thee for a Light to the Gentiles, that thou

mayest be my salvation to the ends of the earth." So this light is saving, and must be divine and supernatural.

He continued travelling to different parts of England, and in 1658, came to John Crook's, in Bedfordshire, "where a General Yearly Meeting for the whole nation was appointed to be held." To this meeting, which lasted three days, many thousands of people came from all parts of the kingdom, so that the towns and inns round about could scarcely contain them. George Fox was largely engaged in the ministry; showing the fallen, corrupt state of man by nature, the necessity of a Redeemer and Saviour, to rescue him from this lost estate, and restore him to that blessed condition from which Adam fell; and the all-sufficiency of Christ Jesus for this glorious purpose—He having come in the flesh, died as a propitiation for the sins of mankind, and now appeared a second time, without sin unto salvation, by his Holy Spirit in the hearts of men, as a swift witness against sin and a guide into all righteousness.

He was also led to open many things respecting the ministry, exhorting those engaged in this weighty work to take care of destroying that which they had built up; and to take heed of many words. The following abstract will give a view of the general heads :—That which cometh from God, reaches to the life, and settles in it. Ministers are to live in that spirit which qualifies them to preach the way of salvation to others. This preserves them in their places, from laying hands suddenly on any, and from smiting their fellow-servants. That which moves any to travel abroad, must preserve them while they are abroad ; and as such are sensible of the dangers which surround them, and keep in the pure fear of the Lord, preservation will be experienced. Though they are favoured with Divine openings to minister to others ; yet for their own growth, they must dwell under the government of the Spirit of Truth, which will keep out the boaster ; and when their service is performed, they are to return to their own habitations. The Spirit of God is weighty, and brings those who obey it to be solid. It preserves out of all foolish imaginations and rashness, and endues with wisdom to walk circumspectly and wisely in the Church of God. None are to be hasty to speak, neither backward when they are called to do so ; for that brings confusion and poverty. Truth is honourable in the eyes of those who are not Friends, and when ministers abide in the Truth, they are kept in esteem ; but if they lose its life and power, they lose their crown ; and getting from under the cross, they may lose their former good condition, crucifying Christ afresh and putting Him to open shame. The practice of uttering words without authority or life, gives rise to formal preaching, and may settle the hearers in formality, whereby much hurt may be done. And take heed of inordinate affections, and seeking a name among men. When those among whom ministers labour receive and own their testimony, there is danger of self-exaltation. But as the Life of Christ and the power of his cross is lived in and abode under, preservation will be known ; and such will have a witness in the hearts of the people, answering to the Divine Witness there. There will be no want of wisdom, or knowledge, or of power, for the Lord is the helper and keeper of all such, and will in due time give them the victory.

After this meeting was over, the officers came with a warrant to apprehend George Fox; but he having walked out of the house into the garden, they missed him and went away disappointed.

About this time, the sufferings of Friends in support of their principles increased; and the prisons, both in England and Ireland, were crowded with them. George Fox wrote to Oliver Cromwell, remonstrating against the cruelty practised towards them, but could obtain no redress. Yet with a strange inconsistency, the protector issued an order for a day of fasting and humiliation, as well as a general collection, on account of the sufferings of the Protestants on the Continent, under the Duke of Savoy, who persecuted them with great severity for their religion. To show how contrary they acted to the Gospel rule of doing as they would be done by, in thus imprisoning Friends, while they professed so much abhorrence to the Roman Catholic persecutions, George Fox wrote a paper and had it printed and circulated, " to show them the nature of a true fast, such as God requires and accepts, and to make them sensible of their injustice and self-condemnation, in blaming the Papists for persecuting the Protestants abroad, while they, calling themselves Protestants, were at the same time persecuting their Protestant neighbours and Friends at home."

The crowded state of the prisons, and the consequent unhealthiness of many of the sufferers, induced Friends to go before the parliament and intercede that they might be suffered to go and lie in the stead of their brethren who were in gaol, that they might have an opportunity of recruiting and breathing a purer air. This indeed was a strong proof of the love which prevailed in the Society at that period, inducing the members freely to give up their time, money, and even liberty, for the help of each other. But it had little effect on their persecutors ; who rather seemed to be exasperated by such evidence of affectionate attachment, and threatened the applicants with being whipped and sent home. George Fox spent some time in London, labouring for the relief of his afflicted brethren, and writing epistles and papers, tending to strengthen their faith, to rebuke sinners, or persuade the high professors to moderation. An Address to the members of Parliament, whom he considered the principal authors of the persecution, is as follows, viz. :—

" O friends, do not cloak and cover yourselves ; there is a God that knoweth your hearts, and that will uncover you. He seeth your way. ' Wo be to him that covereth, but not with my spirit, saith the Lord.' Do ye do contrary to the law, and then put it from you ! Mercy and true judgment ye neglect. Look, what was spoken against such. My Saviour spake against such ; ' I was sick and in prison, and ye visited me not : I was an hungered, and ye gave me no meat : I was a stranger, and ye took me not in.' But they said, ' When saw we thee in prison and did not come to thee ! ' ' Inasmuch as ye did not unto one of these little ones, ye did it not unto me.' Friends, ye prison them that be in the life and power of truth, and yet profess to be the ministers of Christ; but if Christ had sent you, ye would bring out of prison, and out of bondage, and receive strangers. Ye have lived in pleasure on the earth, and been wanton? ye have nourished your hearts, as in a day of slaughter; ye have condemned and killed the just, and he doth not resist you.

"G. F."

CHAPTER V.   1659-1660.

*Attends a Yearly Meeting at Balby—And a General Meeting
at Skipton—Committed to Lancaster gaol—Addresses Charles
II. on his accession to the throne—Receives his discharge by
order of the King.*

CROMWELL dying, his son Richard was declared Protector, and soon after his accession the nation was again involved in intestine commotion.   The probability of a change in the government, and the excitement and confusion consequent on such a state of things, induced a fear in the mind of George Fox, lest Friends should be drawn into parties and strife. He therefore addressed an epistle to his brethren, warning them to keep clear of meddling with any of the powers of the earth, but to mind the Lord and his service.

In 1659, he again travelled through the counties of England, and had large and precious meetings, in which many were convinced.   This was particularly the case in Cornwall; " several eminent people being convinced in that county," says George Fox, " whom neither priests nor magistrates, by spoiling goods or imprisonments, could make to forsake their Shepherd, the Lord Jesus Christ, that had bought them."

About the time of George Fox's visit to these parts, several vessels were wrecked on the coast of England, near the Land's End.   It was the custom, at such times, for both rich and poor to get possession of as much of the wreck as possible, without caring to save the lives of the distressed mariners. It grieved George to hear of such unchristian practices, and he earnestly expostulated against them, in an address which he circulated among the inhabitants. He also encouraged Friends who resided there, to use their exertions in suppressing the practice, and to set a good example, by endeavouring to save the lives of those who suffered shipwreck, and to preserve the property for the rightful owners.

The agitated state of the country increased the difficulties of travelling, as well as the sufferings of Friends; their meetings being often broken up by the soldiers, and they beaten, stoned and dragged away to prison, there to languish in confinement for many months. Complaint of this cruel usage being made to General Monk, who commanded the army, he issued an order requiring both officers and soldiers to forbear disturbing the meetings of Friends; which gave them them some respite.

George Fox continued his journey to Bristol, Nailsworth, Gloucester, Worcester, and Badgely, from whence he went to visit his relatives at Drayton. At Balby, in Yorkshire, a General, or Yearly Meeting of Friends, was held in an orchard, where several thousands of persons, Friends and others, were collected. To this meeting George Fox went; and, standing upon a high stool, began to preach to the people. He had proceeded but a little time, when two trumpeters came riding towards him, sounding their trumpets; and the captain of the troop cried to the people to divide to the right and left, and make way. It proved to be a company of

horse sent from York, more than thirty miles distant, to break up the meeting. George continued
speaking, and the captain bade him come down, for
he must disperse them. George reasoned calmly
with him on the hardship of the case, many having
come a great distance to attend the meeting; and
assured him they were peaceably met for the worship of God, and should separate in a quiet and
orderly manner, as soon as the service of the meeting was over. At length he prevailed with him to
leave a few of his soldiers, to see that all ended
quietly. The captain soon went away, and the soldiers who had to stay, told Friends they might continue their meeting until night, if they chose. " But
we staid," says G. F., " but about three hours after,
and had a glorïous powerful meeting ; for the presence of the living God was manifest amongst us,
and the Seed, Christ, was set over all."

He then proceeded through Warnsworth and
Barton-Abbey to Skipton, where he attended a
General Meeting of Friends from " many counties
concerning the affairs of the church." He had
recommended the institution of this meeting several
years before. It was sometimes attended by members from most parts of the nation, and was useful
in advising and assisting Friends under the multiplied sufferings to which they were subjected.
Representations of these were prepared to be laid
before justices, judges, and the parliament ; and
collections made for the relief of poor Friends and
others. It had stood for several years, and the
civil or military officers had frequently come to disperse Friends, but when they found the object for

which they had convened, they not only passed away without molesting them, but commended the care of the Society in providing for its own poor, as well as its liberality in relieving the wants of others, who were not in religious connexion with it.

In the course of his travels in 1660, George Fox came to Swarthmore in company with his friends Francis Howgill and Thomas Curtis. He had not been there long, before he was arrested under a warrant from Henry Porter, a justice of the peace, and carried to Ulverstone that night, and next morning to Lancaster. The hearing of his case took place before justice Porter, who charged him with many things which as usual he could not, and indeed did not attempt to prove, but committed him to prison. George desired a copy of the mittimus, that he might know for what he was imprisoned. It was refused, and the gaoler was ordered to lock him up in a part of the gaol called "the dark house," and to let none come to him, but keep him close prisoner until he was delivered by the king or parliament.

The numerous falsehoods put in circulation respecting this valiant soldier of Jesus Christ produced some singular notions of his character in the minds of the ignorant class of people. At the constable's house, where they detained him the night of his arrest, they set a guard of *sixteen* men to watch him, some of whom sat in the fire-place lest he should take flight out of the chimney. One of them remarked he did not think "a thousand men could have taken him." Next day, as they were proceeding to Lancaster, one wicked fellow knelt down, and lifting up his hands blessed God that he was taken.   The people seemed disposed to glory in his arrest, but George says, he " was moved to sing praises to the Lord in his triumphing power over them."

The illegality and injustice of this commitment induced Friends to use considerable exertions to obtain his release.   Margaret Fell and Anne Curtis applied in person to king Charles, who had just been raised to the throne, requesting him to send for George Fox, and hear the case himself; which he assented to, and accordingly directed an order to be issued for removing him from Lancaster to London. Various frivolous pretences were used to prevent the execution of the king's mandate : but at length they concluded to send him up, and consulted as to the safest and least expensive mode of conveyance. One of the charges against him was, that he had endeavoured " to raise insurrection, and to embroil the whole kingdom in blood ;" and when it was proposed to escort him with a party of horse, George replied, that if he was such a man as they represented him to be, they had need to send a troop or two of horse to guard him.   But the expense of this mode formed a serious objection.   It was then suggested that the constable and a few of the bailiffs might be sufficient to escort him.   On examination, however, it was found that this would cost more than was convenient for them to pay, and they proposed to him to put in bail for his appearance on a certain day in London.   This he refused to do, asserting his entire innocence of the charges brought against him ; but at the same time he informed them, that if he was set at liberty, he would engage

charges, and the fact that
against him, made way for his
by order of the king, dated 24
after he had been a prisoner at

At the time Charles II.
there were about seven hundre
prisons in England, who had
the governments of Oliver an
The king on his accession to
all at liberty. There seeme
intention on the part of the ki
conscience to his subjects; but
tuous behaviour of some disor
this desirable object. They
monarchy-men, and made an i
of London against the gover
which was to bring great suffer
although they were in no way
disturbers of the peace, but
mony against all plots and i
those persons made pretence
wicked designs, the suspicions
were excited against all who
established religion, and their n
with great violence. George
it was likely to be a time of
remained in London, to bear his
ing brethren, and to encourage
by his example. He was soon
to Whitehall; and while waitin
those who were to examine him
to the people. This being obse
in authority who happened t

to appear before the judges in London, on a certain day of the court term, if the Lord permitted.

After some consultation, they agreed to take his bare word for his appearance; and he whom they had represented as so dangerous a person, was permitted to go at large; and travelled at his leisure up to London, to take his trial on an indictment, charging him with insurrection, sedition, and attempting to shed the blood of his fellow-subjects.

At the time of assize many came to see him, to whom he preached from the gaol windows, and showed them the fluctuations which attended the profession of religion, among the various denominations; each, as it rose into power, persecuting the rest for non-conformity to its formula of faith. All pleaded in their turn, that people " must be subject to the higher power," that is, to whomsoever had the rule; but George Fox, " directed them to Christ Jesus, that they might be built upon Him, the Rock and Foundation that changeth not." He also gave forth the following paper, concerning true religion :—

" True religion is the true rule and right way of serving God. And religion is a pure stream of righteousness flowing from the image of God, and is the life and power of God planted in the heart and mind by the law of life in the heart, which bringeth the soul, mind, spirit, and body to be conformable to God, the Father of spirits, and to Christ; so that they come to have fellowship with the Father and the Son, and with all his holy angels and saints. And this religion is pure, from above, undefiled before God; and is to visit the father-

less, and widows, and :
spots of the world.   S
defiled, spotted religion
themselves from defilei
pure, and below, and
widows, and strangers d(

Besides this, he wrot(
and ·one for the purpose
who were agitated with
He also addressed the k
to the throne of his a
extend mercy and forgi
and to suppress the pro
overspread the nation o
with his accustomed p
exercise forgiveness, an
the laws for arresting t
tion, and also stop perse
not hear his prayers, o1
but blindness and hardn(
him, and the country
Gomorrah, for wickedne

In about three weeks
ment, he appeared at t
court in London.   The
read ; and when they can
sented him as a dangero
up their hands in asto
them if they could be
magistrates of Lancaster
come up alone, if he was
ment alleged.   The g

directed that he should be put in a place of confinement " where he could not stir."   The order was
promptly executed ; but he observed to them, that
although they could confine his body, and shut that
up, yet " they could not stop up the Word of Life."
Through the kind interference of an officer of the
king's bed-chamber, who knew his innocence and
was friendly to him, George Fox was soon discharged ; and, after preaching to the soldiers, he
went to visit a number of his friends, who were
imprisoned in an inn near Whitehall.   Richard
Hubberthorn and he drew up a declaration against
plots and fightings, setting forth the peaceable and
non-resisting principles of Friends, which prohibited
them from being engaged in forcibly setting up or
pulling down any government.   It is as follows :
viz.—

" *A Declaration from the harmless and innocent people
    of God, called Quakers, against all sedition,
    plotters, and fighters in the world ; for the removing
    of the ground of jealousy and suspicion from both
    magistrates and people in the kingdom, concerning
    wars and fightings.   Presented unto the king upon
    the 21st day of the Eleventh Month, 1660.*

" OUR principle is, and our practices have always
been, to seek peace and ensue it, and to follow after
righteousness and the knowledge of God ; seeking
the good and welfare, and doing that which tends
to the peace of all.   We know that wars and fightings proceed from the lusts of men, as James iv.
1, 2, 3 ; out of which lusts the Lord hath redeemed
us, and so out of the occasion of war ; the occasion

of which war and the war itself (wherein envious men, who are lovers of themselves more than lovers of God, lust, kill, and desire to have men's lives or estates) ariseth from the lust. All bloody principles and practices we, as to our own particulars, do utterly deny; with all outward wars, and strife, and fightings with outward weapons, for any end, or under any pretence whatsoever: and this is our testimony to the whole world.

" And whereas it is objected,—

" But although you now say, that you cannot fight nor take up arms at. all; yet if the Spirit do move you, then you will change your principle, and then you will sell your coat and buy a sword, and fight for the kingdom of Christ.

" *Answer*—As for this, we say to you, that Christ said to Peter, ' Put up again thy sword into his place;' though He had said before, he that had no sword might sell his coat and buy one (to the fulfilling of the law and Scripture); yet after, when He had bid him put it up, He said, 'All they that take the sword shall perish with the sword.' And further Christ said to Pilate, ' Thinkest thou, that I cannot now pray to my Father, and he shall presently give me more than twelve legions of angels?' And this might satisfy Peter, after he had put up his sword, when He said to him, he that took it should perish by it; which satisfieth us. And in the Revelation it is said, ' He that killeth with the sword must be killed with the sword; here is the faith and the patience of the saints.' And so Christ's kingdom is not of this world, therefore do not his servants fight; as he told Pilate, the magistrate who crucified Him. And did they not look upon Christ as a raiser of sedition? And did not He say, 'Forgive them?' But thus it is that we are numbered amongst transgressors and numbered amongst fighters. . . .

"That Spirit of Christ by which we are guided is not changeable, so as once to command us from a thing, as evil, and again to move unto it; and we do certainly know, and so testify to the world, that the Spirit of Christ, which leads us into all truth, will never move us to fight and war against any man with outward weapons, neither for the kingdom of Christ, nor for the kingdoms of this world.

"First, Because the kingdom of Christ God will exalt, according to his promise, and cause it to grow and flourish in righteousness; ' not by might, nor by power (of outward sword), but by my Spirit, saith the Lord,' Zech. iv. 6. So those that use any weapon to fight for Christ, or for the establishing of his kingdom or government, both the spirit, principle, and practice in that we deny.

"Secondly, We do earnestly desire and wait, that (by the word of God's power and its effectual operation in the hearts of men) the kingdoms of this world may become the kingdoms of the Lord, and of his Christ; that He might rule and reign in men by his Spirit and truth; that thereby all people, out of all different judgments and professions, might be brought into love and unity with God, and one with another; and that they all might come to witness the prophet's words, who said, ' Nation shall not lift up sword against nation, neither shall they learn war any more,' Isa. ii. 4 ; Mich. iv. 3.

" So we, whom the Lord hath called into the obedience of his truth, have denied wars and fightings, and cannot again any more learn it. And this is a certain testimony unto all the world of the truth of our hearts in this particular, that as God persuadeth every man's heart to believe, so they may receive it. For we have not (as some others) gone about cunningly with devised fables; nor have we ever denied in practice what we have professed in principle; but in sincerity and truth, and by the word of God, have we laboured to be made manifest unto all men, that both we and our ways might be witnessed in the hearts of all. And whereas all manner of evil hath been falsely spoken of us, we hereby speak forth the plain truth of our hearts, to take away the occasion of that offence; that so we, being innocent, may not suffer for other men's offences, nor be made a prey upon by the wills of men, for that of which we were never guilty; but in the uprightness of our hearts we may, under the power ordained of God for the punishment of evil-doers, and for the praise of them that do well, live a peaceable and godly life in all godliness and honesty. For, although we have always suffered, and do now more abundantly suffer, yet we know that it is for righteousness's sake: ' For our rejoicing is this, the testimony of our conscience, that in simplicity and godly sincerity, not with fleshly wisdom, but by the grace of God, we have had our conversation in the world,' 2 Cor. i. 12; which for us is a witness for the convincing of our enemies. For this we can say to all the world, we have wronged no man's person or possessions, we have used no force nor violence against any man; we have been found in no plots, nor guilty of sedition. When we have been wronged we have not sought to revenge ourselves; we have not made resistance against authority, but wherein we could not obey for conscience' sake, we have suffered even the most of any people in the nation.

" We have been counted as sheep for the slaughter, persecuted and despised, beaten, stoned, wounded, stocked, whipped, imprisoned, haled out of synagogues, cast into dungeons and noisome vaults, where many have died in bonds, shut up from our friends, denied needful sustenance for many days together, with other the like cruelties. And the cause of all these our sufferings is not for any evil, but for things relating to the worship of our God, and in obedience to his requirings of us. For which cause we shall freely give up our bodies a sacrifice, rather than disobey the Lord; for we know, as the Lord hath kept us innocent, so He will plead our cause when there is none in the earth to plead it. So we, in obedience unto his truth, do not love our lives unto death, that we may do his will, and wrong no man in our generation, but seek the good and peace of all men. And He that hath commanded us, That we shall not swear at all, (Matt. v. 34,) hath also commanded us, That we shall not kill, Matt. v. So that we can neither kill men, nor swear for nor against them. And this is both our principle and practice, and hath been from the beginning; so that if we suffer, as suspected to take up arms or make war against any, it is without any ground from us; for it neither is, nor ever was in our hearts, since we owned the truth of God; neither shall we ever do it, because it is contrary to the

Spirit of Christ, his doctrine, and the practices of his apostles; even contrary to Him for whom we suffer all things and endure all things.

" And whereas men come against us with clubs, staves, drawn swords, pistols cocked; and do beat, cut and abuse us; yet we never resisted them, but to them our hair, backs, and cheeks have been ready. But it is not an honour to manhood or nobility to run upon harmless people, who lift not up a hand against them, with arms and weapons.

" Therefore consider these things, ye men of understanding; for plotters, raisers of insurrections, tumultuous ones, and fighters, running with swords, clubs, staves, and pistols, one against another, we say, these are of the world; from the foundation of which the Lamb hath been slain; which Lamb hath redeemed us from this unrighteous world. And we are not of it, but are heirs of a world in which there is no end, and of a kingdom where no corruptible thing enters. And our weapons are spiritual, and not carnal, yet mighty through God to the pulling down of the strongholds of sin and Satan, who is author of wars, fighting, murder, and plots. And our swords are broken into ploughshares, and spears into pruning hooks, as prophesied of in Micah iv. Therefore we cannot learn war any more, neither rise up against nation or kingdom with outward weapons, though you have numbered us amongst the transgressors and plotters. The Lord knows our innocency herein, and will plead our cause with all men and people upon earth, at the day of their judgment, when all men shall have a reward according to their works.

" Therefore in love we warn you for your soul's

good, not to wrong the innocent, nor the babes of
Christ, which He hath in his hand, which He tenders
as the apple of his eye; neither seek to destroy the
heritage of God, neither turn your swords backward
upon such as the law was not made for, *i.e.*, the
righteous; but for the sinners and transgressors, to
keep them down. For those are not the peace-makers,
neither the lovers of enemies, neither can they overcome evil with good, who wrong them that be friends
to you and all men, and wish your good and the good
of all people on the earth. If you oppress us, as
they did the children of Israel in Egypt, and if
you oppress us as they did when Christ was born,
and as they did the Christians in the primitive times,
we can say, 'The Lord forgive you;' and leave the
Lord to deal with you, and not revenge ourselves.
And if you say, as the council said to Peter and
John, you must speak no more in that name; and if
you serve us as they served the three children spoken
of in Daniel, God is the same as ever He was,
that lives for ever and ever, who hath the innocent
in his arms.

"Oh! friends! offend not the Lord and his little
ones, neither afflict his people; but consider and be
moderate. And do not run hastily into things, but
mind and consider mercy, justice, and judgment;
that is the way for you to prosper and get the favour
of the Lord. Our meetings were stopped and
broken up in the days of Oliver, on pretence of
plotting against him; and in the days of the Committee of Safety* we were looked upon as plotters

* The Committee of Safety were chosen by parliament
after the resignation of Richard Cromwell. They held the
reins of government until the restoration of Charles II.

to bring in king Charles; and now our peaceable
meetings are termed seditious. Oh! that men
should lose their reason, and go contrary to their
own conscience; knowing that we have suffered all
things, and have been accounted plotters all along,
though we have declared against them both by word
of mouth and printing, and are clear from any such
thing. Though we have suffered all along, because
we would not take up carnal weapons to fight
withal against any, and are thus made a prey upon
because we are the innocent lambs of Christ, and
cannot avenge ourselves! These things are left upon
your hearts to consider; but we are out of all those
things in the patience of the saints, and we know
that as Christ said, ' They that take the sword shall
perish with the sword,' Matt. xxvi. 52 ; Rev.
xiii. 10.

    '' This is given forth, in the year 1660, from the
people called Quakers, to satisfy the King and
his council, and all those that have any jealousy
concerning us, that all occasion of suspicion may
be taken away, and our innocency cleared.

'' POSTSCRIPT.

" Though we are numbered amongst transgressors, and so have been given up to all rude,
merciless men, by which our meetings are broken up;
in which we edified one another in our holy faith,
and prayed together to the Lord that lives for ever,
yet He is our pleader for us in this day. The Lord
saith, ' They that feared the Lord spake often one
to another ' (as in Malachi); which were as his jewels.
For this cause, and no evil doing, are we cast into

holes, dungeons, houses of correction, prisons, they sparing neither old nor young, men nor women, and made a prey on in the sight of all nations, under pretence of being seditious, &c., so that all rude people ran upon us to take possession; for which we say, The Lord forgive them that have done thus to us; who doth and will enable us to suffer; and never shall we lift up hand against any man that doth thus use us; but that the Lord may have mercy upon them, that they may consider what they have done. For how is it possible for them to requite us for the wrong they have done to us? Who to all nations have sounded us abroad as seditious or plotters, who were never found plotters against any power or man upon the earth, since we knew the life and power of Jesus Christ manifested in us; who hath redeemed us from the world and all works of darkness, and plotters that be in it. So we say, the Lord have mercy upon our enemies, and forgive them for what they have done unto us.

"Oh! do as you would be done by; and do unto all men as you would have them do unto you; for this is but the law and the prophets.

"And all plots, insurrections, and riotous meetings, we do deny, knowing them to be of the devil, the murderer; which we in Christ, who was before they were, triumph over them. And all wars and fightings with carnal weapons we do deny, who have the sword of the Spirit; and all that wrong us, we leave them to the Lord. And this is to clear our innocency from that aspersion cast upon us, 'That we are seditious or plotters.'"

No entreaty or persuasion that could be used

served to arrest the fierceness of persecution. Men and women who were known to be Friends could scarcely pass without violent abuse through the streets and highways, on their lawful business, or to procure provisions for their families. Many were haled out of their houses, and some who were sick were cruelly dragged from their beds to prison. Amid this storm of ill usage, Friends continued steadfast to their principles and faithfully attended their meetings, although they went to them with a full expectation of beating, stoning and imprisonment. The prisons were filled with the peaceable Quakers, and accounts were received in London that several thousands had been thrown into gaol in the space of a few weeks. Under a lively sense of the grievous sufferings of his friends, and tender sympathy with them, George Fox addressed them in an epistle of Christian consolation, as follows : —

" My dear Friends,

" In the immortal Seed of God, which will plead its own innocency, who be inheritors of an everlasting kingdom that is incorruptible, and of a world and riches that fade not away, peace and mercy be multiplied amongst you in all your sufferings, who never feared them ; whose backs were not unready, but your hair and cheeks prepared ; who never feared sufferings, as knowing it is your portion in the world, from the foundation of which the Lamb was slain ; who reigns in his glory, which He had with his Father before the world began ; who is your rock in all floods and waves, upon which ye can stand safe, with a cheerful countenance, beholding the Lord God of the whole earth on your side.   So in the Seed of God, which was before the unrighteous world in which the sufferings are, live and feed, wherein the bread of life is felt, and no cause of complaint of hunger and cold. Friends, your sufferings, all that are or have been of late in prison, I would have you send up an account of them, and how things are amongst you, that it may be delivered to the king and his council; for things are pretty well here after the storm.

" G. F.

" London, the 28th of the
Eleventh Month, 1660."

CHAPTER VI. 1660-1662.

*Persecution of Friends in New England—Charles II. issues a
mandamus forbidding any more executions of Friends there
—Statement of the Sufferings of Friends presented to the
King—The legality of Friends' marriages established.*

DURING the year 1660, much blood was shed in
England, in consequence of the change which had
taken place in the government; and Colonel Hacker,
with others who had been active in persecuting
Friends during the ·time of the Protector, was
brought to the gallows. Often had these men been
warned by Friends against their cruelty and persecution, and of the day of retribution, which would
overtake them, when the Lord should arise to plead
the cause of the oppressed, of the destitute widows
and fatherless children whom they had made such,
by their unrelenting severity. That day was now
come; the overflowing scourge entered among them,
and brought a dread and fear over the minds of the
people, so that they who had deridingly nicknamed
Friends, Quakers, were made to tremble and quake
for themselves. Many now would gladly have taken
refuge among this despised people, as a shelter and
hiding-place from the storm; and some, through
the distress that came upon them, were brought to
make open profession of the religion which before
they had persecuted.

In reviewing the trials and hardships which Friends had undergone for their profession, George Fox made these remarks: "Oh, the daily reproaches, revilings, and beatings we underwent amongst them even on the highways, because we could not put off our hats to them, and for saying thou and thee to them. Oh, the havoc and spoil the priests made of our goods, because we could not give them tithes nor put into their mouths; besides casting into prisons, and besides the great fines laid upon us, because we could not swear! But for all these things did the Lord God plead with them. Yet some of them were so hardened in their wickedness, that when they were turned out of their places and offices, they said if they had power they would do the same again. And when this day of overturning was come upon them, I was moved to write to them and to ask them, ' Did we ever resist you when you took away our ploughs and plough-gears, our carts and horses, our corn and cattle, our kettles and platters from us, and whipped us, and set us in the stocks, and cast us into prison ; and all this only for serving and worshipping God in spirit and truth, and because we could not conform to your religion, manners, customs, and fashions? Did we ever resist you? Did we not give our backs to beat, and our cheeks to pull off the hair, and our faces to spit on? . . . . You thought to have wearied us out and undone us, but you undid yourselves ; whereas, we could praise God, notwithstanding all your plundering of us, that we have a kettle, and a platter, and a horse and plough still.' "

Many warnings in various ways were given by Friends to some in power under Cromwell's government, which they not only rejected, but abused them in return for their faithful admonitions. But when king Charles took the throne, most of these lost their places and benefices, and they then confessed Friends had been true prophets to the nation. A priest of much note in Oliver's days, when some liberty was granted, prayed that God would put it into the hearts of the chief magistrates to remove this " cursed toleration." Others prayed against it as intolerable. But after the above priest was turned out of his benefice, a Friend asked him whether he would account toleration accursed now; he shook his head without making any reply.

Although many of those who were imprisoned in consequence of the rising of the Fifth-monarchymen, were soon after set at liberty, as being entirely innocent of any connection with those wild enthusiasts; yet the meetings of Friends continued to be disturbed by the soldiers and rude people. At one time, a company of Irishmen came to the meetinghouse at Pall Mall, with a view of making a riot, but the meeting was over before they got there. George Fox had gone into an upper chamber, and overheard one of them say he would kill all the Quakers, if they were there. George Fox went down to them, and reproved this bloodthirsty man, telling him " *the law* said, ' An eye for an eye, and a tooth for a tooth;' but thou threatens to kill all the Quakers, though they have done thee no hurt. But here is *Gospel* for thee : here is my hair, here is my cheek, and here is my shoulder," turning it to him. This address so surprised the man and his companions, as to induce the remark, that if those were Quaker principles, they had never heard the like before. George replied, that what Friends were in words, the same they were in life. The man who made the threat became quite moderate, and carried himself courteously, although one of his company, who staid with-out the house, said he was so desperate a character that he did not dare to go in with him, fearing he would have done Friends some mischief. Such is the powerful influence which a gentle and peaceable demeanour under provocation, has over the spirits even of persecutors; furnishing strong evidence of the blessed effects of the meek and non-resisting spirit of the Gospel, and of the truth of the declaration, that " a soft answer turneth away wrath."

About this time Friends received an account from New England, that the government there had made a law to banish the Quakers out of their colonies, on pain of death, and that four having returned after banishment were put to death. At the time of their execution, although no intelligence had then reached England of any such cruelty being intended, George Fox had a clear sense of their sufferings, " as perfectly," to use his own words, " as if the halter had been put about my own neck." The intelligence produced much sympathy and feeling for the Society in that country ; and Edward Burrough went immediately to court, and obtained an audience with the King, and told him " there was a vein of innocent blood opened in his dominions, which, if it were not stopped, would overrun all." The king replied, " But I will stop that vein." "Then do it speedily," said Edward, " for we know not how many may soon be put to death." "As speedily as you will," rejoined the King.

" Call the secretary," said he, to one of his attendants, " and I will do it presently." A mandamus was forthwith granted, forbidding the execution of any more of the Quakers: and the King was pleased to appoint one of that Society, who had been banished from New England, on pain of death, to be the bearer of the despatch. Friends hired a master of a vessel for three hundred pounds, to sail in ten days, whether he had freight or not; and after a prosperous voyage they reached Boston in about six weeks. Many Friends went passengers in the ship, and when they arrived in the harbour, word was quickly spread through the town, that a ship-load of Quakers had come; and among them one under sentence of banishment on pain of death.   On the following day, the master of the vessel and the King's messenger went to the house of John Endicott, the governor, and laid before him the King's mandate. After reading it, they all went to the deputy-governor, and showed it to him; the Friends receiving for answer that the King's commands should be obeyed. The matter soon became rumoured through the town, to the great joy of the moderate people; and Friends assembled, with one accord, to offer up praise and thanksgivings to God, who had so wonderfully delivered them from the power of the destroyer. While thus devoutly engaged, one of their brethren came in, who had been laying in irons some time, under sentence of death, and had just been discharged. This added greatly to their joy, and caused them to lift up their hearts and hands in praises to God, who only is able to sustain and deliver those that put their trust in him. Some time after this Governor Winthrop, of Massachusetts, being in England, George Fox had conversation with him respecting the execution of those Friends. The governor assured George that "he had no hand in putting Friends to death, or in any way persecuting them, but was one of those that protested against it."

In the year 1660, while George Fox was in Lancaster gaol, a book called the Battledore was published. It was prepared by two Friends, at his suggestion, and revised, with some additions, by himself, showing by examples, from about thirty different languages, ancient and modern, that "thou" and "thee" to one person, and "you" to more than one, was the proper form of expression. It was widely circulated, and had a good effect in moderating the violence of persecution for adhering to the rules of grammar, few being so fierce against Friends for the use of thou and thee as they had formerly been.

George Fox had now resided in London and its vicinity nearly two years, facing the storm of persecution, which fell heavily on that city, and not only enduring hardness as a good soldier of Jesus Christ, but animating his fellow-professors to suffer cheerfully in support of the same blessed cause. He took a short journey into Essex, and had large meetings among the people; but returned very soon to London, where there was a great field of service to the Lord, the hearts of the people being open to hear and receive the gospel message. Persecution, however, continued; the irregularities of the Fifth-monarchy men being still the pretext for breaking up the meetings of Friends, and casting them into prison. This induced George Fox and Richard Hubberthorn to draw up a statement and present it to the king, showing the hardships which the Society endured in support of its principles and meetings. It is as follows :—

" TO THE KING.

" Friend, who art the chief ruler of these dominions, here is a list of some of the sufferings of the people of God, in scorn called Quakers, that have suffered under the changeable powers before thee, by whom there have been imprisoned, and under whom there have suffered for good conscience' sake, and for bearing testimony to the truth, as it is in Jesus, three thousand one hundred and seventy-three persons ; and there yet lie in prison, in the name of the commonwealth, seventy-three persons that we know of. And there have died in prison in the time of the commonwealth, and of Oliver and Richard, the Protectors, through cruel and hard imprisonments, upon nasty straw, and in dungeons, thirty-two persons. There have been also imprisoned in thy name, since thy arrival, by such as thought to ingratiate themselves thereby to thee, three thousand sixty and eight persons. Besides this, our meetings are daily broken up by men with clubs and arms, though we meet peaceably, according to the practice of God's people in the primitive times; and our friends are thrown into waters, and trod upon till the very blood gushes out of them; the number of which abuses can hardly be uttered. Now this we would have of thee, to set them at liberty that lie in prison in the names of the commonwealth, and of the two

N

Protectors, and them that lie in thy own name, for speaking the truth, and for good conscience' sake, who have not lifted up an hand against thee nor any man; and that the meetings of our friends, who meet peaceably together in the fear of God, to worship Him, may not be broken up by rude people, with their clubs, and swords, and staves. One of the greatest things that we have suffered for formerly, was because we could not swear to the Protectors and all the changeable governments; and now we are imprisoned because we cannot take the oath of allegiance. Now, if yea be not yea, and nay nay, to thee and to all men upon the earth, let us suffer as much for breaking of that as others do for breaking an oath. We have suffered these many years both in lives and estates, under these changeable governments, because we cannot swear, but obey Christ's doctrine, who commands we should not swear at all, Math. v., James v.; and this we seal with our lives and estates, with our yea and nay, according to the doctrine of Christ. Hearken to these things, and so consider them in the wisdom of God, that by it such actions may be stopped; thou that hast the government and mayst do it. We desire that all that are in prison may be set at liberty, and that for the time to come they may not be imprisoned for conscience' and for the truth's sake. And if thou question the innocency of their sufferings, let them and their accusers be brought up before thee; and we shall produce a more particular and full account of their sufferings, if required.

"G. F. and R. H."

It was not from persecution only that Friends suffered. Among themselves persons arose, who, "giving heed to seducing spirits," fell away from a good condition, and became a cause of reproach and trouble to Friends.—The instrument in this schism was John Perrot, who had been a minister in good esteem, and in this capacity had gone to Rome, where he had suffered imprisonment. On his return he seemed to be puffed up with a high conceit of himself; and possessing good natural abilities, he was ambitious to distinguish himself in the Society. He pretended to have clearer views on religious matters than George Fox and others of his brethren, and among other things, objected to the practice of taking off the hat in time of prayer, with which he refused to comply.

Novelties, however absurd, are rarely without admirers, and Perrot had his adherents. The spirit of discord once stirred up was not easily allayed, and some well-disposed Friends became unsettled by it. As is mostly the case, however, with apostates, Perrot, having turned from what he had once known to be right, grew worse and worse, and went into many things which he had formerly testified against. This contributed not a little to convince those who had for a time associated with him, that he was a fallen man, and verified that saying of the apostle, "If I build again the things which I destroyed, I make myself a transgressor." But he stopped not here—conscious of the loss he had sustained by his apostacy—restless and dissatisfied in himself, he became also exceedingly envious of those he had left; and going over to America, obtained an office

in which he was a most rigorous exacter of oaths,
and persecutor of Friends. He threw off the
appearance of a Friend, dressed himself in fashionable apparel, with a sword by his side, and fell into
open sensualities, according to that saying, "Evil
men and seducers shall wax worse and worse, deceiving and being deceived."

During the prevalence of this spirit, George Fox
laboured both by preaching and writing, to arrest its
progress and to rescue those who had been entangled.
He published the following short warning to all who
had gone into the spirit of separation, viz. :

"Whosoever is tainted with this spirit of John
Perrot, it will perish. Mark theirs and his end,
that are turned into those outward things and janglings about them, and that which is not savoury ; all
which is for perpetual judgment, and is to be swept
and cleansed out of the camp of God's elect. This
is to that spirit that is gone into jangling about that
which is below (the rotten principle of the old
Ranters), and gone from the invisible power of God,
in which is the everlasting fellowship. And so,
many are become like the corn on the house-top,
and like the untimely figs, and now clamour and
speak against them that be in the power of God.
Oh, consider ! the light and power of God goes
over you all, and leaves you in the fretting nature,
but of the unity which is in the everlasting light,
life, and power of God. Consider this before the
day be gone from you, and take heed that your
memorial be not rooted out from among the
righteous.

"G. F."

Among other trials which Friends had about this time, the legality of their marriages was called in question, by an action brought in one of the courts of England, to dispossess the child of a deceased Friend of his inheritance in a copyhold estate belonging to his father, who had been married according to the order of Friends. In opening the case, the plaintiff's counsel took the ground that the marriage was not solemnized according to the laws of the realm, and therefore not valid, using moreover many unhandsome expressions respecting the Society. Judge Archer, in summing up the case, observed, " there was a marriage in Paradise when Adam took Eve, and Eve took Adam ; and that it was the consent of the parties that made a marriage. And for the Quakers, he added, he did not know their opinions, but he did not believe what had been said of them, but that they went together as Christians ; and therefore he did believe the marriage was lawful and the child lawful heir." To satisfy the jury more fully, he adduced a case in point ; where a marriage, performed by the simple declaration of the parties before witnesses, that they took each other to be husband and wife, had been questioned, but that its validity and lawfulness were affirmed by the bishops as well as judges. This subject is mentioned by George Fox as one of great interest to the Society ; and the decision obtained so fully settled the question, that it has never since been contested.

The oaths of allegiance and supremacy being now pressed upon Friends, and many imprisoned and some premunired because they could not conscientiously take them, George Fox gave forth this short essay on the lawfulness of swearing.

" The world saith, ' Kiss the book ;' but the book saith, ' Kiss the Son, lest he be angry ;' and the Son saith, ' Swear not at all ;' but keep to yea and nay in all your communications ; ' for whatsoever is more' than these cometh of evil. Again the world saith, ' Lay your hand on the book ;' but the book saith, Handle the word ; and the word saith, Handle not the traditions, nor the inventions, nor the rudiments of the world. And God saith, ' This is my beloved Son, hear him ;' who is the life, and the truth, and the light, and the way to God.

" G. F."

It has already been stated, that during the year 1650, George Fox was prisoner six months in the house of correction at Derby, where he was treated with great severity by the keeper. This man was afterwards brought to a sense of his wickedness, and was in great distress on account of it. As he patiently submitted to the operation of the Spirit of judgment in his own mind, he experienced forgiveness, became convinced of the principles of Friends and a steady member of the Society. At this time he wrote the following letter to George Fox :—

" Dear Friend,

" Having such a convenient messenger, I could do no less than give thee an account of my present condition ; remembering that, to the first awakening of me to a sense of life, and of the inward principle, God was pleased to make use of thee as an instrument. So that sometimes I am taken with admiration that it should come by such a means as it did; that is to say, that Providence should order thee to be my prisoner, to give me my first real sight of the truth. It makes me many times to think of the gaoler's conversion by the apostles. . . Notwithstanding my outward losses are, since that time, such that I am become nothing in the world, yet I hope I shall find that all these light afflictions, which are but for a moment, will work for me a far more exceeding and eternal weight of glory. They have taken all from me; and now, instead of keeping a prison, I am rather waiting when I shall become a prisoner myself. Pray for me, that my faith fail not, but that I may hold out to the death, that I may receive a crown of life. I earnestly desire to hear from thee, and of thy condition, which would very much rejoice me. Not having else at present, but my kind love unto thee and all Christian friends with thee, in haste, I rest thine in Christ Jesus,

"THOMAS SHERMAN.

"Derby, the 22nd of the
Fourth Month, 1662."

From London George Fox travelled through the country, accompanied by John Stubbs and Alexander Parker, visiting Friends and holding meetings until they reached Bristol. Here they understood that the officers had been very rude in breaking up the meetings, and on First-day, while Alexander Parker was preaching in the meeting at Broadmead, they came and took him away. After he was gone George

stood up and spoke to the people for a considerable
time in a powerful manner; all were quiet, and the
assembly broke up peaceably. Information having
got abroad that he was in town, and likely to attend
the meetings, the magistrates threatened to take him,
and raised the trained-band for the purpose. Having
ascertained this to be the case, his friends endeavoured
to dissuade him from going to meeting on the following First-day. George desired them to go to the
meeting, not telling them what he intended doing:
but, after they were gone, he went also, taking a path
which led across the fields. On his way he met
several persons who dissuaded him from going, from
the apprehension that he would be imprisoned. He
was not, however, to be deterred by the fear of suffering, and proceeded to the meeting, where he was
soon engaged in declaring the truth to the people,
and a heavenly, precious meeting they had. After
clearing his mind in testimony, he knelt down in
prayer to God; and at the conclusion of the meeting
observed to his friends, " they might see there was a
God in Israel that could deliver." The assembly
was very large, and dispersed peaceably. The officers
and soldiers having gone to break up another meeting, it occupied so much of their time that this concluded before they arrived, and thus they missed
their object.

After he had left the town, and gone to a neigh-
bouring meeting, the soldiers surrounded the meeting
house at Bristol, saying they should be sure to have
him now; but on looking over the company, and
finding he was not among them, they were greatly
incensed and kept Friends prisoners in the house

most of the day, asking them where George Fox was gone and how they might take him.

Passing through Wiltshire and Berkshire, he came again to London, and after a short stay went northward into Leicestershire, having many large meetings on the way, in which there was great opportunity for spreading the knowledge of the truth. At Swannington he was arrested by Lord Beaumont with a company of soldiers, who rushed into the house with swords and pistols in their hands. Finding nothing on which to ground a commitment, they tendered him the oath of allegiance and supremacy, which he declined taking, having a conscientious objection to all swearing; and after some time, a mittimus was made out for him and the Friends who were with him, charging him with this refusal, and stating that "*they were to have had a meeting.*" It was difficult to procure any one to convey them to prison; most persons being engaged in collecting their harvests, and none liking to be concerned in conveying their peaceable and respectable neighbours to gaol. At length a man was hired for the purpose, who, though paid for it, went with great reluctance. The Friends, five in number, were placed in his cart, and as they rode along some carried their Bibles in their hands and preached Christ to the people, telling them that they were prisoners going to suffer bonds for his name and truth's sake; and a woman Friend carried her spinning-wheel in her lap to afford her employment in prison. The people in the towns through which they passed were greatly affected, and on their arrival at Leicester the innkeeper was anxious to procure their liberty, offering them the privilege of staying at his house rather than they should go to the gaol. But though they acknowledged his kindness, they preferred sharing the lot of their brethren, many of whom were already in prison there.

The man who conducted them thither delivered the mittimus to the gaoler. They requested him to furnish them with some straw, but he replied, " You do not look like men that would lie on straw." After some friendly conversation with the gaoler's wife, they succeeded in obtaining a room, and the liberation of some Friends from the dungeon, for the purpose of participating in the accommodation which they procured. Before George Fox and his companions came into the prison, such was the roughness of the gaoler, that when Friends met together on First-day, if any one prayed, he would come with his mastiff-dog at his heels and pull them to the ground by the hair, and strike them with his staff; the dog, however, of a different temper from his master, would lay hold of the staff and take it out of his hand. George, nothing daunted by his ferocious disposition, gave notice to the felons and debtors that there would be a meeting in the yard on First-day, and any one wishing to hear the word of the Lord declared might come thither. The prisoners assembled accordingly, and held a comfortable meeting, which was kept up during the stay of Friends, and attended by others from the town and country, and some " received the Lord's truth there, who stood faithful witnesses for it ever since."

When the sessions came they were brought before the justices, who tendered the oaths to them again, and, because they steadfastly declined taking them, in obedience to the positive commands of Christ and his apostles, they were remanded to prison. As they went thither they preached the Gospel, the streets being full of people, and could rejoice that they were esteemed worthy to suffer for the testimony of Jesus. Soon after they were settled in the prison an order came from the court that they should all be discharged. Thus, through the kind providence of the Most High, way was made for their escape, when they least expected it. George Fox went to see Lord Beaumont, and showed him a letter from Lord Hastings to the justices of the sessions, requiring them to set him at liberty; but though George had it in his pocket at the time of his trial he did not show it to them. After reading it he seemed troubled in his mind, yet threatened that if they held any more meetings at Swannington he would send them to prison again. George Fox was not to be deterred by threats from the performance of his religious duty, and finding his mind engaged thereto, he held a meeting at Swannington without molestation. From thence he travelled to Twy Cross and through Warwick, Northampton, and Bedfordshire to London; and after tarrying there a short time he went into Norfolk and Cambridgeshire. Here he received intelligence of the decease of Edward Burrough, who, though but a young man, being only about twenty-eight years of age when he died, had, by his faithfulness to the manifestations of the Spirit of truth, grown up to the stature of a strong man in Christ, and become eminently useful in the Society, as a minister of the Gospel. Being sensible how great a grief and loss

his removal would be to Friends, George wrote a
short epistle to them, in order to stay and comfort
their minds.

Passing into Huntingdonshire he came to Lynn,
where he had a favoured meeting, and as he was
going out of the inn-yard where he had lodged, the
officers came to search the house for him ; " So, by
the good hand of the Lord," says he, " I escaped
their cruel hands.   After this we passed through the
counties, visiting Friends in their meetings, and the
Lord's power carried us over the persecuting spirits
and through many dangers ; and his truth spread
and grew, and Friends were established therein :
praises and glory to his name for ever."

CHAPTER VII. 1662-1664.

George Fox is again committed to Lancaster gaol—Conversation with Judge Twisden at the assizes—And with Judge Turner—Again brought before Judge Twisden and sentenced to be premunired.

In 1662, travelling in Kent, with Thomas Briggs, G. F. had a large meeting at Tenterden, at the close of which they walked into the yard, while their horses were getting ready, and saw a captain and large company of soldiers coming, with lighted matches and muskets. They soon came up and told them they must go before the captain. When brought before him, he asked which was George Fox, and, with his usual intrepidity and frankness, George answered, " I am the man." The captain appeared somewhat struck with his readiness, and stepping to him observed, " I will secure you among the soldiers." They seemed to look on George Fox as a person possessing great power and influence, and took no small pains, though very unnecessarily, to guard him. The great parade of muskets and lights excited George's curiosity, and he asked the persons who conducted him, what it meant, desiring them to be civil to their peaceable neighbours. They gave him little satisfaction, but conveyed him to an inn, where he underwent an examination of some length. He answered them with so much prudence, that none

of their accusations would stand. He showed that
Friends were a peaceable people; that their meetings
were for the worship of the Almighty, and that the
Society never meddled with any of the affairs of
government. He then spoke to them respecting
their own states, exhorting them to live in the fear
of God, to walk in his wisdom, and be tender of their
pious neighbours. His discourse had so much effect
that they set him and all the other Friends at liberty.
George parted from them in a friendly manner,
acknowledging that their civility was noble.

At Pulmer, in Hampshire, he attended a monthly
meeting held for the neighbourhood. Previous to
the hour of its collecting the soldiers came to break
up the meeting and imprison Friends, but they came
so early that but few were there. "After they were
gone," says George Fox, " Friends began to come
in apace, and a large and glorious meeting we had,
for the everlasting seed of God was set over all, and
the people were settled in the new covenant of life, upon
the foundation, Christ Jesus." Toward the close of
the meeting, while George was speaking to the
people, a man in gay apparel came up and looked
in at the window; and presently went away to
Ringwood and informed the magistrates that the
soldiers had taken up two or three men at Pulmer, and
left George Fox there preaching to as many hundreds.
The magistrates forthwith dispatched the officers
and soldiers again ; but the man having a mile and a
half to carry the information, and the soldiers as
much to walk back, the meeting was over and
Friends dispersed before they arrived. Thus they
were again mercifully delivered from their persecutors.

After a meeting at Tiverton, in Devonshire, he went to Collumpton and Wellington, and had a large meeting at a butcher's house, where the Gospel was freely preached. Persecution had been very hot in that county some time before, and the meetings of Friends often interrupted, but now they were quiet.

". " The Friends told us," says he, " how they had broken up their meetings by warrants from the justices, and how by their warrants they were required to carry Friends before the justices. And Friends bid them carry them then. The officers told them they must go; but Friends said, nay, that was not according to their warrants, which required them to carry them. Then they were fain to hire carts, and waggons, and horses, and to lift Friends up into their waggons and carts to carry them before a justice. And when they came to a justice's house, sometimes he happened to be from home, and if he were a moderate man he would get out of the way, and then they were forced to carry them before another; so that they were many days carting and carrying Friends up and down from place to place. And when afterwards the officers came to lay their charges for this upon the town, the town's-people would not pay it, but made them bear it themselves, and that brake the neck of their persecution there for that time. The like was done in several other places, till the officers had shamed and tired themselves, and then were fain to give over.

" At one place they warned Friends to come to the steeple-house; and the Friends met together to consider of it, and had freedom to go to the steeple-house and meet together there. Accordingly when they came thither, they sate down together to wait upon the Lord, in his power and Spirit, and minded the Lord Jesus Christ, their Teacher and Saviour; but did not mind the priest. When the officers saw that, they came to them to put them out of the steeple-house again; but the Friends told them, it was not time for them to break up their meeting yet. A while after, when the priest had done, they came to the Friends again, and would have had them go home to dinner; but the Friends told them they did not choose to go to dinner, but were feeding upon the bread of life. So there they sat, waiting upon the Lord, and enjoying his power and presence, till they found freedom in themselves to depart. Thus the priest's people were offended, because they could not get them to the steeple-house, and when they were there, they were offended because they could not get them out again."

During most of the year 1663 he continued travelling through England, and went into Wales, where he " had several precious meetings. The Lord's name and standard was set up, and many were gathered to it, and are settled under the teaching of Christ Jesus, their Saviour, who hath bought them." Coming into the county of Cumberland, where persecution was very hot at that time, Friends asked him if he had come there to go to prison. So eager were the magistrates to stir up the people against Friends, that some offered five shillings, and some a' noble a day to any that would apprehend speakers among the Quakers; but it being now the time of the quarter-sessions, most of those mercenary persecutors had gone thither to get their wages, and Friends held their meetings in quietness.

There was quite an anxiety among the justices to take George Fox prisoner, and it is truly remark-able, and a proof of the preserving power of an over-ruling Providence, that although frequently very near them and apparently exposed to the liability of being arrested, yet he escaped out of their hands. In the open sessions at Kendal in Westmoreland, Justice Flemming offered a reward of five pounds to any one that should take him. On the way to a Friend's house, George met a man coming from the court, to whom this reward had been tendered. As he passed he remarked to his company, " That is George Fox," but did not attempt to molest him ; " for," says G. F., " the Lord preserved me over them all."

Few persons possessed a more undaunted courage and firmness than did George Fox. No danger seemed to alarm or disconcert him, no perils to deter him from the performance of duty. He was ever ready to bear his full portion of suffering for the religion he espoused, and by example as well as precept to encourage his brethren in the faithful maintenance of their principles. Hearing that Colonel Kirby had sent a lieutenant to the house of Margaret Fell, in Swarthmore, to search for him, he started on the following morning for Kirby Hall, where the colonel resided. On being introduced to him, he observed, that understanding he was desirous of seeing him, he had come to visit him to know what he had to say, or whether he had any-

thing against him.   Colonel Kirby seemed taken by
surprise, and said, before all the company, he had
nothing against him.   After much friendly conversation had passed, they shook hands and parted.

Soon after this, Kirby went to London, and the
other justices held a private meeting and granted a
warrant to apprehend George Fox.   Information
was given to him over night, both of the meeting
and the warrant, and he had ample opportunity to
avoid it; but he chose rather to stay and meet the
storm—hoping he should thus shield his friends from
its force.   On the following morning, an officer,
armed with sword and pistols, came to apprehend
him, and carried him before the justices; here he
was examined on various points.   They then tendered
the oath to him, and on his refusal to swear, required
him to appear at the next sessions.   The time appointed coming on, George Fox repaired to Lancaster,
and appeared before the justices, according to his engagement.   The concourse was large, and the court-
house very full; but he made his way to the bar, and
there stood with his hat on.   Silence being ordered,
he addressed the company twice, " Peace be among
you."   The chairman asked him if he knew where
he was.   " Yes, I do," he replied; " but it may be
my hat offends you.   That is a low thing—that is not
the honour that I give to magistrates—for the true
honour is from above.   I hope it is not the hat that
you look upon to be the honour."   After some
further conversation, they bade one of the officers to
take his hat off, and then proceeded to examine him
respecting a pretended plot against the government,
of which he showed himself entirely clear.   Not

being able to find any other charge against him, they tendered him the oaths of allegiance and supremacy, and for his refusal to swear, committed him to prison. He bid the justices and people take notice that he " suffered for the doctrine of Christ and for obedience to his command." Several others were also committed, some for refusing the oaths, and some for attending their religious meetings, so that the gaols were full. Many of the prisoners were poor men, whose families were dependant on their daily labour; and this being now taken from them, their wives went to the justices, who committed them, and told them, if they persisted in keeping their husbands in prison for the truth of Christ and the testimony of a good conscience, they must bring their children to them to be maintained. Their innocence, and the righteousness of their cause, gave them great boldness, and they feared not to plead with and warn their persecutors against their cruelty and hardness of heart.

On the 14th of the month called March, George Fox was brought to the assizes, before Judge Twisden, when the following conversation took place :—

G. F.—Peace be amongst you all.

Judge.—What! do you come into the court with your hat on !

G. F.—The hat is not the honour that comes from God.

Judge.—Will you take the oath of allegiance?

G. F.—I never took any oath in my life, nor any covenant or engagement.

Judge.—Will you swear or no?

G. F.—I am a Christian, and Christ commands

me not to swear; and so does the apostle James likewise; and whether I should obey God or man, do thou judge.

Judge.—I ask you again, whether you will swear or no?

G. F.—I am neither Turk, Jew, nor Heathen, but a Christian, and should show forth Christianity. Dost thou not know that Christians in the primitive times, and some also of the martyrs in Queen Mary's days, refused swearing, because Christ and the apostles had forbidden it? You have had experience enough, how many men had first sworn for the King and then against the King. But as for me, I have never taken an oath in all my life; and my allegiance does not lie in swearing, but in truth and faithfulness; for I honour all men, much more the King. But Christ who is the great prophet, who is the King of kings, who is the Saviour of the world and the great Judge of the whole world, He saith I must not swear. Now, whether must I obey Christ or thee? for it is in tenderness of conscience, and in obedience to the commands of Christ, that I do not swear: and we have the word of a king for tender consciences. Dost thou own the King?

Judge.—Yes, I do own the King.

G. F.—Why, then, dost thou not observe his declaration from Breda, and his promises made since he came into England; that none should be called in question for matters of religion, so long as they lived peaceably? Now, if thou ownest the King, why dost thou call me into question, and put me upon taking an oath, which is a matter of religion; seeing thou nor none else can charge me with unpeaceable living?

Judge.—Sirrah! will you swear?

G. F.—I am none of thy sirrahs. I am a Christian; and for thee, an old man, and a judge, to sit there and give nicknames to prisoners, it does not become either thy grey hairs or thy office.

Judge.—Well, I am a Christian too.

G. F.—Then do Christian works.

The judge again pressed the oath upon him, and he, declining to take it, was remanded to prison, there to remain until the next assizes.

George Fox was not idle while waiting in gaol for the return of the assizes. A Baptist preacher, also a prisoner, challenged Friends to a dispute, and George obtaining liberty to go to his apartment, engaged with him in the controversy. The preacher affirmed, that "some men never had the Spirit of God, and that the true light, which enlighteneth every one that cometh into the world, is natural;" and for proof instanced Balaam, affirming that he had not the Spirit of God. George asserted that Balaam and other wicked men had the Spirit of God, or else how could they quench, vex, grieve, and resist the Holy Ghost, like the stiffnecked Jews? To the second assertion George answered, that the true light, which enlighteneth every man that cometh into the world, was Christ the Word, and that He was divine and eternal, and not natural; and he might as well say the Word was natural, as that the life in the Word was so. And it was expressly said, that men hated the light because their deeds were evil, and would not come to it because it reproved

them—which of course must be in them, as a
reprover.

Some envious persons frequently reminding Friends
of a plot in the north, as though they were impli-
cated in it, he wrote the following paper, to clear
them and their Christian profession of such an unjust
reflection :—

" A Testimony from us the people of God, whom
the world call Quakers, to all the magistrates and
officers of what sort soever, from the highest to
the lowest.

" We are peaceable, and seek the peace, and good,
and welfare of all men and women upon the earth,
as in our lives and peaceable carriages is manifested ;
and we desire the eternal good and welfare of all,
and their soul's everlasting peace. We are heirs of
the blessing before the curse was, and of the power
of God before the devil was, and before the fall of
man. We are heirs of the Gospel of peace, which
is the power of God ; and we are heirs of Christ,
who have inherited him and his everlasting kingdom,
and do possess the power of an endless life. Knowing this our portion and inheritance, this is to take
off all jealousies out of your minds, and out of the
minds of all people concerning us, that all plots and
conspiracies, plotters and conspirators against the
king, and all aiders or assisters thereunto we always
did and do utterly deny to be any of us, or to be of
the fellowship of the Gospel, or to be of Christ's
kingdom, or to be his servants. For Christ said,
' My kingdom is not of this world, if my kingdom

were of this world, then would my servants fight.' And therefore He bid Peter put up his sword for, said He, ' all they that take the sword shall perish with the sword.' Here is the faith and patience of the saints, to bear and suffer all things, knowing, as we know, that vengeance is the Lord's, and He will repay it to them that hurt his people and that do wrong to the innocent; therefore cannot we avenge, but suffer for his name's sake. And we do know that the Lord will judge the world in righteousness according to their deeds; and that, when every one shall give an account to Him of the ' deeds done in the body,' then will the Lord give every man according to his works, whether they be good or whether they be evil. Christ saith, He came not to destroy men's lives; and when his disciples would have had ' fire to come down from heaven,' to have consumed them that did not receive Him, He told them, they knew not what spirit they were of, that would have men's lives destroyed; and therefore He rebuked them, and told them, that he came not ' to destroy men's lives, but to save them.' Now we are of Christ's mind, who is the great prophet, whom all ought to hear in all things, who saith to his, ' Whosoever shall smite thee on the right cheek, turn to him the other also.' This doctrine of his have we learned, and do not only confess Him in words, but follow his doctrine; and therefore do we suffer all manner of reproaches, scandals, and slanders, and spoiling of goods, buf-fetings, and whipping, stripes, and imprisonments, for these many years, and can say, ' The Lord for-give them that have thus served us, and lay not these things to their charge!'   And we know that the Jews' outward sword, by which they cut down the heathen outwardly, was a type of the inward sword of the Spirit, which cuts down the inward heathen, the raging nature in people.   And the blood of bulls, lambs, rams, and other offerings, and that priesthood that offered them, together with other things in the law, were types of Christ, the one offering, and of his blood, who is the everlasting Priest and covenant, Christ, our life, and way to God, and who is the great Prophet and Shepherd, that looks to his flock, and the Head of his church, and the great Bishop of our souls, whom we witness come; and He doth oversee and keep his flock.   For in Adam, in the fall, we know the striving, quarrelling, unpeaceable spirits are in the enmity one with another, and not in peace ; but in Christ Jesus, the second Adam that never fell, is peace, rest, and life.   And the doctrine of Christ, who never sinned, is to ' love one another,' and those who be in the doctrine hurt no man ; in which we are, in Christ, who is our life. Therefore it is well for you to distinguish betwixt the precious and the vile, between them that fear God and serve Him, and them that do not, and to put a difference between the innocent and the guilty, and between him that is holy and pure, and the ungodly and profane ; for they that do not so, bring troubles, burdens, and sorrows upon themselves. And this we write in love to your souls, that ye may consider these things ; for they that hate enemies, and hate one another, we cannot say they are of God, nor in Christ's doctrine, but are opposers of it.   And such as wrestle with flesh and blood, with

carnal weapons, are gone into the flesh out of the Spirit. They are not in our fellowship in the Spirit, in which is the bond of peace ; neither are they of us, nor have we unity with them in their fleshly state, and with their carnal weapons. For our unity and fellowship stands in the Gospel, which is the power of God, before the devil was,—the liar, and the murderer, the man-slayer, and the envious man. Now Christ's mind and his doctrine being to save men's lives, we who are of Christ's mind are out of and above these things. And our desire is, that in the fear of the Lord ye may all live, that in that ye may receive God's wisdom, by which all things were created, that by it all may be ordered to God's glory.
"This is from them that love all your souls, and seek your eternal good."

As a warning to his friends against the spirit of dissension which actuated John Perrot and his company, G. F. published the following :

"Dear Friends,
"Dwell in the love of God, and in his righteousness, that will preserve you above all changeable spirits that be foul and unclean, and that dwell not in the truth but in quarrels. Avoid such, and keep your habitations in the truth. And dwell in the truth and in the word of God, by which ye are reconciled to God. And keep your meetings in the name of Jesus Christ, that never fell ; and then you will see over all the gatherings of Adam's sons and daughters, you being met in the life, over them all, in which is your unity, and peace and fellowship

with God, and one with another, in the life in which we may enjoy God's presence among you. So remember me to all Friends in the everlasting Seed of God. And all they that are gotten into fellow-ship in outward things, their fellowship will corrupt, and rot, and wither away. Therefore live in the Gospel, the power of God, which power of God, the Gospel, was before the devil was. And this fellowship in the Gospel, the power of God, is a mystery to all the fellowships in the world. So look over all outward sufferings, and look at the Lord and the Lamb, who is the First and Last, the Amen: in whom farewell.

" G. F."

In the Sixth Month the assizes were held again, when he was brought before Judge Turner, a jury empannelled, and the justices sworn as witnesses that he refused the oath at the last session. The following dialogue then took place.

Judge.—Did you not refuse the oath at the last assizes?

G. F.—I never took oath in my life; and Christ, the Saviour and Judge of the world, said, " Swear not at all."

The judge seemed not disposed to notice this answer, but again repeated his former question.

G. F.—The words that I then spake to them were, that if they could prove, either judge, justices, priest or teacher, that after Christ and the Apostle had forbidden swearing, they commanded that Christians should swear, I would swear.

Judge.—I am not at this time to dispute whether it is lawful to swear, but to inquire whether you refuse to take the oath or not.

G. F.—Those things mentioned in the oath, as plotting against the king, and owning the pope's or any other foreign power, I utterly deny.

Judge.—You say well in that, but did you deny to take the oath? What say you?

G. F.—What wouldst thou have me to say, for I have told thee before what I did say?

Judge.—Would you have those men to swear that you took the oath?

G. F.—Wouldst thou have these men to swear that I refused the oath?

At this the court burst into a laugh; and George being grieved to see such serious matter treated with levity, asked the judge, "Is this court a play-house? Where is gravity and sobriety? for this behaviour doth not become you."

The indictment being read, George stated that there were many errors in it, which he wished to show. The judge said he would afterward hear whatever he might have to say why judgment should not be pronounced against him. George then addressed the jury, telling them they could not bring him in guilty upon that indictment, for it was wrongly laid, and had many gross errors in it. The judge told him he must not speak to the jury—he would do that himself; and accordingly, he instructed them to bring in a verdict of guilty against the prisoner. On the following morning he was called up to hear his sentence; when the judge asked him what he had to say why sentence should not be pronounced.

G. F.—I am no lawyer, but I have much to say —if ye would but have patience to hear. Is the oath to be tendered to the king's subjects, or to the subjects of foreign princes?

Judge.—To the subjects of the realm.

G. F.—Look the indictment, and ye may see that ye have left out the word subject. So, not having named me in the indictment as a subject, ye cannot premunire me for not taking the oath.

Judge.—It is an error.

G. F.—I have something else to stop judgment. Look what day the indictment says the oath was tendered to me at the sessions there.

Court.—It was the 11th day of January.

G. F.—What day of the week was that session held on?

Court.—On a Tuesday.

G. F.—Then look your almanacs, and see whether there was any sessions held at Lancaster on the 11th day of January, so called.

They accordingly looked, and found that the 11th day was the day called Monday, and that the sessions was on the day called Tuesday, which was the 12th day of that month.

G. F.—Look ye now, ye have indicted me for refusing the oath in the quarter sessions held at Lancaster on the 11th day of January last, and the justices have sworn that they tendered me the oath in open sessions here that day, and the jury upon their oaths have found me guilty thereupon ; and yet ye see there was no session held in Lancaster that day.

The judge, anxious to cover the matter, or find some excuse for so inexcusable a blunder, asked, "Did not the sessions *begin* on the 11th day ?" To which it was answered, "No ; the session held but one day, and that was the 12th."

Judge.—This is a great mistake, and an error.

Justices.—[In a passion, and stamping.]—Who hath done this? Somebody hath done it on purpose.

G. F.—Are not the justices here who have sworn to this indictment, forsworn men in the face of the country? But this is not all: I have more yet to offer why sentence should not be given against me. In what year of the king was the last assise here holden, which was in the month called March last?

Judge.—In the sixteenth year of the king.

G. F.—But the indictment says it was in the fifteenth year.

This also was acknowledged to be an important error, and the court appeared to be vexed at the exposure thus made of their irregular proceedings. George proceeded to show other similar defects in the instrument on which he was prosecuted, until the judge desired him to stop and say no more, for he had enough. To which George Fox replied, "If thou hast enough, I desire nothing but law and justice at thy hands: for I do not look for mercy."

Judge.—You must have justice, and you shall have law.

G. F.—Am I at liberty, and free from all that ever hath been done against me in this matter?

Judge.—Yes: you are free from all that hath been done against you. But, [starting up in a rage, he added,] I can put the oath to any man here, and I will tender you the oath again.

G. F.—Thou hadst examples enough yesterday, of swearing and false swearing, both in the justices and in the jury.

But determined that he should not escape, he again tendered the oath to him; and notwithstanding the unfairness of such a procedure was clearly laid before him, and the hardship of the prisoner's case, who had been so long in gaol, without any cause whatever, yet he persisted in his unrighteous course.   He ordered the clerk of the court to give him the book. George took it into his hand, looked into it, and with great composure said, " I see it is a Bible; I am glad of it."   The oath was then read, and the judge asked him whether he would take it or not.   To which George answered, " Ye have given me a book here to kiss and to swear on; and this book which you have given me to kiss, says, ' Kiss the Son,' and the Son says in this book, *Swear not at all;*" and so says also the Apostle James.   Now I say as the book says, and yet ye imprison me.   How chance ye do not imprison the book for saying so?   How comes it that the book is at liberty amongst you, which bids me not swear, and yet ye imprison me for doing as the book bids me; why don't you imprison the book?

This short but conclusive argument put the judge somewhat out of temper, and he replied, " Nay, but we will imprison George Fox."

He reminded them of the oaths taken by the justices to an indictment full of errors, and of his offering, if any of them could convince him that Christ or his apostles had altered the command against swearing, they should see that he would swear.   He told the jury it was for Christ's sake that he could not swear; and therefore warned them not to act contrary to the witness for God in their consciences, for before his judgment seat they must all be brought. "As for plots, and persecution for religion, and popery, I do deny them in my heart; for I am a Christian, and shall show forth Christianity amongst you this day. And it is for Christ's doctrine I stand."

The jury found the indictment against him, and the judge, calling him to the bar in the afternoon, asked him what he had to say to it. George desired he might have a copy of it, and time given until the next assizes, to examine it. After some discourse, they committed him to prison until the next assize; and Colonel Kirby gave orders to the gaoler to "keep him close and suffer no flesh alive to come at him, for he was not fit to be discoursed with by men." The gaoler accordingly put him into an apartment in the tower, where the smoke and damp from the rooms of the other prisoners came up so thick that it stood like dew upon the walls, and sometimes a lighted candle could scarcely be seen. At times he was almost suffocated, and the under-gaoler was so afraid of breathing the smoke, that George could hardly persuade him to come and unlock one of the upper doors, to ventilate the room. "Beside," says he, "it rained in upon my bed, and many times when I went to stop out the rain in the cold winter season, my shirt would be mucked with the rain that came in upon me, while I was labouring to stop it out. And the place being high and open to the wind, sometimes as fast as I stopped it, the wind being high and fierce would blow it out again. In this manner did I lie all that long, cold winter, till the next assize; in which time I was so starved with cold and rain, that my body was greatly swelled and my limbs much benumbed." It would seem as though they wished to destroy him.

At the assizes held the 16th of the month called March, George Fox was again brought before the court, Judge Twisden being on the bench. While he was showing the errors in this second indictment, the judge called to the gaoler, "Take him away—take him away," which was according done. After he was gone the jury brought in a verdict of guilty, and the court recorded him as a premunired person, though he was not called to hear the verdict, nor was sentence pronounced; which was contrary to law. There is no doubt the court were afraid to give him an opportunity of showing why sentence should not be pronounced, lest his acute discrimination should discover some flaw in the indictment, and subject them to another mortifying exposure.

CHAPTER VIII.   1665-1667.

Removed from Lancaster to Scarborough Castle—Visited there by Lady Fairfax, Dr. Whitby, and others, with whom he discoursed on religious subjects—Is liberated from his confinement by order of Charles II.—Engaged in establishing meetings for discipline.

GEORGE FOX was now laid by in prison, and from the bitterness of his persecutors there seemed little probability that he would soon be released.   Speaking of his confinement he says, " By reason of my long and close imprisonment in so bad a place, I was grown very weak of body, but the Lord's power was over all, and supported me through all, and enabled me to do service for Him, and for his truth, and people, as the place would admit."   The service which is here spoken of consisted in writing answers to several books, and publishing the views of the Society on the subject of tithes.

The justices were so incensed at the manner in which George Fox had exposed them at the sessions, that they determined, if possible, to get him removed from Lancaster.   Colonel Kirby often threatened that " he should be sent far enough, and beyond sea;" and in about six weeks after the assizes, they got an order from the king and council for his removal, which they forthwith proceeded to execute, but without letting him know where they intended

P

carrying him. He was so weakened by the cruel usage he received as to be scarcely able to walk or stand; and they offered him wine to drink, which he refused. George remonstrated earnestly against their taking him away, because he had been illegally treated at the sessions; that no sentence of premunire having been pronounced on him, that he knew of, he was the sheriff's prisoner and not the King's, and therefore could not be removed by the King's order. But remonstrance was in vain—they placed him on horseback; and though so stiff and feeble as scarcely to be able to sit there, yet one of the company had the cruelty to lash the horse with his whip, to make him skip and leap, and then would tauntingly look him in the face and say, "How do you do, Mr. Fox?" to which George meekly replied, that it was not civil in him to do so. They conveyed him through Bentham, Giggleswick, York, and Malton, to Scarborough castle, which was to be the place of his imprisonment.

Continuing very weak, and subject to frequent turns of fainting, they sometimes allowed him to out under care of a sentry, after he first came there; but this kindness was soon exchanged for a course of great severity. They thrust him into an open room, where the rain came in and the chimney smoked exceedingly. The governor, Sir Jordan Crosslands, coming to see him, he represented the cruelty of his case to him, but could obtain no improvement of it. After spending above fifty shillings of his money in excluding the rain and smoke, his persecutors finding the room was now tolerable, removed him from it to another far worse, open to the sea, and in which there was neither chimney nor fire-hearth. The water drove in and run over his bed, and on the floor, so as to make it necessary to bale it up, and when his clothes were wet he was not allowed a fire to dry them. These hardships further impaired his health, his body became benumbed with cold, and his limbs swelled far beyond their natural size. In this suffering situation they refused to allow his friends to come to him, or to bring him suitable food, so that he was obliged to hire a person to supply him, and it sometimes happened that the soldiers would take it away from her as she was fetching it. Although they thus excluded his friends, yet they frequently brought other persons to gaze at, or to contend with him; and many disputes he had with such respecting his religious opinions. Some of these interviews he thus notices, viz. :

" Another time there came one called Dr. Whitty, who was esteemed a great doctor of physic, with Lord Falconbridge, and the governor of Tinmouth Castle, and several knights. And I being called to them, this Whitty undertook to discourse with me, and asked me, ' What I was in prison for ?' I told him, ' Because I would not disobey the command of Christ, and swear.' He said I ought to swear my allegiance to the King. Now he being a great Presbyterian, I asked him, whether he had not sworn against the King and house of lords, and taken the Scotch covenant ? And had he not since sworn to the King ? And what then was his swearing good for ! ' But my allegiance,' I told him, ' did not consist in swearing, but in truth and faithfulness.'

So after some further discourse, I was had away to my prison again; and afterwards this Dr. Whitty boasted in the town, amongst his patients, that he had conquered me. When I heard of his boasting, I told the governor, ' It was a small boast in him to say, he had conquered a bondman.' And I desired to bid him to come to me again when he came to the castle. He came again a while after, with a matter of sixteen or seventeen great persons, and then he ran himself worse on ground than before.. For in discourse he affirmed before them all, that Christ had not enlightened every man that cometh into the world; and that the grace of God, that brought salvation, had not appeared unto all men, and that Christ had not died for all men. I asked him what sort of men those were which Christ had not enlightened ? and whom his grace had not appeared to, and whom he had not died for? He said ' Christ did not die for adulterers, and idolaters, and wicked men.'' Then I asked him, whether adulterers and wicked men were not sinners ? and he said, ' Yes.' ' And did not Christ die for sinners ?' said I. ' Did he not come to call sinners to repentance ?' ' Yes,' said he. ' Then,' said I, thou hast stopped thy own mouth.' So I proved that the grace of God had appeared unto all men, though some turned it into wantonness, and walked despitefully against it; •and that Christ had enlightened all men, though some hated the light. Several of the people that were present confessed it was true ; but he went away in a great rage, and came no more at me.

" There came another time the widow of him who was called the old Lord Fairfax, and with her a great company; and one of the company was a priest. I was moved to declare the truth to them, and the priest asked me, why we said thou and thee to people? for he counted us but fools and idiots for speaking so. I asked him, ' Whether they that translated the Scriptures, and that made the grammar' and accidence, were fools and idiots, seeing they translated the Scriptures so, and made the grammar so, thou to one, and you to more than one, and' left it so to us?' And if they were fools and idiots, then why had not he and such as he, that looked upon themselves as wise men, and that could not bear thou and thee to a singular, altered the grammar, accidence, and Bible, and put the plural instead of the singular? But if they were wise men that had so translated the Bible, and had made the grammar and accidence so, then I wished him to consider whether they were not fools and idiots themselves, that did not speak. as their grammars and Bibles taught them; but were offended with us, and called us fools and idiots for speaking so? Thus the priest's mouth was stopped; and many of the company did acknowledge the truth, and were pretty loving and tender; and some would have given me money, but I would not receive it."

With Dr. Cradock, an episcopal priest, G. F. had much conversation on the lawfulness of oaths under the Gospel, at the close of which he acknowledged that " in Gospel times every thing was to be established out of the mouths of two or three witnesses, but there was to be no swearing then." George then asked him why he forced oaths upon Christians, contrary to his own knowledge; and

why he excommunicated Friends.   The doctor
answered, " For not coming to church."   George
thus replied to him : " Why, ye left us above
twenty years ago, when we were but young lads and
lasses, to the Presbyterians, Independents, and Baptists, many whereof made spoil of our goods, and
persecuted us because we would not follow them.
Now, we being but young, knew little then of your
principles, and the old men that did know them, if
ye had intended to have kept them to you, and have
kept your principles alive, that we might have
known them, ye should either not have fled from us
as ye did, or ye should have sent us your epistles,
and collects, and homilies, and evening songs : (for
Paul writ epistles to the saints, though he was in
prison).   But they and we might have turned Turks
or Jews for any collects, homilies, or epistles we
had from you all this while.   And now thou hast
excommunicated us, both young and old, and so
have others of you done ; that is, ye have put us
out of your church, before ye have got us into it,
and before ye have brought us to know your principles.   And is not this madness in you, to put us
out before we were brought in ?   Indeed, if ye had
brought us into your church, and, when we had been
in, if we had done some bad thing, that had been
something like a ground for excommunication, or
putting out again.   ' But,' said I, ' what dost thou
call the church ?"   ' Why,' said he, ' that which you
call the steeple-house.'   Then I asked him,
' Whether Christ shed his blood for the steeple-
house ? and purchased and sanctified the steeple-
house with his blood.   And seeing the church is

Christ's bride and wife, and that He is the head of the church, dost thou think the steeple-house is Christ's wife and bride, and that He is the head of that old house, or of his people?' 'No,' said he, 'Christ is the head of his people, and they are the church.' 'Then,' said I, 'but you have given the title, church, to an old house, which belongs to the people; and you have taught people to believe so.' I asked him also, why he persecuted Friends for not paying tithes?' 'And whether God did ever give a command to the Gentiles that they should pay tithes? And whether Christ had not ended tithes when He ended the Levitical priesthood that took tithes? And whether Christ, when He sent forth his disciples to preach, had not commanded them to preach freely as He had given them freely? And whether all the ministers of Christ are not bound to observe this command of Christ?' He said, ' He would not dispute that.' Neither did I find he was willing to stay on that subject; for he presently turned to another matter, and said, ' You marry, but I know not how.' I replied, ' It may be so: but why dost thou not come and see?' Then he threatened that he would use his power against us, as he had done. I bid him to take heed; for he was an old man. I asked him also, where he read, from Genesis to the Revelations, that ever any priest did marry any? And I wished him to show me some instance thereof, if he would have us come to them to be married; for, said I, ' thou hast excommunicated one of my friends, two years after he was dead, about his marriage. And why dost thou not excommunicate Isaac and Jacob, and Boaz and Ruth; why dost thou not use thy power against these ?   For we do not read that they were ever married by the priests ; but they took one another in the assemblies of the righteous, in the presence of God and his people ; and so do we.   So that we have all the holy men and women that the Scriptures speak of, in this practice, on our side.' Much discourse we had ; but when he found he could get no advantage of me, he went away with his company."

G. F. makes the following remarks respecting these occurrences, viz., " With such sorts of people I was much exercised while I was there, for most that came to the castle would desire to speak with me, and great disputes and reasonings I had with them.   But as to Friends, I was a man buried alive ; for though many friends came from far to see me, yet few were suffered to come at me, and when any Friend came into the castle about business, if he looked but towards me they would rage at him.

. It was the general impression among those who were instrumental in detaining him a prisoner, that he possessed great influence over the minds of the people, and of course could turn them for or against the government.   The political convulsions which had agitated the nation, and embroiled it in civil war, and the recent restoration of the existing form of government, produced a want of confidence in its stability.   The minds of the people had not yet become settled, and of course there was a constant apprehension lest some new disturber should arise, and occasion fresh difficulties.   The high pretensions to religion which had characterized the ruling party under Cromwell, and the extraordinary excitement which prevailed on that subject, naturally tended to make the rulers suspicious of all those who were distinguished for their strictness, or who dissented from the form of worship established by law.

These circumstances were made use of by his enemies, to prejudice persons in authority with the opinion that George Fox and his friends were disposed to meddle with political affairs, and their meetings held for that purpose.

From this cause they were subjected to much suffering, not only in the disturbance of their assemblies for Divine worship, and the seizure of their property, often to the loss of everything moveable, but confinement in prisons where they were crowded so close, and the atmosphere became so pestilential, that scores of them died. It is a remarkable fact, that amid all this complicated suffering, there was scarcely an instance of any Friend flinching from the faithful maintenance of his testimony. They were united to each other by the strongest ties of sympathy and love; which led them cheerfully to offer their bodies to lie in prison instead of their brethren, and their property to maintain those who were in necessitous circumstances. Even their persecutors were forced to exclaim with admiration at the nearness and disinterestedness of their affection, " See how these Quakers love one another;" and to remark that they never could put the Society down while they continued to be connected by such a tie. A most sacred regard to the principles of their religion seemed to be the paramount feeling of their minds. To preserve their profession from every shade of reproach—to

keep themselves unspotted from the world—and to
live and walk as strangers and pilgrims on earth,
seeking another and better country, were the primary
objects of their concern. No marvel if the Society
increased, and the blessed cause of Christ prospered
in such hands, for the daily language of their meek
and self-denying lives preached with convincing
energy, and held forth the winning invitation,
Come and "have fellowship with us; and truly our
fellowship is with the Father and with his Son Jesus
Christ."

While the place which George Fox's ministry and
blameless life had procured for him among the people, was made a pretext for the cruel treatment he
experienced; the ignorant persons by whom he was
surrounded were too much prejudiced to perceive that
his peaceable and non-resisting principles formed an
effectual barrier against his interference in political
affairs. The officers of the castle often threatened
him with hanging, telling him the king had ordered
him there on account of the great interest he had
with the people, and that if any insurrection occurred,
he would be hung over the prison wall as a terror
to others. This induced him to tell them, that if
that was it they desired, and it was permitted
them, he was ready; for he never feared death
nor sufferings, but was known to be an innocent,
peaceable man, free from all plottings, and one that
sought the good of all men.

At length his meek and patient endurance of suffering, and the blamelessness of his conduct and conversation, softened the hearts of some of his keepers;
and, the governor of the castle going up to London,

George desired him to speak to Sir Francis Cobb in his behalf. This he did, and considerable interest was excited in his favour. His friends, John Whitehead and Ellis Hookes, drew up a relation of his imprisonment, and carried it to Esquire Marsh, through whose interference it was laid before the King, and an order for his release obtained. The subject of the mandate was, " that the King being certainly informed that George Fox was principled against plotting and fighting, and had been ready at all times to discover plots rather than to make any, therefore his royal pleasure was that he should be discharged from imprisonment." No sooner was the order obtained, than John Whitehead, anxious for the release of his friend and brother, set off for Scarborough, and presented it to the governor, who, with great nobility assembled his officers, and, without demanding any bond or sureties for his future peaceable conduct, freely discharged his prisoner, and presented him with the following passport :

" Permit the bearer hereof, George Fox, late a prisoner here, and now discharged by his Majesty's order, quietly to pass about his lawful occasions without any molestation. Given under my hand at Scarborough castle, this first day of September, 1666.
" JORDAN CROSSLANDS,
" Governor of Scarborough Castle."

The constancy and faithfulness of this devoted servant of Jesus Christ, not only wrought on the minds of his persecutors to convince them of his innocence, but also produced feelings of tenderness, towards Friends. On parting with the governor, George offered him a present as an acknowledgment of his civility ; but he courteously declined ; saying that, "he would do whatever good he could for him and his friends, and never do them any hurt." And afterward, if at any time he was ordered to send down soldiers from the castle, to break up their meetings, he would privately charge them "not to meddle," and continued kind to Friends until his dying day. A great change was also visible in the conduct of the soldiers and officers at the castle. Before George was discharged, they treated him with much more respect, and in speaking afterwards of his integrity and firmness, said, " He is as stiff as a tree, and as pure as a bell, for we never could bow him. This imprisonment lasted nearly three years.

George Fox, as well as other of the first Friends, sometimes had a presentiment of important events. While confined in Lancaster castle, public report of the warlike operations of the grand Turk excited fears in many that he would overrun Christendom, but George told several persons that he had seen him turn backward; and within a month the news reached England that he had been defeated.

"Another time," he says, "as I was walking in my chamber, with my eye to the Lord, I saw the angel of the Lord with a glittering drawn sword stretched southward, as though the court had been all on a fire. Not long after, the wars brake out with Holland, and the sickness brake forth, and afterwards the fire of London ; so the Lord's sword was drawn indeed."

No sooner was George Fox set at liberty, than he resumed his labours in the ministry of the Gospel; travelling to Whitby, Burlington, Oram, Malton, and Hull, until he came to York; visiting the meetings of Friends by the way, and strengthening his brethren in their religious principles. Several attempts were made to arrest him in his journey, but through the goodness of Divine Providence they all failed. The meetings were generally large and quiet, and there appeared an openness to receive his testimony. At Synderhill Green he had a general meeting, to which a large number of people came. The priest of the place hearing of it, sent the constable to the justices to procure a warrant for apprehending Friends; but although they rode their horses so hard as almost to spoil them, yet the notice being short and the distance considerable, the meeting was ended before they arrived with the warrant. On the way from the meeting, George Fox learned that some of the officers were searching the Friend's house where he was going, in order to take him; but he not having arrived, they were disappointed in their object. As he proceeded toward it, he met the constables, wardens, and justice's clerk coming away, and passed through them; but they, not knowing it was he, suffered him to go unmolested. Friends all escaped their malicious designs; "for," says he, "the Lord's power frustrated them: praised be his name for ever."

George Fox continued his journey through several of the counties of England, until he came to London, "having many large and precious meetings among the people. But I was so weak," adds he, "with

lying almost three years in cruel and hard imprisonments, and my joints and my body were so stiff and
benumbed, that I could hardly get on my horse, or
bend my joints, nor well bear to be near the fire or
to eat warm meat, I had been kept so long from it.
Being come to London I walked a little among the
ruins, and took good notice of them. And I saw
the city lying according as the word of the Lord
came to me concerning it several years before."

It becomes the members of the Society of Friends
in the present day, often to reflect seriously on the
sufferings which their forefathers endured for the
support of those principles and testimonies which
they have handed down to us. We live in a day of
great outward ease, wherein we are permitted to
exercise our conscientious views on the subject of
religion without molestation. Fines and imprisonment, and corporeal punishments are no longer inflicted on us; and this happy exemption has been in
some measure purchased for us by their faithfulness
and perseverance. If we duly estimate the privilege
we enjoy; if our hearts are warmed with gratitude
to that merciful Providence who has thus wrought
our deliverance, and made our lot easy, compared
with the path which our predecessors trod, we shall
feel those principles and testimonies very precious to
us, and be religiously concerned to live so watch-
fully in the fear of the Lord that nothing in our
example or conduct may lessen their value or importance, or cast a shade over the purity of our high
profession. Our birthright in the Society of Friends,
and the privileges which attach to it, may justly be
compared to a precious inheritance, purchased for us

by the stripes and sufferings of our ancestors; it becomes us, therefore, to set a proportionate value upon it, and permit nothing to rob us of so rich a treasure.

The difficulty which occurred in the Society from the conduct of John Perrot, has already been noticed. His entire departure from the Christian principles he had once professed, and the looseness of his conduct subsequent to his apostacy, convinced many who had been caught with the spirit of separation that he was in error. Through Divine goodness, their minds were prepared to see and condemn their misconduct and separation, and to return to the bosom of the church. On this subject George Fox remarks :—

" About this time, some that had run out from truth and clashed against Friends, were reached unto by the power of the Lord, which came wonderfully over, and made them condemn and tear their papers of controversy to pieces. Several meetings we had with them; and the Lord's everlasting power was over all, and set judgment on the head of that that had run out. And in these meetings (which lasted whole days) several that had run out with John Perrot and others, came in again, and condemned that spirit that led them to keep on their hats when Friends prayed, and when they themselves prayed. And some of them said, that Friends were more righteous than they; and that if Friends had not stood they had been gone and had fallen into perdition."

From London, George Fox proceeded through Kingston and Reading to Bristol, where Friends were assembled from several parts of the nation, and after having much service at the meetings held there, he returned again to London. Among the great numbers who had joined in profession with the Society of Friends, it was to be expected there would be some less faithful than others, who might go into things not convenient for them, and which, if suffered to pass uncorrected, would tend to dishonour the high profession which they made. There were also many poor Friends, made so by the depredations of merciless persecutors, and widows and orphan children, some of whose parents had died in prison, who required the care and attention of Friends, that all might be duly provided for, and the profession of truth preserved from any just cause of blame or reproach.

For these reasons George Fox soon found it expedient to establish an order in the infant Society, and to hold meetings for its due maintenance, as well as for ascertaining the situation of Friends in different parts, and extending such relief or assistance as cases might require. The first meeting of this description that we have any account of was held at Balby, near Doncaster, in Yorkshire, in 1656. It appears, however, that he had recommended the establishment of such meetings several years before, and probably some were held accordingly, though no account of them has come to us. General or Yearly Meetings, as they were sometimes called, were frequently held in England prior and subsequently to this period; but they appear to have been for worship only, and not for the transaction of Church affairs. Respecting a meeting at Skipton in 1660,

George Fox says, " To it came many Friends out of most parts of the nation; for it was about business relating to the church, both in this nation and beyond the seas. Several years before, when I was in the north, I was moved to recommend to Friends the setting up of this meeting for that service; for many Friends suffered in divers parts of the nation, and their goods were taken from them contrary to the law, and they understood not how to help themselves, or where to seek redress. But after this meeting was set up, several Friends that had been justices and magistrates, and others that understood something of the law, came thither and were able to inform Friends, and to assist them in gathering up the sufferings, that they might be laid before the justices, judges, or parliament. Now this meeting had stood several years; and divers justices and captains had come to break it up, but when they have understood the business Friends met about, and have seen Friends' books, and accounts of collections for relief of the poor, how we took care, one county to help another, and to help our friends beyond the seas, and provide for our poor, that none of them should be chargeable to their parishes, the justices and officers would confess that we did their work, and would pass away peaceably and lovingly, commending Friends' practice. And sometimes there would come two hundred of the world's poor people and wait there till the meeting was done (for all the country knew we met about the poor); and then after the meeting was over Friends would send to the bakers for bread and give every one of those poor people a loaf, how many soever there were of them;

for we were taught "to do good unto all, though especially to the household of faith."

This Christian principle of maintaining their own poor and contributing also to the relief of others, has been steadily practised by the Society down to the present period; and it recommends to its members individually the exercise of liberality and benevolence toward all, according to the means which it has pleased Divine Providence to bestow on them. As the cares of the Society for its members increased with their numbers, the necessity of convening meetings for business more frequently became obvious; and instead of holding them once a year only, and for several counties, they were subsequently held every three months, and one for each county where Friends were settled. These were called Quarterly Meetings, and extended the requisite care over the Society within their respective limits. In the year 1675 a meeting was established in London, the object of which was to receive accounts of the sufferings of Friends from all parts of the kingdom, and to render such advice and assistance as might be requisite. This was called, "The Meeting for Sufferings;" and its duties were gradually extended to other objects, until at length it became the representative body of the Yearly Meeting during its recess.

In the year 1666, on his return from Bristol to London, George Fox recommended the setting up of Monthly Meetings, for the more close and intimate inspection into the state of the Society, and the conduct of its members, as well as to render proper assistance to such as might be in necessitous circumstances. To use his own words, they were "to take care of God's glory, and to admonish and exhort such as walked disorderly or carelessly, and not according to truth." Hitherto they had had only Quarterly Meetings, which embracing a considerable district of country as well as a large number of members, it was more difficult to oversee them with that vigilance which he thought requisite; but Monthly Meetings including smaller precincts, the care of the church could be more readily extended to each individual case. Several of the Monthly Meetings were embraced in one Quarterly Meeting, which exercised a supervisory jurisdiction over them, and rendered such advice and aid as cases might require. Of the feelings which led him to this service, he says, " Whereas Friends had had only Quarterly Meetings ; now truth was spread and Friends were grown more numerous, I was moved to recommend the setting up of Monthly Meetings throughout the nation. And the Lord opened to me and let me see what I must do, and how the men's and women's Monthly and Quarterly Meetings should be ordered and established in this nation and other nations; and that I should write to them, where I came not to do the same." Believing himself thus called to establish these meetings in the Society, he travelled through most parts of the nation, opening to Friends the necessity for a wholesome order and discipline in the church, that all might be preserved in unity and harmony, consistent with their profession ; and in nearly all places such meetings were accordingly instituted. Monthly and Quarterly Meetings being thus organized, the next step was to unite them all in one general Yearly Meeting, which was done in the year 1672, when the Yearly Meeting first assembled in London, and has been continued to the present period. This meeting exercises a general care and guardianship over all the others, which regularly report their state to it, and receive such counsel and rules for the government of the meetings and members within their respective limits, as may seem necessary.

It was many years, however, before the Society was thus organized, or Monthly Meetings established in all the counties. George Fox had to encounter much opposition and calumny from some unfaithful members, who, not liking to submit to the salutary restraints which meetings for discipline introduced, nor to be circumscribed within the limits which good order prescribed, cried out against them as an arbitrary imposition; and against him in particular as one who assumed too much in the church, and 'was lording over the heritage of God. These succeeded for a time in spreading disaffection and discontent, and forming a separate party who pleaded for greater liberty, and for being left to the guidance of the Spirit of Truth in themselves, without any church government or control.

These dissatisfied persons carried their opposition so far, that notwithstanding the brotherly admonition of Friends and affectionate endeavours to reclaim them, they ran into an open schism and set up separate meetings. The chief instruments in this work of discord were John Wilkinson, John Story, William Rogers, and Thomas Crisp, the two latter of whom wrote against the Society. Their plea, as is usually the case with schismatics, was oppression and imposition on the part of their brethren; and although they first took up the pen professedly to vindicate their own principles and conduct, yet the bitterness of their spirit soon evinced itself, by endeavours to destroy the Christian reputation of their quondam brethren, upbraiding them with every inconsiderate or imprudent act committed by any in profession with the Society, publishing, on the slightest grounds, whatever report they thought would throw a shade of doubt over its character, and taking every opportunity of showing their malevolence towards those with whom they had once enjoyed fellowship and communion. This schism was the source of much sorrow and suffering to Friends, and it was some years before it was got rid of. After their separation, jealousies and dissensions arose among themselves, and they soon decayed and fell into oblivion.

The beneficial effects of the Discipline were soon apparent, in preserving the members faithful in the support of the principles and testimonies of the Society, and in clearing it of the reproach of such as walked disorderly. George Fox was next concerned to write letters to his brethren in Ireland, Scotland, Holland, Barbadoes, and the provinces of North America, advising them to settle such meetings among them.

Speaking of the happy results flowing from the institution of the Discipline he says : " Since the time these meetings have been settled, many mouths have been opened in thanksgivings and praise, and many have blessed the Lord God, that ever He did send me forth in this service : yea, with tears have many praised the Lord. For now all coming to have a concern and care for God's honour and glory, that his name be not blasphemed, which they do profess; and to see that all who profess the truth, do walk in the truth, in righteousness and in holiness, which becomes the house of God, and that all order their conversations aright, that they may see the salvation of God; all having this care upon them for God's glory, and being exercised in his holy power and Spirit, in the order of the heavenly life and Gospel of Jesus, here they may all see and know, possess and partake of, the government of Christ, of the increase of which there is to be no end. Thus the Lord's everlasting renown and praise is set up in every one's heart that is faithful; so that we can now say that the Gospel order established amongst us is not of man, nor by man, but of and by Jesus Christ, in and through the Holy Ghost. And this order of the Gospel, which is from Christ the Heavenly Man, is above all the orders of men in the fall, whether Jews, Gentiles, or apostatized Christians, and will be when they are gone. For the power of God, which is the everlasting Gospel, was before the devil was, and will be and remain for ever. And as the everlasting Gospel was preached in the Apostles' days to all nations, that all nations might come into the order of it through the divine power, which brings life and immortality to light, that they who were heirs of it, might inherit the power and authority of it; so now, since all nations have drunk the whore's cup and all the world hath worshipped the beast (but they whose names are written in the book of life from the foundation of the world, who have worshipped God in spirit and truth, as Christ commanded), the everlasting Gospel is to be and is preached again (as John the divine foresaw it should) to all nations, kindreds, tongues and people."

While engaged in his journey through England, setting up meetings for discipline, G. F. felt his mind drawn to London, whither he repaired, and found that some disorders had arisen for want of duly observing the advices given on the subject of marriage, of which he thus speaks, viz.: "After we had visited Friends in the city, and had stayed there a while, I was moved to exhort them to bring all their marriages to the men's and women's meetings, that they might lay them before the faithful there; that so care might be taken to prevent those disorders that had been committed by some. For many had gone together in marriage, contrary to their relations' minds; and some young, raw people, that came among us, had mixed with the world. And widows had married and not made provision for their children by their former husbands, before their second marriage; although I had given forth a paper concerning marriages about the year 1653, when truth was but little spread over the nation, advising Friends, who might be concerned in that case, that they might lay it before the faithful in time, before any thing was concluded; and afterwards publish it in the end of a meeting, or in a market. And when all things were found clear, they being free from all others, and their relations satisfied, then they might appoint a meeting on purpose, for the taking of each other in the presence of at least twelve faithful witnesses. Yet these directions not being observed, and truth being now more spread over the nation, it was therefore ordered that marriages should be laid before the men's Monthly and Quarterly Meetings, or as the meetings were then established; that Friends might see that the relations of those that proceeded to marriage were satisfied, and that the parties were clear from all others, and that widows had made provision for their first husband's children, before they married again, and what else was needful to be inquired into; that so all things might be kept clean and pure, and done in righteousness to the glory of God. And afterwards it was ordered in the same wisdom of God, that if either of the parties, that intended to marry, came out of another nation, county, or Monthly Meeting, they should bring a certificate from the Monthly Meeting to which they belonged; for satisfaction of the Monthly Meeting before which they came to lay their intentions of marriage."

CHAPTER IX.   1667-1670.

Interesting visit to Justice Marsh, and conversation with a Papist—Establishes a school at Waltham Abbey and at Shacklewell—Visits Ireland—Discussion on Election and Reprobation—Is married to Margaret Fell—Severe persecutions under the new Conventicle Act.

GEORGE FOX spent considerable time in the city of London, visiting the meetings of Friends and attending to the affairs of the Society; of which a large portion of the burden and care devolved on him. He also visited his old friend Justice Marsh, who had often showed much kindness to him and his brethren. He was now very civil and courteous, inviting George to dine with him; but, though pressed to do so, he was not free to comply. He had always manifested an unwillingness to bring himself under any obligations to the rich, or great, or powerful of this world, lest it might prove a snare to him, or to mingle with them on terms of familiarity, any further than he thought his religious duties required. Several persons of distinction were at dinner with him when he was introduced, and the Justice addressing one of them who was a Papist, observed, "Here is a Quaker, which you have not seen before." This introduced a conversation on several points of doctrine : viz.—

Papist.—Do you own the christening of children?

G. F.—There is no Scripture for any such practice.

Papist.—What! not for christening children!

G. F.—Nay—the one baptism by the one Spirit into the one body, we own: but to throw a little water on a child's face, and say that is baptizing and christening it,—there is no Scripture for this.

Papist.—Do you own the Catholic faith?

G. F.—Yes. But neither the pope nor the Papists are in the Catholic faith; for the true faith works by love and purifies the heart. And if they were in that faith that gives victory, by which they might have access to God, they would not tell the people of a purgatory after they were dead. So that neither priests nor Papists, that hold a purgatory hereafter, are in the true faith; for the true, precious, divine faith, which Christ is the author of, gives the victory over the devil and sin, that had separated man and woman from God. And if they (the Papists) were in the true faith they would never use racks, prisons, and fines, to persecute and force others to their religion that were not of their faith. For this was not the practice of the apostles and primitive Christians who witnessed and enjoyed the true faith of Christ; but it was the practice of the faithless Jews and heathens so to do. But seeing thou art a great and leading man among the Papists, and hast been taught and bred up under the pope, and seeing thou sayest there is no salvation but in your church, I desire to know of thee what it is that doth bring salvation in your church?

Papist.—A good life.

G. F.—And nothing else?

Papist.—Yes—good works.

G. F.—And is this it that brings salvation in your

church,—a good life and good works?   Is this your doctrine and principle ?

Papist.—Yes.

G. F.—Then neither thou, nor the pope, nor any of the Papists know what it is that brings salvation ?

Papist.—What brings salvation in your church ?

G. F.—That which brought salvation to the church in the apostles' days, the same brings salvation to us, and not another, viz., the grace of God, which, the Scripture says, brings salvation, and hath appeared to all men ; which taught the saints then and teaches us now.   And this grace, which brings salvation, teaches to deny ungodliness and worldly lusts, and to live godly, righteously, and soberly.   So it is not the good works, nor the good life that brings the salvation, but the grace.

Papist.—What ! doth this grace, that brings salvation, appear unto all men ?

G. F.—Yes.

Papist.—Then I deny that.

G. F.—All that deny that are sect-makers, and are not in the universal faith, grace, and truth which the apostles were in.

" Then he spake to me about the mother-church ; and I told him the several sects in Christendom had accused us, and said, we forsook our mother-church. The Papists charged us with forsaking their church, saying, Rome was the only mother-church.   The Episcopalians taxed us with forsaking the old Protestant religion, and they said theirs was the reformed mother-church. The Presbyterians and Independents blamed us for leaving them, and each of them said theirs was the right reformed church.   But I said, if we could own any outward city or place to be the mother-church, we should own outward Jerusalem, where the Gospel was first preached by Christ himself and the apostles; where Christ suffered, where the great conversion to Christianity by Peter was, where were the types, figures, and shadows, which Christ ended, and where Christ commanded his disciples to wait until they were endued with power from on high. So if any outward place deserved to be called the mother, that was the place where the first great conversion to Christianity was. But the apostle saith, (Gal. iv. 25, 26,) 'Jerusalem which now is, is in bondage with her children; but Jerusalem, which is above, is free, which is the mother of us all.' And we can own no other, neither outward Jerusalem, nor Rome, nor any sect of people for our mother, but Jerusalem which is above, which is free, the mother of us all that are born again, and become true believers in the light, and who are grafted into Christ, the heavenly vine. For all who are born again of the immortal seed, by the word of God, which lives and abides for ever, feed upon the milk of the word, the breasts of life, and grow by it in life; and cannot acknowledge any other to be their mother, but Jerusalem which is above. 'Oh!' said Squire Marsh to the Papist, 'you do not know this man. If he would but come to church now and then, he would be a brave man.'

"After some other discourse together, I went aside with this Justice Marsh into another room, to speak with him concerning Friends; for he was a justice of peace for Middlesex, and being a courtier, the other justices put much of the management of matters upon him. He told me he was in a strait how to act between us and some other dissenters. ' For,' said he, ' you cannot swear, and the Independents, Baptists, and Fifth-monarchy-people say also they cannot swear ; and therefore,' said he,' how shall I know how to distinguish betwixt you and them, seeing they and you all say, it is for conscience' sake that you cannot swear?' I answered, ' I will show thee how to distinguish. For they, or most of them, thou speakest of, can and do swear in some cases, but we cannot swear in any case. If a man should steal their cows or horses, and thou shouldst ask them whether they would swear they were theirs, many of them would readily do it; but if thou try our Friends, they cannot swear for their own goods. Therefore, when thou puttest the oath of allegiance to any of them, ask them, whether they can swear in any other case, as for their cow or horse ? Which, if they be really of us they cannot do, though they can bear witness to the truth.' Hereupon I gave him a relation of a trial in Berkshire, which was thus. A thief stole two beasts from a friend of ours. The thief was taken and cast into prison, and the Friend appeared against him at the assizes. But somebody having informed the judge that the man that prosecuted was a Quaker, and could not swear, the judge, before he heard what the Friend could say, said, ' Is he a Quaker? And will he not swear? Then tender him the oaths of allegiance and supremacy.' So he cast the Friend into prison, and premunired him, and let the thief go at liberty that had stolen his goods. Justice Marsh said, ' That judge was a wicked man.' ' But,' said I,

' if we could swear in any case, we would take the oath of allegiance to the King, who is to preserve the laws that preserve every man in his estate. Whereas others, that can swear in some cases to preserve a part of their estates, if they be robbed, will not take this oath to the King, who is to preserve them in their whole estates and bodies also. So that thou mayst easily distinguish, and put a difference betwixt us and other people.'

" This Justice Marsh was afterwards very serviceable to Friends in this and other cases; for he kept several, both Friends and others, from being premunired; and when Friends have been brought before him, in the times of persecution, he set many of them at liberty. And when he could not avoid sending to prison, he sent some for a few hours, or for a night. At length he went to the King, and told him, he had sent some of us to prison contrary to his conscience, and he could not do so any more. Wherefore he removed his family from Limehouse, where he lived, and took lodgings near James's Park. He told the King that, if he ' would be pleased to give liberty of conscience, that would quiet and settle all; for then none could have any pretence to be uneasy.' And indeed he was a very serviceable man to truth and Friends in his day."

During this year George Fox visited a priest, who some years before had been very bitter against him, declaring he would kill him if he ever met him again, and that he would lose his head if George was not knocked down within a month; yet now he had become very affectionate, and expressed his gladness at seeing him; his wife had joined the

Society. Many such instances he met with in the course of his travels, where violent persecutors were softened by his meekness and integrity, and the patience with which he suffered for righteousness' sake, evincing the truth of that saying of Holy Scripture, "When a man's ways please the Lord, he causeth even his enemies to be at peace with him."

Having succeeded in settling the Meetings for Discipline, his enlarged mind was engaged on the subject of education; and he recommended the establishment of two schools, one for boys at Waltham, and one for girls at Shacklewell, "for instructing them in whatsoever things were civil and useful in the creation;" thus embracing a wide range, and showing that he held no narrow views of the benefits of good instruction. These schools were accordingly established, and existed for many years. He frequently visited them, and appeared deeply interested in their prosperity.

Leaving London he proceeded through Surrey, Sussex, and into Yorkshire, having many meetings by the way; and although the constables threatened to arrest him, yet through the protecting care of the Lord he escaped their hands. At York he attended the Quarterly Meeting, which was very large, many having joined the Society by convincement; and so sensible were Friends of the benefits resulting from the support of the Discipline, that requests came up for the establishment of several additional Monthly Meetings.

Coming into the neighbourhood of Scarborough, where he was so long a prisoner, the governor,

Jordan Crosslands, sent to invite him to his house,
saying, "surely I would not be so unkind as not to
come and see him and his wife." George accordingly
went, and was very kindly received. From thence
he went into the neighbourhood of his old persecutor Colonel Kirby, who had threatened, if ever he
came near him he would send him to prison again,
and offered forty pounds to any one who would
arrest him. George held a meeting not far from his
house, but the Colonel was seized with a fit of the
gout, which prevented him from walking, and none
of his neighbours seemed inclined to avail themselves of the proffered reward, so that George
passed away unmolested, after a very large meeting
"in which the Lord's power and presence was
eminently amongst them."

He went on through Staffordshire and Cheshire,
having many large and favoured meetings, and being
drawn to visit his brethren in Ireland, he came to
Liverpool to take shipping. He was accompanied
in this engagement by Robert Lodge, James Lancaster, Thomas Briggs, and John Stubbs; and after
a short passage landed at Dublin, where they attended the week-day meeting, and "the life and
power of God appeared greatly in it."

From thence he proceeded through the island,
visiting most of the principal towns, as well as the
settlements of Friends; and although envy and ill-
will stirred up some to persecute him, yet through
the goodness of the Shepherd of Israel, he escaped
out of their hands. "The Lord," says he, "disappointed all their counsels, and defeated all their
designs against me, and by his good hand of Provi-

dence preserved me out of all their snares, and gave us many sweet and blessed opportunities to visit Friends, and spread truth through that nation. For meetings were very large, Friends coming to them far and near, and the world's people flocking in. And the powerful presence of the Lord was preciously felt with and amongst us, whereby many of the world were reached, and convinced, and gathered to the truth. And the Lord's flock was increased, and Friends were greatly refreshed and comforted in feeling the love of God. Oh, the brokenness that was amongst them, in the flowings of life! so that in the power and spirit of the Lord, many together have broken out into singing, even with audible voices, making melody in their hearts."

While at James Hutchinson's, several persons came to see him, for the purpose of conversing with him on election and reprobation. Of the manner in which he treated the subject he gives the following account :—

" You say that God hath ordained the greatest part of·men for hell; and that they were ordained so before the world began; for which your proof is in Jude. And you say Esau was reprobated, and the Egyptians, and the stock of Ham. But Christ saith to his disciples, ' Go, teach all nations;' and Go into all nations, and preach the Gospel of life and salvation. Now if they were to go to all nations, were they not to go to Ham's stock, and Esau's stock? Did not Christ die for all? Then for the stock of Ham and of Esau, and the Egyptians. Doth not the Scripture say, God will have all men to be saved?' Mark, ' all men ;' then

the stock of Esau, and of Ham also. And doth
not God say, ' Egypt my people ;' and that He
would have an altar in Egypt ? Isa. xix. Were
there not many Christians formerly in Egypt ? And
doth not history say, that the bishop of Alexandria
would formerly have been pope ? And had not God
a church in Babylon ? I confess his ' word came unto
Jacob, his statutes and his judgments unto Israel ;'
the like was not to other nations. For the law of God
was given to Israel ; but the Gospel was to be preached
to all nations, and is to be preached :—The Gospel of
peace and glad tidings to all nations. ' He that
believeth is not condemned, but he that believeth not
is condemned already ; so the condemnation comes
through unbelief. And whereas Jude speaks of
some that were of old ordained (or written of before) to condemnation, he doth not say, before the
world began ; but ' *written of old*,' may be referred
to Moses's writings, who writ of those whom Jude
mentions, namely, Cain, Corah, Balaam, and the
angels that kept not their first estate ; and such
Christians as followed them in their way, and
apostatized from the first state of Christianity, which
were and are ordained for condemnation by the light
and truth, which they are gone from. And though
the apostle speaks of God's loving Jacob and hating
Esau, yet he tells the believers, We all ' were by
nature children of wrath, even as others.' This
includes the stock of Jacob, of which the apostle
himself was and all believing Jews were. And thus
both Jews and Gentiles were all concluded under sin,
and so under condemnation, that God might have
mercy upon all through Jesus Christ. So the elec-

tion and choice stands in Christ : ' and he that believeth on him is not condemned, but he that believeth not is condemned already.'   And Jacob is the
second birth, which God loved ; and both Jews and
Gentiles must be born again, before they can enter
the kingdom of God.   And when you are born
again, ye will know election and reprobation; for
. the election stands in Christ, the Seed, before the
world began ; but the reprobation lies in the evil
seed since the world began."

In the passage home they encountered a violent
storm, from which the vessel was in considerable
danger ; but in the blessed assurance that the Lord's
power was over both sea and land, and that he could
'control the winds and the waves as he saw meet, his
mind was preserved calm and peaceful.   Landing
at Liverpool he proceeded through Lancashire and
. Cheshire, into Gloucestershire ; and at Nailsworth
he found a report in circulation, that George Fox
had turned Presbyterian—that a pulpit had been
prepared for him, and set up in a yard, and that
there would be a thousand people there the next day,
to hear him preach.   The occasion of this report was,
that a certain John Fox, an itinerant Presbyterian
preacher, was in the neighbourhood, and gave out
that he was to preach on the following day at
the appointed place.   The news soon spread, and
George being, through ignorance or design, substituted for John, the idea that the Friend had turned
Presbyterian,attracted a large company.   They were
soon disappointed, however, in the character of the
preacher ; and learning that the real George Fox
was close by, several hundreds left the Presbyterian

and came to Friends' meeting, where they were sober and attentive, being directed, says he, "to the grace of God in themselves, which would teach them and bring them salvation."

Passing through Gloucestershire, he proceeded to Bristol, where he met with Margaret Fell, widow of Thomas Fell, one of the judges of the Welsh courts; a man highly esteemed for his piety, moderation, and good sense. She was the daughter of John Askew, of Lancashire, descended of an ancient and honourable family, and born in the year 1614. After their marriage, her husband and herself, being much engaged for their spiritual welfare, sought the company of the most serious people, and often had prayers and other religious exercises in their own family. While in this inquiring state of mind, George Fox came to their house at Swarthmore, in 1652, and so effectually declared the truths of the Gospel, that Margaret, her children, and several of the servants were convinced. The judge was at that time in London. On his return the priests and justices of the neighbourhood gave him such an account of the Quaker principles as greatly incensed him; but George Fox returning to his house soon after, had a conversation with him, and so fully answered all his doubts and objections, by the Holy Scriptures, as entirely to convince his judgment; and although he did not join in membership with the Society, yet he permitted a meeting to be settled at his house, which continued there nearly forty years. He died in the year 1658. His widow was much engaged in travelling through the nation, attending the meetings of Friends, and visiting such as were under suffering or affliction; and was often concerned to plead with persons in authority for the release of those who were imprisoned. It was while on a visit to one of her daughters that George Fox met her at Bristol. They had long been intimately acquainted, and companions in suffering; and for a considerable time previous to this, he had believed it would be right they should be joined in marriage; which he had communicated to her, though not with an expectation of proceeding therein at that time. "Wherefore," says he, "I let the thing rest, and went on in the work and service of the Lord, as before, according as the Lord led me; travelling up and down in this nation, and through the nation of Ireland. But now after I was come back from Ireland and was come to Bristol, and found Margaret Fell there, it opened to me from the Lord that the thing should be now accomplished. And after we had discoursed the thing together, I told her, if she also was satisfied with the accomplishing of it now, she should first send for her children; which she did. And when the rest of her daughters were come I asked both them and her sons-in-law, if they had any thing against it, or for it, desiring them to speak; and they all severally expressed their satisfaction therein. Then I asked Margaret, if she had fulfilled and performed her husband's will to her children. She replied, 'The children knew that.' Whereupon I asked them, whether if their mother married they should not lose by it. And I asked Margaret, whether she had done any thing in lieu of it, which might answer it to the children. The children said, she had answered it to them, and desired me to speak no more of that. I told them I

was plain, and would have all things done plainly;
for I sought not any outward advantage to myself.
So our intention of marriage was laid before Friends,
both privately and publicly, to the full satisfaction of
Friends, many of whom gave testimony thereunto,
that it was of God.   Afterwards, a meeting being
appointed on purpose for the accomplishing thereof,
in the public meeting-house at Broad-Mead in
Bristol, we took each other in marriage; the Lord
joining us together in the honourable marriage,
in the everlasting covenant and immortal Seed of
life.   In the sense whereof, living and weighty
testimonies were borne thereunto by Friends in the
movings of the heavenly power, which united us
together.   Then was a certificate, relating both the
proceedings and the marriage, openly read, and
signed by the relations and by most of the ancient
Friends of that city; besides many other Friends
from divers parts of the nation.

"We staid about a week in Bristol, and then
went into the country together to Oldstone; where,
taking our leave of each other in the |Lord, we
parted, betaking ourselves each to our several service; Margaret returning homewards to the North,
and I passing on into the counties in the work of
the Lord, as before.   I travelled through Wiltshire,
Berkshire, Oxfordshire, Buckinghamshire, and so to
London, visiting Friends: in all which counties I
had many large and precious meetings."

George Fox was about forty-five, and his wife
fifty-five years of age, at the time of their mar-.
riage.

While in London he addressed an epistle to the

Quarterly Meetings, advising them to ascertain what widows or other poor Friends had children of a proper age to place apprentice, and that the meetings should be at the expense of procuring them suitable situations among Friends, where they might be taught useful trades, so as to maintain themselves, and assist their parents, or brothers and sisters. He recommended that each Quarterly Meeting should place out four in a year, if there were that number of suitable objects within its limits.

From London he passed through Essex, Hertford, Cambridge and Huntingdonshire, and wrote to his wife to meet him in Leicestershire; but instead of finding her there, as he expected, he was informed that she had been haled out of her house, and conveyed to Lancaster prison, by an order from the king and council to re-commit her on an old premunire, from which she had been regularly discharged more than a year before. On receiving this intelligence he returned through Derbyshire and Warwickshire to London, " having many large and blessed meetings, and being sweetly refreshed amongst Friends" in his travels.

On reaching London, he hastened Mary Lower, and Sarah Fell, two of his wife's daughters, to the king, to acquaint him of the treatment of their mother; and, if possible, to procure a discharge for her. After persevering application, and some difficulty, they at length obtained an order to Sir John Otway, directing him to write to the sheriff of Lancaster, and signify the king's pleasure that she should be released. She was now fully set at liberty, as they apprehended, from the old premunire against her.

The act passed by parliament in the year 1664, for suppressing the meetings of Friends and other dissenters, having expired, another was enacted in 1670, the force of which fell heavily on Friends. When the First Conventicle Act, as it was termed, was passed, which was in 1661, Friends appeared before the committee of the house, and earnestly remonstrated against it, showing the injurious tendency it would have on their rights and liberty as subjects and as Christians. But though supported by Waller the poet, Mallet, Sir John Vaughan, and other distinguished members, who spoke on the occasion, their petitions were disregarded. Each succeeding law was made more severe at the instigation of the church party, who appeared determined to exterminate Friends, if persecution would effect it. On the passage of this last act, the persecutors set themselves to work with fresh appetite and diligence. The ease of conviction, when there was no jury in the way, nor any of the delay and trouble usually attendant on court trials, rendered it an important acquisition to the plunderers. A single justice of the peace could decide the case, and when the Quakers only were concerned, all fear of resistance being removed, no extortion was too great to practise.

Archbishop Sheldon issued a pastoral letter on the occasion, in which he directs all ecclesiastical judges and officers " to take notice of all non-conformists, holders, frequenters, maintainers, and abettors of conventicles, especially of the preachers or teachers in them, and of the places wherein they are held; ever keeping a more watchful eye over the cities and great towns, from whence the mischief is for the most part derived, unto the lesser villages and hamlets. And wheresoever they find such wilful offenders, that then with a hearty affection to the worship of God, the honour of the king and his laws, and the peace of the church and kingdom, they do address themselves to the civil magistrate, justices, and others concerned, imploring their help and assistance for preventing and suppressing the same, according to the late act in that behalf made and set forth.

"What the success will be we must leave to God Almighty; yet I have this confidence under God, that if we do our parts now at first seriously, by God's help and the assistance of the civil power, considering the abundant care and provision the act contains for our advantage, we shall in a few months see a great alteration in the distractions of these times."

The Bishop of Peterborough, declared publicly in the steeple-house at Rowel, after he had commanded the officers to put this act in execution, "Against all fanatics it hath done its business, except the Quakers; but when the parliament sits again a stronger law will be made, not only to take away their lands and goods, and also to sell them for bondslaves."

John Chapple, the priest of Broughton, in Lincolnshire, perceiving that the constable of his parish was not forward in arresting his neighbours, and making distraints on their property, for peaceably assembling to worship God, sent him a letter to quicken his diligence; in which he says, "I cannot but wonder that any king's officer should be so back-

ward in executing the laws, as I find you to be."
. . . " I have sent my man on purpose to join with
you in giving information to the justices concerning
the late conventicle at Broughton ; and if you refuse
to act, I have ordered my man to make his complaint
to the bench. If your landlord, Mr. Pierpont, be
informed how you and others have behaved yourselves
in this business, I know that he will not thank you
for your remissness ; for whatever his tenants at
Broughton may be, sure I am he is a person more
zealous for the church."

When encouragement, persuasion, and threats
from the professed ministers of religion, were
superadded to the temptation which the law presented to the cupidity of informers, it were no
wonder if the storm of persecution raged violently.
Indeed, it is difficult to conceive, much more to
describe, the hardships which Friends endured.   In
the hope of moving some of the magistrates and
justices to greater moderation, George Fox, while
in London, wrote the following pathetic address to
them : viz.

" Oh, Friends, consider this act, which limits us
to five ; that but five may meet. Is this to do as
ye would be done by?   Would ye be so served
yourselves ?   We own Christ Jesus as well as you,
his coming, death, and resurrection ; and if we
be contrary-minded to you in some things, is not
this the apostle's exhortation, to wait till God hath
revealed it?   Doth not he say, ' Whatsoever is not
of faith, is sin?'   And seeing we have not faith in
things which ye would have us to do, would it not be
sin in us if we should do contrary to our faith ? And

why should any man have power over any other
man's faith, seeing Christ is the author of it ?   When
the apostles did preach in the name of Jesus, and
great multitudes heard them, and the rulers forbad
them to speak any more in that name, did not they
bid them judge whether it were better to obey God
or man ?   Would not this act have taken hold of
the twelve apostles and seventy disciples; for they
met often together ?   And if there had been an act
or law made then, that not above five should have
met with Christ, would not that have been an
hindering Him from meeting with his disciples ?
And do you think that He (who is the wisdom of
God) or his disciples, would have obeyed it ?   If
such a law had been made in the apostles' days, that
not above five might have met together, who had
been different minded from either the Jews or the
Gentiles, do you think the churches of Christ at
Corinth, Philippi, Ephesus, Thessalonica, or the
rest of the gathered churches, would have obeyed it ?
Oh, therefore, consider ! for we are Christians, and
partake of the nature and life of Christ.   And strive
not to limit the Holy One ; for God's power cannot
be limited, and is not to be quenched.   And Do
unto all men as ye would have them do unto you ;
' for this it the law and the prophets.'

" This is from those who wish you all well, and
desire your everlasting good and prosperity, who
are called Quakers ; and seek the peace and good
of all people, though they do afflict us, and
cause to suffer.

" G. F."

He also addressed a short letter to his suffering brethren, encouraging them to stand fast in their testimony, and bear with Christian patience and resignation the trials which were permitted to come upon them.   It is as follows :—

" All my dear friends, keep in the faith of God above all outward things, and in his power that hath given you dominion over all. The same power of God is still with you to deliver you as formerly ; for God and his power is the same ; and his Seed is over all, and before all ; and will be, when that which makes to suffer is gone. So be of good faith in that which changeth not ; for whatsoever any doth against the Truth, it will come upon themselves, and fall as a millstone on their heads. And if be that the Lord do suffer·you to be tried, let all be given up. Then look at the Lord and his power, which is over the whole world, and will be when the world is gone. And in the Lord's power and truth rejoice, friends, over that which makes to suffer, in the Seed which was before it was ; for the life, and truth, and the power of God is over all. And all keep in that ; and if ye do suffer in that it is to the Lord.

" Friends, the Lord hath blessed you in outward things ; and now the Lord may try you, whether your minds be in the outward things, or with the Lord that gave you them ? Therefore keep in the Seed, by which all outward things were made, and which is over them all. What! shall not I pray, and speak to God, with my face towards heavenly Jerusalem, according to my wonted time ? And let not any

one's Delilah shave his head, lest such lose their
strength; neither rest in its lap, lest the Philistines
be upon you.   For your rest is in Christ Jesus;
therefore rest not in anything else.

" G. F.

" London, the 12th of the
        Second Month, 1670."

It was not by precept only, however, that he
endeavoured to strengthen his brethren. His example
was in consonance with what he recommended to
others.   On the next First-day, after the act came in
force, like an undaunted soldier of Christ, he repaired
to Gracechurch-street meeting, where it was expected
the violence of the storm would fall.   On his arrival
he found the street full of people, and a guard set to
keep Friends out of the house : he soon began to
preach, and had proceeded but a little while, when
the constable and soldiers came, and pulling him
down, conveyed him to the mayor's house.   This
officer treated him with great mildness, and he
gives the following animated account of the whole
scene : viz.

" After I had spoken a while, the constable came
with an informer and soldiers ; and as they plucked
me down, I said, ' Blessed are the peace-makers.'
The commander of the soldiers put me among the
soldiers, and bid them secure me, saying to me, ' You
are the man I looked for.' They took also John
Burneyate, and another Friend, and had us away
first to the Exchange, and afterwards towards Moor-
field.s As we went along the streets the people were

very moderate. And some of them laughed at the constable, and told him, ' We would not run away.' The informer went with us unknown, till falling into discourse with one of the company, he said, ' It would never be a good world till all people came to the good old religion that was two hundred years ago.' Whereupon I asked him, ' Art thou a Papist ? What ! a Papist informer ? for two hundred years ago there was no other religion but that of the Papists.' He saw he had ensnared himself, and was vexed at it ; for as he went along the streets I spoke often to him, and manifested what he was. When we were come to the mayor's house, and were in the court-yard, several asked me, ' how and for what I was taken.' I desired them to ask the informer ; and also know what his name was: but he refused to tell his name. Whereupon one of the mayor's officers, looking out of a window, told him, ' He should tell his name before he went away ; for the lord mayor would know by what authority he intruded himself with soldiers into the execution of those laws which belonged to the civil magistrate to execute, and not to the military.' After this he was restless, and eager to be gone ; and went to the porter to be let out. One of the officers called to him, saying, ' Have you brought people here to inform against, and now will you go away before my lord mayor comes ! Some called to the porter not to let him out ; whereupon he forcibly pulled open the door and slipped out. No sooner was he come into the street but the people gave a shout, that made the street ring again, crying out, ' A Papist informer ! A Papist informer !' We desired the constable and soldiers to go forth and rescue him out of the people's hands, fearing lest they should have done him a mischief. They went, and brought him into the mayor's entry, where he staid awhile : but when he went out again, the people received him with such another shout. Whereupon the soldiers were fain to go and rescue him once more ; and then they had him into an house in an alley, where they persuaded him to change his periwig, and so he got away unknown.

" When the mayor came, we were brought into the room where he was, and some of his officers would have taken off our hats ; which he perceiving, called to them and bid them let us alone, and not meddle with our hats ; for, said he, they are not yet brought before me in judicature. So we stood by, while he examined some Presbyterians and Baptist teachers ; with whom he was somewhat sharp, and convicted them.. After he had done with them, I was brought to the table where he sat ; and then the officers took off my hat. And the mayor said mildly to me, ' Mr. Fox, you are an eminent man amongst those of your profession ; pray will you be instrumental to dissuade them from meeting in such great numbers ? for, seeing Christ hath promised that where two or three are met in his name, He will be in the midst of them, and the king and parliament are graciously pleased to allow of four to meet together to worship God, why will not you be content to partake both of Christ's promise to two or three and the king's indulgence to four ? ' I answered to this purpose : that Christ's promise was not to discourage many from meeting together in his name, but to encourage the few, that the fewest might not forbear to meet, be-

cause of their fewness.   But if Christ hath promised
to manifest his presence in the midst of so small an
assembly, where but two or three were gathered in
his name, how much more would his presence abound
where two or three hundred are gathered in his name !
I wished him to consider whether this act would not
have taken hold of Christ, with his twelve apostles,
and seventy disciples, if it had been in their time,
who used to meet often together, with great numbers.   However, I told him that this act did not
concern us ; for it was made against seditious meetings, of such as met under colour and pretence of
religion, to contrive insurrections, as (the act says)
late experience had shown ; but we had been sufficiently tried and proved and always found peaceable ;
and therefore he should do well to put a difference
between the innocent and the guilty.   He said, ' The
act was made against meetings, and a worship not
according to the liturgy.'   I told him, ' According
to ' was not the very same thing ; and I asked him,
whether the liturgy was according to the Scriptures.
And whether we might not read Scriptures, and
speak Scriptures.   He said, Yes.   I told him, This
act took hold only of such as did meet to plot and
contrive insurrections, as late experience had shown ;
but they had never experienced that by us.   Because
thieves are sometimes on the road, must not honest
men travel therefore ?   And because plotters and
contrivers have met to do mischief, must not an
honest, peaceable people meet to do good ?   If we
had been a people that did meet to plot and contrive
insurrections we might have drawn ourselves into
fours ; for four might do more mischief in plot-

ting than if there were four hundred, because four might speak out their minds more freely one to another than four hundred could. Therefore we being innocent, and not the people this act concerns, we keep our meetings as we used to do; and I said, I believed that he knew in his conscience we were innocent. After some more discourse he took our names, and the places where we lodged, and at length, inasmuch as the informer was gone, set us at liberty."

Being again at liberty, he returned immediately to Gracechurch-street meeting, and the people having generally dispersed, he went to a Friend's house and sent to know how it fared with his brethren at the other meetings. Some had been kept out of their meeting-houses, and others taken to prison; but were discharged in a few days. The firmness and patience of Friends in meeting this storm, was of great benefit to their religious profession, being at once a testimony to their innocence and integrity, and a noble assertion of the right of liberty of conscience. " A glorious time it was," says George Fox, " for the Lord's power came over all, and his everlasting Truth got renown. For as fast as some that were speaking were taken down, others were moved of the Lord to stand up and speak, to the admiration of the people; and the more because many Baptists and other sectaries left their public meetings, and came to see how the Quakers would stand." After some time the heat of persecution began to abate, and meetings became more quiet, on which George Fox left the city and went into Middlesex, Buckinghamshire, and Oxfordshire. At Reading he found nearly all the Friends in prison, with whom, and several others that

came in, he had a religious meeting, in which they
were refreshed with the power and presence of the
Lord.

From Reading he proceeded into Hampshire,
Berkshire, Sussex, and Kent, holding meetings
among Friends to their comfort and edification ; and
although it was a time of severe persecution through
the nation, yet the Lord preserved him in a remarkable manner out of the hands of his enemies, and
strengthened him for his service.

CHAPTER X.   1671-1673.

Embarks for Barbadoes—Is earnestly concerned for the religious welfare of the Negroes and Indians—Publishes an Address to the Governor and Council of Barbadoes—Visits Jamaica, Maryland, New England, Long Island, Rhode Island, New Jersey, Delaware, Maryland, Virginia, Carolina—Embarks for England, and arrives in safety at Bristol.

THE great increase of wickedness and licentiousness throughout the kingdom, after the restoration of King Charles the Second, was a source of much sorrow to Friends and other religious persons. Many of the latter being driven away by the cruelties practised towards dissenters, expressed their sense that if Friends did not stand their ground, the nation would be overrun with drunkenness, debauchery, and excess. The awful sense of this flood of sin and wickedness, which as a mighty torrent was sweeping through the land, deeply affected George Fox; and such was the grief and exercise of his mind, that it seriously impaired his health. With considerable difficulty he reached the house of a Friend at Stratford in Essex, where he was confined many months, his sight and hearing being almost gone, and his body so enfeebled that his friends thought he could not long survive. During this season of conflict he was much engaged in prayer to the Lord that he would be pleased to prosper truth, and preserve justice and equity in the land, and bring down iniquity, oppression, falsehood, profanity, and licentiousness.

s 2

In the spring of 1671, he was removed to London, though still very weak; and finding that the measures he had before taken for procuring his wife's liberty had been frustrated by her persecutors, he caused another application to be made to the King in her behalf, which was successful. A discharge under the great seal was obtained, liberating both her person and estate from the forfeiture passed upon her; and after ten years' imprisonment, at different periods, she was once more set at liberty, and joined her husband in London.

They attended the Yearly Meeting there, which was very large, and a strengthening heavenly season; wherein, says he, "the Lord's power was over all, and his glorious, everlastingly renowned Seed of Life was exalted over all." Having been for some time drawn in spirit to visit his brethren in America, after this meeting was over he took leave of his wife, and embarked on the 12th of the Sixth Month, on board the yacht *Industry*, Thomas Foster, master, bound for Barbadoes. A considerable number of ministers, who were engaged for the same service, accompanied him.

When they had been at sea about three weeks, they were chased by a Turkish man-of-war, which gained fast upon them; and the prospect of falling into their hands put the captain and crew into great terror. It was on Seventh-day evening, and the moon shining clear, they could perceive the vessel nearing them, and now almost close enough to speak; when the captain came to George Fox to know what should be done, observing that if the mariners had taken Paul's counsel, they would not have suffered the damage they did. George told them "it was a trial of faith, and therefore the Lord was to be waited on for counsel." After a time of mental retirement and waiting on the Lord, it was shown him, that the Lord's power was round about them, and would preserve them from harm. He then told them to put out all the lights except the one they steered by, and for all in the ship to be as quiet as possible, and that they should tack about and steer their right course. They did so, but still the vessel gained upon them, and was now so close that the passengers were much alarmed. The watch cried out " They are just upon us ;" and rising up in his berth, George looked through a port hole and perceived it was so. He was about to get up and go on deck, but remembering it had been shown him that the Lord's power was between them and their pursuers, he returned again to bed. Soon after this the moon went down, and a fresh breeze springing up, they escaped out of their hands, though they had come so close that it seemed almost impossible.

The next day being First-day, according to their custom they held a public meeting in the ship for the worship of God, and returned thanks to him for this deliverance.

On the 3rd of the Eighth Month they anchored in Carlisle Bay in Barbadoes. The hot climate of the West Indies did not agree with G. F.'s health, already enfeebled by the imprisonments and hardships he had suffered, and it was some weeks before he was able to travel much.

When he had recovered a little, he attended the Meetings for Discipline, and laboured to promote good order amongst them. He exhorted them to take more care respecting the order of marriages, that persons of too near kindred should not marry : and also in cases of second marriage, that due respect should be paid to the memory of the deceased companion, and a sufficient time elapse before any proceedings were had toward another connexion. Some of the children of Friends having married at a very early age, he admonished against it, and showed the unfitness of such childish marriages. He also advised that marriages, births, and burials should be regularly recorded in distinct books kept for the purpose ; and likewise the testimonies against such as persisted in walking disorderly, and the repentance of such as were restored. He recommended the purchase of convenient and decent burial-places ; and gave advice relative to the timely making of wills, and the care of legacies · left by Friends for public uses. " Then as to their Blacks or Negroes, I desired them," says he, " to endeavour to train them up in the fear of God, as well them that were bought with their money, as them that were born in their families, that all might come to the knowledge of the Lord ; and so with Joshua, they might (every master of a family) say, ' As for me and my house, we will serve the Lord.' I desired them also that they would cause their overseers to deal mildly and gently with their Negroes, and not use cruelty toward them, as the manner of some hath been and is, and that after certain years of servitude they should make them free."

His comprehensive mind seemed to perceive, as at a glance, what would tend to promote the welfare of his brethren, both in a religious and moral sense; so that there is scarcely a feature in the admirable code of Discipline now existing in the Society, that did not originate with this extraordinary man. His concern for the welfare of the African race in the colonies, evinces the benevolence of his feelings. In numerous letters written subsequently to this period, he earnestly enjoins the duty of instructing them and the Indian natives in the principles of Christianity.

In an epistle to Friends in America concerning their Negroes and Indians, written in 1679, he says " All Friends, everywhere, that have Indians, or Blacks, you are to preach the gospel to them and other servants, if you be true Christians; for the gospel of salvation was to be preached to every creature under heaven. Christ commands it to his disciples, ' Go and teach all nations, baptizing them in the name of the Father, Son, and Holy Ghost.' And this is the one baptism with the Spirit into one body, which plunges down sin and corruption, which hath gotten up by disobedience and transgression. For all have been plunged into sin, and death from the life; for all died in Adam; then they have been all subjected by the evil spirit which hath led them out of the truth into the evil; and therefore must all be baptized into the death of Christ, and put on Christ if they have life.

" And also, you must preach the grace of God to all Blacks and Indians; which grace brings salvation, that hath appeared unto all men, to teach and instruct them to live godly, righteously, and soberly: which grace of God is sufficient to teach and establish all true Christians, that they may appear before the throne of grace.

" And also, you must teach and instruct Blacks and Indians, and others, how that God doth pour out his Spirit upon all flesh in these days of the New Covenant, and New Testament ; and that none of them must quench the motions of his Spirit, nor grieve it, nor vex it, nor rebel against it, nor err from it, nor resist it ; but be led by his good Spirit to instruct them, and with which they may profit in the things of God.   Neither must they turn from his grace into wantonness, nor walk despitefully against the Spirit of grace, for it will teach them to live soberly, godly, and righteously, and season their words.

" And also, you must instruct and teach your Indians and Negroes, and all others, how that Christ by the grace of God, tasted death for every man, and ' gave himself a ransom for all, to be testified in due time ;' and is the propitiation, not for the sins of Christians only, ' but also for the sins of the whole world : ' and how that he doth enlighten every man that cometh into the world, with his true Light, which is the Life in Christ, by whom the world was made."

Another, dated 1681, to Friends in Carolina, contains the following, viz.—

" And if you had sometimes some meetings with the Indian kings and their people, to preach the Gospel of peace, of life, and of salvation to them. For the Gospel is to be preached to every creature ; and Christ hath tasted death for every man, and died for their sins, that they might come out of death and sin, and live to Christ, ·that died for them ; who hath enlightened them with the Light, which is the Life in Himself; and God pours out of this Spirit upon all flesh; that is, upon all men and women. And the grace and favour of God appears unto all men; so that all may believe in his Light, and walk in his Holy Spirit, and receive his grace, which will teach them to live godly, &c., and bring them salvation: so that you may come to see the light of Christ's glorious Gospel set up in those parts. And God hath promised he will lift up an ensign unto the nations. And again, ' There shall be a root of Jesse, which shall stand for an ensign to the people; to it shall the Gentiles seek.' And again he saith, ' For the earth shall be full of the knowledge of the Lord, as the waters cover the sea.' So, I desire that that part of the earth may be filled with the knowledge of the Lord."

In 1687, he addressed his brethren in West Jersey and Pennsylvania, on several subjects connected with their religious welfare. In this communication, he remarks :—" And sometimes you should have some meetings with the Indian kings and their councils, to let them know the principles of truth; so that they may know the way of salvation, and the nature of true Christianity, and how that Christ hath died for them, who tasted death for every man. And so the Gospel of salvation must be preached to every creature under heaven; and how that Christ hath enlightened them, who enlightens all that come into the world. And God hath poured out his Spirit upon all flesh; and so the Indians must receive God's Spirit; for ' the grace of God, that bringeth salvation, hath appeared to all men : ' and so let them know, that they have a day of salvation, grace and favour of God offered unto them; if they will receive it, it will be their blessing."

He had several large public meetings in Barbadoes, to which most of the principal officers and persons of the Island came, and many were convinced. Some false reports having been industriously spread there by the enemies of Friends, as that they denied Jesus Christ, &c., after one of those meetings, Colonel Lyne, a sober, discreet man, remarked, " Now I can gainsay such as I have heard speak evil of you, who say you do not own Christ, nor that He died; whereas I perceive you exalt Christ in all his offices beyond what I have ever heard before."

But these scandalous reports had been so widely circulated, that George Fox thought it his duty, in conjunction with some other Friends, to draw up a paper in the name of the Society, to clear it of these charges. They accordingly prepared and published the following address to the governor and council, which, for soundness of doctrine, and clearness and force of expression, has rarely been surpassed :—

" Whereas many scandalous lies and slanders have been cast upon us, to render us odious; as that ' We do deny God, and Christ Jesus, and the Scriptures of truth, &c.' This is to inform you, that all our books and declarations which for these many years have been published to the world, do clearly testify the contrary. Yet, notwithstanding, for your satisfaction, we do now plainly and sincerely declare,

" That we do own and believe in God, the only wise, omnipotent, and everlasting God, who is the Creator of all things, both in heaven and in the earth, and the Preserver of all that He hath made ; who is God over all, blessed for ever ; to whom be all honour and glory, dominion, praise and thanksgiving, both now and for evermore !

" And we do own and believe in Jesus Christ, his beloved and only begotten Son, in whom He is well pleased ; who was conceived by the Holy Ghost, and born of the Virgin Mary ; in whom we have redemption through his blood, even the forgiveness of sins ; who is the express image of the invisible God, the first born of every creature, by whom were all things created that are in heaven and that are in earth, visible and invisible, whether they be thrones, or dominions, or principalities, or powers ; all things were created by Him.

" And we do own and believe that He was made a sacrifice for sin, who knew no sin, neither was guile found in his mouth ; and that He was crucified for us in the flesh, without the gates of Jerusalem ; and that He was buried, and rose again the third day by the power of his Father, for our justification ; and we do believe that he ascended up into Heaven, and now sitteth at the right hand of God. This Jesus, who was the foundation of the holy prophets and apostles, is our foundation ; and we do believe there is no other foundation to be laid but that which is laid, even Christ Jesus : who, we believe, tasted death for every man, and shed his blood for all men, and is the propitiation for our sins, and not for ours only but also for the sins of the whole world : according as John the Baptist testified of him, when he said, ' Behold the Lamb of God, which taketh away the sin of the world.' John i. 29.

" We believe that He alone is our Redeemer and
Saviour, even the Captain of our salvation (who saves
us from sin, as well as from hell and the wrath to
come, and destroys the devil and his works), who is
the Seed of the woman that bruises the serpent's
head, to wit, Christ Jesus, the Alpha and Omega,
the First and the Last. That He is (as the Scriptures of truth say of Him) our wisdom and righteousness, justification and redemption; neither is there
salvation in any other, for there is no other name
under heaven given among men, whereby we may be
saved. It is He alone who is the Shepherd and
Bishop of our souls: He it is who is our Prophet,
whom Moses long since testified of, saying, ' A prophet shall the Lord your God raise up unto you of
your brethren, like unto me; him shall ye hear in
all things, whatsoever he shall say unto you : and it
shall come to pass, that every soul which will not hear
that prophet shall be destroyed from among the
people.'   Acts iii. 22, 23.

" He it is that is now come, and ' hath given us
an understanding, that we know him that is true.'
And he rules in our hearts by his law of love and of
life, and makes us free from the law of sin and death.
And we have no life but by Him; for He is the
quickening Spirit, the second Adam, the Lord from
heaven, by whose blood we are cleansed, and our
consciences sprinkled from dead works, to serve the
living God. And he is our Mediator, that makes
peace and reconciliation between God offended and
us offending; He being the Oath of God, the new
covenant of light, life, grace, and peace, the Author
and Finisher of our Faith.

" Now this Lord Jesus Christ, the heavenly man, the Emmanuel, God with us, we all own and believe in ; Him whom the high-priest raged against, and said He had spoken blasphemy; whom the priests and the elders of the Jews took counsel together against, and put to death; the same whom Judas betrayed for thirty pieces of silver, which the priests gave him as a reward for his treason; who also gave large money to the soldiers to broach an horrible lie, namely, that his disciples came and stole Him away by night whilst they slept. And after He was risen from the dead, the history of the acts of the apostles sets forth how the chief priests and elders persecuted the disciples of this Jesus, for preaching Christ and his resurrection. This, we say, is that Lord Jesus Christ, whom we own to be our life and salvation.

" And as concerning the Holy Scriptures, we do believe that they were given forth by the Holy Spirit of God, through the holy men of God, who (as the Scripture itself declares, 2 Pet. i. 21) ' spake as they were moved by the Holy Ghost.' We believe they are to be read, believed, and fulfilled, (He that fulfils them is Christ;) and they are ' profitable for doctrine, for reproof, for correction, for instruction in righteousness, that the man of God may be perfect, throughly furnished unto all good works,' 2 Tim. iii. 16, 17 ; and are able to make wise ' unto salvation, through faith which is in Christ Jesus.'

" And we do believe that the Holy Scriptures are the Words of God ; for it is said in Exodus xx. 1, ' God spake all these words, saying,' &c., meaning the ten commandments given forth upon Mount Sinai.

And in Rev. xxii. 18, saith John, ' I testify unto
every man that heareth the words of the prophecy of
this book, if any man shall add unto these, . . . and if
any man shall take away from the words of the book
of this prophecy,' (not the Word), &c.   So in Luke
i. 20. ' Because thou believest not my words.'   And
so in John, v. 47, xv. 7, xiv. 23, xii. 47.   So that
we call the Holy Scriptures, as Christ and the apostles
called them, and holy men of God called them, viz.,
the words of God.

" Another slander and lie they have cast upon us,
' That we should teach the Negroes to rebel ;' a
thing we utterly abhor and detest in our hearts ; the
Lord knows it : who is the Searcher of all hearts,
and knows all things; and so can witness and testify
for us, that this is a most abominable untruth.   For
that which we have spoken and declared to them, is,
to exhort and admonish them to be sober, and to
fear God, and to love their masters and mistresses,
and to be faithful and diligent in their masters'
service and business; and then their masters and
overseers would love them, and deal gently and
kindly with them.   And that they should not beat
their wives, nor the wives their husbands ; neither
should the men have many wives.   And that they
should not steal, nor be drunk, nor commit adultery,
nor fornication, nor curse, nor swear, nor lie, nor
give bad words to one another, nor to any one else ;
for there is something in them, that tells them they
should not practise those nor any other evils.

" But if they, notwithstanding, should do them,
then we let them know, there are but two ways, the
one that leads to heaven, where the righteous go ;

and the other that leads to hell, where the wicked and debauched, whoremongers and adulterers, murderers and liars go. To the one the Lord will say, ' Come, ye blessed of my father, inherit the kingdom prepared for you from the foundation of the world ;' to the other he will say, ' Depart from me, ye cursed, into everlasting fire, prepared for the devil and his angels :' so the wicked go into ' everlasting punishment, but the righteous into life eternal.' Matt. xxv. Now, consider, friends, it is no transgression for a master of a family to instruct his family himself, or for some others to do it in his behalf; but rather it is a very great duty incumbent upon them. Abraham and Joshua did so. Of the first, we read, the Lord said (Gen. xviii. 19), ' I know that Abraham will command his children, and his household after him ; and they shall keep the way of the Lord, to do justice and judgment, that the Lord may bring upon Abraham that which he hath spoken of him.' And the latter, we read, said (Josh. xxiv. 15), ' Choose you this day whom ye will serve : . . . but as for me and my house, we will serve the Lord.'

" We do declare, that we do esteem it a duty incumbent on us to pray with and for, to teach, instruct, and admonish those in and belonging to our families : this being a command of the Lord, the disobedience whereunto will provoke his displeasure ; as may be seen in Jer. x. 25, ' Pour out thy fury upon the heathen that know thee not; and upon the families that call not on thy name ;' Now, Negroes, Tawnies, and Indians, make up a very great part of the families in this island; for whom an account will be required by Him who

comes to judge both quick and dead at the great
day of judgment, when everyone shall be rewarded
according the deeds done in the body, whether they
be good, or whether they be evil ;—at that day, we
say, of the resurrection both of the good and of the
bad, of the just and the unjust, when ' the Lord
Jesus shall be revealed from heaven with his mighty
angels, in flaming fire, taking vengeance on them that
know not God, and obey not the Gospel of our Lord
Jesus Christ, who shall be punished with everlasting
destruction from the presence of the Lord, and from
the glory of his power; when he shall come to be
glorified in his saints, and to be admired in all them
that believe in that day.' 2 Thess. i. 7-10. See also
2 Pet. iii. 3, &c."

Having spent upwards of three months in Barbadoes, he went to Jamaica ; where he staid about
seven weeks preaching the Gospel and turning the
people to the light of Christ Jesus in their consciences, by which they would be reproved for their
sins, and show their duty to God and to man. On
the 8th of First Month, 1672, he and the Friends
with him embarked in a vessel bound for Maryland,
and had a long and tempestuous passage of nearly
seven weeks, respecting which he says, " We went
on board the 8th of the First Month, 1671-2 ; and
having contrary winds, were a full week sailing
forwards and backwards, before we could get out of
sight of Jamaica. A difficult voyage this proved,
and pretty dangerous, especially in our passing
through the gulf of Florida, where we met with many
trials by winds and storms. But the great God, who
is Lord of the seas and of the land, and who rideth

upon the wings of the wind, did by his power preserve us through many and great dangers, when by extreme stress of weather our vessel was divers times like to be overset, and much of our tackling broken. And indeed we were sensible that the Lord was a God at hand, and that his ear was open to the supplications of his people. For when the winds were so strong and boisterous, and the storms and tempests so great, that the sailors knew not what to do, but were fain to let the ship go which way she would, then did we pray unto the Lord, and the Lord did graciously hear and accept us, and did calm the winds and the seas, and gave us seasonable weather, and made us to rejoice in his salvation. Blessed and praised be the holy name of the Lord, whose power hath dominion over all, and whom the winds and seas obey.

" We were at sea betwixt six and seven weeks, in this passage from Jamaica to Maryland. But some days before we came to land, after we had entered the bay of Patuxent-river, a great storm arose, which cast a boat upon us for shelter; in which were divers persons, both men and women, people of account outwardly in the world. We took them in ; but the boat was lost, with five hundred pounds worth of goods in it, as they said. They continued on board us several days, not having any means to get off; and we had a good meeting with them in the ship. But provisions grew short, for they brought in none with them ; and ours, by reason of the length of our voyage, was well nigh spent when they came to us : so that, with their living upon it too, we had now little or none left. Whereupon

George Pattison took a boat, and ventured his life to get to shore; the hazard whereof was so great, that all but Friends concluded he would be cast away. Yet it pleased the Lord to bring him safe to land; and in a short time after, the Friends of the place came to fetch us to land also, in a seasonable time, for our provisions were quite spent.

" We partook also of another great deliverance in this voyage, through the good providence of the Lord, which we came to understand afterwards. For when we were determined to come from Jamaica, we had our choice of two vessels that were both bound for the same coast. One of these was a frigate, the other was called a yacht. The master of the frigate, we thought, asked unreasonably for our passage; which made us agree with the master of the yacht, who offered to carry us ten shillings a-piece cheaper than the other. We went on board the yacht, and the frigate came out together with us, intending to be consorts during the voyage; and for several days we sailed together: but what with calms and contrary winds, we were in a while separated. After that, the frigate, losing her way, fell among the Spaniards; by whom she was taken and robbed, and the master and mate made prisoners; afterwards, being retaken by the English, she was sent home to her owners in Virginia. Which when we came to understand, we saw and admired the providence of God, who preserved us out of our enemies' hands; and he that was covetous fell among the covetous."

On landing in Maryland they found John Burneyate, an eminent minister in the Society, preparing to return to England. Having been for some time engaged in visiting Friends and others in America, he had appointed a general meeting for those parts, intending to take his leave. George Fox and his companions arrived just in time to attend this meeting, which was very large and held four days ; and, after the public service was over, they continued together to transact the affairs of the Church, which gave George a good opportunity for explaining and enforcing the discipline and good order of the Society.

After this meeting the Friends separated to their respective labours in the work of the Gospel, George going over to the eastern shore of Maryland, where he had a large meeting, to which by invitation came some of the Indian chiefs, who heard the word willingly and behaved with sobriety.

Next day, George Fox and his companions commenced their journey towards New England. Much of the country through which they had to pass was an uninhabited wilderness, traversed only by Indian hunters, and thickly set with bogs and morasses. There were few houses to stop at, and often, after a hard day's journey, they had to lodge in the woods, or put up in Indian wigwams, and sometimes they would see neither man nor house in some days' ride. But through the protecting care and providence of the Lord they travelled safely, and reached Oyster Bay on Long Island, in time for the Half-year's Meeting held there. Here he was instrumental in correcting some abuses which had been introduced by the Ranters, a wild, fanatical people who were a great trouble to Friends. Respecting these he remarks : " The Half-year's Meeting began next

day, which was the first day of the week, and lasted
four days. The first and second days we had public
meetings for worship, to which the people of the
world of all sorts might and did come. On the
third day of the week were the men's and women's
meetings, wherein the affairs of the church were
taken care of. Here we met with some of the bad
spirits, who were run out from Truth into prejudice,
contention, and opposition to the order of Truth,
and to Friends therein. These had been very trouble-
some to Friends in their meetings there and there-
abouts formerly, and 'tis like would have been so
now; but I would not suffer the service of our men's
and women's meetings to be interrupted and hindered
by their cavils. Wherefore I let them know that if
they had anything to object against the order of
Truth which we were in, we would give them a
meeting another day on purpose. And indeed I
laboured the more, and travelled the harder to get
to this meeting, where it was expected many of
these contentions people would be; because I understood they had reflected much upon me when I was
far from them. So the men's and women's meetings being over, on the fourth day we had a meeting
with those discontented people, to which as many of
them as would did come, and as many Friends as
had a desire were present also ; and the Lord's power
brake forth gloriously, to the confounding of the
gainsayers. And then some of those that had been
chief in the mischievous work of contention and
opposition against the Truth, began to fawn upon me,
and cast the matter upon others ; but the deceitful
spirit was judged down and condemned, and the
glorious Truth of God was exalted and set over all ;

and they were all brought down and bowed under: which was of great service to truth and great satisfaction and comfort to Friends : glory to the Lord for ever !"

Having laboured much on Long Island in the ministry of the Gospel, he proceeded eastward through Rhode Island, holding meetings where there were settlements. The Yearly Meeting for Friends of New England and other colonies adjacent, held six days ; four of which were spent in general public meetings for worship, to which a great concourse of other people came, the governor, deputy-governor, and several justices being of the number. G. F. remarks that he had " rarely observed a people, in the state wherein they stood, to hear with more attention, diligence, and affection, than generally they did during the four days together ;" which was also taken notice of by other Friends. In the two meetings for the affairs of the Society, he communicated advice and instruction on the proper order of the church, and several meetings for the care of the poor and the promotion of a consistent conduct amongst the members were concluded to be established. " When this great and general meeting on Rhode Island was ended, it was somewhat hard," he says, "for Friends to part; for the glorious power of the Lord, which was over all, and his blessed truth and Life flowing amongst them, had so knit and united them together, that they spent two days in taking leave one of another, and of the Friends of the island ; and then, being mightily filled with the presence and power of the Lord, they went away with joyful hearts to their several habitations, in the several colonies where they lived."

Accompanied by the Governor and many others, he went to Providence, where he held a great meeting in a barn, and proceeded from thence to Narraganset. Here also a large company assembled at a justice's house, people from the country coming in who had never heard of Friends. They were much affected, and manifested a strong desire after the Truth. In one place they talked of hiring him for their minister; not understanding the principles of Friends. George concluded it was time for him to be gone, for if their eye was so much to him or to any other person, they would not come to the great Teacher, Christ Jesus. "This hiring of Ministers," he remarks, "had spoiled many, by hindering them from improving their own talents; whereas our labour is, to bring every one to their own teacher in themselves."

Having cleared his mind of New England, he returned to Shrewsbury in New Jersey, though not without encountering many perils by land and water, owing to the wilderness state of the country. In crossing the rivers they generally had to make use of a canoe for themselves and baggage, and to swim the horses by the side of it, which was frequently dangerous.

At Middletown Bay, near Shrewsbury, they had a large and good meeting. Hiring Indian guides, they set out for the lower provinces, and were five days in getting to New Castle in Delaware, where the governor received and entertained them kindly, and offered his house for a meeting. This they accepted, and following being the First-day, they had a large assembly. There had never been a meeting in this town nor anywhere near; but this, says George, was "a very precious one; many of the kind people, both men and women, were tender and confessed to the Truth, and some received it—blessed be the Lord for ever."

Leaving Newcastle they went through Delaware, holding meetings where there were settlements, to a General Meeting near Third-Haven Creek, on the eastern shore of Maryland. This was very large, it being computed there were more than a thousand persons present at it; many of whom came in boats, so that the creek was almost as thickly covered with them as the Thames, near London. "It was a heavenly meeting, wherein the presence of the Lord was gloriously manifested, and Friends were thereby sweetly refreshed, and the people generally satisfied, and many convinced; for the blessed power of the Lord was over all—everlasting praises to his holy name for ever."

Proceeding on their journey, they went through Maryland and Virginia, into Carolina, enduring great hardships from the extreme badness of the ways; there being no open roads, but only paths through the wilderness, and in many places deep bogs and swamps, so that they were commonly wet up to the knees, and lay out in the woods at night. Yet they were mercifully preserved from any serious injury from the exposure. There appeared to be great openness among the people to receive them, and they met with very little opposition. At one place, a doctor contended against the universality of the light of

Christ, asserting that the Indians had it not. George therefore called an Indian to him, and asked him whether or not, when he spoke falsely or did any wrong action, there was not something in him which reproved him for it. To which he readily answered there was, and that it reproved him, and made him feel ashamed when he had done or spoken wrong.

Soon after this he went to a settlement of Indians, and by an interpreter preached the Gospel to them, " showing them that Christ did die for all men— for their sins as well as for others, and had enlightened them as well as others." They received him kindly.

Having travelled through most of the provinces where there were Friends, and preached the Gospel of salvation to the people, George Fox felt himself at liberty to return to his own country. Robert Widders and James Lancaster had been his companions during most of his journey ; in a review of which he remarks : " Having travelled through most parts of that country, and visited most of the plantations thereabout, and had very good service for the Lord in America, having alarmed the people of all sorts where we came, and proclaimed the day of God's salvation amongst them, we found our spirits began to be clear of those parts of the world, and to draw towards Old England again. Yet we were desirous and felt freedom from the Lord to stay till the general meeting for that province of Maryland was over, which drew nigh, that we might see Friends generally together before we departed. Wherefore spending our time in the interim, partly in visiting Friends and friendly people, and in having meetings about the

Cliffs and Patuxent, and partly in writing answers to some cavilling objections which some of Truth's adversaries had raised and spread abroad to hinder people from receiving the truth, we were not idle, but laboured in the work of the Lord until that general provincial meeting came on, which began the 17th of the Third Month, and lasted four days. On the first of these days the men and women had their meetings for business, wherein the affairs of the church were taken care of, and many things relating thereunto were opened unto them to their edification and comfort. The other three days were spent in public meeting for the worship of God, at which divers of considerable account in the government and many others of the world's people were present; who were generally satisfied, and many of them reached: for it was a wonderful, glorious meeting, and the mighty presence of the Lord was seen and felt over all; blessed and praised be his holy name for ever, who over all giveth dominion!"

After attending this general meeting, which was in the Spring of 1673, they embarked for England the 21st of Third Month, and cast anchor in King's-road, Bristol-harbour, the 28th of the month following. "We had in our passage," he observes, "very high winds and tempestuous weather, which made the sea exceeding rough; the waves rising like mountains, so that masters and sailors wondered at it, and said they never saw the like before. But though the wind was strong, it sate for the most part with us, so that we sailed away before it; and the great God, who commands the winds, who is Lord of heaven, of earth, and the seas, and whose wonders are seen in the deep, He steered our course, and preserved us from many imminent dangers. The same good hand of Providence that went with us and carried us safely over, watched over us in our return and brought us safely back again—thanksgivings and praises be to his holy name for ever."

His wife, with several of her children, and some friends from London, soon joined him at Bristol ; and after having meetings there, he proceeded through the midland counties to the house of his wife's son-in-law, John Rouse, at Kingston-upon-Thames. Here he made a short stay, and then went to London, where he was much engaged in attending meetings, and in getting replies written and printed to several abusive works which had recently come out against the Society ; some of them by the Socinians.

CHAPTER XI.   1673-1679.

Disputes with a priest on perfection— Committed to Worcester gaol as a prisoner for life—Refuses a pardon from the King— Is brought before the judges of the King's Bench by habeas corpus, and discharged by proclamation—Embarks for Holland with William Penn and Robert Barclay—Returns to the Yearly Meeting at London—Addresses those who opposed the establishment of the discipline—Retires to Swarthmore, from whence he issues many epistles.

GOING from London into Worcestershire, he was arrested after a large meeting in the parish of Tredington, by a warrant from Henry Parker, a justice of the peace, and, with his son-in-law, Thomas Lower, sent to Worcester gaol.   When they had been some time there, they thought it best to lay their case before the lord-lieutenant of the county and other officers ; which they did by the following address :—

" These are to inform you, the lord-lieutenant (so called), and the deputy-lieutenants, and the justices of the county of Worcestershire, how unchristianly and inhumanly we have been dealt withal by Henry Parker, a justice (so called), in our journey or travel towards the north.   We, coming to our friend John Halford's house, on the 17th day of the Tenth Month, 1673, and some friends bringing us on the way, and others coming to visit us there, towards night there came the aforesaid justice, and a priest called Rowland Hains, of Hunniton, in Warwickshire, and demanded our names and places of abode. And though we were not in any meeting, but were discoursing together when they came in, yet he made a mittimus to send us to Worcester gaol. Now whereas he says in his mittimus, that complaint had been made to him of several by-past meetings of many hundreds at a time; we know nothing of that, nor do we think that concerns us. And whereas he says further, that no satisfactory account of our settlement or place of habitation appeared unto him; this he contradicts in his own mittimus, mentioning therein the places of our abode and habitation; the account of which we satisfactorily and fully gave him. And one of us (Thomas Lower) told him, that he was going down with his mother-in-law (who is George Fox his wife,) and with his sister, to fetch up his own wife and child out of the north into his own country. And the other of us (George Fox) told him, that he was bringing forward his wife on her journey towards the north, who had been at London, to visit one of her daughters, who had lately lain in. And having received a message from his mother, an ancient woman in Leicestershire, that she earnestly desired to see him before she died, he intended, as soon as he had brought his wife on her journey as far as Causal, in Warwickshire, to turn over into Leicestershire, to have seen his mother and relations there, and then to have returned to London again. But by his interrupting of us in our journey, and taking the husband from his wife, and the son from his mother and sister, and stopping him from visiting his wife and child so remote off, we were forced to get strangers, or whom we could, to help them on their journey, to our great damage and their hindrance. We asked the priest, whether this was his gospel, and their way of entertaining strangers? And we desired the justice to consider whether this was doing as he would be done by? But he said, he had said it, and he would do it. And whereas he says, we refused to give sureties; he asked only George Fox for sureties; who replied, he was an innocent man, and knew no law he had broken; but he did not ask Thomas Lower for any, as if it had been crime and cause enough for his commitment that he came out of Cornwall. And if we were at a meeting, as he says in his mittimus, he might have proceeded otherwise than by sending us to gaol, to answer the breach of the common laws; and yet he showed us no breach of any, as may be seen in the mittimus. So we thought fit to lay before you the substance of his proceedings against us, hoping there will more moderation and justice appear in you towards us, that so we may prosecute our intended journey.

" GEORGE FOX.
" THOMAS LOWER."

They, however, obtained no redress, and were kept in prison until the Eleventh Month following, when they were brought before the justices at the sessions, and Thomas Lower discharged; but they tendered the oaths of allegiance and supremacy to George Fox, and, on his refusing to take them, re-committed him to prison. His friends soon after obtained a writ of habeas corpus, in virtue of which he was taken up to London, to be heard before the judges of the king's bench; and it was generally believed he would have been discharged but for the malice of Justice Parker, who endeavoured to incense the judges against him; and finally procured an order remanding him to Worcester assizes for trial. To Worcester he accordingly went in the First Month, 1674, without any guard or attendant, and in a few days after was called before the judges at the assizes, who were very friendly; but Parker's enmity appeared unabated, and he prevailed on the judges to turn him over to the sessions for trial. They would not, however, send him to gaol, but gave him the liberty of the town, and permission to lodge at a Friend's house until the sessions.

During this time he had a dispute with a priest, who undertook to prove that the Scriptures are the only rule of life. Failing to adduce proof of this, G. F. had a suitable opportunity of opening to the audience the use and excellency of the Holy Scriptures, and also of showing that a manifestation of the Spirit is given to every man to profit withal, and that the grace of God which bringeth salvation, hath appeared unto all men, teaching to deny ungodliness, and worldly lusts, and to live soberly, righteously, and godly in this present world.

" Another time," says he, " there came a common-prayer priest, and some people with him, and he asked me, if I was grown up to perfection? I told him, ' What I was, I was by the grace of God.' He replied, ' It was a modest and civil answer.'

Then he urged the words of John, ' If we say that
we have no sin, we deceive ourselves, and the truth
is not in us.'   And he asked, ' What did I say to
that ?'   I said, with the same apostle, ' If we say
that we have not sinned, we make him a liar, and his
word is not in us,' who came to destroy sin, and
to take away sin.   So there is a time for people
to see that they have sinned, and there is a time for
them to see that they have sin ; and there is a time
for them to confess their sin, and to forsake it, and
to know the blood of Christ to cleanse from all sin.
Then the priest was asked, ' Whether Adam was not
perfect before he fell ? and whether all God's works
were not perfect ?'   The priest said, ' There might be
a perfection as Adam had, and a falling from it.'
But I told him there is a perfection in Christ above
Adam, and beyond falling ; and that it was the work
of the ministers of Christ to present every man perfect in Christ ; and for the perfecting of them they
had their gifts from Christ ; and therefore they that
denied perfection denied the work of the ministry,
and the gifts which Christ gave for the perfecting of
the saints.   The priest said, ' We must always be
striving.'   I told him it was a sad and comfortless
sort of striving, to strive with a belief that we
should never overcome.   I told him also that Paul
who cried out of the body of death, did also thank
God, who gave him the victory through our Lord
Jesus Christ.   So there was a time of crying out
for want of victory, and a time of praising God for
the victory.   And Paul said, ' There is therefore now
no condemnation to them which are in Christ Jesus.'
The priest said, Job was not perfect.   I told him,

God said Job was a perfect man, and that he did shun
evil; and the devil was forced to confess that God had
set an hedge about him; which was not an outward
hedge, but the invisible, heavenly power.   The priest
said, ' Job said, He chargeth his angels with folly,
and the heavens are not clean in his sight.'   I told
him, that was his mistake, it was not Job said so
but Eliphaz, who contended against Job.   ' Well,
but,' said the priest, ' what say you to that Scripture, The justest man that is sinneth seven times
a day?' ' Why truly,' said I, ' I say there is no such
Scripture;' and with that the priest's mouth was
stopped.''

At the sessions the grand jury found a bill against
him for not taking the oath, and he was required to
give bail for his appearance to take his trial at the
next court.   But being conscious of his own innocence, he declined on principle entering into any such
bonds, and was consequently sent to prison.   Such,
however, was the confidence some of the justices had
in his word, that in a few hours he was discharged,
without any bond or bail, simply on his promise to
appear at the next quarter-sessions, if life and health
permitted.   He accordingly attended, and though he
showed a number of gross errors in the indictment,
sufficient to quash it, yet the presiding magistrate determined to force it to trial, and accordingly got a jury
to convict him of twice refusing to take the oaths; the
punishment of which was the loss of liberty, of all his
goods and chattels, and to be imprisoned for life—
which sentence they pronounced against him, and sent
him to Worcester gaol.   Here he had a very severe
attack of illness, which continued a considerable time,

and brought him so low that his life was despaired of. But the Lord showed him that he had more service for him to perform before he took him to himself. Application was made to the King in his behalf, who readily offered a pardon for him, and even urged the acceptance of it. George, however, being sensible that he had done no wrong, and thinking that the acceptance of a pardon would look like giving countenance to the unjust proceedings against him, refused to accept it—" For," says he, " I had rather have lain in prison all my days than come out in any way dishonourable to Truth."

On the 11th of the Twelfth Month he was again brought by habeas corpus, before the judges of the King's Bench at London, of whom Chief Justice Sir Matthew Hale was one; and the indictment being examined, it was found so full of errors that all the judges gave their opinion that it was void. Some envious persons present endeavoured to persuade the court to tender the oaths to him again—saying he was a dangerous man to be at liberty; but Chief Justice Hale said he had indeed heard some such report, but he had heard many more good reports of him; and, with the other judges, ordered him to be discharged by proclamation. Thus, after an unjust imprisonment of nearly fourteen months he was honourably set at liberty.

Soon after this he went to Swarthmore, the residence of his wife; and his constitution being much impaired, both by the hardships he had endured, and his severe illness in Worcester prison, it seemed necessary that he should have some rest for the recovery of his strength and health. He accordingly remained there until the First Month, 1677, during which time he was mostly engaged in writing epistles to Friends and others in various parts of the world ; also some tracts explanatory of the religious principles of the Society, and in collecting and arranging others which he had before published.

Early in 1677 he set out for London, and taking meetings in his way reached that city in time for the Yearly Meeting. This meeting was large and favoured with the presence of the Lord, in a sense of which " the affairs of truth were sweetly carried on in the unity of the Spirit, to the satisfaction and comfort of the upright-hearted ;—blessed be the Lord for ever." In the Fifth Month following, accompanied by William Penn, Robert Barclay, and several other Friends, he embarked for Holland, and visited most of the meetings of Friends in that country, and assisted in establishing a Monthly and Quarterly Meeting among them, and also a Yearly Meeting, to be held at Amsterdam, for Friends in Holland, the Palatinate, Embden, Hamburgh, Frederickstadt, Dantzick, and other places in Germany. At Harlingen he had a public meeting, which was attended by Socinians, Baptists, Lutherans and other professors, amongst whom was a physician and a priest. After he had preached pretty largely, opening the happy state that Adam and Eve were in whilst they kept God's commands, and abode in paradise ; and the woe and misery that came upon them when they departed from his teaching, and hearkened to the serpent, transgressed God's command, and were driven out of paradise ; and set forth the way whereby man and woman might come into that happy state again; the priest, an ancient grave man, stood up just as he concluded, and putting off his hat, said, " I pray God to prosper and confirm that doctrine, for it is truth, and I have nothing against it."   He was obliged to leave the meeting to preach to his own congregation, but sent a message of love to George Fox, and that he had shortened his own meeting half an hour, in order that he might return and hear more of that good doctrine—though when he arrived the meeting was closed.

A Lutheran minister attended a meeting which George Fox held at Haarlem, and at the close said, he had heard nothing but what was according to the word of God, and desired that the blessing of the Lord might rest upon Friends and their assemblies. Others confessed to the truth, saying, " they had never heard things so plainly opened to their understandings before."   Two German priests, of considerable note, also visited him for the purpose of conferring with him on some points, when he took the opportunity to declare the way of truth, opening to them how they might come to know God and Christ, and his law and Gospel; and showing them that they could never know it by study nor philosophy, but through the Spirit of God opening it to them.   The men went away well satisfied.

His services in those parts appear to have been well received, not only by the members of his own Society, but by serious people of other professions; and after a stay of about three months, during most of which he was industriously engaged in travelling, he returned to London.

From this time until the Yearly Meeting in the

Third Month following, he was engaged in visiting Friends in various parts of the nation, settling them in the good order and discipline which had been established; and endeavouring to convince some gainsayers who were opposed to it. These however proved contentious, and endeavoured to prejudice the minds of others against him, as one who took too much upon him, and was disposed to lord it over the Society. These unjust and unkind accusations he bore with Christian meekness and forbearance; and fearing lest some of the young convinced and tender minds might be deceived by those disaffected members, he laboured much both in word and by writing, to guard his friends against that dissatisfied and contentious spirit.

He had several very satisfactory meetings at Bristol, many Friends being there from different parts of the kingdom. And though some unruly persons treated him in an unchristian manner, yet he was preserved in the heavenly patience which can bear injuries for Christ's sake. The more they laboured to vilify him, the more the love of sincere friends abounded towards him. Great was the unity that prevailed amongst these; and some who had been betrayed by their adversaries, seeing their bitterness and envy, broke off from them, for which they had cause to bless the Lord.

He arrived in London about two weeks prior to the Yearly Meeting. Friends having laid their sufferings before parliament, he joined them in their endeavours to procure relief from prosecutions under the law against popish recusants. The hopes of redress, which they entertained, were disappointed by an unexpected prorogation of parliament. He represents the Yearly Meetings as having been a heavenly season, in which the glory and majesty of the Lord, and love, wisdom, and unity were signally manifest. Numerous testimonies were borne against that ungodly spirit, which sought to make rents and divisions, but none spoke in its defence.

He remained in and about London several weeks; and some of those who had gone from the simplicity of the Gospel into improper liberty, labouring to draw others after them, opposed the order and discipline which, in Divine wisdom, was instituted for the preservation of the Society in consistency with its religious profession. They made a great clamour against its prescriptions, and by their plausible insinuations beguiled the simple, and furnished pretexts to the slightly-attached members to throw off its restraints.

After the Yearly Meeting he visited Friends in several of the counties of England, where he had "very precious meetings and very good service among Friends and other people, for there was great openness;" and in the Seventh Month, 1678, reached his residence at Swarthmore. Whether at home or abroad, the care of the churches and a righteous concern for the honour and promotion of the cause of Christ daily rested upon him; and he spared not himself, but laboured diligently, as the Lord called him thereto. And although he was enfeebled, and his limbs greatly swollen and stiffened by exposure to wet and cold in noisome and damp dungeons, so that it was painful to him to ride or walk, yet the

lively zeal and energy of his mind abated not, nor his
love for Friends.   In his retirement at Swarthmore,
where he remained nearly a year and a half, he
wrote many excellent epistles to his brethren, some
to warn them against dangers which he saw
threatened the church, some to encourage them to
be bold and valiant in support of the testimonies
of truth, and others to cheer and refresh them under
suffering :—

"My dear Friends,
"Who are sufferers for the Lord Jesus' sake, and
for the testimony of his truth, the Lord God
Almighty with his power uphold you and support
you in all your trials and sufferings, and give you
patience and content in his will, that ye may stand
valiant for Christ and his truth upon the earth, over
the persecuting and destroying spirit, which makes
to suffer in Christ (who bruises his head), in whom
ye have both election and salvation.   And for God's
elect's sake the Lord hath done much from the
foundation of the world, as may be seen throughout
the Scriptures of truth.   And they that touch them
touch the apple of God's eye, they are so tender to
Him ; and therefore it is good for all God's suffering
children to trust in the Lord, and to wait upon Him ;
for they shall be as Mount Sion, that cannot be
removed from Christ their rock and salvation ;
who is the foundation of all the elect of God, of the
prophets and the apostles, and of God's people now
and to the end : glory to the Lord and the Lamb
over all !   Remember my dear love to all Friends,
and do not think the time long ; for all time is in

the Father's hand and power. And therefore keep
the word of patience, and exercise that gift. And
the Lord strengthen you in your sufferings, in his
holy Spirit of faith. Amen.   "G. F.
    " Swarthmore, the 5th of the
        Twelfth Month, 1678."

In an epistle which he addressed to the Yearly
Meeting that occurred during his stay at Swarthmore,
we find the following excellent paragraphs :—
    " My desire is, that all your lights may shine as
from a city set upon a hill, that cannot be hid; and that
ye may be the salt of the earth, to salt and season it,
and make it savoury to God, and you all seasoned
with it. Then all your sacrifices will be a sweet
savour to the Lord, and ye will be as the lilies and
roses, and garden of God, which gives a sweet smell
unto Him, whose garden is preserved by his power;
that is the hedge that hedges out all the unruly and
unsavoury, and the destroyers and hurters of the
vines, buds, and plants, and God's tender blade,
which springs up from his seed of life; who waters
it with his heavenly water and word of life every
moment, that they may grow and be fruitful; that so
He may have a pleasant and fruitful garden. And
so here all are kept fresh and green, being watered
every moment with the everlasting holy water of life
from the Lord, the fountain. So, my dear friends, my
desire is, that this heavenly Seed, that bruises down
the head of the serpent, both within and without, may
be all your crowns and lifes, and ye, in Him, one another's crown and joy, to the praise of the Lord God
over all, blessed for evermore. This holy Seed will

outlast and wear out all that which the evil seed, since the fall of man, hath brought forth and set up. And as every one hath received Christ Jesus the Lord, so walk in Him in the humility which He teaches. And shun the occasions of strife, vain janglings, and disputings with men of corrupt minds, who are destitute of the truth; for the truth is peaceable, and the Gospel is a peaceable habitation in the power of God (which was before the devil was); and his wisdom is peaceable and gentle, and his kingdom stands in peace. Oh! his glory shines over all his works. And in Christ Jesus ye will have peace, who is not of the world; yea, a peace that the world cannot take away: the peace which ye have from Him was before the world was, and will be when it is gone. So they are not like to take his peace away from his people. This keeps all in that which is weighty and substantial over all chaff, and will be when it is gone. Glory to the Lord God over all for ever and ever! Amen.

"And now, my dear friends, the Lord doth require more of you than he doth of other people, because He hath committed more to you. He requires fruits of his Spirit, and of the light, and of the Gospel, and of the grace, and of the truth. For herein is He glorified, as Christ said, in your bringing forth much fruit,—fruits of righteousness, holiness, godliness, virtue, truth, and purity; so that ye may answer that which is of God in all people. And be ye valiant for his everlasting, glorious Gospel, in God's holy Spirit and Truth, keeping in the unity, and in the holy Spirit, light, and life, which is over death and darkness, and was before death and darkness was. In this Spirit ye have the bond of peace, which cannot be broken except ye go from the Spirit, and then ye lose the unity and bond of peace, which ye have from the Prince of peace.

"The world also does expect more from Friends than from other people; because you profess more. Therefore you should be more just than others in your words and dealings, and more righteous, holy, and pure in your lives and conversations, so that your lives and conversations may preach. For the world's tongues and mouths have preached long enough; but their lives and conversations have denied what their tongues have professed and declared.

"And, dear friends, strive to excel one another in virtue, and that ye may grow in love, that excellent way which unites all to Christ and God; and that all may stand up for God's glory, and mind that which concerns the Lord's honour and glory, that in no wise his power may be abused, nor his name evil spoken of by any evil talkers or walkers; but that in all things God may be honoured, and ye may glorify Him in your bodies, souls, and spirits, the little time ye have to live. So my love to you all in the Holy Seed of life, that reigns over all, and is the first and last, in whom ye all have life and salvation, and your election and peace with God, through Jesus Christ, who destroys him that hath been betwixt you and God; so that nothing may be betwixt you and the Lord but Christ Jesus. Amen."

CHAPTER XII.　1680-1686.

*Returns to London—Addresses an epistle of tender sympathy
to his suffering brethren—Embarks a second time for Holland
—Charles II. grants an order for a general release of Friends
from prison—G. F. bequeaths his freehold Property in England for the service of the Society.*

SETTING out from home early in 1680, he travelled
through Westmoreland, Lancashire, and Yorkshire.
Coming to York at the time of the assizes, he
interested himself in behalf of several Friends then
suffering imprisonment there.　He also attended the
Quarterly Meeting, which was a satisfactory and
refreshing season; and proceeded by slow stages
toward London, which he reached in time for the
Yearly Meeting.　Of this annual solemnity he says,
"a blessed opportunity the Lord gave us together,
wherein the ancient love was sweetly felt, and the
heavenly life flowed abundantly over all."　Soon after
this he visited two boarding-schools for Friends'
children, the establishment of which he had promoted, and now felt a lively interest in their right
support.　One was at Shacklewell, for the education
of girls; and the other for boys, kept by Christopher
Taylor, at Edmonton.

Returning to London he spent most of the winter
there, assisting Friends in their endeavours to induce
the parliament to grant some relief to the hardships

and grievances they endured in various parts of the kingdom, and labouring in other ways for the promotion of the cause of righteousness in the earth. After the Yearly Meeting he made a short visit to some parts of Bucks, Berks, and Oxon, again returning to London ; which city and its vicinity became his principal residence during the remainder of his life.

He was much engaged in correspondence with Friends in different parts of the world, advising and assisting in cases of difficulty, and exerting himself for the preservation and prosperity of the infant Society. London being a central situation, where Friends from all parts resorted, and where a large portion of the concerns of the church were transacted, it seemed more convenient for him than the secluded situation of Swarthmore. Suffering still continuing severe upon Friends in this city, he felt himself bound to attend their meetings in order to encourage them, both by word and example, to stand fast in the testimony to which God had called them ; and at other times he went from house to house visiting those who were despoiled of their goods for truth's sake. At the instance of rapacious informers, the magistrates proceeded against Friends without giving them a hearing, by which many suffered both unjustly and illegally. In conjunction with others he drew up a remonstrance against their conduct, and Friends appealing from their decisions, several were acquitted and the informers defeated, which moderated the justices and brought relief to the sufferers.

An election for sheriffs coming on, George Fox wrote the following short address, to show the candidates the unreasonableness of expecting Friends to vote for those who would persecute them, and also took an opportunity to bring some of their testimonies into view:

" Do any here in London, who stand to be chosen sheriffs, own that Christ that was crucified without the gates of Jerusalem, to be the light of the world, which ' lighteth every man that cometh into the world ;' who saith, ' Believe in the light, that ye may be the children of light ?' And is any of you against persecuting people for their religion and worship of God in spirit and truth, as Christ commandeth? For Christ said ' My kingdom is not of this world,' and therefore he doth not uphold his spiritual worship and pure religion with worldly and carnal weapons. And Christ said, ' Swear not at all ; ' and his apostle James saith the same : but will not you force us to swear, and so to break Christ's and his apostle's commands, in putting oaths to us? And Christ saith to his apostles, ' Freely ye have received, freely give :' Will not you force us to give tithes and maintenance to such teachers as we know God hath not sent?   Shall we be free to serve and worship God, and keep his and his Son's commands, if we give our voices freely for you? for we are unwilling to give our voices for such as will imprison and persecute us, and spoil our goods."

" But whatever they were that stood to be chosen," says he, " I observed there was a heat and strife in the spirits of the people that were to choose ; wherefore I writ a few lines to be spread amongst them, directed thus :—

" To the people who are choosing sheriffs in London :

" All keep in the gentle and peaceable wisdom of God, which is above that that is earthly, sensual, and devilish ; and live in that love of God that is not puffed up, nor is unseemly, which envieth not, but beareth and endureth all things. And in this love ye will seek the good and peace of all men, and the hurt of no man. Keep out of all heats, and be not hot-headed, but be cool and gentle, that your Christian moderation may appear to all men ; for the Lord is at hand, who beholds all men's words, thoughts, and actions, and will reward every one according to their works ; and what every man soweth, that shall he reap."

It being understood that the meetings would be disturbed on a certain First-day, he remained in the city to be present, though he felt an inclination to go to a meeting in the country. William Penn accompanied him to Gracechurch-street, where they both preached the Gospel. Several constables with their staves came in, and bade William Penn desist and come down, and the soldiers stood with muskets in the yard. George closed the meeting with prayer. He and William Penn withdrew, as was their custom, to a room near the meeting-place ; and lest the constables should suppose they wished to shun them, a Friend went down and informed them they might come up if they had any business with them. They had conversation with one of them, in which he admitted a doubt of the propriety of arresting them

by his warrant on First-day; but to release him from
all difficulty, Friends offered to go to the alderman
who granted the warrant, thereby proving their devotion to the cause of Christ, and willingness to subject
themselves to suffering, rather than that the officer
should suffer; but the affair terminated without their
appearing.

Under an affecting sense of the trials to which his
brethren were subjected, he addressed them an epistle
of tender sympathy and encouragement. He thus
introduces it :—" As sufferings continued very sore
and heavy upon Friends, not only in the city but in
most parts of the nation, I drew up a paper, to be
presented to the King; setting forth our grievances
therein, and desiring redress from him in those particular cases which I understood were in his power.
But not having relief from him, it came upon me to
write an epistle to Friends, to encourage them in
their sufferings, that they might bear with patience
the many exercises brought upon them, both from
the magistrates and by false brethren and apostates;
whose wicked books and filthy slanders did grieve
the upright-hearted. This epistle I writ at Dalston,
whither I went to visit an ancient Friend that lay
sick.

" Friends and brethren in Christ Jesus, whom the
Lord hath called and gathered unto Him; in Him
abide; for without Him (to wit, Christ) ye can do
nothing, and through him ye can do all things; who
is your strength and support in all your trials, temptations, imprisonments, and sufferings, who, for Christ's
sake, are 'accounted as sheep for the slaughter:'
nay, in all these things we are more than conquerors,

through Him that loved us. And, therefore, friends, though ye do suffer by the outward powers, ye know that the prophets, Christ, and the apostles suffered by the unconverted.

" And though ye do suffer by false brethren and false apostates for a time, and by their filthy books and tongues, whose tongues indeed are become no slander, let them speak, write, or print what they will; for the sober people even of the world hardly regard it. And it is well they have manifested themselves to the world, that their folly may proceed no further; though to the utmost of their power they have showed their wicked intent to stir up the magistrates, professors, and profane against us, and to speak evil of the way of truth. But God's judgments will overtake them, and come upon them as sure as they have come upon those that are gone before them. Let their pretence be never so high, mark their end; for they will fall like untimely figs, and wither like the grass on the top of the house. Though they may seem to flourish, and make a boast and a noise for a time, yet the Seed is on the head of such, which will grind them to powder; which seed bruises the serpent's head. Therefore in this Seed, Christ, who is your sanctuary, rest, peace, and quiet habitatation, who is the First and Last, and over all, in Him walk; for the Lord taketh pleasure in his people that are faithful and that serve and worship Him. And therefore let the saints be joyful in glory; and the God of peace, ' the God of all grace,' who hath called us into his eternal glory by Christ Jesus, after that ye have suffered awhile, make you perfect; stablish, strengthen, settle you; ' casting all your care upon him, for he careth for you.'

" And, beloved, ' think it not strange concerning the fiery trial which is to try you, as though some strange thing happened unto you ;' . . . . ' for it is better, if the will of God be so, that you suffer for well-doing than for evil-doing ;' and ' rejoice, inasmuch as ye are partakers of Christ's sufferings.' ' Wherefore let them that suffer according to the will of God, commit the keeping of their souls to him in well-doing, as unto a faithful Creator.' ' For unto you it is given, in the behalf of Christ, not only to believe on him, but also to suffer . for his sake.' So it is given, or is a gift from Christ, to suffer for his name; and therefore, as I said before, rejoice, inasmuch as ye are partakers of Christ's sufferings. ' And, if ye be reproached (or evil spoken of) for the name of Christ, happy are ye ; for the spirit of glory and of God resteth upon you : on their part he is evil spoken of, but on your part he is glorified.'

" And, therefore, ' if any man suffer as a Christian, let him not be ashamed, but let him glorify God on this 'behalf.' Though now for a season ye are in sufferings, and trials, and temptations, ' that the trial of your faith, being much more precious than of gold that perisheth, though it be tried with fire, might be found unto praise, and honour, and glory,' . . ' who are kept by the power of God, through faith, unto salvation.' Therefore mind your keeper, wherever ye are, or what sufferings soever ye be in ; and mind the example of the apostle, how he suffered trouble as an evil doer, unto bonds. But the word of God is not bound, which is everlasting, and endures for ever; and they who are in that which is not everlasting and doth not endure for ever, cannot bind the Word. And the Apostle said, ' I endure all things for the elect's sake; that they may also obtain the salvation which is in Christ Jesus, with eternal glory;' mark, ' with eternal glory.' And if we suffer with Christ, we shall also reign with Christ, who abide faithful.

" Therefore ' strive not about words to no profit :' but ' shun profane and vain babblings, for they will increase unto more ungodliness;' so that ye may be vessels ' of honour, sanctified and meet for' Christ your ' master's use, and prepared unto every good work.' Follow after righteousness, godliness, faith, love, patience, and meekness. And fight the good fight of faith with your heavenly weapons : which faith is victory (or gives victory), by which ye lay hold on eternal life, and have access unto God, ' who will render to every man according to his deeds : to them who, by patient continuance in well-doing, seek for glory, and honour, and immortality, eternal life; but unto them that are contentious, and do not obey the truth, but obey unrighteousness, indignation and wrath, tribulation and. anguish upon every soul of man that doth evil; . . . but glory, honour, and peace to every man that worketh good.' Christ said to his disciples, ' If the world hate you, ye know that it hated me before it hated you. If ye were of the world, the world would love his own : but because ye are not of the world, but I have chosen you out of the world, therefore the world hateth you.' . . . . . And, ' If they have persecuted me, they will also persecute you.' And John in his general epistle to the church saith, ' Marvel not, my brethren, if the world hate you.   We know that we have passed from death unto life, because we love the brethren.'   And Christ, in his prayer to his Father, saith of his followers, ' As thou hast sent me into the world, even so have I also sent them into the world. . . . . And the glory which thou gavest me I have given them, that they may be one, even as we are one.'   And therefore all ye that know God and Jesus Christ (whom to know is eternal life), and are partakers of his glory, keep the testimony of Jesus, and be valiant for his truth upon earth, that ye may be all settled upon Christ, the rock and foundation.

" G. F.

" Dalston, the 3rd of the
   Eighth Month, 1682."

Friends were now often compelled to meet out of doors as near as they could to the meeting-houses, yet sometimes they unexpectedly obtained a quiet, peaceable meeting within the house.   At one time G. F. wished to visit a sick Friend a mile or two out of town, but hearing that the King had ordered the mayor to put the laws in execution against dissenters, and that the magistrates therefore intended to nail up the doors of the meeting-house, he was not willing to go away, but went to Gracechurch-street, where, notwithstanding the threats, they had a large and good, and very quiet meeting.

On another occasion, when the doors were guarded by constables with their staves, and they refused him and others entrance, they assembled in the yard.   A Friend commenced speaking whom they ordered to be silent, and grew angry at his persisting. George Fox laid his hand on the constable and desired him to let the friend alone; when he ceased, George stood up and said they " need not come against us with swords and staves, for we are a peaceable people, and have nothing in our hearts but good will to the King and magistrates, and to all people upon the earth. And we did not meet under pretence of religion to plot and contrive against the government, or to raise insurrections, but to worship God in Spirit and in truth. And we had Christ to be our Bishop, and Priest, and Shepherd to feed us and oversee us, and He ruled in our hearts; so we could all sit in silence, enjoying our Teacher; so to Christ, their Bishop and Shepherd, I did recommend them all." He was also moved to pray; when the people, constables, and soldiers put off their hats, and the power of the Lord was felt to be over them. Such was the influence of the solemnity, that on parting, one of the constables took off his hat and desired the Lord to bless them. Thus the Holy Spirit at times raised a testimony in the hearts of their enemies, that Friends were " true men" and sought the welfare of all.

At the Yearly Meeting of 1683, he was much concerned lest Friends from the country should be imprisoned at London while in attendance there. But he says the Lord was with us, his power preserved us, and gave us a sweet and blessed opportunity to wait upon Him, and be refreshed together in Him, and to perform those services for his truth and people, for which we met. In consideration of the great spoiling of goods to which Friends were then subjected, he felt very desirous that while suffering for their religious principles, they might not do it at the

expense of justice to those who had credited dealers
with goods.   He accordingly drew up the following
epistle, which shows the soundness of his views, as
well as the tenderness of his scruples, and presented
it to the Yearly Meeting for consideration, by which
it was approved and sent among Friends throughout
the nation.

    " Dear Friends and brethren in the Lord Jesus
                    Christ,
    " Who is your only sanctuary in this day of storm
and persecution, spoiling of goods and imprisonments.
Let every one's eye be unto Him, who has all power
in heaven and earth given unto Him ; so that none
can touch an hair of your head, nor you, nor anything ye have, except it be permitted or suffered in
this day to try his people, whether their minds be
with the Lord, or in the outward things. And now,
dear friends, take care that all your offerings may
be free, and of your own, that has cost you something ; so that ye may not offer of that which is
another man's, or that which ye are entrusted withal,
and not your own, or fatherless or widows' estates ;
but all such things ye may settle and establish in
their places.
    " You may remember many years ago, in a time
of great persecution, there were divers Friends who
were traders, shopkeepers, and others, who had the
concerns of widows and fatherless, and other people's
estates in their hands. And when a great suffering,
persecution, and spoiling of goods came upon Friends,
there was especial care taken that all Friends that did
suffer, what they did offer up to the Lord in their

sufferings might be really their own, and not any others' estates or goods which they had in their hands, and were not really their own ; so that they might offer up that which they had bought and paid for, or were able to pay for. And afterwards several letters came out of the country to the meeting at London, from friends that had goods of the shop-keepers here at London upon credit, which they had not paid for ; who writ to their creditors whom they had their goods of, entreating them to take their goods again.

"And some Friends came to London themselves, and treated with their creditors, letting them understand how their conditions were, that they lay liable to have all that they had taken from them ; and told them, they would not have any man to suffer by them : neither would they by suffering offer up anything but what was really their own, or what they were able to pay for. Upon which several took their goods back again that they had sent down, and this wrought a very good savour in the hearts of many people, when they saw that there was such a righteous, just, and honest principle in Friends, that would not make any to suffer for their testimony ; but what they did suffer for the testimony of Jesus it should be really and truly their own, not other people's. And in this they owed nothing to any but love. So in this every man and woman stands in the free offering, a free people, whether it be spiritual or temporal, which is their own ; and in that they wrong no man, neither inwardly nor outwardly. Ornan said unto David, 'Take the threshing-floor to thee . . . and I give thee the oxen also for burnt offerings, and the threshing instruments

for wood, and the wheat for the meat-offering, I give
it all.   And King David said unto Ornan, Nay, but
I will verily buy it for the full price ; for I will not
take that which is thine for the Lord, nor offer burnt-
offerings without cost' (1 Chron. xxi. 22, &c.); so
it should be his own, and so should it be every man's
that offers.   So you may see here that David would
not accept of another man's gift for an offering to the
Lord ; he would not offer up that which cost him
nothing, but it should be really his own.   A good
man, ' will guide his affairs with discretion.'

> " Let this be read in your Monthly and Quar-
> terly men's and women's meetings.

" G. F.

" London, the 2nd of the
Fourth Month, 1683."

It does not appear that George Fox took any considerable journey until the spring of 1684, when he
found his mind engaged to visit his brethren in Holland once more.

On the 31st of the Third Month, in company with
several friends, he set out for Harwich to take shipping, and stopping a night at Colchester by the way,
concluded to stay and be at meeting there next day.
Although no notice of this conclusion was given, yet
the information of his being there spread ; and a great
concourse of people assembled, so that Friends feared
the magistrates would have taken alarm and broken
up the meeting.   But it proved otherwise, and " a
glorious meeting we had," says George ; " truly the
Lord's power and presence was beyond words, for I
was but weak to go into a meeting, and my face (by
reason of a cold I had taken) was sore, but God

was strong, and manifested his strength in us and with us; and all was well; the Lord have the glory for evermore for his supporting power."

They had a fine run of sixteen hours, and landed at the Briel in Holland, whence they went to Rotterdam, and next day to Amsterdam to attend the Yearly Meeting. This afforded him an opportunity of seeing Friends of those countries generally collected, and they had a refreshing time together in the love of God.

He was visited by many pious, inquiring people, some of them men of note in the world; who with some of their teachers came to the public meetings he held, and were very attentive to the truths of the Gospel which he and his companions declared amongst them.

After spending several weeks travelling among Friends in different parts of Holland, he embarked for England on the 16th of Fifth Month, and landing at Harwich, went to the house of his son-in-law, William Mead, at Gooses, near Hare-street, to rest and recruit his enfeebled body.

Although he ceased from much travelling after this time, yet his enlarged and active mind was diligently engaged in labours of Christian love, writing epistles to his brethren, attending to the sufferings of those who were under persecution, visiting the sick and afflicted and ministering to their consolation, besides being frequently engaged in public testimony in religious meetings; thus imitating the example of his Divine Master, in going about and doing good to the bodies and souls of men.

The nation being much agitated by political con-

tests and popular disaffection, George Fox was concerned on account of his brethren, lest they should be
drawn into the spirit of the contending parties, contrary to the known testimony of the Society, and to
the neglect of their religious duties. He therefore
wrote an epistle, " to caution all to keep out of the
spirit of the world, in which the trouble is, and to dwell
in the peaceable truth."

He was also much grieved at seeing the increase of
the pride of life, and gaiety in dress, even among some
who made profession with Friends; on which account
he wrote an address, showing how unbecoming such
things were in a Christian, and contrary to the examples of the holy men and women of old.

The closeness of the air of London, and the confinement incident to a city life, proved too much for his
enervated constitution, and, after a few weeks' stay,
he was obliged to retreat to some country place in
the vicinity, mostly to Gooses, or to Kingston-upon-
Thames.

Coming into London from the country, in the First
Month, 1686, he exerted himself in advising and
aiding Friends in prosecuting their appeals at the
sessions at Hicks' Hall, and they generally succeeded.
In consequence of the frequent representation of their
hardships to the King, he gave orders for releasing all
who were imprisoned for conscience' sake, and whom
it was in his power to discharge. The prison doors
were opened, and hundreds of Friends, some of whom
had been long confined, were discharged. It was
cause of great joy to friends to see their faithful
brethren again at liberty, and attending the Yearly
Meeting, after their long seclusion from society, and

their accustomed labour in the Lord's work.   A precious refreshing meeting it was.

On an occasion of so much rejoicing, George Fox
felt desirous not only that Friends might ascribe the
deliverance to the Lord from whom all our mercies
come, but also might show forth their gratitude by a
holy life and conversation.   For the purpose of inciting them to these duties he wrote the following
letter :—

   " Friends,

" The Lord, by his eternal power, hath opened
the heart of the King to open the prison doors, by
which about fifteen or sixteen hundred are set at
liberty ; and hath given a check to the informers, so
that in many places our meetings are pretty quiet.
So my desires are, that both liberty and sufferings
all may be sanctified to his people : and Friends may
prize the mercies of the Lord in all things, and to
Him be thankful, who stilleth the raging waves of
the seas, and allayeth the storms and tempest, and
maketh a calm.   And therefore it is good to trust in
the Lord, and cast your care upon Him who careth
for you.   For when ye were in your gaols and
prisons, then the Lord did by his eternal arm and
power uphold you, and sanctified them to you.   And
unto some He made them as a sanctuary, and tried
his people, as in a furnace of affliction, both in
prisons and spoiling of goods.   And in all this the
Lord was with his people, and taught them to know
that 'the earth is the Lord's, and the fulness thereof ;'
and that He was in all places, ' who crowneth the
year with his goodness.'

" Therefore let all God's people be diligent, and careful to keep the camp of God holy, pure, and clean, and to serve God and Christ, and one another in the glorious, peaceable Gospel of life and salvation; which glory shines over God's camp, and his great Prophet and Bishop, and Shepherd is among or in the midst of them, exercising his heavenly offices in them; so that you his people may rejoice in Christ Jesus, through whom you have peace with God. For He that destroyeth the devil and his work, and bruises the serpent's head, is all God's people's heavenly foundation and rock to build upon; which was the holy prophets' and apostles' rock in days past, and is now a rock of our ages, which rock, and foundation of God, standeth sure. And upon this, the Lord God establish all his people. Amen.   " G. F.

  " London, the 25th of the
    Seventh Month, 1686."

Thus did this faithful minister of Christ and overseer of the church watch over the flock; warn, encourage, or reprove them, as he saw occasion, and endeavour, in the ability which the Holy Spirit confers, to build them up in the most holy faith. In such works of love he spent the residue of his days; adding thereto many acts of liberality, both of a public and private nature; having through life cherished that divine charity which is ever ready " to do good and to communicate," and which teaches that temporal treasures are but trusts committed to our care, to be used for the glory of God and the good of his creatures.

One of his gifts of a public nature, being a little remarkable in some particulars, as well as in the manner of its conveyance, may serve to illustrate the character of this great and good man. It is as follows, viz. :—

" *George Fox's declared intention and motion for his giving up Petty's house and land for ever, for the service of the Lord and the people called Quakers.*

"The eternal God, who hath, in and by his eternal powerful arm, preserved me through all my troubles, trials, temptations and afflictions, persecutions, reproaches and imprisonments, and carried me over them all, hath sanctified all these things to me, so that I can say, all things work together for good to them that love God, and are beloved of Him.

"And the Lord God of the whole heaven and earth, and all things therein, both natural and spiritual, hath been, by his eternal power, my preserver, and upholder, and keeper, and hath taken care and provided for me, both for temporals and spirituals, so that I never did want ; and have been content and thankful with what the Lord provided for me.

"And now the Lord hath done much good to me, and to his name, truth, and people, to whom I have offered up my spirit, soul, and body, which are the Lord's, made and created for his glory. And also I do offer and give up freely to the Lord for ever, and for the service of his sons, daughters, and servants, called Quakers, the house and houses, barn, kiln, stable, and all the land, with the garden and orchard, being about three acres of land, more or less; with the commonings, peats, turfings, moss, and whatsoever other privileges that belong to it, called Swarthmore, in the parish of Ulverstone.

" And also my ebony bedstead, with the painted curtains, and the great elbow-chair that Robert Widders sent me; and my great sea-case or cellaridge, with the bottles in it. These I do give to stand in the house as heir-looms, when the house is made use of for a meeting-place; so that a Friend may have a bed to lie on, and a chair to sit in, and a bottle to hold a little water to drink.

" It being free of land, and free from all tithe both great and small; and all this I do freely give up to the Lord, and for the Lord's service and his people's, to make it a meeting-place of.

" It is all the land and house I have in England; and it is given up to the Lord, for it is for his service, and for his children's.

" George Fox."

" I do and have given up Petty's, which I bought of the children Susannah Fell, and Rachel Fell, for seventy-two pounds; for God's people to meet in, when they do not meet at Swarthmore Hall; and let the rest of the ground and malt-house maintain the meeting-house, which may be made fit, either the barn or the house, as the Lord shall let Friends see which is best; and to slate it, and pave the way to it, that so Friends may go dry to their meeting. And let or set part of the house and land to maintain itself for ever for the Lord's service. And you may let any poor honest Friend live in part of the

house.   And so let it be for the Lord's service to the
end of the world; and for his people to meet in, to
keep them from the winter cold and the wet, and the
summer heat.''

The foregoing extracts are from papers dated at
Kingston-upon-Thames, the 13th of Twelfth Month,
and the 22nd of First Month, 1686-7, which appear
to have been sent to his son-in-law, Thomas Lower,
who lived at Marsh Grange, in Lancashire.

In a letter to T. L., dated 28th of Second
Month, 1687, on the subject, he says : '' With
my love to thee and thy wife, with thy mother,
and brother, and sister, at Swarthmore, and thy
children, and the rest of friends, in the Holy
Seed of Life, that reigns over all.   Dear Thomas,
I have sent thee a copy of my mind concerning
Petty's, which thou mayst privately show to thy
mother, and the list of the names.   You that live in
the country may know which of these are the fittest
to put into the deed of trust.   Choose out first, four
of the most faithful and substantial friends in this
list, or other that you may approve of, to join your
four brothers, unto whom the first deed of trust is to
be made; and then you eight are to make it over by
a deed of uses, to ten or twelve Friends more : you
may consider, who are fit to put into that second
deed.   The four names that are to be joined with
you, thou must send up as shortly as thou canst, that
so the deed may be confirmed as soon as may be.

'' This will be a confirmation of what has all along
been in thy mother's mind ; that the meeting will be
continued at Swarthmore.   And as concerning the
ten or twelve Friends more, unto whom you are to

make a deed of uses, the names of them may be considered afterwards when this is done. And as concerning the meeting-place itself, whether the barn or the house, I shall leave it to you. But if the barn will do better; if you could make it wider, may be it may be better, because there will be the house to go into, and the ground may be so raised, that you may go up a step or two into the meeting-house; and it will be more wholesome. And the yards are low, which may be raised and laid dry; and you have stones enough, and poor men to get them. And I would have all the thatch pulled off the houses, and laid in a heap to rot for manure to be laid upon the close; and let all the houses be slated, and the walls about it to be made substantial to stand, and laid in lime and sand.

" And I would have a porch made to the meeting-place, on the common side, from the yard; and with rubbish and earth, as before, you may raise the yard and floors. And I would have the meeting-place large, for truth may increase. The barn made as wide again, which you may do with pillars, or otherwise, which I leave to thee and the workmen; and I would have thee take Robert Barrow's advice in it. If you think fit to have the kiln continued, you may fit it up, if it be worth the charge of doing. But these things I must leave to you.

" I would have it gone about, and prepare things beforehand, as soon as you can; when you have viewed it, and see what you will want; either lime, sand, wood, or stone. And I would have Robert Barrow to do it, if he can. And I would have next winter an orchard planted where you see fit; you may get some trees to set in it where thou sees fit. And I would have some trees set about the close, .and if thou wilt set some of thy fir-trees there, thou may. And when all is done and fitted completely for the Lord's service and his people's, let it stand till there be occasion for it. I desire thee to be very careful in this thing, and let it be done as soon as may be; for it is not for myself, but for the service of the Lord and his people; and let it be done substantially.

" And as for the affairs of truth, in the general things are pretty well, and meetings are quiet both in England and beyond the seas. The Lord keep his people in his fear and in humility, in this time of liberty; that they do not forget Him; for there is danger in a time of liberty, as in a time of suffering, for that to get up which will not stand faithful: but my desire is that all may walk worthy of the Lord's mercies. So no more, with my love to you."

In another letter he further directs :—" And you may mind to buy all the things at the best hand, beforehand, to be ready. I am in the same mind still, not to put any Friend to a farthing charge. But if Friends of the meeting, or thereaway, will come with their carts, and help to fetch stone, lime, wood, sand, or slate, I shall take it kindly ; or to get stone off the common, if need be; and you may speak to Joseph Sharp, for he is a willing man to help in any thing.

" The twenty pounds of J. R.'s which you are to receive, I have and do order for that service; and the fifteen pounds thou hast in thy hands of Jane and

Robert Widders, I order for that service, and for the building; and the five pounds Susannah brought up I took of her, and what more ye do want, when it is wanted let me know. And so, dear Thomas, my love is to thee and all the rest of Friends in the holy and peaceable truth, that is stronger than all they that be out of it. And God Almighty keep you in it, and in the order of it. Amen.

" G. F."

CHAPTER XIII.   1686-1690.

*Retires to Kingston—His health and strength much declined—
Issues frequent Epistles to his friends—His last to Friends
in Ireland — Attends Gracechurch-street Meeting — After
which he was taken ill—His death and burial—Sketch of his
character—Observations on his Contemporaries.*

A PAPER which George Fox wrote towards the close
of the year 1686, concerning the Church of Christ,
exhibits a view of the purity and redemption from
the unsettled spirit of the world which, through perseverance, the members of Christ's body are favoured
to attain, by the power of the Holy Spirit.   It also
contains a declaration of his faith in the propitiatory
offering and sacrifice of Christ for the sins of all mankind, and in his mediation between God and man.
It is as follows:—

" They are living members, and living stones,
which are built up a spiritual household, and are the
children of the promise, and of the seed and flesh of
Christ ; and as the apostle saith, ' members of his
body, of his flesh, and of his bones.'   They are the
good seed, and are the children of the everlasting
kingdom written in heaven, and have put on the
Lord Jesus Christ.   And they sit together in the
heavenly places in Christ Jesus, and so are clothed
with the Sun of righteousness, Christ Jesus, and have

the moon under their feet, Rev. xii.　So all changeable things that are in the world, and all changeable
religions and changeable worships, and changeable
way, and fellowships, and churches, and teachers in
the world are as the moon ; for the moon changes,
but the sun doth not change.　And so the Sun of
righteousness never changeth, nor sets, or goes
down ;　but all the ways, religions, and worships, and
fellowships of the world, and the teachers thereof,
change like the moon.　But the true church, which
Christ is the head of, which is in God the Father of
our Lord Jesus Christ, which church is called ' the
pillar and ground of truth,' whose conversation is in
heaven,—this church is clothed with the Sun, Christ
Jesus, her Head, who doth not change, and hath all
changeable things under her feet.

" These are the living members, born again of the
immortal Seed by the word of God, and feed upon
the immortal milk, and live and grow by it.　And
such' are the new creatures in Christ Jesus, who
makes all things new, and sees the old things pass
away.　And his church, and all his members, which
are clothed with the sun, their worship is in the spirit
and in the truth, which doth not change. . . .　And
likewise the church of Christ, their religion is pure
and undefiled before God, that keeps from the spots
of the world, &c., and their way is the new and living
way, Christ Jesus.　So the Church of Christ, that is
clothed with the Sun, that hath the moon and all
changeable religions and ways under her feet, hath
an unchangeable worship, religion, and way, and
hath an unchangeable rock and foundation, Christ
Jesus, and an unchangeable High Priest, and so are

children of the New Testament, and in the everlasting covenant of light and life.

" And now all that profess the Scriptures both of the New and Old Testament, and are not in Christ Jesus, the apostle tells them they are reprobates if Christ be not in them. And therefore these that be not in Christ cannot be clothed with Christ, the Sun of righteousness, that never changes. And they that be not of Christ be under the changeable moon, in the world, in the changeable things, in the changeable religions, and ways, and worships, and teachers, and rocks, and foundations. But Christ, the Son of God and Sun of righteousness, doth not change : in whom his people are gathered, and sit together in the heavenly places in Him, and so are clothed with Christ Jesus, the Sun, who is the mountain that filleth the whole earth with his divine power and light. And so all his people see Him and feel Him both by sea and land. So He is in all places of the earth felt and seen of all his. And Christ Jesus saith to the outward professors, the Jews, ' Ye are from beneath; I am from above; ye are of this world,' to wit, that is beneath; and so their religions, worships, ways, teachers, faiths, beliefs, and creeds are made of men, and are below, and of this world that changeth like the moon. And ye may see their religions, ways, worships, and teachers, they are all changeable like the moon ; but Christ, the Sun, with which the church is clothed, doth not change, nor his church; for they are spiritually-minded, and their way, worship, and religion is spiritual, from Christ, who is from above and not of this world. For Christ hath redeemed you from the world, and their changeable rudiments and elements, and old things, and their changeable teachers, and from their changeable faiths and beliefs. For Christ is the Author and Finisher of his church's faith, who is from above, and saith, ' Believe in the Light, that ye may be the children of the Light.' And it is given them not only to believe, but to suffer for his name. So this faith and belief is above all forms and beliefs which change like the moon.

" And God's people are an holy nation, a peculiar people, a spiritual household, and royal priesthood, offering up spiritual sacrifices acceptable to God by Jesus Christ; and are zealous of righteous, godly, good works, and their zeal is for that which is of God against the evil which is not of God.

" And Christ took upon Him the seed of Abraham; He doth not say the corrupt seed of the Gentiles. So according to the flesh He was of the holy seed of Abraham and of David, and his holy body and blood was an offering and a sacrifice for the sins of the whole world, as a Lamb without blemish, whose flesh saw no corruption. And so by the one offering of Himself in the New Testament and New Covenant, He has put an end to all the offerings and sacrifices amongst the Jews in the Old Testament. And Christ, the holy Seed, was crucified, dead, and buried, according to the flesh, and raised again the third day, and his flesh saw no corruption. Though He was crucified in the flesh, yet quickened again by the Spirit, and is alive, and liveth for evermore, and hath all power in heaven and earth given to Him, and reigneth over all, and is the One Mediator betwixt God and man, even the Man Christ Jesus.

" And Christ said He gave his flesh for the life of the world; and the apostle saith, his flesh saw no corruption; so that which saw no corruption He gave for the life of the corrupt world to bring them out of corruption. And Christ said again, ' Whoso eateth my flesh and drinketh my blood hath eternal life. . . . For my flesh is meat indeed, and my blood is drink indeed.' He that eateth my flesh and drinketh my blood, dwelleth in me, and I in him.' And he that eats not his flesh and drinks not his blood, which is the life of the flesh, hath not eternal life.

" Now as the apostle saith, ' If one died for all, then were all dead.' Now all coming spiritually to eat the flesh of Christ, the second Adam, and drink his blood, his blood and flesh gives all the dead in Adam· life, and quickens them out of their sins and trespasses in which they were dead. And so they come to sit together in the heavenly places in Christ Jesus, and so are living members of the church of Christ that He is the head of, and are clothed with the Sun, the Sun of righteousness, the Son of God. . . .

" These see the people how that they do change from one worship to another, and from one religion to another, and from one way to another, and one church to another, and yet their hearts are not changed. And the letter of Scripture is read, but the mystery is hid; they have the sheep's clothing, the outside, but are inwardly ravened from the Spirit, which would bring them into the lamb's and sheep's nature. The Scripture saith, all the uncircumcised must go down into the pit; and therefore all must be circumcised with the Spirit of God, which puts off the body of death, and sins of the flesh, that came into man and woman by their

disobedience and transgressing of God's commands.
I say, all must be circumcised with the Spirit, which
puts off the body of death and sins of the flesh,
before they come up into Christ, their rest, that
never fell, and be clothed with Him, the Sun of
righteousness.   " G. F."

Nothing appears to have occupied his thoughts
so much as the character and offices of the Lord
Jesus Christ. It was the constant theme of his
ministry. The requisitions of the Mosaic Law, the
prophecies of the ancient prophets and the expe-
riences of holy men as recited in the Old Testament,
were often brought forward by him to confirm the
authority of Christ as Head of the church, and the
indispensable obligation to keep his commands; the
doctrines of his propitiation, mediation, and intercession, and of the illuminating power of his Spirit
in the hearts of all mankind. The following memo-
randum shows the train of his thoughts and the
subjects which were uppermost in his mind.

" While I was at Kingston, one day, meditating
on the things of God, some particular observations
arose in my mind concerning the first, and the
second or last Adam. As that,

" The first man Adam was made on the Sixth-day
of the week; and Christ, the second Adam, was
crucified on the Sixth-day of the week.

" The first Adam was betrayed by the serpent in
the garden of Eden; and Christ our Saviour, the
second Adam, was betrayed by Judas in a garden
near Jerusalem.

" Christ arose from the dead on the first day of

the week; and they that do believe on Him are entered into Christ their rest: the Christians do meet together to worship God on the first day of the week; and on the first day of the week it was, that God said, ' Let there be light, and there was light.' The Jews' rest was on the seventh day of the week, which was given to the Jews as a sign of the eternal rest of the Lord, sanctifying them, after they came out of the land of Egypt: for before that time the Lord had not given to man and woman his outward sabbath-day to keep, neither in the old world, nor after in Abraham's time, nor in Isaac's, nor in Jacob's time; until the Jews came out of Egypt to Mount Sinai in the wilderness. And then, there the Lord gave the law, and his sabbath, as a sign, in the old covenant, of Christ the eternal rest in the new covenant: and they that believe do enter into Christ their rest.

" Adam, the first man, is the root from whence we all spring naturally; and Christ is called the last or second Adam, because He is the beginning and root of all them that are spiritual.

" ' The first man Adam was made a living soul:' and Christ, ' the last Adam, was made a quickening spirit.'

" Christ by the grace of God tasted death for every man, that they might all come into favour with God; ' and that every tongue should confess, that Jesus Christ is Lord, to the glory of God the Father.' "

In another paper he says: " But though Christ is said to be of the seed of David, and of Abraham, as his generation is declared by Matthew and Luke;

yet Christ was not born 'of the will of the flesh, nor of the will of man, but of God.' For He was conceived by the Holy Ghost, and not by the will of man but by the will of God, born of the Virgin, and supposed to be the son of Joseph, but was the Son of God. And his name was called Jesus, because He should 'save his people from their sins;' and Emmanuel, God with us. And Christ 'took not on Him the nature of angels, but he took on Him the seed of Abraham' (as I said before), and so, 'was made of the seed of David according to the flesh; and declared to be the Son of God with power, according to the spirit of holiness, by the resurrection from the dead.' So the generation of Christ is a mystery. And Christ saw his seed or word to grow up in his disciples; and 'Christ in you the hope of glory,' the apostle calls 'the mystery which hath been hid from ages and from generations; but now is made manifest to his saints' (or sanctified ones,) Col. i. 26, 27; 'Whom we preach; warning every man, and teaching every man in all wisdom, that we may present every man perfect in Christ Jesus,' Col. i. 28. For in Christ, the second Adam, all are made perfect and complete; and in Adam in the fall, all are deformed and made imperfect; so out of Christ all mankind are imperfect and deformed, let them paint and dress themselves with the sheep's clothing, and with the form of godliness, of the prophets', and Christ's and his apostles' words never so much; yet if Christ be not in them, they are uncomplete, imperfect, deformed, reprobates. But the apostle tells the church of Christ, 'Ye are complete in Him which is the head of all principality and power,' Col. ii. 10, for He hath all power in heaven and earth given to Him, Matt. xxviii. 18. And so all the saints are made perfect and complete in Christ Jesus. Blessed be the Lord God over all for ever, through Jesus Christ. Amen, Amen.   "G. F.

    " Kingston, the 15th of the
        First Month, 1686-7."

Having his mind "continually exercised in the things of God, the sense of his infinite goodness and mercy to mankind in visiting them after they had transgressed and rebelled against Him, and providing a way and means for their return to Him again," being deeply impressed upon him, he wrote the following :—

" The devil, who is out of the truth, tempted man and woman to disobey God; and so drew them into the fall from the truth. So it is the devil that hath stopped men's eyes, and ears, and hearts, from the truth, who is called the god of this world; who hath blinded the eyes of infidels, or heathen. But Christ who bruises the serpent's head, and destroys the devil and his works, doth open men's hearts, and eyes, and ears ; who is their Saviour and Redeemer, and giveth life eternal to his people, that obey him and his truth. Blessed be the Lord for ever through Jesus Christ, who hath tasted death for all men, to bring them out of the death of Adam ; and is a propitiation for the sins of the whole world, and ' gave himself a ransom for all, to be testified in due time.' For as by

Adam's transgression and disobedience, death and
condemnation came upon all men, so by Christ's
obedience unto death, justification of life is come
upon all men : and he that believeth in Christ hath
eternal life; but he that doth not is condemned
already.   But God would have all men to be saved,
and come unto the knowledge of the truth, as it is in
Jesus, who is their Saviour; and in Him there is no
condemnation.

" G. F."

While at Kingston in 1687, G. F. says that his
spirit being continually exercised towards God, he
had many precious openings of divine matters, some
of which he committed to writing.   He holds forth
in the following extracts his full belief in the eternal
divinity of our Lord Jesus Christ, and in his glorifi-
cation at the right hand of the Father.

" And ' Christ is the image of the invisible God,
the first born of every creature, for by him were all
things created, that are in heaven and that are in
earth, visible and invisible, whether they be thrones
or dominions, or principalities or powers, all things
were created by him and for him, and he is before all
things, and by him all things consist; and he is
the head of the body, the church; who is the
beginning, the first-born from the dead.'

" The blind Jews that disobeyed God crucified Christ
Jesus: and the outward christians that live and walk
not in Christ, but in sin and evil, though they do make
an outward profession of Christ, yet they do crucify to
themselves Christ afresh.   But as to Christ himself

He is ascended far above all principalities, thrones, powers, and dominions; so that they cannot put Him to death, or crucify Him any more, as to Himself; but what the killers, and crucifiers, and persecutors do now upon the earth, it is against Christ, as in themselves, and in his members; as Christ said to Saul, why persecutest thou me? For what is done to his members, Christ takes as done to Himself, Matt. xxv. 40. And they that did not visit Christ, but persecuted Him in his members, they persecuted Christ in themselves first."

He continued visiting the meetings of Friends in and about London as his health permitted, and attended the Yearly Meeting in 1688; which he says was a very refreshing season, the Lord vouchsafing to honour these assemblies with his living, glorious presence in a very plentiful manner.

His health and strength now declined so much that he was scarcely able to sit a meeting through; and when he did, he often had to retire to a chamber contiguous, as soon as it was over, in order to lie down. " Yet," says he, " did not my weakness of body take me off from the service of the Lord; but I continued to labour in meetings and out of meetings, in the work of the Lord, as the Lord gave me opportunity and ability."

In the year 1689, he attended the Yearly Meeting in London, as he had done for some years previous; and in the autumn retired to the house of his son-in-law, William Mead, where he spent the winter, seldom going out, except a few times to attend the meeting where they belonged, which was about half a mile distant. He however frequently held meetings in the house with the family, and such as came to visit him, feeling the great benefit as well as duty of waiting often upon the Lord, and worshipping Him in as public a manner as bodily health would permit.

In the Second Month, 1690, he went up to London, and attended the Yearly Meeting there in the Fourth Month following, for the last time. It was a favoured season, in which the wonted goodness of the Lord was manifested, to the comfort and refreshment of Friends. When the meeting was over he made a short excursion into the country, returning to the city again in the Seventh Month, where he continued until the time of his decease. He was almost daily with Friends at some one of their meetings in that place, and engaged at other times in writing to his brethren.

For several years before his death he wrote, annually, a postscript to be added to the Yearly Meeting's epistle. The following, showing the fulness and firmness of his faith in Christ, was appended to the epistle issued by the last meeting of that kind which he attended :—

" All Friends, everywhere, that are alive to God through Jesus Christ, and are living members of Christ the Holy Head, be still and stand still in the Lord's camp of holiness and righteousness, and therein see the salvation of God, and your eternal life, rest, and peace. And in it you may feel and see the Lord's power is over all; and how the Lord is at work in his power, and ruling the nations with his rod of iron, and is breaking (in the nations) the old leaky vessels and cisterns to pieces, like the potter's vessels, that will not hold his living water of life; who are erred from the Spirit. But blessed be the Lord God of heaven and earth, who, by his eternal arm and power, hath settled all his people upon the living, holy rock and foundation, that stands sure; whom He hath drawn by his Spirit to his Son, and gathered them into the name of Jesus Christ, his only begotten Son, full of grace and truth; who hath all power in heaven and earth given to Him. Whose name is above every name under the whole heaven, and all his living members know there is no salvation given by any other name under the whole heaven, but by the name of Jesus: and He, their salvation, and their living Head, is felt in the midst of them in his light, life, spirit, grace, and truth, and his word of patience, wisdom, and power; who is his people's Prophet, that God hath raised up, in his New Testament and Covenant, to open to them; and their living Shepherd, that hath purchased, redeemed, and bought them with his precious blood. And Christ, the living One, feeds his living sheep in his living pastures of life, and his living sheep know their living Shepherd's voice, with his living bread and water, and follow Him; and will not follow any of the world's hirelings, nor thieves, nor robbers, nor climbers, that are without Christ, the door. And likewise Christ's living children know Christ, the Bishop of their souls, to oversee them with his heavenly and spiritual eye, that they may be preserved in his fold of life, and go no more forth. And also they know Christ, their holy Priest, that by the grace of God tasted death for them, and for every man, and is a propitiation for their sins; and not for their sins only, but also for the sins of the whole world: and by the one offering up of Himself, 'he hath perfected for ever them that are sanctified.' And such an high priest becomes Christ's sheep in his new covenant and testament, 'who is holy, harmless, undefiled, separate from sinners, and made higher than the heavens;' who is not made a priest after the order of Aaron with his tithes, offerings, &c. ; but He makes an end of all those things, and hath abolished them, and is made an High Priest after the power of an endless life, who ever liveth to make intercession for his people; and 'is able also to save them to the uttermost that come unto God by Him;' who is the one holy Mediator betwixt God and man, and who sanctifies his people, his church, that He is head of, and presents them to God without spot, or wrinkle, or blemish, or any such thing; and makes them 'an holy priesthood, to offer up spiritual sacrifices, acceptable to God by Jesus Christ,' who is King of all kings, and Lord of all lords in the earth; so an holy, heavenly King who hath all power in heaven and earth given to Him; and rules in all the hearts of his sheep and lambs by his holy, divine, precious faith, that is held in all the pure consciences of his people: which holy faith, Christ, the holy One, is the author and finisher of. By which holy faith all the just live, and in which holy, divine, and precious faith all the just and holy ones have unity; and by it they do quench all the fiery darts of Satan; and by this holy, divine, and precious faith they have access to the pure God, in which they do please Him. And Christ, 'who is set on the right hand of the throne of the Majesty in the heavens,' in his New Testament and New Covenant, is the 'Minister of the sanctuary and of the true tabernacle, which the Lord pitched, and not man.'   And therefore all the lambs and sheep of Christ must feel this holy Minister in their temple and sanctuary, who ministers spiritual, holy, and heavenly things to them in their sanctuary and tabernacle.   For all the tabernacles and sanctuaries, that are built or pitched by man, men make ministers for them ; and such ministers are of men and by men, with their worldly sanctuaries and tabernacles of men's pitching, by men's hands.

" And now, all dear friends and brethren everywhere, that are the flock of Christ; ' Christ our passover is sacrificed for us.'   Therefore let us all keep this heavenly feast, of our passover in his New Testament and Covenant, not with old leaven, neither of malice nor wickedness ; but let all that be purged out, with the sour old leavened bread, that all may become a new lump : and so keep this heavenly feast of Christ, our heavenly passover, ' with the unleavened bread (mark, with the unleavened bread) of sincerity and truth.'   My desires are that all the flock of Christ everywhere may keep this heavenly feast of Christ ; our heavenly passover, with his heavenly ' unleavened bread of sincerity and truth.'   Amen.

" G. F."

After making a visit to several places near London, attending and appointing some meetings, he returned to the city ; and the parliament then sitting had a bill before them concerning oaths, and one respecting clandestine marriages. He, with other Friends, attended the house, and had interviews with the members, to guard against the insertion of any clause in the bill which would militate against them.

He again retired to the country for a short period, where he wrote two epistles—one addressed " to Friends in the ministry," as follows :—

" All friends in the ministry, everywhere, to whom God hath given a gift of the ministry, and who use to travel up and down in the gift of the ministry, do not hide your talent, nor put your light under a bushel ; nor cumber yourselves, nor entangle yourselves with the affairs of this world. For the natural soldiers are not to cumber themselves with the world ; much less the soldiers of Christ, who are not of this world ; but are to mind the riches and glory of the world that is everlasting. And therefore stir up the gift of God in you, and improve it, and do not sit down, Demas-like, and embrace this present world, that will have an end ; lest ye become idolators. But be valiant for God's truth upon the earth, and spread it abroad in the day-light of Christ, you who have sought the kingdom of God, and the righteousness thereof, and have received it and preached it ; which stands in ' righteousness and peace, and joy in the Holy Ghost.' As able ministers of the Spirit sow to the Spirit, that of the Spirit ye may reap life everlasting. And go on in the Spirit, ploughing with it in the purifying hope ; and threshing, with the power and Spirit of God, the wheat out of the chaff of corruption, in the same hope. For he that looks back from the spiritual plough into the world, is not fit

for the spiritual and everlasting·kingdom of God;
and then he is not like to press into it, as the faithful do. Therefore you that are awakened and are
come to righteousness, and to the knowledge of the
truth, keep yourselves awakened in it: then the
enemy cannot sow his tares in your field; for truth
and righteousness are over him, and before he was.
So my desires are that all may fulfil their ministry,
that the Lord Jesus Christ hath committed to them;
and then by the blood (or life) and testimony of Jesus
you will overcome the enemy that opposes it, within
and without. And all you that do preach the truth, do
it, as it is in Jesus, in love; and all that are believers
in Jesus, and receivers of Him, He gives them power
to become the sons of God, and so joint-heirs with
Christ; whom He calleth brethren; and He gives.
them the water of life, which shall be a well in them,
springing as a river up to eternal life; that they may
water the spiritual plants of the living God. So that
all may be spiritual planters and spiritual waterers;
and may see with the spiritual eye the everlasting,
eternal God over all to give the increase, who is the
infinite fountain. So my desires are that you may
be kept out of all the beggarly elements of the world,
which is below the spiritual region, to Christ the
Head; and may hold Him, who bruiseth the head of
enmity, and was before it was; so that ye may all be
united together in love, in your Head, Christ, and
be ordered by his heavenly, gentle, peaceable wisdom
to the glory of God. For all that be in Christ, are
in love, peace, and unity. And in Him they are
strong, and in a full persuasion; and in Him, who is
the first and last, they are in a heavenly resolution

and confidence for God's everlasting honour and
glory.   Amen.

> "From him who is translated into the kingdom of
> his dear Son, with all his saints, a heavenly
> salutation.   And salute you one another with a
> holy kiss of charity, that never faileth.
>
> "G. F.
>
> " Ford-Green, the 25th of the
>   Ninth Month, 1690."

The other was more particularly for Friends in
the ministry who were gone to America, as follows :—

" Dear friends and brethren, that are ministers,
and exhorters, and admonishers, that are gone into
America and the islands thereaways. Stir up the
gift of God in you, and the pure mind, and improve
your talents ; that ye may be the light of the world,
a city set upon an hill, that cannot be hid.   And let
your light shine among the Indians, and the blacks,
and the whites; that ye may answer the truth in them,
and bring them to their standard and ensign, that
God hath set up, Christ Jesus. ' For from the rising
of the sun even to the going down of the same,' God's
name shall be great among the Gentiles ; and in every
temple or sanctified heart, incense shall be offered up
to God's name.   And have salt in yourselves, that
ye may be the salt of the earth, that ye may salt it ;
that it may be preserved from corruption and putre-
faction : so that all sacrifices offered up to the Lord
may be salted and seasoned, and be a good savour

to God. And all grow in the faith and grace of Christ, that ye may be not like dwarfs; for a dwarf shall not come near to offer upon God's altar; though he may eat of God's bread, that he may grow by it. And friends, be not negligent, but keep up your Negroes' meetings and your family meetings; and have meetings with the Indian kings, and their councils and subjects everywhere, and with others, and bring them all to the baptizing and circumcising Spirit, by which they may know God, and serve and worship Him. And all take heed of sitting down in the earth, and having your minds in the earthly things, coveting and striving for the earth : for to be carnally minded brings death, and covetousness is idolatry. There is too much strife and contention about that idol, which makes too many go out of the sense and fear of God; so that some have lost morality, and humanity, and the true Christian charity. Oh! therefore, be awakened to righteousness, and keep awakened; for the enemy soweth his tares, while men and women sleep in carelessness and security. Therefore, so many slothful ones go in their filthy rags, and have not the fine linen, the righteousness of Christ; but are straggling and ploughing with their ox and their ass, in their woollen and linen garments, mixed stuff; feeding upon torn food, and that dieth of itself, and drinking of the dregs of their old bottle, and eating the sour, leavened bread, which makes their hearts burn one against another. But all are to keep the feast of Christ, our passover, ' with the unleavened bread of sincerity and truth.' And this unleavened bread of life from heaven makes all hearts and souls glad and joyful,

and lightsome and cheerful, to serve and love God,
and to love and serve one another in the peaceable
truth ; and to keep in the unity of God's spirit, which
is the bond of the Lord of lords, and the King of
all kings his peace.   In this love and peace God Almighty keep and preserve all his people, and make
them valiant for his truth upon the earth, to spread
it abroad both in doctrine, and good life, and conversation.   Amen.

" All the members of Christ have need one of another.   For the foot hath need of the hand, and the
hand hath need of the foot ; the ear hath need of the
eye, and the eye of the ear. So that all the members
are serviceable in the body which Christ is the head
of ; and the head sees their service.   Therefore let
none despise the least member.

" And have a care to keep down that greedy
earthly mind, that raveneth and coveteth after the
riches and things of this world ; lest ye fall into the
low region; like the Gentiles or Heathen, and so lose
the kingdom of God that is everlasting ; but seek that
first, and God knows what things ye have need of ;
who takes care for all both in heaven and in the
earth.   Thanks be unto God for his unspeakable gifts,
both temporal and spiritual !

" G. F.

" Tottenham, the 11th of the
    Tenth Month, 1690."

The last production of this kind bears date the day
before he was taken ill, and is addressed to Friends
in Ireland, to console and encourage them under the
sufferings they were then enduring.

The following day he went to Gracechurch-street meeting, in which he was engaged in testimony and prayer, in a powerful and affecting manner. As soon as the meeting was over, he withdrew to the house of Henry Goldney, a friend who lived near, remarking that he felt the cold strike to his heart as he came out of the meeting; yet added, "I am glad I was here—now I am clear, I am fully clear." He laid down to rest himself, but finding the sensation of coldness increase, he soon after went to bed, with symptoms of increasing weakness. His mind, which for a long course of years had been engaged, under the influence of the universal love of God, in endeavouring to promote the everlasting welfare of mankind and to draw souls to Christ, rose superior to the infirmities and pains of the frail tenement it occupied, and still evinced a lively and unabated interest in the promotion of this glorious cause.

He sent for several of his particular friends, and, at this awful crisis, communicated to them his mind respecting matters connected with the welfare of the church, and his desire for the spread of Friends' books; that those principles which he had so long personally advocated might thereby be diffused in the earth.

The triumphant state of his mind, amid the decay of expiring nature, was manifest by his expressions to those who visited him: "All is well—the Seed of God reigns over all, and over death itself. And though I am weak in body, yet the power of God is over all, and the Seed reigns over all disorderly spirits."

A few hours before his death he was asked how

he found himself; and with that fortitude and indif-
ference to corporeal suffering for which he had been
remarkable through life, he replied, " Never heed;
the Lord's power is over all weakness and death.
The Seed reigns; blessed be the Lord."   Enjoying
the use of his mental faculties to the last, and that
victory over death which is the gift of God, through
Jesus Christ our Lord, he contemplated his approaching change with a holy quietude and composure, and
even closed his eyes and mouth himself, at the time
that life was expiring.

In this heavenly and prepared frame, his spirit
quitted its earthly tenement, on Third-day, the 13th
of the Eleventh Month, 1690, between the hours of
nine and ten at night; he being then in the 67th
year of his age.   His dying-bed was surrounded
by many of his beloved friends, who, though they
could but rejoice in his eternal gain, yet were deeply
affected with their own and the church's loss.   Three
days after his decease, his body was conveyed to the
meeting-house in Gracechurch-street, where a large
and solemn meeting was held, for about two hours;
during which time ten Friends, among whom were
George Whitehead, William Penn, and Stephen
Crisp, spoke in testimony, and Thomas Green
closed the meeting with prayer.   The company,
which William Penn estimates at two thousand—and
Robert Barrow states the number much higher—then
proceeded to Friends' burial-ground, in Bunhill-fields,
where the corpse was committed to the grave.   Several
friends bore testimony to the sufficiency of that
Divine Power which had raised up and qualified
this extraordinary man for the work of his day, and

enabled him to adorn the doctrine of God his Saviour in a consistent life and conversation.

Having now closed the life of George Fox, it may not be uninteresting to make some general remarks on his outward affairs, and also on the estimation in which he was held by his contemporaries who were most intimately acquainted with his character.

From the fact of his being almost constantly engaged in the work of the ministry, it is obvious that he could not undertake any business which required his personal attention, nor of course any which would yield him much profit. But he had a mind contented with a little, and so far from seeking to be rich, he even refused it when circumstances placed it in his power. It appears that he was part owner of two vessels which sailed out of Scarborough, and he had also a small share in some other business. The reader of these sketches will remember that, in the early part of his life, he mentioned his having enough to keep himself from being chargeable, and also to administer to the wants of others. Mention is made in several of his letters of small sums of money lodged in the hands of different friends, and from the best estimate that can be made, his whole property appears to have been about seven hundred pounds, exclusive of one thousand acres of land in Pennsylvania, which, he says, William Penn gave him : but it does not appear ever to have come into his possession so as to be of any benefit to him. His property was probably all patrimonial ; for though Margaret Fell was a woman of large estate, he seems scrupulously to have avoided enriching himself by it. Previously to his marriage to her, he sent for her daughters, and, in the presence of their mother, inquired if their father's will had been fulfilled, and whether their mother's estate was so settled, that they would not be the losers by her marriage with him. To which they replied it was, and desired him to speak no more of it. " I told them," says he, " I was plain and would have all things done plainly, for I sought not any outward advantage to myself."

Though much separated from his nearest connexions, yet in the various relations of a son, husband, and father-in-law, he appears to have conducted himself so as to gain the tender affection of all; and his wife's children, in a written testimonial to his memory, say that they found him a tender father who never failed to give them wholesome counsel; and that the esteem they entertained for him in early life was increased by a longer and more intimate acquaintance.

His mental faculties were clear and vigorous; and though deprived of the benefit of much education, yet he cultivated various branches of knowledge. He was the friend, instead of the enemy, of useful learning, and not only promoted the establishment of several schools which he frequently visited, but spent considerable time in acquiring a knowledge of one or more of the ancient languages. " A divine and a naturalist," wrote W. Penn, " and all of God Almighty's making." A piece of ground which he owned at Philadelphia, he gave for a botanical garden for " the lads and lasses of the city to learn the habits and uses of the plants."

In person he was tall and rather corpulent, his

countenance manly, intelligent, and graceful; and his manners, says William Penn, "civil beyond all forms of breeding." If some of his expressions sound more plain and harsh than is agreeable to the refinement of modern times, we should recollect the temper and manners of the age in which he lived were very different from the present, and that such forms of speech were then common. There is, however, a remarkable change observable in this respect toward the latter part of his life, his writings at that period breathing a mildness which is peculiarly grateful. His contemporary biographer says, "he was of an innocent life—no busybody, nor self-seeker, neither touchy nor critical. What he said was very inoffensive if not very edifying. So meek, contented, modest, easy, steady, tender, it was a pleasure to be in his company. A most merciful man, as ready to forgive as unapt to take or give an offence."

His ministry was deep, searching, powerful; and though not ornamented with the elegances of literature, he possessed the tongue of the learned in another and higher sense, and could speak "a word in due season to the conditions and capacities of most, especially to them that were weary and wanted soul's rest, being deep in the divine mysteries of the kingdom of God."

Not only was he frequently engaged in opening the doctrines of the Christian faith in a clear and convincing manner, but having a sense and discernment given him of God respecting the states of his auditory, he spake to them under the leading of the Holy Spirit very pertinently, to their admiration and convincement; an instance of which was related by an ancient woman Friend as follows : viz.

" And now, friends, I will tell you how I was first convinced. I was a young lass at that time, and lived in Dorsetshire, when George Fox came to that country; and he having appointed a meeting, to which people generally flocked, I went among the rest; and in my going along the road, this query arose in my mind : ' What is it that I feel which condemneth me when I do evil, and justifieth me when I do well ? What is it ?" In this state I went to the meeting. It was a large gathering, and George Fox rose up with these words : ' Who art thou that queriest in thy mind, what is it that I feel, which condemneth me when I do evil, and justifieth me when I do well ? I will tell thee what it is. Lo ! He that formeth the mountains and createth the wind, and declareth unto man what is his thought; that maketh the morning darkness, and treadeth upon the high places of the earth; the Lord, the God of Hosts is his name. It is He by his Spirit that condemneth thee for evil and justifieth thee when thou dost well. Keep under its dictates, and it will be thy preserver to the end.' " To this narration the ancient friend added, " It was the truth, the very truth; and I have never departed from it."

" But above all," says Willam Penn, " he excelled in prayer. The inwardness and weight of his spirit; the reverence and solemnity of his address and behaviour, and the fewness and fulness of his words, have often struck even strangers with admiration, as they used to reach others with consolation. The most awful, living, reverent frame I ever felt or beheld, I must say, was his, in prayer. And truly it was a testimony that he knew and lived nearer to the

Lord than other men; for they that know Him most will see most reason to approach Him with reverence and fear."

As has been the case with many other eminent and faithful servants of Christ, he had to endure opposition and envy from some jealous spirits in his own Society, who grudged him that authority and dignity with which the Truth clothed him, and sought to lessen his services and prejudice the minds of others against him. Here again William Penn remarks respecting him: " He bore all their weakness and prejudice, and returned not reflection for reflection; but forgave them their weak and bitter speeches. And truly I must say, that though God hath visibly clothed him with a Divine preference and authority—and indeed his very presence expressed a religious majesty—yet he never abused it, but held his place in the church of God with great meekness, and a most engaging humility and moderation. For upon all occasions, like his blessed Master, he was a servant to all, holding and exercising his eldership, in the invisible power that had gathered them; with reverence to the Head, and care over the body. I write by knowledge, and not report, and my witness is true; having been with him for weeks and months together on divers occasions, and those of the nearest and most exercising nature, and that by night and by day, by sea and by land, in this and in foreign countries; and I can say I never saw him out of his place, or not a match for every service or occasion."

Thomas Ellwood, another contemporary and intimate friend of George Fox, sums up his character in the following manner :—

" He was valiant for the truth; bold in asserting it; patient in suffering for it; unwearied in labouring in it; steady in his testimony to it; immoveable as a rock. Deep he was in Divine knowledge; clear in opening heavenly mysteries; plain and powerful in preaching; fervent in prayer. He was richly endued with heavenly wisdom; quick in discerning; sound in judgment; able and ready in giving, discreet in keeping, counsel; a lover of righteousness; an encourager of virtue, justice, temperance, meekness, purity, chastity, modesty, humility, charity, and self-denial in all, both by word and example. Graceful he was in countenance; manly in personage; grave in gesture; courteous in conversation; weighty in communication; instructive in discourse; free from affectation in speech or carriage. A severe reprover of hard and obstinate sinners; a mild and gentle admonisher of such as were tender and sensible of their failings. Not apt to resent personal wrongs; easy to forgive injuries; but zealously earnest where the honour of God, the prosperity of truth, the peace of the church, was concerned. Very tender, compassionate, and pitiful he was to all that were under any sort of affliction; full of brotherly love; full of fatherly care : for indeed the care of the churches of Christ was daily upon him, the prosperity and peace whereof he studiously sought. Beloved he was of God; beloved of God's people; and (which was not the least part of his honour) the common butt of all apostates' envy; whose good, notwithstanding, he

earnestly sought.   He lived and died the servant of
the Lord."

Having completed these brief sketches of the life
and character of George Fox, it may not be improper to make a few observations on the men who
were his early companions in religious fellowship.

The religious Society of Friends, in the beginning,
consisted of persons who were earnestly seeking that
inward acquaintance with God and with his Son
Jesus Christ, which is life eternal.   Many of them
were highly esteemed, in the several religious professions of the day, for their uncommon piety and great
experience, being punctual in the performance of all
their religious duties and regular in partaking of the
ordinances.

But notwithstanding their faithfulness to the degree of knowledge they had received, their minds
were not at rest.   They did not experience that
victory over sin and that true settlement which their
souls longed for ; and hence they were led to believe
that a purer and more spiritual way than they had
yet found, was to be obtained.   They felt that they
needed to know more of the power of Christ in their
hearts, making them new creatures ; renewing them
up into that divine image which was lost in Adam's
fall, and sanctifying them, body, soul, and spirit,
through the Holy Ghost.

Great were their conflicts and earnest their prayers
that they might be brought to this blessed experience ; but looking without, instead of having their
attention turned inward, they missed the object of
their search.   They frequented the preaching of the
most eminent ministers, spent much time in read-

ing the Holy Scriptures, in fasting, meditation, and prayer, and became increasingly strict in their lives and in their religious performances.

Many of them were deeply versed in Scripture knowledge and familiar with the religious controversies of the day; and some, after wearying themselves with the multitude and severity of their religious performances, without finding the expected benefit from them, separated from all the forms of worship then known, and sat down in a very simple way, earnestly looking and praying for the fuller manifestation of the power of Christ, in redeeming them from sin and giving that peace which passeth all understanding.

In this humble, wrestling, seeking state, the Lord was graciously pleased to meet with them, sometimes without any instrumental means, and at others through the ministry of his anointed servants whom He sent amongst them. Then were they brought to see that that which made them uneasy in the midst of their high profession and manifold observances, and raised fervent desires after a nearer acquaintance with the God of their lives, was nothing less than the Spirit of the Lord Jesus Christ, striving with them in order to bring them from under the bondage of sin into the glorious liberty of the children of God.

They were brought to feel that they had been resting too much in a mere historical belief of the blessed doctrines of the Gospel—the birth, life, miracles, sufferings, death, resurrection, ascension, mediation, atonement and divinity of the Lord Jesus, all of which were then readily assented to by Christian pro-

fessors—but had not sufficiently looked for and abode
under the heart-cleansing and sanctifying power of
the Holy Spirit or Comforter, to seal those precious
truths on the understanding, and give to each one
a living, practical interest in them; so that they
might indeed know Christ to be *their* Saviour and
Redeemer.

They perceived that, while partaking of the outward bread and wine, and resting in that, they had
overlooked the true communion, in which Christ
comes into the soul and sups with it, causing it to
partake of that living bread which comes down
from heaven, and the new wine of his kingdom, by
which its spiritual strength and enjoyment are renewed. That the baptism in water was a mere
external rite, which could neither wash the soul from
pollution nor initiate it into the church of Christ,
and that they must therefore experience the one
spiritual baptism by the Holy Ghost and fire; "not
the putting away of the filth of the flesh, but the
answer of a good conscience towards God, by the
resurrection of Jesus Christ."

It was indeed the dawning of a new day to their
souls; and as they attended in simple obedience
to the discoveries of this divine Light, they were
gradually led further into the spirituality of the
Gospel dispensation. The change which it made in
their views was great, and many and deep were their
searchings of heart, trying the fleece both wet and
dry, ere they yielded; lest they should be mistaken,
and put the workings of their own imaginations for
the unfoldings of the Spirit of Christ. But as they
patiently abode under its enlightening. operations,

every doubt and difficulty was removed, and they were enabled to speak from joyful experience of that which they had seen, and handled, and tasted of the good word of life.

As Adam was originally created in the image of his Maker, free from every defilement, and fell from this blessed condition by yielding to the temptations of the devil; and as Christ came to restore man from the effects of the fall and bring him back to his primeval condition; so they believed that such as fully embraced the religion of Christ would have power given them over sin and be enabled to follow Him in all things; in conformity with his blessed commandment, "Be ye therefore perfect, even as your Father which is heaven is perfect."

Our Lord Jesus Christ having left it as a standing testimony to all his disciples, that without Him they could do nothing; that it is the Spirit which quickeneth, the flesh profiting nothing, they found that they could no longer pray, preach, or sing in their own wills, when and as they pleased, but must wait to receive a divine qualification, and feel the Spirit of Truth moving them thereto, and so helping their infirmities that they might perform those services acceptably to God.

Hence they came to see that no qualifications derived from human learning or ordination, could make a man a minister of the Gospel; but that this was a divine gift received from Christ himself, as the great Head of his church; and that the ability to preach or pray aright must be derived from the immediate moving and inspiration of his Holy Spirit.

As George Fox travelled through England preaching this fundamental doctrine of the light of Christ in the conscience, and calling men away from a dependence on traditional knowledge and outside religion, by which Gospel truth and power had been overlaid, to the teachings of the Holy Spirit, he found many persons prepared to receive his testimony, and to acknowledge that this was what their thirsty souls had long been panting after. To this circumstance may in part be attributed the great convincements which took place, and the rapid increase of the Society; for although the adoption of those principles soon brought on them the ridicule, reproach, and even the cruel persecution of their former associates and friends, yet they joyfully embraced them, counting nothing too dear to part with in order to purchase the blessed truth, and that peace and settlement they had so long sought in vain.

It is no cause of surprise that minds thus happily brought to experience the blessed effects of the doctrine, should dwell much in their writings and ministry on the immediate teachings of the Holy Spirit. It was indeed the burden of the word with them; and as it struck at the very foundation of Satan's kingdom, so he strove hard to misrepresent and pervert it.

They were charged with setting up this doctrine, in opposition to the coming in the flesh, and the propitiatory sufferings and death of the dear Son of God, as well as to his divinity and mediation: which false accusation they promptly denied, asserting that since they had come to the teachings of his Spirit in their hearts, they had been brought to a more true,

reverent, and living sense of his unmerited mercy in
coming into the world to die for sinners, and all his
blessed offices in the work of man's salvation, than
they ever had before.

In answer to the charge of denying or under-
valuing the Holy Scriptures, they declared, that those
precious writings were in great measure a sealed
book to them, until they were opened by the Spirit
which influenced the holy men of old who wrote
them ; and that, through its enlightening influences,
the beauty, harmony and consistency of the Scriptures were clearly set before the view of their minds,
and the saying truths recorded therein livingly sealed
upon their understandings.

In reading the writings of the first members of the
Society of Friends, we are struck with the numerous
quotations from both the Old and New Testament,
which they adduced to prove the truth of their
doctrines. That they were deeply versed in those
Sacred Writings, and diligent readers of them, is
obvious from this fact, as well as from the memoirs
of their lives. Their sermons also were fraught with
Scripture language, illustrating and establishing, by
its high authority, the great truths they enforced.
By precept likewise, as well as practice, they recommended the duty of diligently and devoutly reading
the Holy Scriptures ; not as a mere dry, customary
performance, without interest or a feeling of the individual application and importance of the truths
they contain, but as a serious yet delightful engagement, in which the mind ought to be turned to the
Lord, in reverent desire that He would be pleased to
bless it as a means of religious instruction and com-

fort, and, by the effusions of his Holy Spirit, enlighten the heart to understand, and availingly apply to our benefit, what we read.

From an early period in the history of the Society, this Christian duty has been often enjoined by the Yearly Meetings as well as by individual Friends. There is probably no community of Christian professors, who have evinced the same solicitude that all its members should be made acquainted with the Holy Scriptures, and be frequently engaged in reading them. Parents are earnestly encouraged to instruct the infant minds of their children in the saving truths contained in those Divine Writings, and to excite them to a reverent esteem of them; and in order that all may be reminded of their duty in this respect, the query is annually to be answered by each of the subordinate meetings: "Is it the care of all Friends to be frequent in reading the Holy Scriptures? and do those who have children, servants, and others under their care, train them up in the practice of this religious duty?"

As "the natural man [or man in the fallen and unregenerate state, which by nature belongs to him] receiveth not the things of the Spirit of God, for they are foolishness unto him; neither can he know them, because they are spiritually discerned," our first Friends contended, and the Society to the present time holds the sentiment, that the saving knowledge of the doctrines of Christian redemption, contained in Holy Scripture, is only obtained through the influences of the Holy Spirit, opening and enlightening the understanding to apprehend them aright, and sealing them upon the heart by his powerful operations. They asserted, therefore, that in order to arrive at this essential and experimental knowledge, it was necessary that the people should come to the teachings of the same eternal Spirit by which the Scriptures were given forth; for holy men of old wrote them as they were moved by the Holy Ghost. Not that they believed we were to expect the same degree of divine illumination which those pre-eminently favoured instruments enjoyed, nor yet that we are to wait for a divine revelation to induce us to read the Sacred Volume; but that, in our daily perusal of them, we should endeavour to have our minds directed to Him in whom are hid all the treasures of wisdom and knowledge. While the mysteries of redemption are only revealed to the babes in Christ, there are a multitude of precepts and narratives contained in the Bible, fraught with interest and instruction, intelligible to the humblest capacity, and of daily application to the duties of life. We cannot become too conversant with these, nor ponder them too often or too seriously with reference to our own conduct and conversation. It is not, therefore, to discourage from the diligent perusal of this blessed book, that the Society enjoins the necessity of seeking the aid of the Holy Spirit, savingly to open and apply the doctrines it contains, but rather to encourage all, in the performance of this important duty, to apply in faith to·Him who opened the understandings of his disciples formerly to understand the Scriptures; that so we may realize the truth of the apostle's testimony, that they are "profitable for doctrine, for reproof, for correction, for instruction in righteousness: that the man of

God may be perfect, thoroughly furnished unto all good works;" and that they are able to make "wise unto salvation through faith which is in Christ Jesus."

Their belief in a divine communication between the soul of man and its Almighty Creator, through the medium of the Holy Spirit, by which the Christian may be "led into all truth," did not at all lessen their regard for the authority of the Holy Scriptures as the test of doctrines. They constantly professed their willingness that all their principles and practices should be tried by them; and that whatsoever any, who pretended to the guidance of the Spirit, either said or did which was contrary to their testimony, ought to be rejected and condemned as a Satanic delusion; and also, that "what is not read therein nor may be proved thereby, is not to be required of any man that it should be believed as an article of faith."

With these views of the spirituality of the Gospel, and the authority of Holy Scripture, they were led to the cordial acceptance of those precepts of our blessed Saviour and his apostles, which so strikingly enforce what are termed the *testimonies* of the Society, viz., against war, oaths, and a hireling ministry, against the pride of life and worldly compliance in extravagant and costly attire and living, the use of the plural language to a single person, and of flattering titles and compliments; against all intemperance in eating or drinking, vain amusements, conversation, and jesting; in short, whatever was inconsistent with the gravity of men, who were "looking for and hastening unto the great day" of righteous retribution, and who therefore desired to pass the time of their sojourning here in the fear and favour of God.

In the midst of a corrupt and licentious age, their godly example was as a light that could not be hid, and which the surrounding darkness only served to render more conspicuous. Silently, but steadily it made its way to the hearts of the people, in the face of contempt, ridicule, and persecution, and finally disarmed their enemies and even extorted from them reluctant commendation. Principles, for the promulgation of which they suffered deeply in person and estate, were subsequently acknowledged as truth by a large portion of Christian professors, and some of their testimonies have so generally obtained as to have modified the legal codes in England and America, and given a new aspect to judicial proceedings. When we contemplate the spread of those Christian doctrines which our forefathers maintained almost alone, and remember that they have lost none of their truth or excellence, that their benign influence in promoting the happiness and true interests of mankind is not lessened, and that they are among the loveliest features and highest privileges of the Christian religion, the importance of maintaining them inviolate assumes a most serious character. Had the members of the Society stood in that degree of faithfulness to which they are individually called, we cannot say how much more extensively those principles would have prevailed, or what still greater influence they might have had in promoting the kingdom of the dear Son of God. In proportion to the advantages bestowed upon us, our responsibility as a community and as individuals is increased; and it is a serious reflection that, if we are not improving them and walking answerably thereto, we are retarding the diffusion of Gospel light and knowledge, and, as far as our influence extends, delaying the coming of that day when "the kingdoms of this world" shall "become the kingdoms of our Lord and of his Christ."

Every individual, however humble his sphere in life, exercises an influence over those around him, which, under divine guidance, may be made subservient to the advancement of religion. That the most important results often arise from small beginnings, the history of our forefathers in the truth furnishes abundant evidence. Their zeal and devotion, their constancy and faith, nay, the whole tendency of their example, presents an awakening call to their successors in religious profession, to press earnestly after the attainment of the same holiness in life and conversation, agreeably to the exhortation of the apostle : Brethren, be followers together of us, "and mark them which walk so as ye have us for an ensample : for our conversation is in heaven ; from whence also we look for the Saviour, the Lord Jesus Christ, who shall change our vile body, that it may be fashioned like unto his glorious body, according to the working whereby he is able even to subdue all things unto himself."

THE END.

LONDON:

R. BARRETT AND SONS, PRINTERS,

MARK LANE.